What readers are saying about
KAREN KINGSBURY'S
books

"If you had an official fan club I'd love to be the president! . . .
I am so hooked on your books. My goal is to collect them all and
share them with my friends, family, neighbors and coworkers!"

—Peggy

"I can't find the words to describe the emotions I went through
reading the entire Redemption series. God bless you, Karen, for
letting Him use your pen and hand and of course your heart to put
words of such magnitude on paper to bless us all so much!"

—Darlene

"You are the best writer ever. I get so excited when I walk into a
Christian bookstore and see one of your new books sitting there."

—Jessica

"Thank you for your beautifully written books. They make me
laugh, they make me cry, and they fill my heart with a love that can
only be God once again touching my heart and my soul."

—Natalie

"Okay, where's the next one? I know it's sitting in a warehouse
somewhere and you are making us wait! (Just kidding!) Karen,
there isn't a person I know who doesn't read your books and hold
you and your family in their prayers!"

—Rachel

"Life-changing books! I haven't been much of a reader until now! I have fallen in love with all of the Baxters. Thank you for letting me grieve my mother's death in a whole new light. . . . I have recommended the series to everyone I come across."　—Peggy

"I have fallen away from the almighty God many times. But always reading one of your books reminds me as to why I desperately need Him in my life. Thank you!"　—Nichole

"I loved the Redemption series and have shared it with various women in my church. Everyone has the same answer: 'I loved it!' We ALL laughed and cried. Your writing is an inspiration to all!"　—Rachel

"*Let Me Hold You Longer* is breathtaking! My friend read this story to me—the first night we both left our new babies overnight. And by the end, the two of us were bawling. She bought me my own copy for Mother's Day, and I read it to everyone . . . and each person cries as I read the words. I now buy it for every baby shower I go to. I think every parent should own or read this book. I read it as often as I can."　—Shannon

"My husband is equally hooked on your books. It is a family affair for us now! Can't wait for the next one."　—Angie

"The words God gives you in your stories have such power to reach my emotions. No other author has been able to do that!"　—Diane

"Every time our school buys your next new book, everybody goes crazy trying to read it first!"　—Roxanne

"Recently I made an effort to find GOOD Christian writers, and I've hit the jackpot with Karen Kingsbury!"　—Linda

Karen KINGSBURY

Found

TYNDALE HOUSE PUBLISHERS, INC.
Carol Stream, Illinois

Visit Tyndale's exciting Web site at www.tyndale.com

Visit Karen Kingsbury's Web site and learn more about her Life-Changing Fiction at www.KarenKingsbury.com

TYNDALE and Tyndale's quill logo are registered trademarks of Tyndale House Publishers, Inc.

Found

Designed by Jennifer Lund

Edited by Lorie Popp

Scripture quotations are taken from the *Holy Bible,* New International Version®. NIV®. Copyright 1973, 1978, 1984 by International Bible Society. Used by permission of Zondervan Publishing House. All rights reserved.

Published in association with the literary agency of Alive Communications, Inc., 7680 Goddard Street, Suite 200, Colorado Springs, CO 80920.

Library of Congress Cataloging-in-Publication Data

Kingsbury, Karen.
  Found / Karen Kingsbury.
    p. cm.
  ISBN-13: 978-0-8423-8745-3 (pbk. : alk. paper)
  ISBN-10: 0-8423-8745-5 (pbk. : alk. paper)
  I. Title.
  PS3561.I4873F68 2006
  813'.54—dc22   2006014552

Printed in the United States of America

09 08 07 06
8   7   6   5   4   3   2   1

To Donald, my prince charming

In this season of life, with you working as full-time teacher here at home
for our boys, I am maybe more proud of you than ever. I am amazed
at the way you blend love and laughter, tenderness and tough standards
to bring out the best in our boys. Don't for a minute think that your role
in all this is somehow smaller. You have the greatest responsibility of all.
Not only with our children but in praying for me as I write and speak
and go about this crazy, fun job God has given me. I couldn't do it without
you. Thanks for loving me, for being my best friend, and for finding
"date moments" amidst even the most maniacal or mundane times.
My favorite times are with you by my side. I love you always, forever.

To Kelsey, my precious daughter

You are sixteen, pushing seventeen, and sometimes I find myself barely able
to exhale. The ride is so fast at this point that I can only try not to blink,
so I won't miss a minute of it. Like the most beautiful springtime flower,
I see you growing and unfolding, becoming interested in current events and
formulating godly viewpoints that are yours alone. The same is true in dance,
where you are simply breathtaking onstage. I believe in you, honey.
Keep your eyes on Jesus, and the path will be easy to follow.
Don't ever stop dancing. I love you.

To Tyler, my beautiful song

Can it be that you are thirteen and, yes, taller than me? Just yesterday people
would call and confuse you with Kelsey. Now they confuse you with your
dad—in more ways than one. You are on the bridge, dear son, making the
transition between Neverland and Tomorrowland and becoming a strong,
godly young man in the process. Keep giving Jesus your very best, and
always remember that you're in a battle. In today's world, Ty, you need
His armor every day, every minute. Don't forget . . . when you're up
there onstage, no matter how bright the lights, I'll be watching from
the front row, cheering you on. I love you.

To Sean, my wonder boy

Your sweet nature continues to be a bright light in our home. It seems
a lifetime ago that we first brought you—our precious son—home from Haiti.
It's been my great joy to watch you grow and develop this past year, learning
more about reading and writing and, of course, animals. You're a walking
encyclopedia of animal facts, and that, too, brings a smile to my face. Your
hugs are something I look forward to, Sean. Keep close to Jesus. I love you.

To Josh, my tender tough guy

You continue to excel at everything you do, but my favorite time is late
at night when I poke my head into your room and see that—once again—
your nose is buried in your Bible. You really get it, Josh. That by being
strong in Christ, first and foremost, you'll be strong at everything else.
Keep winning for Him, dear son. You make me so proud. I love you.

To EJ, my chosen one

You amaze me, Emmanuel Jean! You have become a different little boy while
attending your daddy's home school. In every possible area you have
improved. I see you standing straighter and taller, articulating more,
making eye contact, and feeling confident and proud. I know that Jesus
is leading the way and that you are excited to learn the plans He has for you.
But for you, this year will always stand out as a turning point.
Congratulations, honey! I love you.

To Austin, my miracle child

Can my little boy be eight years old? I love that you still wake up every now
and then and scurry down the hall to our room so you can sleep in the middle.
But most of all I love your tender heart. Just last week you looked at me and
said, "Mommy, you're so pretty." Talk about making my day! Then you were at
a basketball game with us, and you sat on Daddy's knee and hooked your arms
around his neck and said, "You're my best friend, Daddy. Thanks for loving
me." Wow . . . it's so wonderful to see a reflection of my own heart in you, my
littlest son. I thank God for your health, precious boy. I love you.

And to God Almighty, the Author of life,

who has—for now—blessed me with these.

ACKNOWLEDGMENTS

This book couldn't have come together without the help of many people. First, a special thanks to my friends at Tyndale, who have believed in this series and worked with me to get this book to my readers sooner than any of us dreamed possible. Thank you!

Thanks to my amazing agent, Rick Christian, president of Alive Communications. I am amazed more as every day passes at your sincere integrity, your brilliant talent, and your commitment to the Lord and to getting my Life-Changing Fiction out to all the world. You are a strong man of God, Rick. You care for my career as if you were personally responsible for the souls God touches through these books. Thank you for looking out for my personal time—the hours I have with my husband and kids most of all. I couldn't do this without you.

As always, this book wouldn't be possible without the help of my husband and kids, who will eat tuna sandwiches and quesadillas and bring me plates of baked chicken and vegetables when I need the brainpower to write past midnight. Thanks for understanding the sometimes crazy life I lead and for always being my greatest support.

Thanks to my mother and assistant, Anne Kingsbury, for her great sensitivity and love for my readers. You are a reflection of my own heart, Mom, or maybe I'm a reflection of yours. Either way we are a great team, and I appreciate you more than you know. I'm grateful also for my dad, Ted Kingsbury, who is and always has been my greatest encourager. I remember when I was a little girl, Dad, and you would say, "One day, honey, everyone will read your books and know what a wonderful writer you are." Thank you for believing in me long before anyone else ever did. Thanks also to my sisters Tricia and Susan, who help out with my business when the workload is too large to see around. I appreciate you!

Thanks to Katie Johnson, who runs a large part of my business life—everything from my Quickbooks to my calendar. God brought you to me, Katie, and I'll be grateful as long as I'm writing for Him. Don't ever leave, okay? Thanks to Olga Kalachik, whose hard work allows me to operate a significant part of my business from my home. The personal touches you both bring to my ministry are precious to me, priceless to me. Thank you with all my heart.

And thanks to my friends and family who continue to surround me with love and prayer and support. I could list you by name, but you know who you are. Thank you for believing in me and for seeing who I really am. A true friend stands by through the changing seasons of life and cheers you on not for your successes but for staying true to what matters most. You are the ones who know me that way, and I'm grateful for every one of you.

Of course, the greatest thanks goes to God Almighty, the most wonderful Author of all—the Author of life. The gift is Yours. I pray I might have the incredible opportunity and responsibility to use it for You all the days of my life.

CHAPTER ONE

THE STORY WAS MORE than any reporter could resist.

A knife-wielding stalker with the delusional belief that she was married to the famous actor Dayne Matthews. The accusation that the same crazy woman had jumped from the dark shadows of Paradise Cove in an attempted murder of an associate of Dayne's. The rescue of that associate by Dayne, the photos that showed him and an unknown woman kissing near the beach earlier that night, and the fact that no one had ever been able to identify her.

Never mind that it was just a deposition. A crew of news vans and photographers surrounded the entrance to the Los Angeles Superior Court this January morning, hoping for a glimpse of the star they couldn't get enough of. Desperate for details beyond what they already knew.

Dayne Matthews sat in the backseat of the rented black Suburban. His attorney, Joe Morris, was driving. They were the only people in the vehicle, and from their position at a stoplight in front of the courthouse, they could see everything. Newscasters and print guys and tabloid photogs scurrying about the scene, searching for the best angle, the fewest shadows, plugging in wires and adjusting lenses as they waited for him to appear.

"They're out in full force." Joe turned the SUV into the parking lot.

"They love a good story." Today's newspaper lay on the seat beside Dayne, and he picked it up. His publicist had spoken with the media and put quite a spin on the facts. The article read: *Dayne Matthews and his unnamed associate will appear in court this morning to give depositions in the case against stalker Margie Madden.*

Dayne chuckled to himself. Katy was coming into court half an hour after him, and she was hardly a mere associate—though that's what the media and the police had believed about Katy since the beginning. An "associate" helping him scout out a location for an upcoming film. Since Katy was an unknown and since they didn't need to release her name until the trial, no one had to know that she was an actress or that she'd turned down the lead role in *Dream On* or that she lived in Bloomington, Indiana. The tabloids had a picture of him kissing an unknown woman earlier that evening on the beach, and he had explained that she was an actress who preferred to stay anonymous. The media had never put the two stories together.

"Let's go." His attorney exhaled hard as he put the vehicle in park. "It'll take a while to get through the throng."

Dayne unbuckled his seat belt and slid toward the door of the Suburban. The explanation he'd given to the press and the police had holes big enough to drive a train through, but none of it was a lie, not really. Katy *was* his associate, in the sense that she'd associated with him in a work setting for a time. And the police didn't care about the tabloid photos of him kissing some woman on the beach. He wasn't on trial after all.

Margie Madden was.

The explanation bought them time. That way Katy could stay

out of the limelight as long as possible. By the time the press heard actual testimony and realized her name, and that she'd been thinking about the role in *Dream On*, the movie would already be released and Katy would be only a small aspect of the story.

Dayne and Joe walked close together, their pace fast and clipped. Joe had flown out from New York City to be here, even though his presence wasn't really necessary. The prosecuting attorney would handle the deposition, and normally witnesses needed no other representation. But Dayne's situation was different. His public persona was at stake any time he did or said anything involving the law. His attorney even planned to have someone out here from the New York office at Dayne's side every moment during the trial.

They were a hundred feet from the courthouse when the swarm of media caught wind of Dayne's arrival. In a rush they pivoted and aimed their cameras. A few nicely dressed newscasters stepped in front of the others, large booming microphones in their hands. The bigger the network, the more likely they were to use his last name.

"Mr. Matthews." A heavily made-up blonde stepped into his path. "Is it true you want the judge in this case to make an example of Margie Madden, and is it true—?"

"No comment." Joe took hold of Dayne's elbow and straight-armed a path through the crowd. "Excuse us."

"Dayne." It was a photographer shouting from a few layers back in the crowd. "Tell us about the associate. Where is she? Isn't she supposed to be—?"

"She's already here." Joe's answer was loud enough for most of them to hear. It was part of the plan, that he would discourage the press from sticking around and waiting for Katy.

The photographer raised his hand and shouted again, "Does she still work with Dayne and in what capacity, since we don't have a name on her and—"

"No comment." Joe kept up his pace. He pulled Dayne along, leaving no room for responses. Dayne sort of liked the help. Maybe if he had Joe around more often, the paparazzi would leave him alone. He stifled a grin at the thought.

The crowd parted easily, and Dayne did his best to look straight ahead, his expression serious. The press would have their requisite photos and footage—Dayne Matthews, Hollywood star, coming to court to give testimony on the crazy stalker who tried to kill his associate. None of them really expected more than that.

Other than passing glances and whispered comments, Dayne and Joe weren't approached again as they entered the building and took the elevator to the eighth floor. Dayne stopped for a minute and looked out the window across the hazy Los Angeles scene. Somewhere out there Katy Hart was back in his city, making her way to the courthouse. Her visit was all he'd been able to think about since Christmas.

"This way." Joe took the lead and headed toward a room at the end of the hall.

They were met by a sharp-looking woman who appeared to be in her midfifties. She introduced herself as the prosecuting attorney. "We have a room set up for you." She gave them a business-like smile. "Follow me."

The attorney explained the proceedings as they walked down another hallway, but Dayne did little more than give an occasional nod in her direction. Joe would handle the details. All he had to do was tell the story while the prosecutor tape-recorded it. For now he could let his mind wander, let himself think about Katy.

He hadn't heard from her since opening night of *Annie*, but she was there when he woke up and when he lay down to sleep. The past few months had been the loneliest of his life. Not that he hadn't had offers. He was in the middle of filming a romantic suspense film opposite Angie Carr, a dark-haired beauty with exotic looks and a penchant for her leading men. They'd met at several functions but never starred in a film together until now.

On the first day of filming she had poked her head out of her trailer and called to him. "Dayne, come here." Her eyes danced, and her smile held the pout she was famous for. "I have a question."

He was in the middle of three things, including a conversation with his agent. But she was his priority as long as they were still establishing chemistry for the film. He jogged to her trailer, stepped inside, and closed the door behind him.

She stood facing him, dressed in nothing but a transparent negligee. "Hi." She took a step closer. "I need your opinion." Another step. "Will this work for the bedroom scene, the one at the beginning of the film?"

He swallowed and put his hand on the trailer door. "I thought the script called for a nightgown."

She pushed out her lips in a pout most men would have found irresistible. She played with a lock of her hair, dropping her chin and looking beyond seductive. "You don't like it?"

"Yeah, well . . ." He let loose a single chuckle and rubbed the back of his neck. "The film's PG-13, so I'm thinking something less see-through."

She grinned. "Oh, well." One more step and now she ran her finger down the length of his arm. "It works for right now, anyway." She nodded toward the set crew outside. "They'll be busy for an hour before they need us." Her face was so close he could smell the mint on her breath. She dropped her voice to a whisper. "Do you know how long I've wanted to practice a love scene with you, Dayne Matthews?"

He gritted his teeth. "Angie, listen . . ." She was stunning, but so what? Did she want him to take her right here on the trailer floor? And if he did, then what? They'd pretend to be hot lovers for a few weeks, and after that he'd be lonelier than ever. Something else too. The peace he'd found in Bloomington wouldn't last if he went back to his old ways.

With gentle hands, he framed her face and drew her close. Then he kissed her forehead. "The film calls for a few kisses— that's all." He searched her eyes. "We'll have time to practice later, okay?"

She could've gotten angry, but she didn't. Instead she took a few steps back, making sure he had a view of her full frame. "I'll look forward to it." She tossed him a confident smile as if to say she wasn't giving up that easily. "Dinner tonight?"

Since then, Angie's attempts had been relentless, just short of desperate, but he'd managed to keep his distance and still build chemistry with her. Working with her had its benefits. She was a professional, brilliant on the screen and fun off it. But she made him feel empty and plastic, the way all of Hollywood made him feel lately.

He was glad for a day off now, and never mind that he'd spend most of it here in a Los Angeles courthouse. He would've looked forward to a day in jail if it meant seeing Katy Hart again.

The attorneys were still talking as they reached a door at the end of the hallway. Dayne glanced at his watch, then toward the elevator. Katy would be here in fifteen minutes.

"This is perfect." Joe opened the door and led the way into a small room. He looked at Dayne. "You ready?"

"Perfectly." Dayne felt a sudden rush of passion toward the job ahead. The stalker had cost him much. This was his chance to get back at her.

The prosecutor followed them inside. "The deposition doesn't start for twenty minutes." She checked the clock on the wall. "I'll grab coffee and be back by then."

"I'll come." Joe set his portfolio on the desk and nodded at Dayne. "Want anything?"

"I'm fine."

The attorneys left, and Dayne took one of the seats. In the

silence he could almost hear his heart beat. Would Katy still have feelings for him? Would the electricity, the emotions that had existed between them still be there after they'd been apart so long? He tapped his fingers on the table. The minutes couldn't drop off the clock fast enough.

He should've brought his Bible, the one Katy had given him. That would've passed the time. He had been reading it lately, taking in a little more of the message every night. Not that he was ready to hit the nearest church or claim himself born again, the way some of his athlete friends had done recently. But the God of the Bible was the same God claimed by his parents, the Baxters, and Katy Hart. Because of that, He was the same God on Dayne's mind more often now.

He was about to step outside and check for Katy when he heard a knock. The attorneys would've come in without waiting, so maybe it was . . .

He stood and opened the door, and before he could take another breath he was looking into her eyes. The same clear blue eyes he'd connected with from the balcony of the Bloomington Community Theater back in November.

"Hi." Katy was breathless. She looked over her shoulder, nervous. "I've never seen so many cameras."

"They didn't know it was you, did they?"

"No." She exhaled, finding her composure. "I slipped past."

He let her in, closed the door, and suddenly they were alone, face-to-face as if no time at all had passed between them. "Katy—" he reached out and took her hands—"you look wonderful."

The faintest blush tinged her cheeks, and she shifted her gaze to the floor. When her eyes found his again, he had the answer he was looking for. The connection was still there. It was in her eyes and in her expression and in the way she ran her thumbs along the tops of his hands. "I didn't think we'd have any time alone."

"We won't have much."

Her smile told him everything she was feeling. But at the same time it cried of resignation. Because here they were again, their emotions leading the way, and yet their time would be measured and counted by the events around them, by the parameters of his world.

"How are you, Dayne?" Katy didn't blink, didn't seem to want to lose a moment of whatever minutes they had together.

"I'm good." He grinned, wanting desperately to keep things light. How was it fair that this visit would end up amounting to little more than another sad good-bye? "What are you working on?"

"*Robin Hood.*" She stifled a laugh. "It's coming together."

"The kids?" He wanted to know, wanted to soak himself in everything about her. "Are they okay?"

"They are. The older kids are still in the Bible study, the one they started after Sarah Jo Stryker's accident." She made a funny face. "Of course, we should probably spend an extra day a week on practice the way things are going."

"Blocking, you mean?"

"No." She laughed. "Trying to stay onstage. I'd be happy with that." Katy talked with her hands when she was excited. Now she released his hands and began illustrating her story. "So there's this scene where Robin's supposed to fly in from the wings on a rope, right?"

"To rescue Maid Marian?"

"Exactly." She took a quick breath. "Marian's standing on a fake tree stump, her hands tied, and he's supposed to swing in, land beside her, and save the day."

Dayne chuckled. He could see what was coming.

"Instead—" Katy demonstrated the swinging motion—"he sails in from the wings and knocks her square on the floor."

"Oh." Dayne made a face. "Was she hurt?"

"Her pride, yes. Her onstage chemistry with Robin, yes." Katy gave him a teasing look. "We decided we'd better just have him run in from now on."

"Sounds good." Dayne saw so much more than her physical beauty. Her enthusiasm and spirit, her joy and excitement for the little things of life. All of it was like getting air after being too long underwater.

"So . . . enough on that." Her tone softened. "How are you . . . really?"

"Well . . ." He found her eyes and held them. "I'm not a Kabbalist."

Her eyes widened, and she looked deeply at him, to the lonely desert plains of his heart. "Really?"

"Tossed it all." He felt his eyes begin to dance. "Some girl said it probably wasn't for me. Told me I needed to find the truth."

"Must've been a smart girl."

"Mmm." He took hold of her hands again, but he kept his distance. "Definitely. In fact, she gave me a Bible."

"A Bible? How interesting." Her eyes twinkled. "What a great idea. You know . . . since, well, it *is* the truth. I mean, if you're looking for it you might as well go to the source."

"That's what I figured." He felt his smile fade. "It's changing me, Katy. I can feel it."

Her expression softened, and what had been playful became serious. She closed the gap between them and slipped her arms around his neck. "Dayne, I prayed for this . . . for you."

He wouldn't have gone to her, wouldn't have crossed the line he'd crossed the last time they were together. But now, lost in her embrace, he couldn't imagine letting her go. Slowly, he worked his fingers along the back of her neck into her hair. She smelled wonderful, like the flowers in Bloomington.

Too soon she pulled back and searched his eyes. "Did you find Jesus? When you read the Bible, I mean?"

His hands were around her waist but only loosely. He looked

beyond her. The question was a good one. He understood for-giveness and peace better. "Have I found Jesus?"

"Mmm-hmm." She angled her head, her soul as transparent as a child's. "When you look past the hurt and sadness of your yes-terdays, is He there?"

A part of his heart sank a little. The answer wasn't what she wanted to hear. "Not yet." He released his hold on her waist and took her hands once more. "But I'm looking."

Disappointment never even flashed in her eyes. She gave him her brightest smile yet. "That's it."

"What?" It was all he could do to keep from kissing her.

"That's what I've been praying for." Her eyes glistened. "That you'll look."

The door opened. They dropped hands and stepped back to keep from being hit.

Joe Morris was the first to enter. He stopped and looked from Dayne to Katy. "Hi. You must be Katy Hart."

"I am." She held out her hand to him. Her cheeks were red, but she rebounded quickly. "I understand the deposition won't take long."

"Not at all."

The prosecutor stepped into the room. She greeted Katy and then Dayne. "We need your testimony on record so we can pre-pare for the case."

Dayne felt the intimacy from a moment ago fade like fog in July. It was no longer a reconnecting, a time to remember why he couldn't get Katy Hart out of his mind. They were in business mode now, and the atmosphere stayed that way for the next hour.

When the lawyers were finished, the group stood and moved to the door. Dayne was about to ask Katy if she wanted to go somewhere, spend some time together before she left. But before he could say anything his cell phone rang.

He checked the caller ID. Kelly Parker. He stuffed his frustration. She rarely called. At least he could politely put her off until later. The two of them hadn't talked much since she'd moved out. He held his finger up to Katy and opened his phone. "Hey."

"Dayne." There was a cry in her voice, one that mixed sorrow and fear. She waited a moment. "I've got bad news. I just found out."

His heart skipped a beat, and he moved to a corner of the room. In the background he heard his attorney start a conversation with Katy. He pressed the phone to his ear. "What is it?"

"There's no easy way to say this." Kelly sighed, and it rattled all the way to his soul. "Dayne, I'm pregnant."

❧

John Baxter was running out of options.

He'd done everything he could to find his firstborn son, everything a person could possibly think of. He'd searched the Internet for information, and he'd gone to adoption sites. He'd made phone calls and connected with people who aided parents in finding their birth children. Now he was down to his last hope.

The chances of finding his oldest son rested completely in the hands of a private investigator. John had hired him a week ago, and now—sitting on his desk—was a message from the man with one simple instruction: *Call immediately*.

He stared at the piece of paper and reached for the phone. Was this it? Had the man found the boy he and Elizabeth had prayed about for so many years? Would he have every bit of information he'd ever wanted in just a few minutes? The possibilities welled up in him and made it hard to breathe.

John closed his eyes and exhaled. *God, meet me in this place. I want to find him so badly, and this is my last chance. Please let there be something to go on—a lead, a phone number, a name. Something.*

He opened his eyes, and they fell on a small frame on his desk. It read: *With God all things are possible. Matthew 19:26.* A smile tugged at the corners of John's lips, and he felt himself relax. *Thanks, God. You always know just what I need.* Whatever the private investigator had to tell him, he wouldn't give up. Not now, not ever.

His palms felt sweaty against the phone's receiver. He took a full breath, picked it up, and tapped out the private investigator's number.

The man's secretary answered and connected him to the PI.

"Tim Brown here." The man was a fast talker, high energy. "How can I help you?"

"Uh . . . this is John Baxter, returning your call." He swallowed hard. "Did you find my son?"

"Yes, John, thanks for calling back." The man's tone became serious, slower than before. "Listen, something's come up in my research. Something very, very important. We need to talk about it in person."

In person? John wouldn't be able to think straight until he heard the news. "Are you sure? Can't you tell me now?"

"Not something like this." Tim rustled some papers. "Can you be here in the morning? Eleven o'clock?" He sighed, and the sound carried his concern across the phone lines. "This is very sensitive. I think you should know right away."

CHAPTER TWO

THE SHOCK WAS STILL SETTING IN.

Dayne clutched his cell phone, but the floor beneath his feet shifted the way it did when an earthquake rolled through the LA area. He was still standing in the corner of the small room, ready to make his way out behind the lawyers, behind Katy Hart. But suddenly a million miles seemed to separate them, as if everyone else had gone ahead to the cars waiting behind the courthouse, and he was being sucked backward, downward into a suffocating tunnel with no way out and daylight fading fast.

Katy turned around and tilted her head. Question marks danced in her eyes. *"You okay?"* she mouthed, her question for him alone.

Just beyond her, the attorneys were talking. But their words ran together. Kelly Parker was still on the other end, silent, waiting. His head hurt. He closed his eyes and whispered into the phone, "Hold on, okay?"

"Look, Dayne . . ." Kelly exhaled, irritated, impatient. "We need to talk."

"I said give me a minute," he hissed, and anger crept into his tone. "I'm at court." Dayne covered the phone and lowered it to his waist. His eyes found Katy's and held. "I have to take this call."

If she was disappointed, she didn't let it show. She looked at her watch. "The attorneys want to pick up lunch and meet in a private room off the lobby of my hotel." She shrugged, and the innocence of it made her look beyond adorable. "Can you go?"

Dayne's attorney pulled out of the other conversation and poked his head over Katy's shoulder. "We need to take separate exits. There's a car waiting for you at the back of the building, Dayne. An officer'll show you the way." Joe put his hand on Katy's shoulder. "She's got her own driver. I'll go on my own, and we'll meet at Katy's hotel. Sound good?"

Dayne's mind was reeling. Kelly was pregnant? How was this happening? He pinched the bridge of his nose, tried to focus. Lunch at the hotel? "Uh . . . sure. Can you tell my driver I'll be five minutes?" He held up his phone. "I have to take this."

"Got it." Joe took a step back. "The driver knows which hotel." He motioned for Katy to follow him. He was already flipping open his cell phone as he turned and headed down the hallway.

"See you there." Katy gave Dayne a little wave and turned to leave. Something in her eyes looked more distant than before. Or maybe it was his imagination, his conscience.

His conscience.

He moved farther into the room, leaned against the wall, and lifted the phone to his ear. With his other hand he braced himself so his knees wouldn't buckle. "Kelly?"

"Dayne, I don't have long. They need me on the set in five minutes."

"Sorry." His mouth was dry, his heart racing. She was pregnant? He was going to be a father? He squeezed his eyes shut. "So what . . . what happens now?"

"Well—" she laughed, but the sound came out more like a cry—"I guess that's up to me."

"Meaning . . . ?" He slid one foot up the wall behind him, bent forward, and dug his elbow into his knee.

"Meaning it's my choice. I'm four months pregnant, but I could fix that in an afternoon."

Abortion. Kelly was talking about getting rid of the baby, and in a rush of memories he could hear his adoptive parents talking to a group of adults. His mother was saying, *"Of all the gifts God has given us, life is the most precious of all. Life at any stage, any season, very young or very old, healthy or sick. Life is God's to give, God's to take."*

And his father was pulling him aside and giving him "the talk," saying, *"Abstinence is God's way, but it's also the only way because once a girl gets pregnant you're a father. No matter what happens after that, you're a father."*

"Dayne!" Kelly was jumpy, her words short and heavy with frustration. "Did you hear what I said?"

"No . . . Kelly, you can't." He felt sick, and the room swayed. Wasn't that the easy answer, what so many in their situation would do? Get an abortion? Eliminate the evidence? But it was all happening too fast. He rubbed his fingers into his brow. "I need time to think."

"You're not listening, Dayne." Kelly sounded more composed. There was noise in the background, probably from the shoot. She was working on a new film, one that starred two other A-list actresses and some unknown new guy. She drew a steady breath. "I want to keep the baby. But I'm not raising a child by myself."

What was she saying? He straightened and stared at the ceiling. "Kelly, you're living with Hawk. How does he feel about this?"

"I'm back at my own house now." Her voice fell. "He knows

about the baby. We talked last night." She hesitated. "He thinks you and I should give it another try."

"Okay." Dayne paced to the other side of the small room. Was this his life they were talking about? Had Kelly and Hawk come to conclusions that would basically decide the course of *his* future? But if a baby was involved and if Kelly was willing to keep it, what choice did he have? His *own* actions had decided the course of his future. "Is . . . is that what you want?"

"Dayne—" she groaned—"I don't know what I want. You're one of my closest friends and for a while there I thought . . ."

She didn't have to finish her sentence. He had thought so too. That if he couldn't have Katy Hart, he might as well have Kelly. She was an actress, someone who would understand his crazy life and all it came with. Because it was her life too. But after spending a few weeks in the fall in Bloomington, after seeing Katy and feeling the way his heart responded every time she was near, he had known.

He could never settle for Kelly Parker.

Not when the real thing was out there. Even if his world and Katy Hart's were so different they never found a way to be together, he could never settle for less than what he'd felt with her.

Until now.

A rush of everything he knew to be true and real and right came at him from every side. The words of wisdom from his adoptive parents, the way his biological family clung so tightly to each other, even the conversations with Katy, the ones they'd had on the trails around Lake Monroe that felt like a lifetime ago.

All the words and whispers came back, and suddenly Dayne knew. It didn't matter how he felt about Kelly, not if they were going to have a baby. He had loved her once, right? What he'd thought was love, anyway. For the sake of their child, he would love her again. He would learn to love Kelly the way she deserved to be loved.

And Katy Hart would be nothing more than a wonderful dream that never had the chance to come true.

"Dayne, you're not talking." Kelly sounded weak, hopeless. "Look, if you're not into this, I can get it taken care of. I'm not raising a kid by myself. Not with the tabs taking potshots at me along the way. If you want out, don't worry about it. I can be done with this in—"

"Kelly!" He didn't raise his voice, but his tone caught her attention. He raked his fingers through his hair and paced across the room to the other side. "I would never ask you to raise a child—*our* child—by yourself." He was breathing faster now, his mind racing with the possibilities. "Should you . . . do you wanna move back in with me? So we can go through this together?"

"It isn't that easy." Defiance colored her words. "I'm not a charity case. If you take me back, it'll be because you want me. Me and no one else but me."

The room was spinning again. Outside in the hall he could hear new voices—new attorneys, no doubt, getting ready to use the room for whatever deposition or hearing came next. He tried to focus. "Okay . . . so you don't want to do this alone. But you don't want to move back in either?"

"What I'm saying is, let's take it slow. Let's start hanging out again and see where it goes." Her tone softened. "There's no one I'd rather have as the daddy for my child. I've seen you with kids—on the sets and on location. I think we have a chance here. Let's at least give it a try."

"Okay." Dayne was still confused. With Kelly four months along, they couldn't only give it a try, could they? They had to make a commitment—to each other and to their unborn child. He stopped and stared at the floor. "When can I see you?"

"Tonight isn't good."

Dayne pictured Katy at the hotel, ready to catch a flight back to Bloomington in the morning. "For me, either."

"What about tomorrow night? We could meet at my place. Eight o'clock."

"All right." Dayne massaged his temples with his free hand. In a single phone call his life had changed. No, more than that. His future had been decided. He had no idea what to say. "Kelly . . . I'm sorry."

"It happens." Possibility rang in her tone. "Who knows? Maybe it was supposed to work out like this. So we would find our way back together."

"Yeah." But Katy Hart's face filled his mind, his soul. He squeezed his eyes shut, willing her smile to disappear. "Yeah, maybe so."

They hung up, and Dayne hung his head. What had just happened? He was going to be a father? He had promised to try and make a future with Kelly Parker? All of it felt like a terrible nightmare, a horrific joke. He felt weak, nauseous. It took nearly a minute before he could force his legs to carry him into the hall to a uniformed officer waiting just outside the door.

"The car's this way."

Dayne nodded and followed the man. He was halfway to Katy's hotel before he made a plan. The information about Kelly and the baby would be a secret to the media and the industry, a secret to the public and even to their friends. But there was one person who had to know before another day passed. A person who would not look back after she knew the reality of what lay ahead.

That person was Katy Hart.

All through lunch, Katy knew.

Something was wrong with Dayne, something about the trial or one of his films or maybe something about her. There was no other explanation. He sat next to his attorney and ate with the rest of them, and whenever someone asked him a question he had an answer. But he was distant and distracted, almost despondent. Most of all, he wouldn't look at her. While they ate salads in a meeting room of her hotel, a space rented by Dayne's lawyer, only rarely did Dayne even glance in her direction.

True, until today they hadn't seen each other since opening night for *Annie*, but the look he'd given her that night and this morning was completely missing now. Katy tried to steel herself against what might be coming. Maybe he had finally realized there could never be anything more than a distant friendship between the two of them. Whatever was wrong, she wanted to be ready for the pain. Months had passed, after all. Dayne wasn't with Kelly Parker anymore, but maybe he'd moved on—the way the tabloids hinted—to Angie Carr, his current costar.

But then why had he seemed so glad to see her at the courthouse earlier?

Dayne's attorney was waving his hand, talking about the press. "They'll eat up the story, folks. I can tell you that much." He took a drink of his iced tea. "Those prelims were dynamite." He pointed at Dayne. "Your testimony alone makes the case a slam dunk."

"Good." Dayne poked his fork around at the wilting lettuce on his plate. "Then let's give Katy a break. She can go home, and I'll be the media circus."

She blinked at him. Go home? Where did this attitude come from? When he was in Bloomington he'd told her several times that whatever was happening between them wasn't finished yet. Not as long as the trial loomed ahead. But now . . .

Joe Morris was saying something about anyone witness to a crime was subject to testify, and that of course there was no way for Katy to get out of testifying. But more than that, Katy could hear Dayne's words: *"Give Katy a break. She can go home . . . go home."*

Katy kept her answers short the last ten minutes of lunch,

talking only when Joe asked her a direct question about her flight or her availability.

Finally, the attorneys stood, and Joe motioned to the prosecutor. "Let's talk out here for a minute."

The prosecutor nodded. She was an intelligent, no-nonsense sort who had kept pace with Dayne's attorney since the meeting at the courthouse.

They left the room, and Katy and Dayne were alone. He lifted his eyes to hers, but he looked weary, as if whatever was eating at him was almost more than he could bear.

"Did I . . . do something?" She pushed back her plate and rested her forearms on the table. She lifted her hands, baffled. "I feel like a stranger over here."

"I'm sorry." Dayne stood, but his movements were slow, troubled. He came to her and took the seat beside her, facing her. "We need to talk."

Katy felt herself grow stiff. She pressed her spine against the back of the chair. *Hide your feelings, Katy. Come on.* "About what?"

Only then did she see it. The hurt in Dayne's expression, the certainty that something had changed or happened. Whatever it was, the look in his eyes was so sad it moved her deeply.

He spoke straight to the loneliest places of her heart. "Later." He looked up for a moment, then back at her. "Meet me at five o'clock tonight. Malibu Beach, a hundred yards south of the pier."

She thought hard, her pulse faster than before. "I'm not sure I know how to get there."

He grabbed a pen and a napkin and wrote her directions. Then he found her eyes. "Please, Katy . . . please come."

Her flight didn't leave until morning. But what about the paparazzi and crazy fans? "We'll get caught."

"Maybe." He bit his lip. Then he came up with a plan: she would tuck her hair into a baseball cap. He would be sitting on the beach behind his house. "If I'm being watched, the moment I see you coming, I'll stand and head up my stairs."

"Okay." This was crazy. How could he live this way, worrying about people taking his picture, tracking his every move? Katy's hands shook as she jotted the details on the napkin.

"If I go inside, you'll stay on the beach for fifteen minutes, act like you're watching the sunset. Then slip in through the door to my stairs. They're fenced off." He gave her a half smile. "Once you're through the door at the bottom, the cameras can't shoot you."

She searched his face for clues. But before she could ask him for a hint, for an idea about what might be so serious, Dayne's attorney returned to the room. The prosecutor was right behind him.

"Look—" Joe checked his watch—"I have to call the office before my flight." He pointed at Katy. "Let's stay in touch over the next few months. The trial should be the first week of May."

Dayne stood and shook his hand. "I'll keep it open."

"Me too." When Katy stood, her shoulder brushed against Dayne's. The contact felt forbidden and wonderful, and it made her realize how much she'd missed him. She took a step to the side, her cheeks warmer than before. She, too, shook the attorney's hand. "I'll wait to hear from you."

The prosecuting attorney nodded. "I might need you both before then. I'll let you know."

"Call me first." Joe chuckled. "That's one client who doesn't do anything without someone from the firm at his side."

"No problem." The prosecutor raised her file in their direction. "I'll be in touch." She slipped her briefcase beneath her arm and left.

As the door opened, Katy caught a glimpse of a crowd in the lobby.

"They found you." Joe grinned as the door closed again.

"Man, they don't ever let up. You got about fifty of 'em out there, Dayne. Someone at the desk must've seen you come in."

"Photographers?" Dayne leaned against the edge of the table. He looked more frazzled than before.

"Fans, I think. Probably a mix. Either way, there's a car outside waiting for you." Joe moved toward the door and turned to Katy. "Better wait until Dayne's been gone awhile before leaving." He motioned to another door. "That one leads to the bank of elevators."

"Fine. I'm going to my room from here."

"Wait at least ten minutes." Joe frowned at Dayne. "Don't you think?"

Dayne slid his hands in his pants pockets. He sighed, and the sound of it filled the room. "Of course."

Joe patted Dayne's shoulder. "I'll call you."

"Thanks." Dayne sounded defeated, beyond tired.

As Joe shut the door behind him, Katy studied Dayne. She could almost read his mind. What sort of life was it if he couldn't spend an hour with a friend, if he couldn't leave a hotel meeting room without making plans to be discreet? She rested against the table too, careful to keep at least a few inches between them. "Crazy."

"Yeah." He shrugged, his eyes still on the door. "I tried to tell you." He cocked his head, his expression softer than before. "It comes with the territory."

He was right. Hollywood was full of people obsessed with a life like Dayne's, drawing seven figures for a film, comfortably at the top of the industry's A-list of actors. But the dream came with a price.

She crossed her arms. "Sounds like you better go."

His bottle of water was still on the table. He took it and downed what was left of it. Then he straightened and faced her. "I'm sorry."

"Don't be." Katy swallowed. Her throat suddenly felt thick, and she worked to find the words. "You can't help it."

"Still . . ." A handful of emotions played out in his expression—frustration, anger, resignation, and finally a longing that was unmistakable. He closed the gap between them, and for a moment he looked as if he might kiss her. But instead he pulled her into a hug. "This isn't how I wanted today to go." When he spoke, his voice sounded strained, as if maybe regret was throwing itself into the mix of feelings tearing at him.

"Me, either." She slid her arms around his neck and allowed the hug to linger. This, their embrace, was wrong, wasn't it? Letting her feelings show this way could never erase the fact that they didn't belong together, that they were too different in every way that mattered. Back home in Bloomington she had trouble convincing herself there was nothing wrong with the feelings she had for Dayne Matthews. The same was true here. But now, in his arms, she didn't ever want to let go.

Dayne nuzzled his face against her hair, and it seemed like he might say something else. But he drew back and took tender hold of her hands. "Tonight?" The sadness was back, a sadness that defied the moment. "Please, Katy."

She breathed in the smell of him, the cologne and faint scent of soap. Why was his tone so heavy? He was used to the throng of autograph seekers and paparazzi, so was there something more? some reason why he'd been different during lunch? Did he feel the impossibility of his feelings for her, the same way she did? She wanted to ask, but he'd made himself clear. Whatever he needed to talk to her about would have to wait until tonight. She gently squeezed his hands and said the only thing she could say, "I'll be there."

Dayne hesitated and then released her fingers. He grabbed his PDA, his eyes on hers as he moved to the door. "Thanks."

"See you." Katy smiled and waited until he shut the door. Only then did she realize she'd been holding her breath. She exhaled and dropped to the nearest chair. On the other side of the door, she could hear loud squeals and shouts, and his name repeated over and over again.

"Dayne . . . Dayne . . . over here, Dayne!"

She hung her head. What was wrong with her? Meeting him at the beach tonight would be a waste of time. She could call him and tell him so, and if he still wanted to talk to her, he could do it then. On the phone. That way she wouldn't be as tempted to forget all the reasons she shouldn't have feelings for him.

But even as she considered calling Dayne instead of seeing him, even as the noise of the throng outside continued, and even as she questioned her sanity, Katy knew without a doubt there was only one place she could possibly be at five o'clock. The place where he would be waiting for her.

Malibu Beach.

CHAPTER THREE

───────────◆═══◆═══◆───────────

T HE SUN WAS SINKING FAST, and so far Dayne hadn't seen any signs of photographers. He wore shorts, an old Michigan sweatshirt, his faded navy baseball cap, and sunglasses. Only the regular media hounds would've recognized him as anyone other than a jogger.

A cool breeze came off the Pacific, but it did nothing to ease the pain in his heart. Kelly was pregnant. He was going to be a father. A dad. This new reality had consumed him since his conversation with Kelly. When Katy came to meet him, what more could he say? The conversation would begin and end with that one fact. Dayne squinted down the beach. It was nearly empty, the way it usually was in January. A few lone fishermen balanced poles off the edge of the pier, and the sandy stretch between him and the parking lot a quarter mile down was dotted with a handful of people.

Still no Katy.

A pair of noisy seagulls swooped low over the surf, looped around, and landed on the wet sand. Dayne pulled up one knee and rested his elbow on it. The timing couldn't have been worse. He had been reading his Bible, trying to figure out why God was so important to everyone who had ever mattered in his life.

But if God cared about him, if God had plans for him the way Katy always said, then why this? Why a baby with a woman he had never really cared for as more than a friend? Was it a lesson of some kind, so he'd have to spend the rest of his life learning to love, loving out of obligation, for the sake of a child?

Dayne looked out over the water. The sky had been brilliant blue all day, and the sunset was already casting a pink glow over the ocean. Whatever God was trying to teach him, Dayne had a pretty strong sense that he and Kelly wouldn't last. He would try, of course. And he would be the best father ever, active in his child's life from the beginning.

One of the two seagulls hopped toward him, stopped, and turned its head one way and then the other.

"No food over here, buddy."

The seagull pecked at something, then took off over the water.

If Kelly wanted to marry him, he'd do that too. It would be better for all of them, really. He and Kelly understood each other, the strange lives they lived. That way the baby would have both parents under one roof. If she'd agree to stay together, he would do it. Kelly was his friend, and he could learn to love her.

If only he could let go of Katy Hart.

That's why he needed to talk to her tonight. So he could close the book on this wonderful, mysterious chapter in his life. So he could say good-bye to the girl who had captured his attention in a handful of minutes on a community theater stage in Bloomington, Indiana.

Movement caught his attention, and he looked to the right. At first he wasn't sure if it was her, but then he knew. Her long blonde hair was tucked into a baseball cap, but nothing could hide the way she walked, the sway of her lithe body as she headed down the sand. Even though she was a hundred yards away, he could feel her eyes on him.

He glanced around, in case a lone photographer was lurking somewhere he'd overlooked. He knew their places—near a cropping of bushes, along one of three staircases, on the hillside beneath one of the closer houses. Every spot was clear.

Dayne leaned back on his hands and stared at the setting sun. He would've wanted this conversation on the beach—because maybe somehow the wind and waves would smooth out the rough edges of the moment. But he couldn't take a chance. Especially in the fading daylight. There might not be a photog hanging around this minute, but they'd be back. And if they caught the two of them together, there was no telling what damage they could do to Katy.

Dayne stood and stretched. She could see him; she'd know where to go. His gaze cast downward, he jogged lightly up the sandy hill to the gate that led to his private stairway. Once he was inside the gate, he took the first six stairs, turned, and sat down, waiting for her.

After fifteen minutes, he heard quick footsteps and the sound of her breathing. She opened the gate and stepped inside without knocking—just the way he'd asked her to do.

She shut the gate behind her and leaned against the fence. Her sides were heaving, her eyes wide. "I . . . I saw you come inside." She bent over and put her hands on her knees. "I ran . . . the rest of the way. Just in case."

He wanted to go to her, wanted to sweep her into his arms and kiss her before either of them had a chance to talk about why she was here. But he forced himself to stay controlled. Katy deserved better. He stood and held out his hand. "Come on. Let's go to the deck."

She looked hesitant, but she took his hand.

The feel of her skin against his almost changed his mind—about the conversation, about the kiss. Even about his allegiance to Kelly. *Find control, Matthews*, he told himself. *You have no choice here*. The temptation passed. He squeezed her fingers and started up the stairs.

He led her through the back door into the house, and around a half wall to the deck slider. The deck had a tinted privacy wall and rail system that allowed a view of the beach but made it harder for passersby or paparazzi to get a clear photo opportunity.

He released her hand. "Want something to drink?"

Katy had her breath back, but she looked nervous. She removed the baseball cap, and her blonde hair tumbled around her shoulders. "Water, thanks."

"Okay." With everything in him he wanted to pretend he was fine, that her being here was simply the fulfillment of how he'd hoped things would go during this stage of the court proceedings. That they were about to share an evening catching up and dreaming about what ifs and maybes. But that wasn't the case. His grin died before it touched his lips. He went inside, found a couple cold bottles of Dasani, and brought them back onto the deck.

Dayne had two lounge chairs and a small wicker sofa on the deck. Katy was already sitting on one end of the sofa, her cap on the adjacent glass-top table. He put the bottled water down next to Katy's hat and took the seat beside her.

The sun had dropped halfway behind the sea. Pinks and oranges streaked across the deep blue sky.

Katy gave him a soft smile. "Gorgeous view."

Dayne studied her, the way the fading sun reflected in her eyes. "Yes." He blinked and turned toward the beach. "I . . . I never get tired of it."

The wind had died down, but still there was the occasional sound of a seagull. Dayne leaned back into the sofa cushion and stretched out his legs. Katy smelled wonderful, something subtle and innocent, like her. He wasn't in a hurry. If the scene they were playing out was on a television screen, he'd hit the Pause button and never touch it again.

She pulled up her legs and turned her body toward him. "Well, I'm here."

"Yeah." He shifted so he could see her better. "Thanks." He nodded toward the beach. "The press hounds aren't around yet. No one saw you come up."

"Then why . . . ?"

"I couldn't take a chance." He sat a little straighter. "It's private here."

"Oh." She nodded, nervous. "Okay." Her expression told him she wanted to say more, wanted to know why he'd asked to meet with her. But she stopped short of saying anything more.

Dayne leaned across her and took his bottle of water. As he did, his arm brushed hers, and the touch made him crazy for wanting her. How could he ask Kelly to move in with him when his feelings for Katy were all-consuming? when he had known from the first day that no one could make him feel the way this woman beside him made him feel?

He opened the water bottle, dropped the plastic cap on the table, and took a sip. He was careful to keep his distance. The ocean air smelled damp and salty, tinged with the faintest hint of seaweed. "You know what I love about the ocean?"

Katy looked out at the water. "What?"

"The sameness of it." He laid his head back against the cushion. This was good, delaying the real conversation. It gave him somewhere to look other than at her. He focused on a wave a few dozen yards out and watched the peaking water make its way steadily to the shore, rising and building, cresting and collapsing in a mound of white foam. "No matter what else happens in a given day, the ocean comes at you the same way. Every hour. Every minute."

"Mmm." She kept her gaze on the ocean for a moment. Then

she turned back to him. "That's not why you asked me here." Her voice was soft, and it mixed with the gentle breeze.

"No." He turned toward her and searched for a way out. There was none. "No, it's not."

She waited, her face filled with questions.

How could he tell her? How could he tell her the truth when doing so would change everything not just now but forever? He ached to be closer to her, to take her in his arms and hug her the way he'd done earlier. But he couldn't even do that. Not with what lay ahead.

Even so, nothing could stop him from reaching out, spanning the distance between them, and taking her hand.

"Dayne . . ." She worked her fingers between his, but the anxiety around the corners of her eyes grew stronger. "Don't do this to me." She began to shiver. "Whatever it is, just tell me."

He drew a long breath. "Kelly Parker called me today when we were leaving the courthouse."

"When we were in the room?"

"Yes." He soothed his thumb along the side of her finger.

Katy seemed to process that for a moment. "You acted different all through lunch."

"Right." He felt sick to his stomach. "Because of what she told me."

He felt her tense up, but she didn't pull away.

Darkness was settling in around them, and Dayne didn't wait another moment. The truth needed to be said, regardless of the outcome. "Katy . . . she's pregnant. Four months." He slid a little closer, holding his breath, waiting for her reaction. "She says . . . the baby's mine."

It took three heartbeats before Katy seemed to understand what he was saying. Then all at once she eased her hand from his and stood. She stared at him, her mouth open, then walked to the edge of the deck and gripped the railing. Gripped it as if she were trying to keep from falling.

He wanted to warn her that whatever photographers had moved in could easily see her there. But he couldn't. He needed her reaction first, needed to know the thoughts that must have been tearing into her heart, her mind.

After a handful of seconds she turned and faced him. "You didn't know?"

Her words were like daggers, and the pain in his heart doubled. Katy deserved the truth, deserved to be set free from the mess his life had become. The mess it had always been. "I had no idea."

"That explains it." Her tone was resigned, as if whatever emotions were playing out in her heart she was determined to let him see just this one. "The way you were at lunch."

"I couldn't tell you there." He wanted to go to her, but he couldn't. Not until she had time to process the news. "I'm sorry."

She sniffed and gave a slight rise of her chin. "What happens now? For you and Kelly, I mean?"

Still seated, he anchored his forearms on his knees and stared at the deck. He wanted to scream or hit something. How could he have been so stupid, so careless? "She and I'll talk tomorrow." He lifted his eyes to hers, but her expression was guarded. Painfully so. "I'll be there for her. I won't be a father like . . ." He almost said it, almost compared himself to John Baxter, the man who had given him up. But the comparison wasn't fair, even in a moment like this. John hadn't had a choice. He wrung his hands. "My child will know me."

Katy crossed her arms. Even in the shadows her face was pale. "So . . . you'll marry her?"

Hollywood wasn't that easy, decisions never that simple. But he understood what she was asking. Now that there was a baby involved, was he going to do the right thing? He laced his fingers together and looked at her, past the block wall and razor wire she'd put up between them. "Yes." This was maybe even harder than the first part. "If that's what Kelly wants."

Katy sighed, but it sounded almost like a cry. She turned around again and faced the surf, her body frozen, thoughts silent. After a minute, he saw her shoulders tremble. The reality hit then. Here was Katy Hart, standing on his deck crying. Because the questions they'd had about each other, about a future together, had all just been answered.

Dayne closed his eyes. A week earlier he'd been flipping channels on TV when he came across a strongman contest. A man with more muscles than limbs was harnessed to a city bus, straining with every step as he pulled it along behind him. Now, as Dayne blinked and stood and closed the distance between them, he felt the same way. The weight of his past was almost more than he could bear.

He came up beside her and pressed his hip into the railing. She wasn't sobbing, wasn't hysterical. Rather a trail of quiet tears fell from her eyes, and her expression made her look a million miles away. He touched her shoulder. "Katy . . ."

She turned to him, and something in her face changed. For the first time since he'd told her about the baby, her heart lay bare for him to see. And in that instant, Dayne knew. He knew that every time he'd ever doubted Katy's feelings for him he'd been wrong. She was in love with him, same as he was in love with her. When it had been only their different worlds keeping them apart, she had held out hope the way he had.

But now . . .

She was shivering harder. "I . . . I should go."

"This isn't what I wanted . . . I never planned for . . ."

"I know." She took a step back. Her eyes were dryer now, and she brushed her thumbs over the tears still on her cheeks. "Don't say anything, Dayne."

There was a rustling on the hillside below and the distinct sound of rapid camera clicks.

Dayne didn't hesitate. He took hold of her arm and pulled her away from the railing.

"What are you—?"

"Paparazzi." Dayne grabbed her baseball cap, handed it to her, and led her into the house. When he'd shut the sliding door behind them, he fell against the wall and groaned. "Why tonight?"

"It's too dark to see anything."

"I hope so." He didn't want to talk about photographers or being found out. Katy was about to run out of his life. He glanced over his shoulder at the deck. "You can't go out that way."

His house was warmer than outside, but still she was shaking. "I need to leave."

He hated that she was so cold. His sweatshirt would be big on her, but it was better than watching her shiver. He pulled it off, turned the sleeves right side out, and handed it to her. "Wear this."

She started to shake her head, but she changed her mind. She slipped it over her head and hugged herself. "Thanks."

They needed a plan if she was going to get out without the tabs capturing every detail. "Come on." He grabbed his keys from the counter and headed for his garage. "I'll drive you to your car. If we get a jump on them, you can be gone before they figure out what happened."

She looked afraid again, but she followed him to his SUV.

Dayne watched in his rearview mirror, and as soon as he pulled onto Pacific Coast Highway he relaxed. "Must've been just one guy. No one's following us."

Katy was silent, her eyes straight ahead. They reached the parking lot in half a minute, and she pointed to her rental car. "There."

Dayne pulled up on the far side of it and killed the engine. Suddenly the paparazzi were forgotten. Because this was good-bye. Given the circumstances, they might not be alone like this ever again. Not even at the upcoming trial.

"Keep looking for Jesus, Dayne." She crossed her arms tight against her middle. She looked like a child, his sweatshirt bulky on her. "Especially now."

The air inside his Escalade felt as if it were being sucked out. She couldn't do this, couldn't just walk out of his life. "We can still talk . . . it's not like we can't be—"

She held up her hand. "Please. It's too late." She smiled, but her eyes glistened. "Wherever you are, know this." She massaged her throat for a moment. "I'll be praying for you." With that she climbed out and shut the door behind her.

"No." The word was for his benefit alone. She was already hurrying to her car. Dayne grabbed his door handle. He couldn't let Katy leave until he told her how he felt. Sure, they'd see each other at the trial in May, but by then he'd be weeks away from being a father. He might even be married to Kelly. He bounded out of his SUV and caught up with her just as she reached the driver's side of her car.

Katy stopped when she saw him, her expression willing him to keep his distance, to not make this any harder than it already was. "I need to go, Dayne."

He slowed his steps. She looked breathtaking in the moonlight, even in his baggy sweatshirt. He came closer so they were only inches apart. "I have to tell you something."

She pressed her back against her car and searched his face.

"It was a mistake, Katy." He reached for her hands. When she didn't pull away, he silently rejoiced. They couldn't go their separate ways without this moment. "I never should've been with Kelly."

"Why?" Katy angled her head. The shine in her eyes became tears, and her chin quivered. "She's part of your world. She was always better for you than I was."

"No." He tightened his grip on her fingers and did the thing he'd been dying to do since she walked through his gate. He pulled her into his arms and held her. It wasn't the embrace of two lovers, but it was a hug that he hoped told her how much he cared, how much he would always care.

When he spoke, he breathed the words into her hair. "There's something you have to know . . . before you leave."

She pulled back just enough to see his face. Her cheeks were wet, and the hurt on her face was once again transparent. "Tell me."

He brushed his cheek against hers, drying her tears. He allowed himself to get lost in her eyes. Even if this were the last time. "Katy Hart, I've loved you since the first day I saw you." The tears were there for him too. He breathed in hard through his nose and stared up at the sky. When he had more control he looked at her again. "If there was a way out, I would've left my world in a minute to be with you." He wanted to kiss her, but he didn't dare. "Don't forget that, okay?"

His admission only made her look sadder. Her tears came faster. She crooked her finger and pressed it to her lips. "Good-bye, Dayne."

He heard the sound just as she was leaning close to hug him once more. The pounding of feet against the pavement, the click of the camera. "Katy, quick . . . go." He shielded her with his body, tried to block the photographer's view, but it was too late. There were two of them now, and they were only twenty yards or so from Katy's car. He could only hope they didn't figure out who she was. He gave her shoulder a gentle squeeze. "I meant what I said."

As fast as she could move, she opened her door and slid inside. It took her only seconds to start the car and back out of the spot. As she did, her eyes met his, and again he was absolutely sure about her feelings. Because the look she gave him said everything her words never had. Not that she had feelings for him or that she'd wondered about what they might've had. More than that.

Even if their connection was ending before it ever really began, she loved him. She loved him as much as he loved her.

He savored her look as long as he could. Then he blinked back tears, turned to the paparazzi, and flashed his famous smile. "Hey, guys, let up." He held out his hands, his expression frozen for the cameras. "I'm all yours."

"Who was she, Dayne?" It was a big, bearded guy. One of the regulars. He was out of breath from running up the beach, but even so he kept snapping pictures. "We'll find out eventually. Come on, tell us."

"Yeah, Dayne." The other guy was a wiry twentysomething—new to the shady business of lurking around the back doors of celebrities. "Make it easy on us. Give us her name."

"All right." He shrugged and gave them a practiced grin. In the distance he heard Katy pull her car onto the highway and speed off. "You caught me. Another day, another actress. What can I say?"

"Was it Kelly Parker? It looked like Kelly." The bearded guy had a line of sweat dripping down the side of his face. "Tell us it was Kelly and we'll leave."

Dayne walked to his Escalade, watching them the whole time, smile still frozen in place. No one would've known that his heart was breaking in half. "Now, now . . ." He kept his voice upbeat, loud enough for them to hear. "Actresses get feisty when you give away their secrets."

"Then it *is* Kelly." The young one jabbed his fist in the air. "I knew it!"

"You guys are too smart for me." Before Dayne climbed into his SUV he waved big. "See ya."

His smile died the moment he slipped behind his tinted glass. She was gone. Katy was gone, and there might never be another moment like that between them again. Not ever.

He turned the key in the ignition and backed up, leaving the photographers standing there wondering. Let them think it was

Kelly. She would be with him soon enough. What mattered was that they didn't know about Katy. That and they hadn't seen his tears, hadn't seen his heartache. As he sped off, he realized that he too was breathless. Not from running up the beach, like the paparazzi. But for pulling off the acting job of his life, smiling for the cameras, playing along.

When all he wanted to do was collapse there on the pavement and cry.

CHAPTER FOUR

JOHN BAXTER SETTLED BACK in the driver's seat and tightened his grip on the wheel. The drive to Indianapolis couldn't happen fast enough. It felt like a lifetime since his phone conversation with Tim Brown, the investigator, but it had only happened the day before. John had wanted to drop everything and head to the man's office. But his appointment wasn't until this morning at eleven.

With no idea what was coming, John had called into his office and asked his secretary to reschedule his appointments. Now it was only a matter of willing the minutes to pass so he could look the investigator in the eye and hear the truth. Whatever the truth was.

He flipped on the radio and hit the button for a country-music station. A commercial was wrapping up, and then the beautiful refrains of a song filled the car. A song he was familiar with. John recognized it before the first words. It was the group Lonestar singing their hit song "I'm Already There." John leaned back against his headrest and turned up the volume.

This was Elizabeth's song, the one she'd listened to so often when she was sick. He remembered her once on the way home from chemotherapy, sitting beside him, thinner than before, her hair almost gone. "I love this song," she told him. She'd reached for his hand. "If things don't go the way we want, if things . . . don't work out—" she smiled at him—"think of me when they play it, okay?"

He listened to the words, words about that special person being there—even when it didn't seem like they were. How that person would be there in the sunshine and the shadows, in the beat of a person's heart or the whisper of their prayers.

Tears stung at John's eyes, and he realized something.

It had been at least a week since he'd cried over losing Elizabeth. Not that he missed her any less. But the idea of missing her was getting more normal all the time, the rhythm of his routine without her more natural. He could still see her, of course. Still see her pale blue eyes, the way they jumped out framed by her thick dark hair. The way it had been before the cancer. The trouble was sometimes the memories weren't in color anymore. More like shades of gray.

He listened to the song some more, hummed along—the way she had done whenever it came on. It was a rainy day, and snow hovered in the forecast, but John didn't care. Elizabeth's dying wish was enough to keep him warm even if he were to open all four windows.

Her dying wish that somehow they find their firstborn.

John clenched his teeth. *God . . . why couldn't we be taking this drive together, she and I? How come we didn't find this investigator sooner?* He waited for a response, but all that came to mind were the words on the plaque on his desk. Words from the nineteenth chapter of Matthew: *With God all things are possible.*

All things.

Then how come Elizabeth hadn't found their son before she died? The questions rolled around like jagged stones in his mind. Or maybe God really did give people a window from heaven. Maybe Elizabeth was clasping her hands in excitement, as anxious as he was about the news that lay just ahead.

And it would be news; it had to be. He'd spent a sleepless night replaying the investigator's phone call. The man must have a find or detail, something important enough to have him come to Indianapolis in person to get the news. That could mean only one thing: Tim Brown, ace investigator, had found his son, his firstborn. It had to be that.

John rejoiced over the possibility, but he had an equal amount of regret. Why hadn't he tried this hard when Elizabeth was alive? She'd wanted the chance to meet their son so badly; the idea of it completely consumed her. But back then it hadn't been a priority for him. All that mattered was keeping her alive, working with her team of doctors, and begging God for another year, one more month. One more day.

At some point near the end of her battle, Elizabeth had peacefully let go of the fight to stay alive. Instead, she focused all her energy on finding their son, whoever he was, wherever he was. The child they'd been forced to give up. She was so adamant about making contact with him that the day before she died she'd convinced herself she had actually met him, that their firstborn had walked into her hospital room and shared an hourlong conversation with her.

At first the drug-induced delusion had made him beyond sad. He had failed her, been unable to bring about her final desire. But now he felt differently about it. Perhaps the dream or hallucination was a gift from God, a way of easing Elizabeth's pain in her dying days.

John drew a long breath. A commercial came on the station, and he turned the channel to classical music. No more sad songs. Not when every song about love or loss seemed written for Elizabeth and him. He squinted and tried to read a road sign up ahead. Indianapolis—10 Miles. The roads were empty; he'd be at the investigator's office in less than fifteen minutes.

His thoughts rolled around some more. The issue with their firstborn son wasn't as secret as it had been when Elizabeth was alive. Ashley knew now, and every few weeks she asked for an update. What was he doing about the search? Whom had he talked to? What investigator was working the case?

She had an uncanny sense about the situation. Last night, hours after the call from Tim Brown, Ashley had phoned him. "Dad, I can't stop thinking about him." Her voice was soft, filled with emotion.

John took a hopeful guess that maybe she was talking about her husband. "Landon?"

She made an exaggerated sigh. "Dad, you know who." She paused, and in the background he could hear Cole chattering away, something about having macaroni and cheese for dinner. Ashley lowered her voice. "My oldest brother."

Of course he knew. Ashley had started a dozen conversations this way since last fall when she found the letter Elizabeth had placed in an envelope marked *Firstborn*. Last night, though, he hadn't wanted to talk about his oldest son. He didn't want anyone to know he was going to the investigator's office until he had had time to sort through the information.

"Honey," he'd finally told her, "there's nothing to say, no news. When I know something, I'll call you."

He took the First Street exit and wound his way into the newer part of downtown. Tim Brown's office was on the fourth floor of a white cement-block building. Snow began falling just as John found an empty meter on the street out front and parked his car.

Five minutes later he stepped off the elevator and into the investigator's sparse quarters.

A woman at the front desk smiled at him. "Mr. Baxter?"

"Yes." John reminded himself to breathe. This was it; whatever had become of their son, he was pretty sure he was about to find out. He stepped forward and brushed a fine layer of snow off his coat. "I have an appointment with Mr. Brown."

"Have a seat." She pointed to a pair of hard-back wood chairs. "Mr. Brown's expecting you."

John did as she asked. The office didn't have much of a view; the building across the street was newer and twice as tall. Without walking over to the window, that was all a person could see.

He had expected the investigator to conform to the stereotypical image: slightly distracted and disheveled, lost in a mass of paperwork and flashing telephone lights. But Tim Brown was different. He was a fast-talking, intense professional, organized in his approach and with a keen eye for details. Details John had never even thought about. What sort of mission work had the adoptive parents done and where might they have done it? What church had they worked with? What was the name of the home where Elizabeth had lived during the last half of her pregnancy?

They were obvious questions. But they couldn't be answered in the court records—all of which were sealed.

Tim Brown had told him there was nothing he could do to open court records. "We're going deeper than that, Mr. Baxter. We'll have to."

John had done his best to cooperate. When his answers were not quite clear or a little hesitant, Tim Brown had pushed him, asking three more questions for every answer John gave. "I'd rather have too much to check than too little," he told John.

That had been a week ago, and now here he was.

The sound of footsteps echoed in the hall, and John drew a long breath. *God, if it's okay, can You let Elizabeth watch? Can You tell her how much I wish she were beside me right now . . . please?*

"Mr. Baxter?" Tim was a compact man with a runner's build.

John stood, and the two shook hands. "Thanks for seeing me."

"Sorry you had to come in. Like I said . . . the information is very sensitive." A seriousness filled the man's eyes. "Why don't you follow me?"

Something occurred to John as he followed him down a boxy hallway. Maybe the investigator wanted to give him this information in person because he'd found something terrible. Maybe their oldest son had enlisted in the service and been killed in action a decade ago. Or maybe he'd died in a car accident or from some sort of illness.

Maybe he was behind bars for some heinous crime.

Those were the sorts of details a PI couldn't possibly feel comfortable sharing over the phone. *Peace, God . . . give me peace. Be with me, whatever the news might be. . . .*

I am with you always, My son.

This time there was no mistaking the small whisper in John's soul. The words were part of Scripture, something he'd read a hundred times before. But he needed them now more than ever. He felt his shoulders relax a little.

"Here we are." Tim Brown opened a door halfway down the hall and moved straight to the simple office chair behind the desk. He motioned to the other one on the opposite side. "Have a seat."

John did. He took hold of the chair arms and focused on feeling the Lord's peace once more. He was about to ask if the news was good or bad, but already Tim was opening a file half an inch thick at the center of his desk.

"Mr. Baxter, I've found your son."

The room began to spin. John leaned forward, studying the investigator's eyes, his face. Was the news that was coming somehow tragic or heartbreaking? John couldn't read the man. He swallowed hard and found the words. "Is he . . . is he alive?"

The man twisted his face, confused by John's question. "Of course." Then his expression eased. "You thought if I wanted you to come in person then maybe . . ."

"Well, yes." John felt warm relief shoot into his veins. "I was concerned." But not anymore. No matter what else the investigator had found, their son was alive. That much alone was enough to make goose bumps rise along his arms and neck.

"Wow . . ." Tim Brown tapped his fist on his forehead a few times. "I'm so sorry. I never meant to put you through that. Sometimes I get so caught up in the answers in front of me that I expect a client to read my mind. I should've told you that I'd found him and he was alive. That much you could've known over the phone."

"Don't worry about it." John wanted the guy to move on. He slid to the edge of his chair and folded his hands on the desk. "What is it then? What did you find?"

The man bit at the inside of his cheek and shook his head. "Once I located your son, once I figured out who he was, my search led me to another investigator in Los Angeles. The two of us have mutual friends in the business. He wouldn't confirm anything, but he did say that he'd worked with your son in the past."

What? The room was spinning again. Their son had hired a private investigator at some point? Tim Brown was on a roll; John stayed glued to every word.

The investigator shifted in his seat. "That got me thinking." He stroked his chin. "If your son had hired an investigator, maybe he knew more about you than you knew about him." He looked at the file. "Sure enough, I found a travel trail on the guy." Tim looked up. "He's been to Bloomington at least twice. Maybe more."

John could hardly exhale. Was the investigator serious? Their son had been to Bloomington? If so, he must know who they were. But then why had he come so far only to avoid making contact?

"Let me see." Tim moved his finger down a page partway through the file. "Here it is. The first time I have record of him traveling to Indiana was the summer before last." He shot a look at John. "Wasn't that when your wife died?"

"Yes." John gave him the date of Elizabeth's death.

"That's what I thought." He turned the file so John could see the dates. "Your son was in Bloomington the day before she died." He paused. "Did you know that?"

John sucked in a sharp breath. "Dear God . . ." He pushed the chair back and stood, clasping his hands at the back of his neck. He finished his prayer silently. *Lord, did he find her? Did she really share an hour with him that day after all?* He moved to the window and stared at the street below. Not for a minute had he believed Elizabeth. But if their son had come, if he'd shared an hour with her, then why hadn't he stayed to meet the rest of the family? Surely Elizabeth would've told him that they were ready and willing—at least he was. The rest of them could've known soon after.

He turned around and leaned against the windowsill. "She told me she met him that day, that he came in and talked to her while we were out getting dinner." He rubbed the back of his neck. "I thought . . . I thought she was delusional from the pain meds and cancer." He squinted against the harsh glare of reality. "But if he found her, why didn't he stay?"

"First of all—" Tim pushed his chair back and kicked one leg over the other—"I hate to presume anything. I don't know for sure if he spent time at the hospital. Just that it appears he was in town that day, and he left later that night."

"One day?" The pieces weren't coming together, weren't making sense the way John needed them to. He gripped the windowsill. "Doesn't that seem strange?"

For a moment Tim looked at the file and then back at John. "Mr. Baxter, I have a lot more to tell you." There it was again. The seriousness in the man's face, the hint that this—whatever lay ahead—was the reason the investigator had called him all the way to Indianapolis.

"Okay." John crossed the room slowly and took his seat once more. "I'm listening."

Tim sorted through the file and made a sound that was more disbelief than utter amazement. "I've never had something like this happen in all my days as an investigator." He studied John's face and hesitated. "Mr. Baxter, your son's in the entertainment business."

John slid forward in his chair. Another wave of relief washed over him. So he wasn't in jail or in a mental facility. He wasn't homeless or living an outcast's life. "That's it?" A small nervous chuckle came from his throat. The young man must be a producer or an agent. "That's the big deal?"

This time Tim laughed. "I don't think you understand." He flipped through the file until he reached a page near the back. "Your son's an actor." He pursed his lips. "One of the most famous actors of our day."

"An actor?" John recognized the feeling coursing through him. Back when the kids were very young, the family would sometimes spend an evening putting together a puzzle. The harder the better. The Baxters developed a technique after a while. Pull the edge pieces out first and try to make the frame. There was always a moment when the sections of the frame suddenly began coming together. That's how he felt now. The picture wasn't clear, but an image was definitely taking shape. He put his hands on the desk. "Would I . . . would I know him?"

"Mr. Baxter—" he turned the folder around and pushed it toward John—"all of America knows him."

John leaned in and realized what he was looking at. There, taped to the bottom of the page, was a photograph cut from a magazine.

A photograph of Dayne Matthews.

John touched the image, stared at it, giving himself time to process the possibility. Again he was on his feet. He paced to the window and back, and for the first time—where his oldest son was concerned—he had more answers than questions. He stared at the ceiling and fought the light-headedness.

He walked back to the window and sat against the sill. No wonder Luke looked like Dayne. They were brothers. Suddenly he remembered something. Elizabeth had mentioned Dayne's name, hadn't she? He pressed his palms to his eyes. Yes, that's exactly what she'd said. His name was Dayne.

And he'd thought that was one more sign that Elizabeth was hallucinating. That somehow she'd remembered Luke's story about meeting Dayne at the law office and how the two of them had looked alike, and her imagination had honed in on the actor's name.

Only she hadn't been hallucinating at all.

If she knew his name, then he must've made it to her hospital room. Which meant . . . tears made his throat feel thick. If nothing else ever came from this meeting, until his last breath John would have peace. Because Elizabeth's final prayer, her dying wish had been answered. Or maybe he was only misunderstanding the man. He let his hands fall to his sides. "You're telling me Dayne Matthews is my son?"

"Yes." He gave a quiet laugh. "I've checked it every which way. Dayne was raised by missionary parents who were killed in a small plane crash in the jungles of Indonesia." He scanned the file. "He grew up in a boarding school for missionary kids, and when he was eighteen, after the death of his adoptive parents, he moved to California and enrolled in UCLA's drama department." The investigator shrugged. "I guess the rest is history."

John stared at the floor and tried to steady himself. Dayne Matthews? The son he and Elizabeth had given up, the child he'd never seen, the boy they'd wondered about all of their lives . . . was Dayne Matthews? The investigator was right. He'd been to Bloomington at least twice, the day before Elizabeth died and again for the filming of his latest movie, the one due out soon. Had Dayne chosen Bloomington because he knew about the Baxters? because he had an interest in them?

Something Tim had mentioned when they first started this

meeting came back. Dayne had hired a private investigator. Maybe that's how he'd found out about his biological family, about Elizabeth's being sick in the hospital. But that left one question. John walked back to the chair and sat down. He searched the man's face across from him. "If he hired an investigator, why haven't we heard from him?"

Tim leaned back, his expression blank. "That's where things get a little hazy." He flipped through the pages of the file. "He's had the chance." The investigator narrowed his eyes. "Something's obviously holding him back. Like I said, he knew about you first. Could be his management team, his studio, something he signed in a contract. Hard to tell with people in his business."

"Yes." John tried not to feel the sting, but it was there anyway. Had Dayne figured out who they were and then changed his mind about meeting them? Did the Baxter family somehow not measure up to what Dayne had hoped to find in his biological family, or had something happened in his conversation with Elizabeth, something that would cause him to keep his distance? Or maybe Tim was right, and there was some reason regarding his career that he had to stay away.

Tim turned his chair and opened a file cabinet. From a folder marked *Baxter*, he pulled out a stack of papers stapled together. "I made copies of everything I found." He slipped the papers into an envelope and handed it to John. "Dayne lives in Malibu, from what I can tell. But I can't get an address. No phone number, either. Couldn't find it." He nodded to the envelope. "You will find an address for the studio that produced his recent film and a phone number for his agent. That might be helpful. His agent's one of the best in the business. Powerful, influential, from what I found out."

"Meaning what?"

Tim lifted his hands and let them fall, clasped, onto the folder on the desk. "Meaning I'm not sure he'll help you. But if you want to contact Dayne, you'd start with his agent."

John stared at the envelope. He'd spent a lifetime longing for the information inside this packet, but he had to wonder if he'd come this far only to reach a dead end. Clearly Dayne knew about them, yet not once had he made contact.

"I've done what I can do." Tim stood. "There's a bill for my services in the envelope. Top sheet."

"Thank you." John rose and shook the investigator's hand. The shock was wearing off. He felt like a man who'd spent a lifetime climbing a mountain only to find out the top wasn't something he could ever reach. "I'll get payment to you later this week."

"Very good."

Tim made small talk for a few more minutes, how he'd worked hundreds of cases and never turned up a celebrity before and how crazy life was for people with Dayne's visibility.

John was glad when he was finally out of the office and into the elevator. He leaned against the wall and pressed the button marked *L* for lobby.

There were dozens of decisions to make. Whether he'd tell Ashley what he'd learned and whether he would tell the family anything at their reunion in April, a chance for everyone to know the truth. Of course, the first decision was whether he'd do what the investigator suggested and call Dayne's agent.

After more than three decades, he finally knew who his son was. Dayne Matthews, mega movie star. John took a long breath and steadied himself. He'd seen the young man last fall filming on location in Bloomington. It was the day he and his friend Elaine had stopped at the farmers' market for blueberries.

No matter which trail his thoughts took, they always came around to that one sad truth: Dayne had known about the Baxters for more than a year and never once connected with any of them except Elizabeth. John clutched the envelope to his side and pictured his firstborn son, the way he'd appeared on the street that day.

No wonder he'd looked so much like Luke.

And that was something else. Certainly if Dayne wanted contact with them he could've started with Luke. Dayne's private investigator would've given him information on the entire Baxter family, which meant he had to know that Luke worked for his very own attorney.

John walked off the elevator, through the lobby, and to his car as another thought hit him. A thought that took his breath away. Luke and Dayne would be working together this spring. Dayne's attorney, Joe Morris, had asked Luke to be available the first part of May to travel to Los Angeles and work in tandem when Dayne's case against the knife-wielding fan went to trial.

"Dad, can you believe it?" Luke had called the week before, excited about the news. "Me! They want me to go with Joe Morris for the Dayne Matthews case." Luke whistled, the kind of whistle John had heard him make hundreds of times over the years after a baseball or basketball game. "They have big plans for me. I mean, I'll just be doing the grunt work, but still." He grabbed a quick breath. "It's a good sign, don't you think, Dad?"

"Absolutely." John had smiled, happy and proud all at once. "That case will have every eye in America on it."

Now John was overwhelmed by the enormity of it.

What's happening here, God? My two sons, strangers, working side by side? The thought was daunting.

John got in the car, took hold of the steering wheel with both hands, and waited before starting the engine. Maybe Dayne was holding out for the perfect time, a week or two when he might be between films and award shows and interviews. Maybe he would call on his own one of these days, John would talk to him, and the whole Baxter family would know in a matter of days.

But maybe not.

The question toyed with him, jabbed at him as he headed back to the freeway. At the trial, when Luke and Dayne found themselves working together, would it be as a legal team?

Or as brothers?

By the time John reached Bloomington he'd made up his mind to call at least one person about the news. A man in Los Angeles who held the key to the next door that separated him from the child he and Elizabeth had given away.

Dayne's agent.

CHAPTER FIVE

────────◆≻⋙◉⋘≺◆────────

ROBIN HOOD WAS SET to take the Christian Kids Theater stage in twelve days, and Katy had never felt less prepared. The parent committees were on target. The program was at the printer, and the props team had collected everything from the two dozen wooden swords to bows and arrows and a hand-painted target for the archery contest.

Al and Nancy Helmes were doing brilliant work with the music, and Rhonda Sanders was bringing together the dance details of everything from the Merry Maiden ballet to the highly choreographed fight scene. Even seven months pregnant, Ashley Baxter Blake was again helping out with sets, and already the forestlike backdrop was breathtaking.

No, the problem wasn't with the people working to make the play a success.

The problem was with her.

The kids needed her fully committed, driven, and intense—the way she'd been with every show up until now. Normally at this point in the production she'd be fine-tuning the details, perfecting the blocking, and cutting precious seconds from the scene changes. Instead, the practices were running together in a blur, and all for one reason.

She was still reeling about Dayne.

Even now, ten minutes before practice, she kept tuning out the conversations around her, ones between Al and Nancy and Rhonda, and even the information CKT area coordinator Bethany Allen was sharing with the production team. They sat at a round table in a small room of the church, Bethany across from Katy, Rhonda on one side of her, Al and Nancy on the other.

Bethany was going over the ticket sales for the show. "We're sold out for every evening performance and one of the Saturday matinees." She checked her notes. "There are still seats available for three afternoon shows."

"What about the school days? Sold out, right?" Rhonda looked at her own notes and then at Bethany.

Bethany poised her pencil over her clipboard. "Actually, no." She frowned. "Half the seats for Tuesday are still open. Two schools pulled out when they heard we are a Christian theater group."

Katy wrote the details on the page in front of her. "We're still trying to get the school district to give us across-the-board approval, the way CKT groups in other parts of the country have done."

"Exactly."

The conversation lasted another few minutes before Bethany led the group in a quick prayer and then went to open the doors of the sanctuary for the kids.

Only after Al and Nancy headed toward the coffeemaker did Rhonda turn to Katy and raise her eyebrows. "Where are you today?" Her voice was low.

"I'm here." Katy put her pen down. A frustrated sigh escaped her lips, and she searched her friend's face. "Do you read the tabloids?"

"Katy . . ." Rhonda knew the truth. She'd known it since the day Katy returned to Bloomington. "Not until after the show's over, remember? You need to focus. No talking about him until then."

Katy waved her hand. "This is different." She kept her tone even. "I'm talking about the tabs. Come on, Rhonda; do you ever read them?"

"In the checkout line at the grocery store." She stood, glancing at the clock that hung over the double doors. "Come on, Katy. The kids are coming in."

"We have a minute." She rose and held her notepad to her side. "'Cause here's what I'm thinking. If Dayne and Kelly are having a baby and if they're back together, then how come there's nothing in the magazines?"

"Katy, let it go." Rhonda stopped and looked at her.

"And how come they keep showing pictures of Kelly with Hawk Daniels?"

The concern in Rhonda's eyes bordered on worry. "It doesn't matter. You know the truth."

Katy looked down at her low-heeled shoes. Rhonda was right, but why'd it still have to hurt so badly a month after she'd returned from LA? Hadn't she convinced herself a year ago that nothing could ever come of her friendship with Dayne Matthews? Of course he was going to be a father, and why not? He and Kelly Parker had lived together after all. If Dayne could have asked Kelly to move in with him, then he never could've been interested in some drama instructor from Bloomington, anyway.

She could hear the kids in the sanctuary, hear them singing and squealing and talking at once as they waited for her. Al and Nancy were warming up on the piano, and the excitement was something she could feel even a room away. She looked at Rhonda. "It's so hard."

"I know." Rhonda came closer and gave her a hug. "We can talk about it later, okay?"

"I have to wait until *Robin Hood*'s finished, remember?"

"Silly." Rhonda took a few steps toward the door. Her eyes held a special knowing sort of compassion. "Rules like that are made to be broken. I'm here whenever you need to talk."

"Thanks." Katy fell in beside her. "We're painting sets tonight. Maybe we can talk then."

"With Ashley here?" Rhonda sounded doubtful. "You don't mind talking about this around her?"

"Not really. She already knows about Dayne and me." Katy gave Rhonda a crooked grin. "He even gave Ashley a ride home one night after *Annie* practice."

"What?" Rhonda's voice was suddenly twice as loud. "You should've invited him back when *I* was here."

"I know. I know." Katy pointed toward the roar of kids in the sanctuary. "Let's go. We can't be late."

"Fine." Rhonda giggled as they ran through the doors and into the other room. "I know where I stand."

They needed to finish two scenes today—the archery contest and the sword fight. Katy took her spot at the front of the kids and studied the faces of the fifty-three kids cast in the show. *God, I need to be at my best today. Please help me stay focused.*

For the first time that afternoon, Katy couldn't feel herself standing in a parking lot at Malibu Beach with Dayne Matthews' arms around her. Instead her mind filled with all they had to accomplish in the next few hours. She did the special CKT clap, and around the room the kids stopped talking as they clapped out the beat in return.

"Okay, you've all read the rehearsal schedule."

In the middle of the room, Bailey Flanigan and her brother Connor were among the first to nod. They were the kids from the family Katy lived with, and though she was careful not to show favoritism, she loved them dearly. They were like family to her, and they were also some of the best behaved and most talented members of the cast.

Katy paced in front of the group, looking into the eyes of each boy and girl she passed. "We have to be at the top of our game today, guys." The words were for her as much as for them. "The fight scene and the archery contest, both in one practice."

She gave directions to the various groups and released them to their assigned places. The sword fighters would take the fellowship hall, where Rhonda would try and complete choreography for a scene that would need to look intense while still somehow safe.

"The key," Rhonda told them before they headed into the next room, "is to treat it like a dance. That way no one will get hurt."

Katy was in charge of the archery contest. The scene would have Kaspar challenge Robin Hood to a competition to win a golden arrow and a kiss from Maid Marian. The main characters would stand upstage on the left side, shooting their arrows across diagonally to the hand-painted target backstage on the right side.

The magic would happen this way. The actors would only pretend to shoot arrows. Instead, they'd grab hold of a thick black-painted rubber tubing attached to the bow. When they drew back, the tubing would take on the appearance of an arrow. Because the actors would look at the target as they released the bow, the audience had the very realistic sensation that an arrow had actually flown across the stage.

Meanwhile, stationed behind the oversized target was a crew member who would quickly pop an arrow out from a predetermined spot behind the target. The black circles on the target were netting, so the boy had a clear view of when Robin Hood released his supposed arrow. If the timing was right on, the eyes of everyone in the audience would be tricked to believe that an arrow had not only been released but that it had landed sharply somewhere near the center of the target.

From the beginning the scene had serious trouble.

Bryan Smythe, a teenager with one of the best voices in CKT, was Robin. He was first to shoot, and he pretended to be lost in the intensity of the moment as he drew back what looked like an arrow. Only as he released it, the target remained completely void of any sign of an arrow.

After eight or nine seconds of silence, the crew member stood up and scratched his head. "Which arrow goes first, the center one or the ones off center?"

"Robin Hood wins the contest." Katy sprinted up the stage steps and hurried to the place behind the target. She took a pen from her pocket and numbered the arrows. "There." She smiled at the crew member. "That'll make it easier."

She returned to her place in the aisle. "Let's try it again."

Bryan lined up, made a keen eye toward the target, and pulled back his rubber tubing. But before he even made a move to release it, an arrow proudly appeared near the bull's-eye. Bryan let his bow fall to his side. He looked at Katy and shrugged.

"Wow . . ." Katy jogged up the stairs again. "Robin's better than we thought."

A round of chuckles came from the older kids positioned around the stage, the ones playing townspeople in the scene.

Bryan grinned at them and took a bow.

Katy moved behind the target and came face-to-face with the boy responsible for the special effect. "Okay, now listen." She took hold of his shoulders. "Timing here is everything. You can see Bryan, right? Through the netting?"

The boy's face was red. "Actually I can only see his knees." He scratched his neck. "I have to sort of guess when he releases the bow."

Katy put her hands on her hips. There had to be a solution. They couldn't have arrows disappearing across the stage, and it wouldn't work to have arrows appearing long before the archer released his bow. She looked at Al and Nancy Helmes, and in a flash an idea came to her.

She snapped her fingers and headed in their direction. "Can you play some sort of edge-of-your-seat-type music? You know, just as Robin Hood and Kaspar are loading their bows and pulling back?"

"Of course." Al grinned at her and rattled off a series of piano notes that was perfect for the moment.

Nancy was sitting beside him on the piano bench. "When they release their bows, Al can play a dissonant chord." She nudged him. "Go ahead."

"Something like this?" Al played a chord that somehow sounded like an arrow whizzing through the air.

"Perfect!" Katy raised her fist in the air. This was the part she loved, watching theater magic come to life. The victory wasn't enough to release her heart of the weight it carried, but she welcomed the distraction. She pointed at the crew member. "Understand what we're doing?"

The boy nodded. "Mr. Helmes plays the build-up music, and then he hits that chord. When he hits it—"

"You pop the arrow through." Katy clapped. "It'll work for sure."

They ran through the scene a few times before the timing was right, but it was the fix she'd been looking for.

After an hour of working the lines and getting the blocking down for the entire scene, Katy was satisfied. She had someone send for Rhonda. "We need to see the sword fight."

This was the scene that worried Katy the most. The swords weren't real, of course. They were cut from wood and painted to look like swords. But they were heavy wooden clubs all the same. If the choreography wasn't right on, boys would be lunging and missing and hitting air, perhaps falling to the stage and landing on their swords, or worse—getting a direct blow from one of the other sword fighters.

The boys filed in, Connor Flanigan among them.

Katy smiled to herself at the picture they made as they took the stage. Each with a sword in his hand, the boys looked like proud, young warriors. The scene would be breathtaking if they could pull it off without injury.

When the clanking of swords had settled down, Katy addressed them. "This will be the part in the play that people talk about an hour after they've seen the show." She kept her tone serious. As much fun as it was to swing a sword at another cast mate, the kids had to realize the potential danger in the scene. "We have to be safe. But if we get this part right, we get the entire show right."

The boys looked even prouder than before.

Katy stifled a grin as she looked them over. "Okay, let's see what you've got."

The fighting was between Robin Hood's men and the men who belonged with the sheriff of Nottingham. When the show was performed, half the boys would be dressed like merry men, in raggedy forest-type costumes. The other half would be in regal attire. The boys knew which were which, and they formed twelve pairs, facing and circling each other with an intensity that was already ominous.

"Good!" Katy stood back and crossed her arms. "I like the emotion."

"Ready?" Rhonda took the spot on the floor near center stage. "Five, six, seven, eight! One, two, three, four . . ." She kept counting as the boys launched into a routine of raising their swords and clanging them against the ones belonging to their opponents, first one way, then another.

Not until the third set of eight counts did three boys move their swords the wrong way. As they did, their face-off partners each brought swords down squarely against the arms of the boys who had messed up.

One boy fell to the floor and grabbed his arm, his face twisted in pain. Another one bent in half and hugged his arm to his middle. The third stood, frowning, and brushed himself off.

"Oh, dear." Katy rushed onto the stage. She looked over her

shoulder at Rhonda, a few steps behind her. "You told them not to go full force, right?"

"Right." Rhonda went to the boy on the floor and helped him to his feet. By then the other two were already looking ready to try again. "Everyone okay?"

A round of nods came from the boys.

"All right, listen." Katy raised her voice so they could all hear her. "We have to remember this is acting, not fighting."

Rhonda exchanged a look with Katy. They had to bite their lips to keep from smiling. "Did everyone hear Katy?" Rhonda took the sword from the nearest boy. "When you swing your sword, you have to *look* like you're swinging it with all your might." She demonstrated by making a face. "But if you really swing that hard and if someone's out of place—" she gestured to the boys who'd been hit—"someone's going to get hurt."

Katy raised her brow. "Everyone got that?"

The group nodded again.

"Okay, follow Rhonda." Katy descended the stairs and took her place to the side.

Rhonda did the same, staying in the middle so she could direct. "Take your places."

Rhonda slowed her count the next time, while Al and Nancy Helmes moved the townspeople into the lobby to finish the opening musical number.

By the time the parents began arriving, Katy was ready to declare her sword-fight scene an abysmal mistake. They had five broken swords, one bloody gash on the lower calf of a ten-year-old boy, and one bruised forehead.

When all the kids had been picked up and the last sword injury had been detailed and discussed with each parent, Katy flopped into a folding chair and stared at the ceiling.

"All right, then." A few feet away, Rhonda leaned against the nearest wall and laughed. "Any other bright ideas?"

Katy sat up. "Helmets." She jabbed her pointer finger at the air above her head. "Plastic swords and helmets."

The door at the back of the room opened, and a very pregnant Ashley Baxter Blake walked in. She had her hand on a cart full of paint cans and supplies. "Landon says I can't carry heavy boxes anymore." She placed her hand on her abdomen and grinned. "Dr. Baxter agrees. But that's because he's my dad."

Katy and Rhonda went to meet Ashley, and the trio crossed the hall. They were using the lobby to paint sets tonight.

When they reached their work spot, Katy gave Ashley a wary look. "You really think that baby's staying in there until April?"

"I know. I'm huge." Ashley stopped and pressed her fist to her lower back. "It was this way with Cole too. I look like I'm carrying triplets."

"Yeah, but you're one of those girls who doesn't look pregnant anywhere else." Rhonda patted her thighs. "I doubt I'll be that lucky when it's my turn."

The group laughed, but a bit of sadness pierced Katy's heart. When would it be time for either her or Rhonda to have children? When would God bring men into their lives who fit the bill of all they were praying for in a husband? Dayne's face filled her mind. Kelly Parker would soon look like Ashley—bursting with life and love and glowing from all her body was going through. And Dayne would be right there beside her.

"Be right back." Rhonda headed for one of the prop-committee dads. "Hey, could you please help me get the backdrop in from Ashley's car . . . ?"

Katy felt the sting of tears. She wasn't ready for this. Just being near Ashley made her feel lonely and left out. As if her time for love and new life might never come. She set the paint cans on one of the tables.

Ashley sat in a chair against the wall and sighed. "It's getting harder to move."

"I'll bet." Katy blinked the wetness from her eyes. She kept her attention on the paint cans, moving them this way and that so she wouldn't have to look at Ashley. She and Ashley were becoming better friends all the time. Her sadness would make no sense at a moment like this. She gave a light sniff and smiled at Ashley. "Landon and Cole must be so excited."

"Landon's worse than my dad." She made a mock look of concern. "'Ashley, are you sure the paint fumes are okay for the baby? Did you take your vitamins? Are you getting enough to eat?'" She laughed. "I told him he was going to wind up in the hospital before I do if he doesn't relax a little."

Katy smiled, but she could feel it stop short of her eyes.

"Hey . . ." Ashley's tone changed. "Everything okay?"

"Yeah." Katy's emotions were skimming along the surface of her heart, but there was nothing she could do about it. "I guess."

Before Ashley could say anything else, Rhonda and the prop dad came huffing through the door, the giant canvas rolled up and balanced on each of their shoulders.

"Where do you want it?" The dad was leading the way.

Rhonda looked like she was doing her best just to keep up.

Katy sprang to one side of a series of tables that had been placed side by side. "Here. Across the tops of these."

Rhonda and the dad lumbered across the lobby and dropped the canvas on the center table.

Rhonda leaned her elbow on the canvas and wiped her other hand across her forehead. "That thing must weigh a hundred pounds." She saluted the dad. "Glad you were here. Thank you."

"No problem. Let me know if you need anything else." He returned to the hallway, where a group of parents were already working on several oversized set pieces.

Rhonda was still out of breath. She rested against one of the tables and looked at Ashley. "How'd you get that thing in your Durango?"

"Landon and one of our neighbors." Ashley stood and

stretched her back. "Landon would've walked it here himself before he'd let me lift a single corner of it."

"He's a good man."

Katy grabbed paint cans and used them to anchor two of the backdrop corners. Rhonda did the same with two other cans. For a few minutes, they talked about the direction the backdrop was taking and how professional it already looked and what an asset Ashley was to CKT.

But when the conversation fell off, Rhonda took a paintbrush from the box in Ashley's roller cart and found her place beside Katy. "All right, friend. I've been waiting all night to hear what's going on."

"See . . ." Ashley was already working on a section of green and gray plants along the right side of the backdrop. "I knew something was wrong."

"Is it that obvious?" Katy looked up. With all she was, she wanted to forget about Dayne Matthews. But he was as much a part of her as her next heartbeat. Maybe if she talked about her feelings for him now, with two of her closest friends, she could talk herself out of caring so much.

"I could see it right away." Ashley slid her chair down a few inches and poised her paintbrush over a section that still had no color. A certainty filled her expression. "Is it Dayne Matthews?"

"Yes." Katy blew at a wisp of her hair. Rhonda knew far more about the situation than Ashley. But Katy appreciated that her friend stayed quiet now. "He told me a month ago that Kelly Parker is pregnant."

"And the baby's his?" Ashley's mouth stayed open, the shock on her face genuine.

Katy dipped her brush into a dark brown paint and dragged it carefully down the length of the biggest tree trunk. "The baby's definitely Dayne's."

"No . . ." Anger flashed in Ashley's eyes. "I saw how he looked at you, Katy. That guy couldn't possibly love anyone the way he loves you. How could he . . . ?"

"Kelly's five months pregnant." Katy felt tears trying to rise up. "She was pregnant before they came here for the filming."

"After the crazy-stalker thing." Rhonda gave a knowing look to Ashley.

"Oh." A resignation came into Ashley's tone. "When you told him the two of you didn't have a chance."

"Right." Katy swirled her brush through the brown paint and wiped off the excess. Her heart hurt just talking about it. "She moved in with Dayne after that, and . . . well, now they're going to have a baby."

For half a minute, none of them spoke. Then Katy stopped her brush midstroke. "So how come I'm not seeing Dayne and Kelly in the tabloids? How come they're not all over the covers by now making plans to get married—like all the other pregnant Hollywood women and their boyfriends? And how come every gossip magazine has pictures of Kelly and Hawk Daniels?" She paused and held the paintbrush over the can. "I mean, have you seen anything in the magazines that makes you think Kelly's back with Dayne?"

"No." Ashley folded her arms. "Definitely not."

Rhonda had moved to the other side of the canvas. "I'm trying to tell her it doesn't matter if the tabs know about the baby yet." She was working intently on painting in a long ivy vine. Her voice was kind, quiet, the humor from earlier gone. She looked straight at Katy. "Bottom line, he's going to be a dad. And he's planning to stay with Kelly, if she'll take him."

A weak moan came from Ashley. She set her brush against the edge of the can and leaned back in her chair. "I'm so sorry, Katy. You should've told me."

"I know." Katy didn't mind the sympathy. But she hated hearing herself explain the situation. It only underscored why she never should've allowed herself to have feelings for Dayne in the first place. "I guess I hate how it sounds. Of course his girlfriend is pregnant." She laughed, but there was nothing funny about the sound. "She was living with him. I mean, what was I thinking? I need to stop dwelling on him."

They talked a little more about the tabloids and the lack of proof that Dayne was indeed making his way back to Kelly. But in the end Ashley agreed with Rhonda. It didn't matter. Dayne Matthews had no place in Katy's life. He was going to be a father.

What more was there to say?

They switched topics, and Ashley talked about her pregnancy.

That led to Rhonda's questions about when it would ever be her turn to fall in love and have children. "I mean, honestly." She took harder swipes at the ivy. "The only guy interested in me right now is ten years older and three inches shorter."

Katy smiled. She liked hearing Rhonda talk about her misadventures in love. It made a very real, very depressing topic seem lighthearted and funny. As if they weren't really wondering whether God had forgotten about them. She pointed her paintbrush at Rhonda. "Hey . . . short's not so bad."

"For you, maybe." Rhonda made an exaggerated look straight down. "How do you talk to a guy when you literally can't see eye to eye?"

They laughed, and the easygoing talk continued. The whole time, Katy tried to convince herself that she was ridiculous to waste another minute thinking about Dayne. Connecting with him, becoming his friend, having feelings for him—all of it was like something from a dream. Who ever heard of a small-town girl falling for a movie star and believing her feelings could actually lead to a relationship?

In some ways Katy wanted to laugh at herself for ever thinking—even in her weakest moments—that the two of them might have a chance. But she couldn't convince her heart. Time and again as the night wore on she had to rope in her feelings, chide herself for remembering Dayne's kiss or the way he looked in the moonlight on Malibu Beach.

Katy was thankful for the backdrop. Otherwise, Rhonda and Ashley would've seen how distracted she was. Rhonda for sure would've figured out that she must still be thinking about Dayne. But since they were determined to finish the canvas, neither of them mentioned it.

After an hour, they stood back and admired their work.

"It's the best yet." Ashley pressed her hand to the small of her back. "Even if this little guy's been kicking the whole time."

"Guy?" Katy faced her friend. "Did you find out?"

"No. We want to be surprised." Ashley giggled. "Cole thinks he's getting a brother. I guess I picked up on it." She looked at her watch. "Good. Landon said he'd be awake until eleven. I'll still have an hour with him."

Again Katy felt the sting of her friend's words. Not that Ashley meant anything by them, but the contrast was just so sharp. Ashley would go home to a man who had loved her since she was in high school. Home to a little boy who adored her and a home where very soon they would bring a new baby.

Katy would go home to the apartment over the Flanigans' garage, alone and with only a handful of social events scattered across the next few months of calendar space.

She helped Ashley pack her rolling cart, and the three of them found their jackets, bundled up, and headed to the parking lot. There was no snow, but the temperature was hovering around ten degrees. Katy and Rhonda helped Ashley load her vehicle and watched her drive off.

"I wonder if she knows how lucky she is." Rhonda looked at the fading taillights on Ashley's vehicle.

"She does." Katy remembered the conversation she'd had with Ashley in the hospital several months ago when they were holding vigil for Sarah Jo Stryker, the twelve-year-old CKT star who died from injuries she received when a drunk driver hit her mother's van last fall. "Ashley sees Landon as a gift from God. Nothing less."

Rhonda gave her a sad smile. "You sounded healthy in there." It was easy to read Katy's eyes, even in the light of the street-lamps. "You know what I mean?"

"About Dayne?" Katy slid her hands into her coat pockets.

"Mmm-hmm." She clutched her dance bag close to her middle. "You need to let him go."

"I have." Katy's answer was quick. The air was icy against her cheeks. But under her jacket she was warm, so much so that she wasn't shivering. "The moment he told me about Kelly I made it clear I had to leave. Obviously."

"Okay." Rhonda angled her head. She seemed to be working hard not to be pushy. She tugged on Katy's jacket sleeve. "If you've let go of him, then good for you. Let's just keep it that way."

They said good-bye and went their separate ways, and only after Katy was getting in the car did she realize something that defied everything she'd told Rhonda and Ashley. How could she claim to be over Dayne when the reason she wasn't cold was because of the cozy oversized sweatshirt she was wearing? The one she'd worn to practice almost every day for nearly a month. A sweatshirt that was warm and thick and gray with MICHIGAN written in block letters across the front.

One that had belonged to Dayne Matthews.

CHAPTER SIX

———⟢⟡⟣———

DAYNE WAS HANGING from a window ledge, his feet dangling against the outside of an old brick building in downtown Los Angeles. Lost to the cameras was the fact that he was only two stories up and a pit of foam rubber lay directly beneath him.

They were filming the toughest scenes, the climax of the romantic thriller he was working on, and every scene was high energy and intense—a life-or-death matter. His costar Angie Carr was supposed to be trapped in the room. The script called for Dayne to vault himself onto the ledge and kick through the window, intending to pull off a surprise rescue.

Instead, he would see through the dirty glass that Angie was working with the con men, that she was in on the dirty deeds. She was one of the bad guys. It was a turning point in the movie, and Dayne had to be at his best. He couldn't afford to think about any of the things that consumed him these days. Not Kelly or the baby, not the faith of his birth parents and adoptive parents.

And especially not Katy Hart.

"All right . . ." The director's voice boomed across the set.

Ron Foster was doing a brilliant job so far. Dayne had worked with the director twice before, and both films were huge successes. Ron would settle for nothing but the best. "Let's move the ladder in."

Between takes when Ron was talking to Angie or blocking some other part of the scene, a ladder would be rolled in beneath Dayne—since there was a limit to how long he could hang from his fingertips. As soon as he could feel something under his feet, he would stand and let go of the window ledge.

Three times already he'd practiced pulling himself onto the ledge, then lowering himself back down when he realized what was happening inside the room. Ron Foster had offered a stunt double for the scene, since the shot was filmed entirely from Dayne's back.

But Dayne liked doing his own stunts.

He'd spent two hours in his home gym every day since Katy left. Physically he was in the best shape of his life—that would have to make up for the fact that every other area was falling apart.

He was rubbing out the kinks in his fingers when Angie slid open the window. She was wearing a revealing tank top, and the makeup team had applied a thin layer of petroleum jelly to her chest and arms, her cheeks and forehead. Even though it was barely seventy degrees in LA today, she gave the appearance of someone overheated. The movie was supposed to take place in Atlanta in July—so the two of them needed to glisten with sweat in almost every scene.

It was the sort of detail Ron was adamant about.

Angie leaned out the window and grinned at him. "You're amazing." She rested her elbows on the sill and cocked her head. She ran one finger along the definition in his upper arm. "Most guys would take the stunt double for a scene like this."

He was balancing on a ladder, leaning one hand against the brick wall. He couldn't go anywhere. "It's a two-story window, Angie." He shrugged one shoulder. "It's not like it's a risk."

"I know." She lightly ran her finger up his neck and tapped the end of his nose. "But swinging yourself onto a window ledge?" Her eyes sparkled. "You're pretty strong, Mr. Dayne Matthews."

Dayne didn't know what to say to that.

Angie had been this way throughout the filming. She was a great actress and a savvy businesswoman. It would've been impossible to miss her beauty and the way she used it to her advantage every possible chance she had. But he truly wasn't attracted to her. Angie Carr had a history of connecting with her leading men. The stories in Hollywood about Angie's love affairs were legendary. Tempting as she could make herself, for a dozen reasons Dayne had no intention of being another notch on her belt.

He glanced over his shoulder to where Ron Foster was standing with a bullhorn, talking to the stunt driver of one of the three cars that would race by when Dayne decided to bail on the rescue of Angie.

He didn't mind interrupting. "How much longer?"

Ron shaded his eyes and looked at him. "Two minutes. Hold tight."

Angie made a quiet chuckling sound. "You enjoy it, don't you?"

He faced her again. "What?"

"Me. Chasing you the way I've done on this film."

"Hmm." Dayne knew better than to anger Angie Carr. Not when their chemistry was so crucial to the film. He grinned and felt his dimples spring to life. "You can tell?"

"Of course." She angled her body, half sitting on the windowsill. Her eyes never left his. "I get what I want, Dayne Matthews." The suggestion in her eyes was so strong she might as well have shouted her feelings from the rooftop. For a moment she pouted her famous lips at him. "Is it Kelly Parker? Is that who you're pining for?"

Dayne kept his cool. Kelly hadn't said anything about her pregnancy. When she did, everyone would know. The tabloids, the television media, and every actor and actress in Hollywood. He switched hands and leaned against the other one. "Who says I'm pining?"

"Well—" she thrust her body closer to him—"you're resisting me pretty well."

"Just testing my strength, Angie." He winked at her. "Figure if I can resist you I can do just about anything."

She smiled, pleased with herself. He silently congratulated himself for saying the right thing. She leaned closer still. "Okay, but you don't have to resist me." Another pout. "I've made that clear, right?"

"Ah, Angie . . . I don't know." He was playing with her, stalling. "You're so hard to read."

"Oh, sure." She slumped a little. "Like the other afternoon when I was in your trailer half dressed waiting for you and you never came?"

He resisted a laugh. "I was working lines." He made a face that implied he'd made a mistake by not following her into the trailer.

"Okay, but come on." She straightened, her expression more curious than before. "It's Kelly, right? That's where your heart is these days?"

Dayne pictured Katy Hart, the way she'd looked standing on his deck in the moonlight . . . "Okay—" he grimaced, giving her a mock look of resignation—"you caught me."

She ignored his teasing. "I knew it." She processed the information for a few seconds. Then she leaned so close he could've kissed her if he wanted to. "You want the bad news now or later?"

Bad news? Dayne didn't react. He steadied himself, and for a moment he considered looking over his shoulder and once more asking Ron Foster how much longer. But something in Angie's tone told him she wasn't kidding. "Bad news?"

"About Kelly." Angie sat up and rolled her eyes. "Come on,

Dayne. The whole world's reading the tabs, and what do you do? Go straight home, hit the gym, and fall into bed by yourself?"

"Pretty much." She'd left out the thinking and missing and aching part, but basically she was right-on. Gone were the days when he would stop at Starbucks and pop into the drugstore a few doors down for a look at the latest celebrity gossip.

Angie clucked her tongue against the roof of her mouth. "It's on the covers of three of them this week."

"Something about Kelly?"

"Yeah." She sang the word with two syllables, as if Dayne were possibly the least informed person on the planet. "Everyone knows. She moved back in with Hawk Daniels."

Dayne was glad for the ladder and the brick wall. In that instant he wouldn't have had the strength to stand on his own, let alone hang from a window ledge. Kelly had moved in with Hawk after they had wrapped up filming *Dream On* in Bloomington. But in January when she had called Dayne with news about the baby, she told him she was back home.

"Well . . ." He kept his smile easy, his tone unaffected. "I guess you're right. I should read the tabs more often."

"She's not worth your time." Angie crossed her arms and made a face. "She's with Hawk; I promise you."

Dayne tried not to react, but his thoughts battled within him. Kelly was back with Hawk Daniels? That explained why she hadn't returned his calls for a week. Here they were four months from becoming parents and so far the whole thing was the best-kept secret in Hollywood.

"All right, places!" Ron Foster bellowed into the bullhorn. Not that he needed one. He was a teetotaler, but even at a nightclub full of drunken celebrities he was the loudest person in the room.

In light of Ron's announcement, people across the set fell silent. He lifted the bullhorn again. "When I raise my hand, I want the ladder removed." He looked toward the window. "You ready, Dayne?"

"Ready." Dayne repositioned himself and gripped the window ledge.

Angie gave him one last smile and returned to her place inside the room.

When Ron raised his hand, two set guys ran over and moved the ladder from view. "Three . . . two . . . one . . . roll 'em."

Dayne heard the slap of the chalkboard, his cue to kick into action. He pushed his feet against the brick as he swung himself onto the ledge. But in that instant, instead of seeing Angie Carr inside the room talking with the bad guys, he saw Katy Hart and Kelly Parker. How could he be in love with one woman and ready to pledge his life to another?

Focus, Matthews . . . come on, focus. He ordered himself to get his head into the scene. As he shifted, looking inside the way he was supposed to, he slipped but caught his balance before he fell. Anger burned in his veins, and he gritted his teeth. Whatever Kelly was doing, he could deal with it later. This scene deserved everything he had.

He peered into the window, swung back down so he was hanging from the ledge again, glanced over his shoulder, and pretended to push himself out from the wall and down onto a moving truck, the one driven by his brother in the movie.

In reality, he landed on his hands and knees in the foam-rubber pit. A stunt double would take the actual jump from the window ledge to the top of the moving truck.

The moment he landed he heard Ron's voice. "Perfect. I'll take it!"

He heard feet jogging in his direction as he climbed a nylon rope ladder on the inside of the foam pit. He kicked his legs over the edge, landed on the ground, and dusted off his hands. Ron must've seen his slip, his near fall, but for some reason he'd let the scene go.

The director was grinning as he reached him. "Did you add that, Matthews? The slip?" He chuckled and adjusted his black baseball cap. "Brilliant move. Very realistic."

Dayne hated to tell him it was a mistake. "Thanks."

"I mean, now we have the star of the show leaping onto a window ledge, getting the shock of his life, and nearly falling in the process." He nodded. "Works, Matthews; works great."

"Right." Dayne gave a halfhearted laugh. "Thanks." He expected Ron to be angry. There was no excuse for him to slip like that. If he wasn't distracted, he would've held on the way he was supposed to.

The rest of the day Dayne doubled his efforts, turning in what the entire cast believed was some of his strongest work on the film so far.

He was exhausted by the time he drove to his house at nine that night. Filming in Los Angeles meant long days, for sure. There was always something else to do, another scene to cut, rough footage to review.

But at least he had home to look forward to when the day was over.

Even though the location shoot in downtown LA was closed to the public, dozens of photographers had found places to lurk and snap pictures. Two of them were tailing him now as he headed along Hollywood Boulevard, but he was pretty sure he could lose them.

He looked in his rearview mirror and made a plan. When there were enough cars around to slow the media hounds, he changed lanes from the right to the left, sped up a ways, cut back into the right lane, and made an immediate turn into the entrance of a gas station and mini-mart.

The move happened so fast that both cars were left stuck in the flow of traffic, unable to follow him.

Dayne drove his Escalade around the back side of the gas station, slipped on a gray knit beanie and a pair of dark glasses, flipped up his coat collar, and made a quick exit from his SUV. His eyes downcast, he rounded the sidewalk, walked into the mini-mart, found the magazine section, and grabbed each of the three tabloids with Kelly Parker's picture on the front.

He slapped a ten-dollar bill on the counter and pretended to look at the arrangement of candy bars and gum just beneath the counter. The checker had a Spanish accent; he didn't seem interested in who was behind the glasses.

Dayne took his change and the bag of magazines, headed to his vehicle, and was back on the road in minutes. Still free of the paparazzi, he took surface streets to Pacific Coast Highway and made his way home without being followed.

When he was inside his house, he dropped to the nearest kitchen chair and spilled the bag of magazines onto his table.

He grabbed the first one, the one that showed Kelly on the balcony of what looked like Hawk's beach house. Kelly was in Hawk's arms, and the two of them were grinning at each other. The headline read: "On Again? Kelly Parker Moves Back in with Hawk Daniels."

Dayne didn't have to flip to the article. If the tabloids had Kelly back with Hawk, chances were that's exactly where she was. He pulled out his cell phone and punched in her number.

She answered on the second ring. "Hello?" He heard voices and loud music in the background.

For a moment Dayne considered hanging up on her. He'd put his entire life on hold so they could try to work something out, so they could be the best possible parents to the baby she was carrying. So why was she being evasive, and how could she have moved back in with Hawk?

The noise in the background grew muffled. "Hello, can you hear me?"

"It's me. Dayne."

"What? Dayne, is that you?"

He drew a long breath. "Kelly, can you get to a quieter place? We need to talk."

There was the sound of her heels clicking on the floor, and then the background noise disappeared almost entirely. "Sorry." She giggled. "I'm at The Zone."

He wasn't sure where to begin. "Did you get my last two messages?"

"Dayne, don't start with me." Her tone was suddenly icy. "Where was this attention before I mentioned the baby, huh?"

The magazine was still staring at him, still shouting at him. "You and Hawk are back together?"

"Are you kidding?" This time her laugh was more nervous. "Don't tell me you believe the tabs! Come on, Dayne—you? After all they've said about your life?"

"They're usually not too far from the truth."

"Well, they are this time, okay?" The attitude was back. She dropped her voice. "Listen, you can't blame me for having fun with my friends. Everything about my life is about to change."

Dayne stood and moved to his sliding door. He hadn't been out on his deck since Katy left. "You plan to party right up until you deliver, or what?"

"I don't appreciate your sarcasm."

"Kelly, please . . ." The anger left his voice. His heart felt heavier than it had all day. He didn't want to be enemies with Kelly Parker. "You and I were best friends back when, remember?" He hesitated. "Tell me you remember."

"I do." Her tone was softer now. "I'm sorry, Dayne." The pretense was entirely gone. In its place was the vulnerable young woman who had gotten lost along the way. "I need a little more time." She paused. "Is that okay?"

Dayne felt his anger stir again, but he kept it out of his voice. "Time for what?"

"To figure things out." She sounded like a little girl. "The premiere for *Dream On* is in a month. I'll be ready then."

"You're five months pregnant now. You wait that long and people will notice, Kelly. Don't you think?"

"No." There was a pout in her voice. "I'm not showing. The doctor says I can hide it until the premiere, no problem."

He rested his forehead against the cool glass. The moon shone on the water, bright enough that he could see the beach was empty. "So that's it, then? We don't talk for another month?"

"We'll talk." Her tone was whiny and flirty all at once. "I'm just not ready to move in and be the mommy. Not yet."

"Fine." He wasn't sure what to say. In the background he could hear someone walk up, talk to Kelly. She seemed to cover the phone and tell the person to hold on, but the guy near her—it was definitely a guy—wouldn't let up. Dayne exhaled hard. "Need to go?"

"Stop . . ." She stifled a giggle. "Listen, can I call you back? Soon, okay. Very soon."

He wanted to tell her not to bother. That she could go party with the night crowd and hang out at Hawk Daniels's house and live her own life for all he cared. But that wasn't how he felt. Not when she was carrying his baby. Whatever rules she wanted to play by, he'd have to live with them. He could hear the guy's voice clearer now, teasing her, asking her to kiss him, to make out with him.

Dayne would know the voice anywhere, the voice of his costar from more than one movie. The voice of Hawk Daniels.

"Hey . . . I gotta go." Kelly didn't sound drunk. At least, he hoped she wasn't drinking—not when she was pregnant. But she sounded beyond distracted, deliriously happy with the attention from Hawk.

"Bye, Kelly." He clenched his jaw and turned back to the kitchen table. "I'll be here when you're ready to talk."

The conversation ended, and Dayne tossed the phone on the table next to the magazines. Then he opened the patio slider and walked out onto his deck. If the paparazzi were hiding in the bushes, so be it. He could stand against his railing and watch the waves if he wanted to.

He took up his place, the spot where he'd stood next to Katy a month earlier. How had everything changed so quickly? Katy was gone, probably for good. He'd called her twice—to see how she was and to apologize for the hurried way their good-bye had ended. She hadn't returned either call.

The seagulls were quiet now, lined up along the base of the bushes, heads tucked under their wings. But the waves were relentless, crashing against the shore time and time again. He lifted his eyes to the moonlit sky and breathed in long and slow.

Where was God in all this?

Everyone who had ever mattered to him believed in God—the God of the Bible. But how was he supposed to connect with that God now, even if he wanted to? The woman he loved was out of his life forever, and the mother of his child was determined to party and club her way through her sixth month of pregnancy.

What was he supposed to do in the meantime? Look for baby furniture? Pick out names?

The breeze was cold against his face, but he didn't care. No matter how he sorted the details of his life, one truth seemed to resonate in his heart: God had never been in his corner. He'd lost everyone who had ever mattered to him, and all of them had an amazing faith. His parents had been forced to give him away, his adoptive parents had died on the mission field, and Katy Hart had walked away believing he was little more than a playboy.

The summary of events made Dayne utter a quiet, sarcastic laugh. No, God had never really been on his side. But even so, here he was—lost and alone—and wondering the way he'd wondered his whole life whether God was real, whether it really mattered how a person lived his life. And why the nicest people always put their trust in a God they couldn't see.

Dayne gripped the railing tighter.

In all his life, there was one person who should've felt the same way, someone who had shared his upbringing and yet came out on the other end with a complete understanding and love for God.

His best friend from boarding-school days—Bob Asher.

Without overthinking the idea, he went back inside, grabbed the phone, and called the Indonesian boarding school for his missionary friend's number.

Eunice—the same secretary who had been there when Dayne and Bob were students—answered. "Ah, yes. Dayne Matthews." She didn't seem to know about his celebrity. "You and that Bob Asher were quite a pair. Thick as thieves, the two of you."

Dayne had no trouble getting the phone number for Bob and his wife in Mexico City. The guy worked as a missionary, of course. Same as his parents.

Dayne dialed the number and waited.

"Hello?" The voice on the other end was groggy.

Dayne squeezed his eyes shut. "Oh, man. Sorry. I forgot how late it was."

There were muffled sounds, and Bob yawned. "What time is it?"

"Almost eleven." Dayne winced. "How 'bout there?"

"Hold on." Bob must've sat up to see his alarm clock. "Almost one."

"Hey, let me call you back tomorrow."

"Is this Dayne?" The fog was obviously clearing from Bob's brain. "Dayne Matthews?"

"Yeah, but, buddy, I didn't mean to wake you." Dayne slipped out through the deck door and sat on the sofa, the one he and Katy had shared when he told her the news. "I'll call later."

"Don't worry about it." Bob chuckled. "I'm awake now." His tone was easygoing, the way it had always been. "What's up?"

Dayne raked his fingers through his hair, and for a moment he was too choked up to speak. "A lot." He bent over his knees and stared at the slats on his deck. "I have questions, Bob. About God." He drew a long breath. "About a lot of things, I guess." He shaded his forehead and pressed his thumb and forefinger against his temples. "I'd sorta like to see you, man."

"Okay . . ." Bob didn't sound surprised or overly anxious. The two were boyhood friends. No amount of fame could change that. Bob thought for a few seconds. "What's your filming schedule?"

"Wraps up mid-March, the premiere for *Dream On* is a few days later, then a week of edits and reshoots." The schedule felt like a lead blanket across the back of his shoulders. "I'm open the end of March."

"Why don't you come here?" Bob sounded wide-awake now. "Rosa and I would love to have you. If you dress right, you'll get a lot less attention here than in the States."

The idea sounded wonderful. Besides, by then he'd know what Kelly had decided, whether she was willing to move in and try to work out something with him for the sake of the baby, or whether she had other plans—plans that would leave him a weekend father at best. His throat felt thick. "You serious?"

"Of course. You could roll up your sleeves and work beside me. That way we'd have all day to talk." He sounded sincere and kind, but something in his tone suggested that he understood. The questions Dayne had were both troubling and serious. "It's been a long time."

"It has."

They made plans to talk again in a couple weeks before they ended the call.

Dayne stood and stared out across the beach once more. With practiced ease, he punched the buttons on his cell phone until Katy's number appeared in the window. He could push the Send button and be moments away from talking to her.

He wouldn't do it, of course. It was too late, and she didn't want to talk to him anyway. But it felt good to look at her number, to know that he was seconds away from her if he wanted to be.

What would she be doing now? Working on *Robin Hood*, the play she'd talked about at the deposition. But had someone new come into her life, someone who could give her the love and devotion she deserved? He stared at the phone a little longer and then snapped it shut and slipped it into his pocket.

Work would have to keep him busy until he could board a plane for Mexico City. Until the shoot wrapped, he would put in twelve-hour days at least. Then the premiere and the edits and after the end of March he still might not have answers about Katy Hart or Kelly Parker.

But if he spent a few days with Bob, maybe he would have something even better, even more life changing. For the first time since he started looking, since he'd found and lost interest in Kabbalah and since he'd known about the faith of the Baxters and Katy, maybe he would have the one thing Dayne could never quite find.

Answers about God.

CHAPTER SEVEN

PLANS FOR THE FAMILY REUNION were coming together quickly, and Ashley couldn't wait. The timing was a little crazy—the reunion was set for two weeks before her due date—but her doctor hadn't seen any reason she should deliver early. No, she wouldn't be playing Frisbee on the shore of Lake Monroe with the kids, but she could do just about everything else.

The reunion was six weeks away, and Ashley was glad they were all getting together for dinner at her dad's house tonight. Landon worked at the fire station until seven, so he'd join them later. Ashley picked Cole up from school and hugged him close.

"That baby's sure getting in the way." Cole grinned at her. He was on the final stretch of first grade and acting older every day. He flung his backpack into the van and buckled himself into the passenger seat. "We're going to Papa's, right?"

"After my errands." She snapped her own seat belt and pulled back into traffic. "Sunset Hills first, okay?"

Cole's eyes lit up. "I love that place. Can we stay a long time?"

"Not real long. I want to say hi to Helen and Bert." She rested her head against her seat and kept her eyes on the road. It had been nearly a month since she'd stopped by Sunset Hills Adult Care Home, long enough for the staff to get comfortable with whoever had filled the latest vacancy.

Her friend Edith had died in January. Dear old Edith, the former beauty queen, the one who had screamed every time she looked in the mirror, believing she was being chased by a witch. Not until Ashley had covered the mirror with a sheet did Edith find any peace. Even so, her Alzheimer's kept taking its toll on her mind, her health. She died in her sleep, her big brown Bible lying open beside her.

Cole shifted so he could see her better. "I kicked a boy today."

The announcement jolted Ashley back to the moment. "Coley!" She cast a glance at her son. Cole was one of the kindest boys she'd ever known. His teachers had always said so. "Why would you kick someone?"

"He needed a kick, Mommy. No one else would give it to him." He shrugged. "So I did."

Ashley was tempted to pull over. She fought to keep her cool. "Cole, no one needs a kick. Why don't you tell me the story."

"Okay, well, you know that mean guy in fourth grade, the one named Brent?"

"Yes." Ashley turned onto Main Street. She was just a few blocks from Sunset Hills. "Brent McHouston, right?"

"Right." Cole didn't look or sound ruffled. Whatever had happened, he felt justified. "So there's this kindergartener named Micah, only he's a little guy, Mommy. Littler than all the other kindergarteners, and he's got forever crutches."

"Forever crutches?" Ashley gave Cole another quick look.

"Teacher said Micah has crutches forever, 'cause he was born that way. You know, Mommy. Forever crutches."

"Okay." Ashley felt her heart begin to melt. "So there's Micah with his forever crutches . . ."

"And me and the boys were playing soccer, but here comes

Micah on his forever crutches, real slow 'cause that's how Micah always comes. Real slow. Only right at that 'zact moment Brent comes up and grabs one of Micah's crutches."

"No! That's terrible."

"I know!" Cole's voice rose a notch. "It is terrible, Mommy. 'Cause Micah fell, and Brent ran all over the playground waving the crutch in the air. And then finally he came back to Micah and pointed at him and laughed."

"He did?"

"Yes, and pointing and laughing are two of the meanest things, Mommy. Case you didn't know."

The light ahead of Ashley turned red, and she eased the van to a stop. Then she looked at Cole. "That's even more terrible, Coley."

"I know. It is more terrible. And all us boys were there watching from behind, but no one did anything about it. So finally I asked myself what Jesus would do if He was playing soccer beside me, you know?"

"Yes." Ashley stifled a grin.

"And I figgered it out! Jesus would walk right up behind that bad ol' Brent and kick him in the leg." Cole smiled sweetly. "That's how come I knew he needed a kick."

"So . . ." Ashley could see where the story was going.

Cole gulped. "I walked right up to that boy and kicked him hard in the back of the leg. He dropped Micah's crutch right then, and he turned around. That's when I kicked him again; only that time I started running." Cole giggled. "I ran and ran, faster and faster, Mommy. That Brent isn't very fast, I found out. He stuck his tongue out at me before we went into class."

"Oh." Ashley ran the details through her head again. "So you actually kicked him twice?"

Cole thought a minute. He held up one finger, then another. He looked a little sheepish. "Two kicks. That's what I meant. He needed two kicks."

The light turned green, and Ashley looked straight ahead. "Did the playground teacher find out? I mean, did you have to go to the principal's office?"

"Sort of." Cole squirmed a little.

"Sort of?"

"Principal and I had a nice visit. So I didn't really think it was the sort of visit where children get in trouble. He told me just because it seems like someone needs a kick, sometimes they just need someone to tell a yard teacher."

"Coley . . ." Ashley gathered her thoughts. "You know better than to kick someone. Even someone mean like Brent McHouston."

"But, Mom—" Cole held out both hands—"he dropped Micah's crutch! Don't you see? The kick worked."

"I see." Ashley had mixed feelings. Again she hid her smile. "Son, it was very nice of you to help Micah, especially when someone stole his crutch that way. But it's never okay to kick someone."

They spent the next few minutes talking about the other ways Cole could've helped Micah. Then they pulled up in front of Sunset Hills.

They were halfway up the sidewalk when Cole puffed out his chest. "Know what Micah said, Mommy? After he had his forever crutch back?"

"What?" She loved the feel of his hand in hers. Especially now, when life was about to get so much busier for all of them.

Cole looked up, his blue eyes sparkling. "He told me I was his hero, and that made me smile. Know why?"

"Why?" They reached the front door, but Ashley hesitated so Cole could finish his story.

"Because Daddy's a hero, and if I'm a hero that means I'm 'zactly like him." He grinned so big she could see the space where he was missing a tooth on the right side. "And what could be better than that?"

Ashley stooped down and hugged him. "I love you, Coley. Know that?"

"I know." He rubbed his nose against hers. "You have to tell me it was wrong to kick bad Brent 'cause you're a grown-up." He gave her a serious nod. "I understand."

They both laughed and spent the next half hour visiting with Helen and Bert. Both were doing better than ever, though Helen still made a point of asking whether the two of them had been checked, a habit she'd had since Ashley worked there. Helen was convinced that spies were trying to invade Sunset Hills.

"We've been checked, Helen." Ashley patted her hand.

Helen looked doubtful. She squinted at Cole and pointed a gnarled finger in his direction. "That one's okay. I recognize him." She waved at the woman working in the kitchen. "He's a firefighter. Put out a fire here once."

Ashley grinned and slipped her arm around Cole's shoulders. Nothing ever really changed at Sunset Hills. Some of the residents had moved on to heaven, no doubt. Precious Irvel and now Edith. But the atmosphere in the home was very much the same.

Bert still spent hours each day shining the saddle Ashley had bought for him on eBay. He was talking more than before, sometimes launching into stories from the old days, back when he was one of the greatest saddlemakers of his time.

The visit was full of warmth and laughter. Afterward Ashley and Cole picked up ingredients to make chili for dinner at her dad's house. They pulled into the driveway of the old Baxter house just as a silver sedan was leaving. Ashley slowed enough to see the driver.

It was Elaine Denning. The woman who had been her mother's friend years ago, the one who was spending time with her father these days. Obviously more time than any of them knew about. Elaine waved, and Ashley did the same. As she did, she felt a strange twist in her heart, a feeling that bordered on betrayal.

"Who's that, Mommy?"

"She's, uh . . ." Ashley swung her van around and parked near the garage. "She's a friend of Papa's."

"Oh." Cole unbuckled his seat belt. "She's pretty."

Cole's comment grated on her. Elaine wasn't pretty, not really. Nowhere near as pretty as her own mother had been. Elaine was short and gray-haired. She looked ten years older than her father. Not that it mattered—her father and Elaine were friends, nothing more.

Ashley and Cole walked to the front door and found her father sitting on the porch swing. The space beside him was empty, as if . . .

"Were you sitting here with Elaine?" Ashley stopped and studied her dad's face. She motioned to Cole. "Sweetie, go check Papa's frog pond." It was in the low forties, warm enough that the sound of frogs was back again. She pointed to the pond. "See if there are any tadpoles yet."

"Hey, you're right! The ice is melted!" Cole waved at her father. "See you in a minute, Papa." He ran full speed toward the pond.

When he was out of earshot, Ashley put her hand on her hip. "Well, am I right?"

"Listen." Her father raised his brow at her. His tone remained calm. "Elaine's my friend, and, yes, occasionally she and I sit here on the swing and talk about our lives."

"Dad . . ." Ashley gritted her teeth so she wouldn't say the first thing that came to mind. But even as she hated knowing that Elaine had sat next to her dad, in the place where her mother had always sat, she knew she was wrong to be angry. None of them had wanted to say good-bye to her mother. But this was all they had left, life without her. Was her father supposed to live alone the rest of his days, without even a friend?

"Uggh . . ." She felt the fight leave her. She set the bag of groceries on the porch and sank down beside him on the swing. "I'm sorry."

"It's okay." He put his arm around her. With the slightest move, he set the swing in motion. "Deep inside—" his eyes met hers—"I don't like it either. But it's a nice day, and neither of us felt like sitting inside."

For a few minutes Ashley didn't say anything. Elaine and her father had a lot in common—both alone without the spouses they'd been with for decades. She watched Cole, bent over the pond, his fingertips in the cold water. *Lord, give me the right words. My dad deserves more than my anger.* She reached for her dad's hand and gave it a squeeze. "Okay. I'm glad you have a friend."

"Thanks." In his voice she heard relief. He patted her abdomen with his other hand. "How're you feeling?"

"Good." She sighed. "Tired but good. I feel like a walking house."

"Your mother always felt that way when she was in her seventh month." His eyes grew soft. "She used to say I would have to roll her out of the house to the hospital by the time the baby finally came."

Ashley pictured that for a minute. She would've been too young to remember much about her mother as a pregnant woman. But hearing this detail now made her feel closer to her mom. Closer and farther away at the same time. "I miss her so much."

"Me too." Her dad's eyes looked wet. "Even now it's hard to believe I won't see her again this side of heaven."

"I know." Ashley drew a long breath. "It seems weird, planning a reunion without her."

Her father smiled, and his eyes glistened. "She'll be there."

Ashley nodded. Her dad was right. They couldn't possibly have a week with all the Baxters gathered in one place and not feel her with them too. Ashley swallowed back the emotion filling her throat. She allowed a few seconds transition. "Who's coming tonight?"

"Everyone around here. Kari and Ryan, Brooke and Peter, and all the kids." He smiled. "I've been looking forward to it all week."

She still had her fingers around her father's. It had been a few weeks since she'd asked, and now was as good a time as any. "Have you heard anything?"

Her dad's expression told her he understood what she was talking about. "Not yet. Nothing but bits and pieces."

Ashley looked out at Cole. "You wouldn't think it would take this long."

"No." He followed her gaze. "I'm doing my best, Ashley."

"I know." She released his fingers, stood, and picked up the grocery bag. "I guess I just have this dream that somehow we'll all be together at the reunion." She looked at him. "Even our older brother."

"Yes." Her father rose and cupped his hands around his mouth. "Any tadpoles yet, Coley? It's pretty early for them."

"I think so!" Cole shot straight up and motioned for his grandfather to come. He pointed back at the water. "They're sleeping, though."

Her dad chuckled. "Looks like I have a little tadpole hunting to do."

For a minute she watched him lumber off to be with Cole. This was what she loved about her dad. He cared about his kids and grandkids so much. When he said he'd been looking forward to the dinner, he was telling exactly how he felt. Never mind that he'd practiced medicine this week or that he'd probably had a hand in saving a few lives because of his daily decisions at work. This was what made him feel alive—being with his family.

Ashley took the groceries inside and in an hour dinner was

almost ready. By then, her dad and Cole were inside watching college basketball on TV.

The house began to fill up around six o'clock when Brooke, Peter, and their two girls arrived.

Maddie, who was a year older than Cole, scrambled inside and raced over to him. She was holding a flutelike recorder. "Coley, I learned a song for you!"

"Really?"

"Yes!" Maddie put the recorder to her lips as the adults filed into the room. With great effort and care she meticulously played "Mary Had a Little Lamb." As the song got underway, Cole bounced along to the beat. When Maddie finished, she raised the recorder in the air and began bouncing alongside Cole. "See!" They exchanged high fives. "That was just for you, Coley!"

Cole ran to Ashley. "Can I have one too, Mommy? Please . . . please can I have a special flute like Maddie's?"

Ashley gave Brooke a pointed smile. "Wow, thanks, Brooke. Can I bring him to your house for practice sessions?"

Kari and Ryan and Jessie and little Ryan arrived then.

"You missed the concert," Cole told them.

"Yes." Ashley grinned at Kari. "Maddie gave a very impressive concert on her recorder."

Maddie jumped around, excited. "I can do it again, Aunt Ashley! Listen!" She launched into another round.

When she was finished, everyone clapped and laughed, and the atmosphere remained upbeat throughout dinner.

Landon arrived just as they were finishing up, and Ashley felt her heart skip a beat. No wonder Cole saw his daddy as a hero. He looked every bit the part, walking through the door with his uniform smudged from smoke.

"Office building," he explained. He brushed his knuckles against his dirty cheek and headed for Ashley. "Someone left a coffeemaker on—at least it seems that way." He leaned down and kissed her, then placed a kiss on the top of Cole's head.

"Did you save anyone, Daddy?" Cole was on his feet, his eyes bright.

"We rescued an older woman." He gave a sad shake of his head. "Must've gotten confused in the smoke and lost her way. They took her to the hospital, but she'll be fine. Just a little smoke inhalation."

Ashley shivered at the words *smoke inhalation*. It was what had nearly killed Landon in a house fire a few years back. This was the part of his job that always kept her on her knees—in close conversation with the Lord. Every day she placed Landon in God's hands. Otherwise she would've been crazy with worry each time he went to work.

Ashley watched her husband dish up a bowl of chili, grab a few slices of bread, and take his place beside her.

She wrinkled her nose. "You stink."

"Yeah." He winked at her. "Fires do that to you."

"Firefighters put out big blazes in all kinds of buildings." Cole gave a serious look to Maddie. "They're also in charge of rescuing people."

Cole continued his explanation, and after a few minutes Maddie looked at him, her brow raised halfway up her forehead. "Yeah, only I already know that, Coley."

Her comeback drew a laugh from everyone at the table except Cole. He gave his cousin a look that suggested there would be more to the discussion later when the grown-ups weren't gathered around.

When they finished visiting, they made a conference call to Luke and Reagan and another one to Erin and Sam. Things were busy at both households, but they were all excited about the upcoming reunion.

"You aren't gonna have that baby early, are you?" Luke's laugh rang over the tinny speakerphone.

The sound of it made Ashley smile. She'd missed Luke more than she had remembered. "The baby's under strict orders: no birth until mid-April."

"Good."

Again they laughed.

By the end of the evening, the family had made plans for everyone to fly in the first Friday in April. Luke and Reagan and their two children—Tommy and Malin, their daughter recently adopted from China—would stay in two of the bedrooms. Erin and Sam and their four girls—Heidi Jo, Amy, Chloe, and Clarisse—would take the other spare bedrooms, since Erin said the little girls liked the idea of sleeping in the same bedroom. Everyone else would camp out at the Baxter house each night as late as possible or use the cots in the basement.

When the plans were set, Brooke and Peter offered to do dishes. Their dad sat with the kids at the dining-room table, playing Scrabble Junior. Hayley was still using a walker to get around. She couldn't play, but she stayed interested, watching everything her sister, Maddie, did.

Landon took Ashley's hand and motioned to the front door. "Wanna take a walk? It's not that cold outside."

She felt her heart soar. She loved this, loved that even now, on a regular day, after a regular dinner, with nothing real to celebrate or mark the moment, Landon still found a way to make every moment special.

Once Ashley had heard a speaker at church, a woman whose message rang with the notion of holding on to every day, every minute. "You must take time to love the people God has put in your life," she had said.

Landon might as well have written her talk.

Ashley smiled at him and pushed back from the table. "If I can get up."

He helped her to her feet, and they put on their coats. They held hands as they went out on the porch. The moon was almost full, and it cast a soft light across the porch and driveway. Landon led her down the steps and put his arm around her shoulders.

"You still smell like smoke." She leaned her head on his shoulder, their steps slow and evenly paced as they headed down the driveway. He was right. It wasn't that cold outside. "Was it bad, the fire?"

"Not really. Lots of paper. I think it burned hotter because of that. Boxes of kindling, that sort of thing."

"You were safe, though?" She stopped and turned into his arms. She'd been wearing flatter shoes lately. They weren't as hard on her back, with the extra weight she was carrying. Now she felt short next to Landon.

"Perfectly." He grinned at her, his expression alive with love and hope and an adoration that had been there since he was a teenager. He brushed his hand along the back of her head. "Has anyone ever told you . . . you have the most beautiful hair?"

She gave a sad laugh. "I miss her. Irvel. Cole and I stopped by Sunset Hills today." Irvel had been Ashley's favorite patient when she worked at the home. Irvel had taught her much about love and life. And always the dear old woman would tell Ashley how lovely her hair was. Even if she'd just said so five minutes earlier.

"I'm glad you still stop in." He allowed his smile to fade some. "Have they replaced Edith?"

"Yes." She bit her lip. "Helen and Bert are doing well."

"Hey." He was studying her, looking as starry-eyed as he had when they had first started dating. He crooked his finger and placed it beneath her chin. "I'm serious about the compliment, though. Have I told you how beautiful you look?"

She arched her back and made an exaggerated push of her belly. "Oh, sure."

"No, I'm serious." There wasn't even a hint of teasing in Landon's voice. "I look at you and I see love the way God meant it to be. New life growing out of a relationship only He could've put together." He brought his lips to hers and kissed her slowly, tenderly.

Ashley returned his kiss, amazed at the passion between them even now. When she eased back, her voice was huskier than before. "Think we'll still have time for this . . . when the baby comes?"

"We might not have time for eating—" he kissed her, nuzzling his face against hers—"but we'll have time for this."

They started walking again. "Cole kicked a boy at school today."

"What?" Landon hesitated, searching her eyes as if maybe she were joking. "That doesn't sound like Cole."

She raised one eyebrow at him. "He was trying to be a hero. Like you." She laughed at the memory. They fell back into an easy pace. "Actually, he was. The boy he kicked was bullying a handicapped child."

"Oh." Landon smiled. "I hope I don't have to punish him for that."

"I think the principal already took care of it." She laughed again. "It was hard keeping a straight face earlier. He'll have to tell you the story."

They were quiet for a minute. Finally Landon stopped and faced her again. He looked up at the moon, the stars. "Can I confess something?" His eyes found hers, and for the first time in a long time, she saw something other than easygoing confidence and love looking back at her.

She saw fear.

"Anything, Landon." She felt no sense of alarm, but she didn't blink, didn't want to miss whatever was coming.

He drew back and cupped his hands gently around her abdomen, around the place where their baby was just starting to kick. "Sometimes I'm afraid."

"Afraid?" The moment seemed surreal. Ashley had the certainty that she would remember this walk as long as she lived.

"Of the birth, of whatever you have to go through." He swallowed, his eyes wider than before. "I couldn't stand it if anything happened to you, Ash."

She brought her hands to his face and framed it. "Landon, honey . . . nothing's going to go wrong." She leaned up, kissed him, and flashed a quick grin. "I've done this before, remember?"

"I know." He exhaled, as if he'd been holding in this secret for too long and now he was relieved it was out. "But I haven't."

She didn't say anything to that. But she kissed him again, longer this time. She wasn't worried at all, not even a little. Still, neither of them could make promises about the future. Everything about their relationship had taught them that much. And she understood what he meant, how he was feeling. Everything about life as they'd known it was about to change. Cole would have to share their attention with his new sister or brother, and no matter what they intended, there would be days when they didn't have time for each other—not enough time, anyway.

Landon seemed to read her thoughts. He ran one finger along her cheekbone. "You know what I picture?"

"What?"

"Bringing the kids over here and taking a walk just like this one. A couple times a week if that's what it takes."

"If that's what it takes for what?" She gave him a teasing look, the kind she always gave him when they were playing with each other this way.

"To make sure you never forget how much . . ." He took her face in his hands and kissed her long and slow. When he pulled back, the love in his expression was so pure and real and deep it took her breath away. "How much I love you, Ashley."

In that moment, she could almost feel God answering a prayer she'd whispered years earlier. It had been a time when she was sitting beside a sick Irvel at Sunset Hills. Irvel had been the most gracious woman Ashley had ever known—apart from her own mother. Though Irvel's husband, Hank, had been dead for nearly a decade, she lived in a world where he was still alive. Just gone for the afternoon, fishing with the boys, she'd say.

The way Irvel adored Hank, the way his love had carried Irvel through long after he was gone, that was the sort of love Ashley had longed for—a sort of love she hadn't even been sure existed. So that night she had prayed about it, asking God that if a love like that existed, could He please move mountains so she could experience it?

And now here they were, and Ashley could see for herself that the love Irvel and Hank shared did indeed exist.

Because it existed in the person of Landon Blake.

CHAPTER EIGHT

JOHN BAXTER had been restless all night.

It wasn't his style to lie to his daughter. Lying went against everything he believed in, and from the moment he did so, he replayed the conversation in his head looking for how he might've avoided being dishonest. Every time he came up with the same answer. There hadn't been any way around it.

Now that he knew the truth about his son's identity, he was doing everything he could to make contact with him. He'd left three messages with Dayne's agent, and still no one had called him back. It wasn't that he was unwilling to tell Ashley what he'd found, but rather he wanted to give her a complete picture.

Because by his actions, Dayne had made it clear that he might not want anything to do with them. If that was the case, fine. John needed to know as much, and then he could tell Ashley the whole truth. Together they could figure out how to tell the others. It was one thing to spring the news on them that they had a biological older brother. But the idea that he had rejected them would make the conversation almost impossible.

That was the reason he couldn't tell Ashley—not yet. He didn't want to mar her thinking about Dayne if maybe the reason he hadn't made contact was because he didn't know what to say, or if the silence from his agent was unintentional. Once Ashley had an inkling that her older brother was famous and might be avoiding them, she would be angry at him before another step could be taken.

In his quiet time with the Lord, John continued to hear the same thing. The verse from Matthew: *With God all things are possible.* For that reason, he held out hope. Maybe Dayne's agent was swamped with messages. Maybe he was unable to get word to Dayne. Maybe he'd tried to return John's call and gotten the numbers wrong.

There were a dozen reasons John could imagine for the man not calling him back. But the more time that passed, the harder it was to imagine a single one of them being true. And now with Ashley asking about her older brother every time they were together, it was especially hard. If he didn't hear from Dayne's agent soon, he'd have to tell Ashley what he knew—even if the details left her jaded.

He was working on the fish pond this afternoon, clearing dead weeds from between the rocks and making a small embankment out of pebbles, a place where Cole and Maddie could get closer to the water without climbing over the bigger boulders that circled the water. He could hardly wait to see Cole's reaction to the changes.

The little landing area was clear of dirt and rocks, so John walked toward the garage for the wheelbarrow of pebbles. In his back pocket was his cell phone. Just in case this was the hour Dayne or his agent chose to call. He squinted in the sunlight, glad that the day was in the fifties, as it had been off and on all week. Unusual for an Indiana February.

It was the sort of day that made him miss Elizabeth more than usual. Even if earlier this morning he'd spent a few hours with

Elaine Denning. They'd met at a coffeehouse near the university because he was desperate to talk about Dayne. Until now, he'd kept the news of his identity to himself—thinking it wasn't right for anyone but his children to know what he'd found. But in light of the silence from Dayne's camp, he needed to tell someone. Elaine, very simply, was the only one who knew about his secret firstborn son but who wasn't emotionally involved.

As he wheeled the pebbles across the driveway and over to the pond, he replayed his earlier conversation with Elaine. . . .

They'd taken a corner table, a little ways from the traffic near the counter. When they were both seated with their coffees, he breathed in deeply. "I found him."

Elaine looked confused at first. "You found who?" Something in his eyes must've clued her in, because she didn't wait for his answer. Her tone changed, soft and incredulous. "You found . . . your older son?"

John nodded. "It's . . . it's very complicated." Whenever he thought about Dayne, he choked up. He massaged his throat. No question the conversation would be difficult. When he could find the words, he looked straight at her, to the place in her heart he knew would understand. "He's an actor, Elaine. A very famous actor."

She searched his face. "Have I heard of him?"

A sad chuckle filled the space between them. "The whole world's heard of him."

"Okay, it's killing me." Her words were slow, laced with shock. "Who is he?"

John glanced over his shoulder, as if someone might be listening. "Dayne Matthews." He leaned back in his chair, feeling the surprise again himself. "It doesn't even sound real saying it. Not yet, anyway."

"Are you serious?" Elaine dropped her voice a notch. "Dayne Matthews is your biological son?"

"Yes." John warmed his fingers against his coffee cup, letting the information sink in for both of them.

"No wonder he looks like Luke."

"Exactly." John gazed out the window. The reality was too new. He still had no real way to put his feelings into words. "The investigator I hired was good. He found out more than I could've dreamed."

Elaine didn't blink. She took a sip of her coffee, waiting for whatever was coming.

"Dayne's been to Bloomington at least twice. The second time was when he was here to film his movie."

Elaine appeared mesmerized, the truth starting to seep into her consciousness. "We were at the farmers' market, and we walked up, stood along the rope for a few minutes, and watched him."

"Yes." John uttered a frustrated sound. "I was twenty feet from my firstborn son, and I didn't know it."

Elaine took another sip. "But he was here before that? For what? To scout locations?"

"I don't think so." John's heart seemed to double in weight. "The investigator thinks he hired a PI of his own, and he was here in Bloomington because he had figured out who we were— who his birth parents were." He narrowed his eyes. "His first visit took place the day before Elizabeth died."

A soft gasp slipped from Elaine's lips. "Elizabeth thought she'd met your son, that he'd been into the hospital room and talked with her for an hour, right?"

"Exactly." John brought his drink to his lips and took a long swig. "I can't prove it really happened, but if Dayne was here . . ."

Elaine sat up straighter. "Then Elizabeth's prayer was answered."

"That's what I'm hoping."

"Okay, so what's so complicated about that?" She angled her head. "He's famous, but he's still your son. If he went out of his way to be with Elizabeth before she died, then he can't be that bad."

"Elaine . . ." John's tone grew as heavy as his heart. "He was here in Bloomington twice. But not once did he call or try to make contact with any of us other than Elizabeth. If he did indeed meet her."

"Oh." Elaine's expression fell. "I hadn't thought of it that way."

"I've left three messages with his agent and heard nothing back." He lifted his hands and let them fall to the table. "What am I supposed to think except that Dayne isn't interested in meeting us? that maybe he can't be bothered or he's afraid we'll want something from him because of his fame?"

"I see." Elaine put her elbows on the table and thought for a moment. "It *is* complicated."

"Last night we were planning the Baxter reunion, and Ashley starts out the evening—before anyone else arrived—by asking me about her older brother, what I've found out and how come the private investigator isn't working harder or faster." He shook his head. "I lied to her, Elaine. What am I going to say, 'Your older brother is Dayne Matthews, but don't think about it too long because he doesn't want to meet us'?"

"That would come across wrong."

"Which is why I lied to her. I told her I didn't know anything yet, because I'm waiting. I need to hear for myself whether Dayne wants contact with us." He took another long drink of his coffee. The frustration felt good, better than the sorrow that usually came over him when he thought about Dayne. He exhaled hard. "What should I do?"

Elaine didn't answer fast. Her patience was one of the many things John liked about her. She was thoughtful, careful, allowing a lifetime of experience and faith to lend credibility to her answers.

Finally she reached out and patted his hand. "We need to pray. Here—" she looked around—"now. Before another minute goes by. We need to beg God for contact of some kind so you'll know. And in the meantime, you have to keep calling."

The sorrow was back, pushing his frustration aside. He let his eyes linger on Elaine's a few moments longer. Then he bowed his head and prayed. Quietly but with a sincerity that came from the depths of his soul, he asked God to allow him contact with either Dayne or his agent and to allow it soon.

"I can't make this happen on my own, Lord. But I believe You've brought me this far for a reason. So please . . . please let me know if I can pursue this further." He swallowed and felt his chin quiver. His voice was shakier than before. "If Dayne doesn't want to know us, God, then could You maybe change his mind? Even just once? There's so much . . ." His voice cracked. He waited until he had his composure back. "There's so much I want to talk to him about. In Jesus' name, amen."

The memory of his prayer from earlier today faded. John dumped the wheelbarrow full of pebbles, then stared into the pond. But before he could whisper another prayer, before he could ask God to open the lines of communication between him and his older son, the phone in his back pocket rang.

Probably Ashley, wondering when his project would be finished so she could bring Cole by. Of his daughters she was the best at keeping contact, staying close, and he appreciated her for it. If Landon was at work, Ashley and Cole visited often. He had no hard feelings about what she'd done last fall when she found the letter marked *Firstborn* in his bedroom and took it home with the intention of giving it to Brooke. He had been hurt by her decision to open it and read it, thereby learning the secret about her older brother. But things between his daughter and him were long since patched up.

He pulled the phone from his pocket, flipped it open, and pressed it to his ear. "Hello?"

"Hello . . . is this John Baxter?" The connection wasn't great, but the man's hesitation was clear.

"Yes." John straightened and winced at the way his back hurt from bending over. "This is he."

The man sounded anxious. "Uh . . . I'm Chris Kane, agent for Dayne Matthews. I believe you've left me a few messages."

John's heart flipped into double time. An airplane was passing overhead, and he covered his other ear so he could hear. "Yes." John's mind raced. Where could he start? The details were so sensitive that he hadn't explained the situation in his message. He'd only mentioned that he was a relative looking to get in touch with Dayne.

He walked slowly back toward the house, begging God for the right words. "Has Dayne told you that he was adopted? that the missionaries who raised him weren't his biological parents?"

"Yes." Something in the agent's tone changed. "I was aware that Dayne hired a private investigator nearly two years ago, and he had some family issues he wanted to look into. Since then, yes. He told me that he was adopted."

John reached the front porch. "Well, recently I hired a PI of my own, so I could find the identity of my firstborn son, a son my wife and I were forced to give up for adoption." He climbed the stairs and sat down on the swing. "I guess there's really no other way to say this." He paused. "I'm Dayne's biological father."

For a moment, the man on the other end said nothing. "Dayne knows about you, Mr. Baxter."

"He does?" John couldn't breathe, couldn't do anything but listen to every detail, every syllable.

"Yes." The agent sighed, and it sounded mixed with frustration or irritation. "He knows about all of you. In fact, against my wishes, he took a trip to Bloomington the summer before last."

"That's what my PI told me." John didn't want to ask if Dayne had seen Elizabeth. But he had to know. He blinked back tears. "He was here the day before my wife died. Her name was Elizabeth. She was . . . Dayne's biological mother."

"Yes, I know that too." Again the man sounded tired, as if

this entire situation was a mess bigger than he had strength to deal with. "My understanding is that he rented a car, drove to the Bloomington hospital with intentions of meeting his birth mother, but then something happened. Something changed his mind."

Changed his mind? John bent over his knees and forced himself to draw a breath. How was that possible when Elizabeth's story seemed to line up with an actual meeting? He closed his eyes. "So . . . he never met her?"

"Not to my understanding." The agent sounded even more frustrated now. "Look, Mr. Baxter, I don't know how to tell you this." The connection was worse than before. "Dayne is a celebrity. He would be wrong to open the door to a biological family at this point in his career. From everything he's told me, he's reached an understanding. An internal understanding. Though he's curious about you and your family, he knows that nearly everyone wants something from him. A brush with fame, money, connections. Something."

John felt sick to his stomach. Each word coming from the agent was like a battering ram, doing solid and permanent damage to his heart and mind, his soul and strength. John didn't have time to respond; the agent was still firing.

"You and your wife gave him up. Another couple raised him. End of story. Any connection at this time would be pointless at best and would raise suspicion in the minds of Dayne and the rest of his team as to your motives." The agent stopped for a moment. "I hope that doesn't sound too harsh, Mr. Baxter. It's simply the reality of Dayne Matthews and the life he lives. It's not like he needs his biological family to accept who he is. Can you understand that?"

For the first time in decades, John felt like saying something he would regret. How dare this pompous man light into him, questioning his motives and assuming the only reason he was making contact was to gain something from Dayne's celebrity status? He gritted his teeth and remained silent.

"You there?" The connection crackled.

John opened his eyes. He stood and supported himself against one of the porch pillars. "I'm here."

"Okay, so what I'm saying is that Dayne's one of the most famous men in the world. This is no time for a reunion with people he doesn't know." The agent tried to soften his tone. "He has too much at stake, too much to lose." Another pause. "I'm sorry, but that's the way it is. Oh, and one more thing." The crackling on the line was bad, but the man's words were clear. "You must keep this news to yourself. This story is the last thing Dayne needs splashed over the tabloids."

John could feel the heat in his face, feel his heart thudding against his chest. "Fine, then. Thank you for returning my call." His words seethed with anger. "Neither you nor Dayne will hear from us again." He flipped the phone closed before the agent could say another word.

For a few seconds John held his breath, certain that he would explode from the fury building inside him. But then he emptied his lungs in a rush and stormed into the house. There was only one place he wanted to be, one place where he could sort through the feelings storming across his soul.

He grabbed his car keys from the hook on the kitchen wall, and ten minutes later he was where he needed to be. At the cemetery. He knew the path well, knew how many steps lay between the place where he always parked and the unassuming headstone that marked Elizabeth's grave.

From the moment he'd hung up, he'd refused to process the conversation, refused to even acknowledge it for fear it would paralyze him. Now, as he reached the place where Elizabeth was buried, the pain was more than he could stand. He fell to his knees and took hold of her tombstone with both hands, the way he would've placed his hands on her shoulders if only she were here.

"It's over." He hung his head, and the sobs blindsided him. "Darling Elizabeth, I t-t-tried . . . but it's over."

That was all he could say, all that was left. Every day John and Elizabeth had prayed for their firstborn son, longed for him, and wondered about him. Twice during Elizabeth's life they had staged a search that had led them nowhere. Her dying prayer—that she might meet their son—hadn't panned out after all. Everything she had said that evening had been a hallucination, just as he had originally assumed.

Whatever had happened to Dayne in his early years, the experience had left him cold and heartless, driven to excel in a career that placed him on center stage and without care enough even to meet his biological mother before she died.

The cemetery was empty this February afternoon, so John let the tears come, let the sorrow have its way with him. His tears spilled onto the grass, over the place where Elizabeth's body was buried. "Why, God?" He moved a little closer, his hands still on the stone, as if by holding it he could somehow hold the woman he had spent decades loving. He rested his forehead against the cool marble. This was the end of the road. The end of the search that John had been willing to spend a lifetime on. "I'm sorry, Elizabeth. S-s-so sorry."

He would have to tell Ashley now, tell all of the children. They deserved to know that their parents had a terrible secret. They had messed up as young lovers, and they had lived with the pain of their mistake to this day.

John leaned back on his heels and stared at the marker. Above the two dates—her birth date and death date—it read only *Elizabeth Baxter, devoted wife and mother*. That summed it up, really. He reached out once more and took hold of the stone. Tears still streamed down his face, tears for everything they'd lost by giving up their oldest son and tears for the fact that Dayne had come so close to connecting with them and then had changed his mind.

"I'm sorry, honey. I tried." Finally, tears for the most painful part of all, the part that was left now that Elizabeth was gone. He would always have a firstborn child out there, a young man who lived a public life and whose movies he could follow in the media anytime he wanted to. He would always have pictures, always have knowledge of how Dayne was doing.

But after today, he would never—not ever—have him as a son.

Chris Kane pushed back from his desk, stood, and faced his window. LA was crystal clear this afternoon, a day when he would've been better off to take a walk on the beach or hike the Santa Monica Mountains. Instead he had had to make that phone call, had to deal with this John Baxter character before the guy somehow found another way to Dayne.

Because Dayne Matthews could never know about this phone call.

Ever since Dayne had started talking about his biological family, he'd been different. Not as edgy or social, more of an introvert. For a while Chris had figured it was more about the girl, the drama instructor in Bloomington. But the more time that passed, the more sure he was that all of it was troubling Dayne. The biological family, the girl, the whole city of Bloomington for that matter.

There were days when Chris feared that Dayne would up and move to Indiana and never look back. He took hold of the window frame and shuddered. He couldn't have that, not for a minute. Dayne was a brilliant actor, only barely scraping the surface of what he was capable of. The last thing he needed was some misplaced set of emotions geared toward small-town life in Middle America.

He needed to be at nightclubs, making the social scene. He needed a different actress on his arm every other month—something to keep the tabloids talking about him. Oh, sure, Chris's clients could complain about the paparazzi, but none of them had enough money to buy the free ink those photographers gave them every week.

Chris kept track of these things. Dayne hadn't made a cover of one of the rags in a month. Last time his face was only a two-inch box, a mention because of the deposition in the case of the crazy fan's attack. The fan would be good for stirring up interest, but it would be short-lived.

It wasn't just the attention from the paparazzi that seemed to be waning—it was Dayne's intensity. In the past he had attacked roles, conquering them and leaving his director and costars and audience collectively breathless. Chris hadn't seen *Dream On* yet, but he'd heard rumors. Dayne was slipping. Dayne had lost his edge. Dayne wasn't what he once was.

As his agent, Chris understood what was happening. Dayne hadn't lost his edge, not really. The simple fact was this: Dayne was distracted. Chris stared at the traffic on busy Mulholland Drive below. He was Dayne's agent, his gatekeeper. It was up to him to protect Dayne from himself—especially when it came to his career.

He thought about the conversation with John Baxter. Okay, so he'd stretched the details, made some of them up. Dayne would be furious with him if he ever found out, which he wouldn't. He could hear in the Baxter guy's tone that he was finished. The man probably figured if Dayne didn't want anything to do with his family, so be it.

Which was exactly what Chris wanted him to feel. Because Dayne Matthews needed to get his head out of the past, out of the clouds, out of some misdirected set of emotions that had him longing for a life he could never live. He was a movie star, a celebrity. Chris had told the Baxter man the truth. Dayne had no time for exploring his roots. He owed his very best acting to his audience and directors and agent.

Chris sighed and returned to his desk. There was a price to pay for being famous, and in the long run Dayne would certainly rather pay it.

Even if it meant a little sacrifice here and there along the way.

CHAPTER NINE

THE RESTAURANT WAS DARK, the waiters dressed in white tuxedos. Katy was surprised. She'd driven by the café a dozen times each week on the way to and from CKT practice. Never had she realized the atmosphere inside was so formal. She smoothed her skirt and rested her elbows on the linen table-cloth.

Her date was in the restroom, and she was glad for the break.

The conversation had been stiff and painful, though the guy seemed comfortable with the fact. Terrence C. Willow, attorney-at-law, was thirty-two years old. His aunt was one of the CKT moms, and like so many others she had insisted on setting Katy up. At least for dinner.

From the beginning Katy wanted to protest, but common sense got the better of her. If she didn't date, she'd never meet a man she might fall in love with, never find the person God had for her, and worst of all never get married. Not that being single was so bad, not for some people.

But long ago when she pictured how she would spend her late

twenties, she pictured having children of her own—not getting set up by every well-meaning mom in town. Between Rhonda and her, there'd been more blind dates than in all of Bloomington combined. Katy was sure of it.

On paper, Terrence sounded promising. He was a water-skier and a hiker, he volunteered time with his church's junior high group, and his ultimate career goal was to sit on a bench in a Bloomington courtroom. His latest job had him working at the district attorney's office downtown—clearly a strong step toward becoming a judge.

The CKT mom had shown Katy his picture; he was nice-looking. Tall, thin—a little too thin—blond hair and glasses. The quiet, sensitive sort, Katy figured. A guy with strong morals and intentions, ready to spend his life putting away the bad guys. If she was going to fall for someone, why not Terrence C. Willow?

That's what Jenny Flanigan had told her the other night.

She had just come home from practice and joined Jenny and her husband, Jim, at the kitchen bar over a bag of microwave popcorn.

Jenny had given her a teasing look. "Heard you have a hot date Saturday night."

Katy rolled her eyes. There it was again. One of the downfalls of working with dozens of kids every week. News traveled faster than lightning. Obviously Terrence's aunt had told her children, and they in turn had told a number of other CKT kids. Which meant that all of CKT was holding its breath wondering if Saturday night would be the night Katy Hart might fall in love.

She was grateful she'd never told the CKT families about Dayne.

Only the Flanigans and Tim Reed knew about Katy's connection to him, and since Dayne was a movie star, even they hadn't taken the situation seriously. More like the two of them were acquaintances, and that was enough. Katy Hart was friends with Dayne Matthews. Wow! Never for a minute did anyone except her closest friends consider that maybe she and Dayne might have something more serious, something real.

She had nodded to Jenny and given her a lopsided grin. "Me and Terrence C. Willow. Attorney-at-law."

Jenny made a funny face. "Is that what he calls himself?"

"No." She did a quick laugh. "That's what his aunt calls him. I think to impress me."

"Have you talked to him?" Jenny took a handful of popcorn and put a few pieces in her mouth. "Did he call you or how did it work out?"

"I gave the okay and he called me." She looked at Jim. "On paper he's a nice guy, but the phone call was short. A minute maybe."

"I like that." Jim grinned and stuck his chest out. "My kind of man, not long on words."

"Yeah, well, let's hope he's a little longer on words Saturday night. Otherwise I'll be giving a three-hour monologue."

They had all chuckled, and Katy changed the subject to the recent play run of *Robin Hood*. Despite her troubled heart, the play had been a beautiful testimony to the talents and efforts of the CKT kids. Alice Stryker had come to several of the shows, connecting with the kids in a way she had never connected with her own daughter, Sarah Jo, while she was alive. Watching her was heartbreaking and inspiring at the same time.

Jenny confirmed what Katy had suspected—though she wasn't always home to see it. Alice Stryker had been coming to Bible studies at the Flanigan house. "She's close to giving her life to the Lord." Jenny reached across the popcorn bag and took her husband's hand. She gave him a knowing look. "She knows she can't make it on her own; that's for sure."

"Our talk the other night was pretty deep." Jim looked at Katy. "I had two crying women on my hands."

Katy smiled. She loved that about the Flanigans. Yes, they might ask her questions about an upcoming date but only because they honestly cared for her. Jenny often said, "The Flanigan family is in the business of helping people." Katy couldn't have agreed more. Jim and Jenny were more concerned with loving and leading people to the Lord than about anything else. That alone was the heartbeat of their home, the focus for not only their lives as a couple but for the lives of their six children—the three they'd birthed and the three they'd adopted from Haiti.

The conversation from the other night faded, and in the corner of her eye, Katy saw Terrence making his way back to the table. He wasn't bad looking. In fact, most women would've found him handsome. Or at the least, cute.

But something about him seemed staid and uptight, something Katy couldn't really put into words. She set her hands back in her lap and straightened a little. "Hi." She smiled.

"Hi." He sat down and slid his chair in. "Did the waiter come by?"

Katy hadn't paid attention. She'd been so caught up in memories of the other night that she hadn't noticed. She looked around the room and then back at Terrence. "I don't think so."

He glanced at his watch. "We've been here five minutes, right? Wouldn't you say?"

She felt suddenly as if she were on a game show, as if the questions he asked needed to be answered quickly and correctly or she'd be booted off the program. "Uh . . ." She took a fast sip of her ice water. "I think so. Five sounds right."

"Well—" he grinned, but it never quite reached his eyes— "that's a percentage point."

Katy lowered her brow, confused. "A percentage point?"

"It's a system I have." He checked his watch again. "The waiter makes his first stop to the table within five minutes or I dock a percentage point from his tip." He waved his hand in the air. "I have a whole system."

"Oh." Katy stared at her water. No wonder he wanted to be a

judge. She could only hope she'd never wind up in his court-room.

Across from her, Terrence had his hands on the table, doing something. Katy lifted her eyes just enough to see. He was straightening his silverware, spacing the pieces so they were exactly a finger's width apart from each other.

She felt her eyes get big. If she didn't start talking she would either burst out laughing or run for her life. She cleared her throat. "So . . . did you see *Robin Hood*?" It was a safe question. Katy was pretty sure the answer was yes. After all, Terrence's cousins were in the play.

Terrence gave a thoughtful nod. He stroked his chin, creating a buildup that would've been appropriate if she'd asked him his position on the death penalty.

Before he could open his mouth, the waiter breezed over to the table, breathless.

Katy looked at Terrence and wondered how many percentage points the waiter would lose if he didn't come by the table for a full seven minutes.

The waiter's name tag read Bart. He smiled at them and whipped out a pad of paper. "Hi, folks. How're you doing?"

Terrence lifted his chin, giving the guy a look that screamed disdain. He glanced at his watch once more, and his expression became pointed. "You must be very busy."

Bart poised a pencil over his paper. "Not anymore. What can I get for you to drink?"

Katy stifled a grin.

The waiter had a soft physique and a hairline heading north. But his eyes sparkled, and there was humor in his voice from the moment he said hello. Without meaning to, Katy checked his ring finger. Empty. If things with Terrence didn't get better fast, she could always leave her number for Bart.

Terrence looked at her. "Katy? Something to drink?"

"Yes." She felt her spirits lifting. It was just one date. If it continued at the pace it was going, she would always have something fun to share with Rhonda later. "Sprite, please. With a cherry in it."

"Really?" Terrence said the word under his breath. His look made her feel as if she'd ordered a Bacardi on the rocks. He waited a beat before turning back to Bart. "I'll stick with water." He pushed back slightly from the table and crossed his arms. "Tell us about the specials."

Bart seemed to realize that Terrence wasn't in the mood for laughs. His smile faded, and he gave a very serious presentation of the fresh seafood and other specials.

"Fine." Terrence slid his chair close to the table once again. "Give us a few minutes, please."

Bart looked at Katy and narrowed his eyes. "You direct the Christian Kids Theater, right?"

"Right." She smiled at him. "Have you seen our shows?"

"Definitely." The guy was more easygoing than Terrence could ever hope to be. "My little sister's Hannah Warman. She's been a townsperson in a few plays."

"A very good one at that." Katy cocked her head. "I thought you looked familiar."

"Well—" he pointed to the kitchen—"I'll get your Sprite."

Terrence was fiddling with his silverware again, and in the time it took him to straighten his salad fork, Bart gave Katy a look—one that suggested he felt sorry for her. She gave him the hint of a smile, and before he turned around, he did the same. Yes, Bart was certainly an option.

Once he was gone, Terrence frowned. "You eat cherry garnishes?"

"Yes." Again Katy had the urge to laugh, but she restrained herself and forced a dignified look. "Yes, I do."

Terrence raised his eyebrows. "You know they're loaded with chemicals and red dye, don't you? I mean, you do know that, right?"

"Now, Terrence—" she waved her hand, pretending to give him a mock brush-off—"how many chemicals could there be in a single cherry garnish?"

"Forty-seven, Katy." He looked alarmed at her naïveté. "You said you eat *them*, right? Meaning . . . more than one a year?"

"Actually . . ." Katy sucked in her cheeks. When she had control she nodded. "More than one a month, probably."

"That's very dangerous." He gave a discouraged shake of his head. "You have no idea how many carcinogens are in a single cherry garnish. Too many to count."

"I guess I better hope they die off in the Sprite." She forced the corners of her mouth upward. "Right?"

"I wasn't going to say anything." He leaned back in his chair and crossed his arms. "Sprite is loaded with sodium and sugar." He shook his finger at her, the way Jim Flanigan shook his finger at the family dog when he chewed up a pair of socks. "Most people know about the sugar, but the sodium . . . truth is, most weight gain comes from sodium. You probably didn't know that. Of course, sugar causes type 2 diabetes, but excess weight is a by-product of a high-sodium diet."

"Oh?" Katy stared at her date. Rhonda was going to love this one. "Is that right?"

"It is. Not that you need to worry about weight. Not yet, anyway." He made an *L* with his finger and thumb and rested his chin on his thumb. With his finger framing his cheek, he looked like a lecturing professor. Or like he was trying to make a statement about himself.

Terrence went on. "They've done studies about sodium, on the damage it does to organs. Half the pesticides in America amount to little more than sodium chloride." He hesitated, as if he only then realized that she might not know what sodium chloride was. "That's the, uh, chemical compound that makes up table salt." He gave a final nod of his head. "Sodium's a deadly deal."

He was just saying "deadly deal" when Bart returned with her Sprite. He paused and looked from Katy to Terrence and back to Katy again. Tentatively, he set the drink in front of her, giving her a look that only she could see. She covered her mouth to keep from giggling. When he straightened he addressed Terrence. "A few more minutes?"

"Yes, thanks." Terrence lifted his menu, and Bart left for another table.

Katy pulled her Sprite close, positioned the straw between her lips, and sucked up a long swig. Longer than usual. She stopped short of saying *ahhhh* as she swallowed.

Terrence looked at her, glanced at her drink, and shrugged sadly.

While she still had his attention, she bit the fruit off the stem, chewed the cherry a few times, and swallowed it. She could feel her eyes dancing. "Some of the best-tasting carcinogens out there." She slid her glass partway toward him. "Take a drink, Terrence. Live on the wild side."

He seemed to understand that she was teasing him, joking around. He chuckled but held up his hand. "Can't do it. Haven't had pop since I was twelve. It's a personal thing."

"Okay." Katy pulled her drink close again. "Your loss."

Terrence looked as if he might launch into an explanation of exactly how many other chemicals were contained in an eight-ounce serving of Sprite. But he changed his mind and smiled. "I like you, Katy Hart. You have spunk."

"Yes." She raised her glass in a mock toast. Dinner dates were few and far between in her world. She was going to have fun if she had to make it happen by herself. "My organs are full of deadly sodium, but I do have spunk."

His smile faded and he chuckled. "Maybe we should look at the menu."

Terrence was a strict believer in no red meat. She didn't find that out until after she ordered the big-and-beefy sirloin burger.

His expression told her that he would've preferred eating a table-spoon of salt over anything from a cow.

When the meal had finally been ordered, he found his way back to the topic of *Robin Hood*. "I thought your approach was a little too comical."

Katy was taking her last sip of Sprite just as he said the words *too comical*, and for some reason his words pushed her over the edge. A burst of laughter caught her completely off guard, and she sprayed Sprite across the table. A fine mist of it must've hit Terrence in the face because he scowled, and in a slow, exaggerated show of disgust, he dabbed his cheeks with his linen napkin.

"Sorry." She put her hand over her mouth. Had she really just done that? Sprayed Sprite on her date?

The night went from bad to worse.

Over the course of the evening Katy received enough lecture time to qualify for college credit. Terrence spoke about the virtues of waterskiing with one ski versus two and how he'd been practicing and perfecting the art since he was twelve. Ironically, the same year he swore off pop forever.

Katy stopped listening when he launched into his opinion about the failing criminal-justice system and the need for stricter penalties for repeat offenders. Even if she agreed with him, she couldn't bear to listen. Not a minute longer.

The fact that Terrence could go on for full ten-minute sessions without so much as offering her a word in response was a good thing. It gave her time to think about how different the night could have been, how she could've been sitting on a balcony overlooking Malibu Beach getting lost in the eyes of a man who seemed perfectly made for her. How he could've been taking her into his arms and kissing her, promising her he'd find a way out of the jungle of celebrity, telling her he'd do whatever he could to be with her. And she could've been sitting across from him, believing him, knowing that nothing could ever keep them apart.

She could've been doing all of that if it weren't for two obvious reasons. First, the man sitting across from her was not Dayne Matthews but Terrence C. Willow, attorney-at-law.

And there was no getting around the second reason. No matter how she played it over in her mind, Dayne wasn't making any promises to her. He was making them to Kelly Parker, the woman who would have his child in just a few short months.

CHAPTER TEN

DAYNE CHECKED HIS APPEARANCE in the mirror and straightened his bow tie. Mitch Henry, the director of *Dream On*, had asked him and three of the movie's other male leads to consider the premiere a black-tie affair. Dayne didn't mind.

Black was certainly the right color. This was, after all, the day of reckoning for him and Kelly Parker.

In the mirror he could see the phone sitting on the nightstand beside his bed. What was Katy Hart doing tonight? Was she on a date or working with her theater kids? Had she put him out of her mind, or did it only take the sight of a telephone to make her want to throw away logic and dial his number? Like it did for him.

He felt the familiar pain in his heart. After tonight, he'd have to make more of an effort to forget about Katy. It wouldn't work to be finding love with the mother of his child while he was still drawn moment by moment to another woman. This was the night everything would be worked out.

He'd given Kelly Parker exactly what she'd asked for—a full month to figure things out, to stop running from the fact that she was pregnant and start thinking about how they were going to handle being parents. She had promised she'd make time for him at the premiere. It was slated to start in two hours, and already he had a car waiting for him outside.

Yes, Kelly had taken every bit of the time she'd asked for. During the past weeks, she'd called once. Not that he didn't hear what she was doing and who she was with. The tabloids still shouted the news that she and Hawk Daniels were an item, living together. A week ago, two of the rags ran pictures of Hawk and her dancing at Club Twenty-One. The photo showed Kelly wrapped in Hawk's arms, the two of them kissing as if there weren't another person in the room.

Strange that the photo didn't bother Dayne. He had looked at it for half a minute, then pushed the magazine aside. If Kelly was caught up with Hawk again, then the news tonight was bound to be pretty straightforward. "Thanks for the offer," she would probably tell him, "but I'll have the baby on my own." And Hawk would probably be attending the premiere with Kelly.

Of course that wouldn't do. What if Dayne didn't want his baby being raised by a wild-partier type like Hawk Daniels? If Kelly wouldn't make an attempt at getting back together with her baby's father, shouldn't he have a say in how his baby was raised? And what would the tabs say? Anyone could do the math. Kelly might not stay with a guy for years at a time, but she was loyal in a relationship. And she had been in a relationship with him when she got pregnant.

Before long, the whole world would know that much.

Peace would only come by believing her. She may have acted crazy lately, but now she was ready to be serious, ready to talk to him and maybe work things out so the two of them could see if they might have a future together. He had to believe that's what was coming.

He held on to the thought as he slipped out the garage door to the waiting limousine and all the way to the Hollywood premiere, half an hour away.

Almost as soon as he stepped out onto the red carpet, he saw Kelly, with Hawk a few feet ahead of her. She looked dazzling in a formfitting, floor-length silver gown slit all the way up one leg. Her appearance caught him by surprise. There was no sign of her pregnancy, nothing about her physical appearance that would give away the fact that she was going to have a baby.

Hundreds of people had shown up for the chance to glimpse the cast of *Dream On*. Paparazzi took up the front row on either side, and behind them a throng of people jumped and waved and held cameras high overhead in hopes of a picture to take home.

"Dayne! Dayne Matthews, over here!" The shouts came from every direction, from both sides of the roped-off carpet.

Like a politician, Dayne held up his hand and grinned in one direction, then in another. For an instant, he wondered what he might be doing right now if he'd been raised in Bloomington, if he'd studied theater at the University of Indiana and fallen in love with Katy Hart. Middle of March . . . Saturday night? He'd probably be taking Katy out to dinner and maybe hanging out with the Baxters. Instead here he was, caught between a thousand flashing lights, dead center in a place where everyone loved him and no one—not even Kelly Parker—really knew him.

He stopped and signed a few autographs, first on one side, then on the other. He cared about the people who would come out on a chilly night just to wave hello. These were the people who made up his fan base, the ones who would shell out ten bucks for a movie when it might be all they could afford for a week's worth of entertainment. In many ways they had made him who he was, and he appreciated them.

It wasn't their fault, the prison he sometimes felt he was in. They didn't understand, didn't realize the life they'd created for him.

"Hi!" He waved to a little girl balanced on the shoulders of a man who looked like her father. Dayne turned a few feet. "Hello!"

He took his time, waving and smiling and signing scraps of paper and baseball caps and T-shirts. Not for fifteen minutes did he finally make his way through the double doors into the private party area. Every sort of delicacy had been catered in for the event—part of the push to convince the media that *Dream On* would definitely be one of the smash hits of the year.

Kelly and Hawk and a handful of film editors and assistant directors were standing by the punch bowl laughing. Dayne kept his pace slow, watching Kelly. As his eyes made their way down to her waist, he stopped. She was six months pregnant. Wasn't that what she'd told him? No matter what sort of great condition she was in she should be showing some kind of bump, right?

So why was her stomach so flat?

People were milling around Dayne, bidding him hello, and engaging him in a few minutes' conversation here and there, but he couldn't keep his eyes off Kelly. Six months pregnant? Maybe her math was off. Or maybe she'd hired a personal trainer, someone to help get her abs in rock-hard shape now—before the baby came. Also, though her figure was stunning, she didn't look radiant. Her face was paler than usual, and her eyes looked sunken—as if maybe she'd been sick.

Dayne turned his back to Kelly and answered a question from one of the select members of the media invited to the party. Yes, that had to be it. Morning sickness. No wonder she hadn't called. Between the sickness and the fact that things hadn't worked out between them the first time, of course Kelly was confused.

He glanced at her over his shoulder, but she still had her attention elsewhere. She had to know he was here, but she hadn't even looked in his direction. And though she and Hawk were making the rounds separately, talking to other people and playing the part of the genial cast mate, Dayne caught Hawk drifting back to Kelly every few minutes. They would exchange a few quiet words and a knowing touch to the elbow or shoulder, and then Hawk would be on his way again.

Dayne was still watching her when Mitch Henry approached him, his whole face taken up with a grin. "I heard the news!"

Dayne's heart skipped a beat. Mitch Henry knew about Kelly's pregnancy? He felt the blood leave his face. "I . . . I, uh . . ." What should he say? No one knew yet, so how come Mitch was suddenly beaming with—?

"You heard it, right? We picked up another hundred theaters!"

"Oh." Dayne laughed, and his heart slid back into a regular rhythm. "Right. That."

Mitch crossed his arms and studied him. "You doing okay, Matthews? You don't look so good."

"I'm great . . . fine." He turned on the smile. "How about you? Working on another film?"

Mitch took a step closer and dropped his voice. "You're not fine. I know you better than that."

Dayne allowed a nervous chuckle. "Ah, Mitch." He held his hands out to the sides. "You got me; I didn't eat my Wheaties this morning."

"You know what I wish?" his director asked. "I wish I knew whether it was Kelly Parker—" his eyes tried to find a deeper place in Dayne—"or Katy Hart who was making you look like this."

Dayne felt like he'd been kicked in the gut. "Well . . ." He inhaled sharply but played it off, not letting Mitch see more than his smile. "You remembered her name."

"Of course I remembered." Mitch was holding a plate of food. He took a cracker, scooped up a mound of caviar, slipped it into his mouth, and chewed a few times. "She was brilliant on camera, Matthews. Every week I'm tempted to call her, just to get her in one of my films."

"Really." For some reason the idea bothered Dayne. Katy had been right to turn down the part in *Dream On*. The fame and spotlight would've changed her life—changed her, even. She was better off in Bloomington, where the simplicity of her charm and beauty couldn't be touched.

Mitch picked up another cracker and pointed it at Dayne. "One of these days I just might do it. I might make the call." He cocked his head, as if once again he was trying to see the feelings Dayne was hiding from him. "Maybe if she were a part of *this* world, the two of you wouldn't have such a hard time figuring it out."

Dayne was listening more intently than he let on. He snatched a carrot from Mitch's plate and willed a teasing look into his eyes. "Figuring what out?"

Mitch frowned at Kelly and then shot a whisper at Dayne. "That it was never Kelly. It was Katy Hart." He glanced over one shoulder and then the other. "And that the two of you are crazy about each other."

"Nah." His answer was fast, but it sounded forced even to him. "Katy's old news."

"Very well." The director slowly stroked his chin. "Can I make one observation?"

"Okay." Dayne was uncomfortable with the subject. Normally he was better at hiding his feelings, but Mitch was spot-on here. Still he had no choice but to make light of everything the director was saying. He grinned. "I'll humor you."

Mitch glanced at Kelly again. When his eyes found Dayne's there was a knowing there. "You never looked at Kelly the way you looked at Katy." He lowered his plate of food. "No matter what I tried on the set, I couldn't match it, couldn't find the look I caught on a simple audition tape when I had Katy Hart in the studio."

Then Mitch really did know. Dayne kept the grin, but the director's words cut him deep. "All right. I guess, thanks for that." He nodded to the punch. "All this talking's made me thirsty. Catch you later." He took a few steps in Kelly's direction, but he pointed back at his director. "You need to tell me about your current film."

Mitch Henry smiled. Then he turned to mingle with a group of minor-role players, excited young actors gathered around the dessert table.

Dayne wiped the side of his hand across his brow. Was he that easy to read? He was an actor after all. If he couldn't hide his feelings any better than that, how could he convince Kelly he wanted to make another go at it?

How could he convince himself?

He stared at her, ten yards away. Kelly Parker. When had things between them gotten so strained? And how would he set them in the right direction here, now? He came up along her right side and blended into the conversation she was having with the movie's producer.

The man was rattling off snippets from recent reviews and going on about financial projections for the film. "It's going to be huge, I tell you." He nodded at Dayne. "In no small part because of how both of you played the screen." With cultured practice he leaned in and kissed each of Kelly's cheeks. "I'll let you two visit." He shook Dayne's hand. "Good to see you."

"You too, sir." Dayne didn't have a casual relationship with the producer. The man was Hollywood royalty, a serious player in the moviemaking industry, a producer with a golden touch for turning movies into megahits. Dayne's agent had long since coached him to handle the man with great respect.

When he was gone, Dayne turned to Kelly and touched her hand. "Hi." They were alone, though not for long at a premiere party like this one. For all the frustration she'd caused him since that phone call in January, he was happy to see her. She had been his friend first, and maybe friendship would allow them a bridge to whatever came next. "How are you?"

"Good." She gave him a shy look. "I thought you were avoiding me."

"No." He studied her. "I was waiting. I didn't want to rush you."

"Oh." She shifted her eyes and looked at something off to the side.

He followed her gaze, and there was Hawk. He turned away as soon as he saw Dayne. It wasn't the time to talk about whatever was going on. Dayne looked back at Kelly's face. "Can we talk? Later?"

"Dayne . . ." She took hold of his hands and made the slightest shake of her head. "I have plans."

Plans? He steadied himself. "With someone else?" He found his smile, but he wanted to yell at her. "You told me to wait for the premiere. That you needed to figure things out and we could talk tonight." He ran his thumbs along the palms of her hands. Anyone watching would've assumed they were still a couple the way they'd been during the filming of *Dream On*.

Kelly seemed resigned at Dayne's reminder. She nodded toward a side door. "There's a private patio out there. We still have half an hour before the movie."

This wasn't the way it was supposed to happen. They were supposed to watch the film and then find somewhere to talk. Two people couldn't make plans for a baby and a lifetime of sharing a parenting role in half an hour. But maybe he needed to hear what she had to say now. Then they could figure out how the rest of the evening would go. He glanced at the door. "Give me half an hour after the movie, during the party. Before your plans."

She bit her lip, and for a single instant she looked across the room at Hawk. "Okay. Fine."

Soon the crowd gathered for the movie. For Dayne it passed in a blur. He sat with Mitch Henry, and when it came to the scenes in Bloomington, he felt a catch in his heart. If there were a way through the screen, through the film and into that town he'd be there in a minute. The talk with Kelly wasn't going to be good—he could already feel her pulling away. Whatever the future held it didn't look promising.

The producer was right about the movie. It was fantastic,

upbeat and funny, emotional and sensitive. Women across the country would love it. Dayne had already seen most of it in the editing room, but watching it on the big screen at the premiere was always a pinnacle moment.

When it was over, the party in the lobby area changed. A pop rock band had been brought in to entertain, and the crowd seemed to swell. Dayne watched Kelly, watched her do what she'd been doing earlier—making the rounds and returning to Hawk every ten minutes or so.

After two hours of celebrating, Kelly found Dayne. She tried to smile, but her look was pained. "Can you talk?"

Dayne pushed back his chair. "Absolutely." He stood and nodded to the other people at his table. They suspected nothing. Most of them were three drinks into the night and wouldn't even notice his absence.

He followed Kelly through the crowd. Moving like two people used to having every eye in the room on them, she led him toward the patio door, occasionally giving him a demure smile and nodding along the way to assistant directors and editors and the crew involved in making the film. The lights were dimmed, and everyone was busy celebrating. No one seemed to think anything of the two of them heading off together.

At the door she turned to him. "The patio should be open, even though it's cold out." Kelly's words were clipped, nervous sounding.

"Okay." Dayne reached out and took Kelly's hand. He was glad to have privacy from the photographers and media members and especially from Hawk Daniels.

Out on the patio, Dayne watched Kelly's posture change, watched her exhale hard and walk across the cement to the wrought-iron railing surrounding an old oak tree. She leaned on it and hung her head. "Maybe we should talk later. After the party."

"I thought you had plans." Dayne came closer. Why wouldn't she look at him? "Isn't that what you said?"

"I do." She uttered a quiet, frustrated cry, and the smell of alcohol mingled with her breath. She kept her gaze downward. "I don't know."

He wanted to shout at her. She shouldn't be drinking. Anyone knew alcohol was bad for unborn babies. But this didn't seem the time—not yet. He came closer still and gently lifted her chin. "You don't know what, Kel?" He saw fear and confusion on her face, and for the first time since hearing the news about the baby, Dayne felt truly sorry for her. Even though she'd promised to be ready to make a decision by now, clearly she was still scared to death. This couldn't be easy for her either. He softened his tone. "What don't you know?"

She was quiet, and her hands began to tremble.

"Kelly, listen. You won't have to have this baby alone. I want to try again. That's what tonight is about for me." His heart rate doubled. Katy Hart's face tried to come to mind, but he refused it. His lips were suddenly dry. "We were friends first, and maybe this . . . the baby will help us give things more of a chance."

For the first time tonight, he didn't see fear or confusion or coyness or uncertainty in Kelly's eyes. He saw guilt. Guilt and regret.

"I don't know how to tell you, Dayne."

It was his turn to feel confused. "Tell me what?"

She looked at him a long time, and her eyes gave him a window to all she was feeling. First the guilt, then remorse, and finally something that mixed love with regret. The emotions took turns with her expression and made her appear vulnerable. Something Dayne hadn't seen in Kelly since they first moved in together.

She reached up and brushed her fingertips against his cheek. "Do you know how much I loved you, Dayne?"

He covered her hand with his own. "I care about you too. I always have."

A sad laugh sounded in her throat. "See? Even now you can't tell me you love me."

"Kelly . . ." What was he supposed to say? "I did love you . . . you know I did." But even as he said the words, he felt like a liar. Love—the sort of love she was talking about—would take weeks, months. As they spent more time together, as they made plans for their baby, he was bound to feel love for her.

But Kelly was shaking her head. "You never loved me, Dayne." There were tears in her eyes. "Not like you loved her."

For the slightest instant he was going to ask, "Who?" Whom had he loved more than Kelly? But the answer was as obvious as the brick wall surrounding them. And it was an answer Kelly already knew. Dayne looked at the ground near his shoes. But Katy was gone. He and Kelly were about to be parents, so there simply was no Katy Hart. Now he needed to convince Kelly. He lifted his eyes and tried to look convincing. "I haven't talked to her since the day you told me about the baby." He moved his hands to her shoulders. "I want to do the right thing here, Kelly."

Tears pooled in her eyes. "There is no right thing." She looked weak, as if her knees could buckle at any moment. "I've loved you for years, Dayne. Only after I moved out did I finally make myself understand that you would never—not ever—love me the way I loved you. Don't you see? I don't want you to work at loving me." Anger crept into her tone. "You want to do the right thing? Can you hear yourself?" She jerked away from him. "This isn't 1950. You don't have to stay around and try to make it work just because you got me pregnant." She wheeled around, stormed across the courtyard, and faced the wall on the other side.

Why was she acting like this? They both had to see that the situation wasn't ideal. What was wrong with agreeing to try, to look for whatever love might be created between them?

He crossed the patio, glancing at the door as he passed it. Ten minutes had slipped by; they didn't have much longer. The others must have sensed that he and Kelly needed time to talk. But if they didn't hurry, Hawk was bound to come looking for them. Dayne came up behind her and once more placed his hands on her shoulders. "Kelly, don't do this. Not now." He kept his voice low, his mouth a few inches from her ear. "I care about you or I wouldn't be here."

"You don't care about me!" She whipped around and glared at him, the tears on her cheeks little more than reflections of her anger. Then she seemed to remember where she was and who she was. The lines on her forehead eased, and she gathered herself into a more composed, upright position. "You care about the baby. That's what this is all about."

Dayne opened his mouth, but he couldn't find the words to refute her. "What's wrong with that?" He didn't raise his voice, but he was more frustrated than before. "We wouldn't be the first couple who found a way to love each other because of a child, right? I mean, right?"

She studied him. "Dayne . . ." The vulnerability from a moment ago was gone, and in its place was a look that screamed vindication. She ran her hands over her flat abdomen and narrow waist. "There is no baby, okay? Can't you figure it out?"

"No baby?" Dayne's head began to spin. What was she saying? How could she let him believe there was a baby all this time if . . . "You weren't . . . you weren't really pregnant?"

She groaned, and the sound of it was riddled with pain. A fresh layer of tears began pooling in her eyes. "I had an abortion, okay?" She took a step back and ran her hands down her sides. "Women six months pregnant don't look like this."

Dayne couldn't breathe, couldn't speak. He staggered back a few steps and grabbed hold of the railing around the tree. "Without . . . without telling me?" The shock was suffocating him, coming at him from every side. The baby . . . the one he'd been planning for these past few months . . . was dead? He felt horrified, numb, and nauseous all at the same time. "Are you serious?"

She came to him with fury in her steps. "Yes, I'm serious." She glared at him, but her heart must've been breaking also because tears streamed down her face. "You didn't—" a sob stopped her sentence short—"you didn't love me, Dayne! Why in the world would I want to have your baby?"

He felt furious and faint. She was telling him the truth; sometime since their last conversation she'd had an abortion without so much as a phone call to let him know. He grabbed a quick breath and doubled over, his hands on his knees. The loss grew and swelled in his heart until the enormity of it threatened to suffocate him.

Slowly, he straightened and studied her features. Whatever she had become, he no longer knew her. She was cold and callous and cruel. "You never even . . . you never called."

"Look." Her expression told him she was scared to death, that she regretted what she'd done. But her tone told an entirely different story. "I didn't have to call you." She pressed her hand over her heart. "It's my body, my pregnancy. It was my choice to end it—mine alone."

"Sure, Kelly . . ." Dayne's heart was breaking for the child they'd lost. It was all he could do to keep his composure. "Sure, tell yourself that." He motioned to the door and the party beyond it. "You've got the right lingo; that's for sure. All that garbage sounds neat and tidy, the way everyone in Hollywood sounds. Your body . . . your choice . . . your right to have an abortion."

"I don't need to hear this." She spat the words at him and moved toward the door.

"Wait!"

She hesitated and looked as if she was trying to hold on to her anger. That way she couldn't give in to the regret he'd seen earlier. "Hurry, Dayne. I told you . . . I have plans."

"Okay." Tears choked his voice now, tears of anger and hurt.

"You can tell me about your rights. But deep inside you know the truth." His chin was quivering, and a lifetime of sorrow welled in his heart. "Our baby was growing inside you, the first child for both of us." He jabbed himself in the chest. "*My* child, Kelly." The reality of what had happened was still hitting him, still tearing into him like shrapnel from a lethal roadside bomb. "I had nothing to say about it, and now that child is dead."

She crossed her arms and drilled her eyes into him. "Please, Dayne . . . don't be so dramatic. We had sex. I got pregnant. I had an abortion." She tilted her chin, once again the proud, controlled actress—the one she'd been on Hawk Daniels's arm earlier. She took one more step toward the door. "I wasn't even five months along when I had it. So there never was a child."

Dayne let his hands fall to his sides, defeated. "You can tell yourself whatever you want, Kelly." Images came to his mind, photos of aborted babies he'd seen in science class. He shuddered and struggled to find his voice. "But don't—not for one minute—tell yourself there was never a child."

Her expression was harder than it had been all night. She looked like a bored teenager, tired of a lecture from Dad. She put her hand on the doorknob and shot him one more dagger. Then without saying good-bye, she reentered the party, shutting the door behind her.

Dayne was still reeling. He held on to the railing with both hands and let his head hang. *Dear God, how can this be happening?* He squeezed his eyes shut. He hadn't talked to God since hearing the news about the baby back in January. He wasn't even sure he believed in God anymore—not if He had allowed Kelly to get pregnant, even though Dayne didn't love her.

But now his thinking seemed to border on insanity.

"God . . ." The word was a desperate cry, a strained whisper. "It wasn't You; it was me. All along it's been me." The tears came, and he did nothing to stop them. He was the one who had asked Kelly to move in with him, the one who had been stung by Katy's rejection after the crazy knife-wielding fan's attack, the one who had then allowed lust to take the place of love.

The fact that Kelly got pregnant wasn't God's way of abandoning him. Rather it was the natural consequence of sleeping with Kelly, of acting in direct opposition to everything his adoptive parents had ever tried to teach him. All of it had been his fault, and he deserved to have it change his life forever.

Only now the worst thing of all—the baby was dead. Just yesterday he'd stopped at a Wild Oats grocery store and seen a mother cradling her newborn. Beside her, a man wearing a wedding ring pushed their cart. For a moment—until the first fan came up asking for an autograph—Dayne just watched. That would be him in a few months, pushing a cart, supporting Kelly, and taking turns holding a tiny infant. As he watched, he could almost feel the weight of the child in his arms, almost hear the little cries of the baby that was about to be his.

His tears came harder. Now there would be no child, no baby to hold. "Was it a girl or a boy, God?" His question rattled around in his mind and echoed across his soul. Whatever their baby was, the child was in heaven now.

Dayne believed that as surely as he believed in oxygen.

And if he believed that, then he had to believe in God as well—the God who was listening to him, weeping with him even now. His lifestyle, his choices had led to this. Kelly truly believed the lies she'd been told: that abortion was a choice, an option. Her body, her call.

Of course the people who fought for such a travesty never really looked in a woman's eyes, never saw the regret and pain like what he had seen deep in Kelly's expression. She was hurting. No matter what lies she told herself, she knew deep down that he was right. There most certainly had been a child, an unborn baby.

And now there wasn't.

"God . . . help me." He squeezed the words through clenched

teeth. Last fall he had done what his birth mother had asked, what she had written to him in the letter on the back of her photograph. He had forgiven. Forgiven his birth parents for giving him up, for not fighting harder to keep him. Forgiven his adoptive parents for choosing the mission field over giving him a normal childhood.

And he had asked forgiveness from Kelly for how he had treated her.

But this . . . how could God ever forgive him for taking part in the death of a child? For that matter, he must've been crazy to sleep with a woman when he didn't know her opinions on something as crucial as the right to life. And what did he think she'd been doing this past month? Had he really thought she was making plans for a nursery between nights of partying and flaunting her relationship with Hawk Daniels?

He should've seen this coming weeks ago.

The truth was, he was every bit as guilty as Kelly. "I'm sorry, God . . . I'm so sorry."

My son, come to Me . . . let Me find you while you still may be found.

Dayne straightened and looked over his shoulder, turning one direction and then the other. Who had said that? The words felt like they had been whispered, carried on the night breeze that sifted across the small, private patio. A chill ran down his spine. *God . . . was that You?*

There was no audible response, but now he had a new sense of strength, of peace.

He dragged his hands across his cheeks and looked inside. It was dark enough in the party room that he could make it through the place without anyone asking what was wrong. People at movie premieres were concerned with making connections and looking good for the cameras. Every one of the gossip rags and even *People* magazine would run a full spread on this premier event—so impressions were everything.

The photographers had gotten hundreds of shots of him earlier, so he could smile big and leave the party without causing a stampede. He leaned against the iron railing and gazed into the sky. He felt stronger, yes, but the hurt was no less overwhelming. He'd thought about his baby every day since Kelly had first told him. Boy or girl? His dark blond hair or Kelly's? Blue eyes or brown? Would the child have been interested in drama and the arts or crazy for sports? He would never know now, not this side of heaven. Never hear his child's voice or see his baby's smile. The loss was so great it took his breath.

No, it wasn't the right timing, and no, Kelly wasn't the right person. But none of that was the baby's fault. Dayne pressed his fists into his middle. His first child was dead. The tragedy hurt deeply. As he stood there, as he let the breeze dry the remaining dampness in his eyes, there was only one place he wanted to be now, one person who could help him take the next step toward finding God—if God truly was calling him.

A woman with pale blonde hair and cornflower blue eyes, who at the very least would point him in the right direction. And something else . . . something no one he knew in Hollywood could ever do. She would grieve with him and ache with him for a hurt that would stay until he drew his last breath. She would understand how great his pains were and that his regret would last for a lifetime. She would feel his sadness because of a series of bad decisions he could never, ever take back.

And most of all she would cry with him because of a baby who lived in heaven now, a child who would not have the chance to live and grow and become on this earth. His arms hurt at the emptiness of it, because he never got to meet his baby.

Because his first child would forever be a baby he never even had the chance to hold.

CHAPTER ELEVEN

ASHLEY HAD THE FEELING her father was hiding something from her. Landon was at the fire station this Saturday afternoon, and she and Cole were on their way to the Baxter house to go over plans for the reunion. The whole ride there, Ashley replayed in her mind a few of the recent conversations she'd had with her dad.

Every time she asked her father about her older brother, he was vague. "How's it coming with the search?" she had asked him a few nights ago. "Anything new from the private investigator?"

"Uh . . ." Always there seemed to be a slight hesitation. "No, nothing yet." Frustration echoed in his voice. "You'll be the first to know, Ashley. I promise you."

Ashley leaned forward and clicked on the radio.

"Put on eighties, okay, Mom?" Cole piped up from the backseat. "Daddy always lets me listen to the eighties."

She laughed, and the sound of it temporarily erased her suspicions. "You're the only kid in Bloomington who listens to eighties, Cole. I just want you to know that."

"I don't just like eighties." In the rearview mirror she saw him grin. "I like country too. 'Specially that song about coming home."

"'Who Says You Can't Go Home'?"

"Yeah." Cole giggled. "I love that song!"

She turned to the eighties station and relished the feeling. A Bryan Adams song was half over, and the instant Cole heard it, he started moving to the music. She took a deep breath. These were the moments she would always remember. She and Cole, music filling the van, bopping around town together as if he'd always be young and she'd always have him in the backseat.

By the time they reached the Baxter house, Ashley's mind had taken a dozen different trails—thoughts about how wonderful it would be to see Luke and Erin. How much she'd missed them and how she couldn't wait to see their kids and how they'd grown. Also how sad it was that their mom wouldn't be there, and that brought her full circle to her father.

And why he didn't seem to be getting anywhere with finding their older brother.

The reunion was the perfect place for all of them to meet him—if he were willing and able to come, of course. The timing had seemed perfect before, but now that it was the middle of March they were running out of days. It would take a miracle to make a connection with their brother in only two weeks.

Her dad was outside waiting for them, sprinkling bits of food into the frog pond. Ashley took hold of Cole's hand, and they started toward him.

"Good news!" Her dad smiled at them. "I bought a few dozen goldfish." He stared at the water. "They love the place."

"Goldfish!" Cole released her hand and ran toward the pond. "To keep the frogs company, you mean?"

"Exactly." Her father rubbed Cole's hair and pulled him close for a hug. He looked at Ashley. "How are you feeling?"

"Good." She couldn't move as fast as Cole, but she was sleeping all right. "The baby's not as active as before." She put her hand on what used to be her waist. "But I can't blame him. Not much room left in there."

Her dad chuckled. "I think you're right." He pointed at the water. "Come look at the fish."

"Yeah, Mommy, Papa's right." Cole dropped to his knees and lowered his face inches above the water. "You never saw such happy goldfish." He gave her a lopsided grin. "They have little fish smiles on their faces."

Little fish smiles. She loved this about Cole, his enthusiasm for life, his imagination. "Wait till Maddie sees them."

"Yeah!" He jumped to his feet, tugging at his grandpa's sleeve. "Can we ask her to come now, Papa? Can we?"

"I think Aunt Brooke's bringing the girls by later. Uncle Peter has some work at the hospital."

"Goodie!" Cole pumped his fist. Then he dropped to his knees again and stared at the fish. "I wish I had a net so I could catch 'em."

Her father frowned. "Maybe we should wait on that."

"Yeah." Cole looked over his shoulder. "Until they've been here awhile."

Ashley stood at her father's side and watched Cole. "The pond looks great."

"You noticed?" His voice rang with pride.

"Of course." Ashley pointed to the pebbly landing. "You made a place for the kids to kneel down closer to the water."

"Right." He nodded to the ring of large rocks. "Cleared the weeds too." He slipped his arm around Ashley. "Remember the fishpond I made for you kids when you were little?"

Ashley laughed. "Of course." The years peeled back, and the memories were vivid once more. "Luke and I spent three summers around that pond."

"That's right." He chuckled, his tone nostalgic. "Always Luke and you, my tomboy."

"Didn't the fish have babies?"

"Babies?" Cole spun around, his eyes wide. "Fish can have babies?"

"Yes." Her dad grinned big. "When your mommy was a little girl our fish had babies and grandbabies and great-grandbabies. So many fish we had to catch some of them and give them to neighbors down the street."

"I remember that. Luke and I wading through the pond with our little nets."

"Really?" Cole turned back to the pond. "When these fish have babies and there gets to be so many like that, maybe you could let me and Maddie be the catchers." He squinted against the glare of the sun. "'Cause I think I'd be a really good catcher, Papa."

A pair of geese flew overhead and landed in the front field, fifty yards away.

Cole spotted them immediately. He stood and took soft running steps in the direction of the birds. "Watch what a good catcher I am, Papa." He spoke with a loud whisper.

Long before Cole reached the geese, they lifted and settled another twenty yards from him.

With him out of earshot, Ashley took a step toward the pond and then faced her father. This was as good a time as any. "You know what I'm going to ask you?"

It took only a few seconds for the knowing look to fill her dad's eyes. "About your older brother?"

"Right." She smiled. This didn't need to be an awkward subject between them. She just wanted to know where he was, who he was. And if her father was having such a hard time finding him, then maybe she should take over the search. "I guess it feels like every time I bring him up you change the subject. Like you don't want to talk about him."

Her father gave her a slow nod and shaded his eyes. "I know."

A heavy sigh rattled on his lips, and his shoulders seemed to slump a few inches. "I'm sorry."

"I mean, Dad—" she took his hand—"maybe it's too much for you. I'd be happy to take over, maybe make a few calls to the investigator, see if I can't get him more enthused about finding him, where he is and who he is and whether he'd want to—"

"Ashley." He brought his free hand to her shoulder and looked deep into her eyes. "The PI found your brother."

Ashley had to hold tight to her father's hand so she wouldn't drop to her knees. This was hardly the news she'd expected to hear. Her throat was suddenly dry and tight, and she swallowed so she could think of what to say. Even then all she could manage was "He found him?"

"Yes." But instead of joy and elation, there was fresh sorrow in her dad's expression. "But the news isn't good."

Not good? A handful of possibilities flashed across Ashley's mind. He was sick or dead, or maybe he'd done some horrible thing. Her legs and arms trembled, and she waited, breathless.

"It's a closed door, Ashley. He doesn't want anything to do with us."

"What?" Outrage immediately replaced the shock working its way through her body. Her baby began to kick, and she motioned to the porch swing. In the distance Cole was still chasing the pair of geese. "Let's go sit down."

Storm clouds were gathering in the distance, and in a few hours there was bound to be thunder and lightning. But for now Ashley appreciated the sunshine on her back as they crossed the driveway. The news chilled her to the bone. How could her brother turn down his entire birth family without ever knowing them?

She steadied herself against her father until they were seated on the swing. Then she looked at him, angry and desperate for answers. "Tell me everything, Dad." Her words were dry. "Start at the beginning."

"I should've told you sooner. I've known about him for two months now."

"Two months?" Ashley raised her voice. She gripped the arm of the swing and angled her large body so she could see her father better. She worked to lower her tone. "Dad, two months?"

"I wanted to make sure."

"Make sure of what?"

"That he didn't want contact with us." He looked sad and tired and old, sunk against the back of the swing. "I've done everything I can do."

"You mean you talked to him?"

"Not exactly." Her dad seemed ready to say more, but he stopped himself. "Last month I talked to a man who works for him. He told me in no uncertain terms that your brother wants nothing to do with us. There's no getting around the truth, Ash. He's made his decision."

Ashley held her breath and then released it all at once. "Well, what's his name? Who is he?" She clenched her fists and dug them into her knees. "I'll call him. Maybe that'll change his mind."

"No, Ashley." He sat a little straighter. "I've reached a dead end. There's nothing more I can do."

Tears stung the corners of her eyes. "But that isn't fair. We never got to know him." She stood slowly, went to the porch railing, and leaned against it. Cole was back at the fishpond, crouched down and pointing at the water as if he were counting the goldfish. Two hot tears fell from her eyes and onto her cheeks. "If he knew us, he'd be sorry he ever missed a day."

"I know." His tone was sad but unbending. This wasn't a topic with any give in it whatsoever. "I'm sorry, Ashley."

"So what's his name?" She turned around and leveled her gaze at him. "Where does he live, and what does he do for a living?" She couldn't stop herself. She had a hundred questions, and now in a single conversation she had to deal with the fact that she might *never* have answers to any of them. "Is he married? Are there nieces and nephews out there somewhere? Have you seen his picture or—?"

"Ashley . . ." He held out his hands. "Enough."

"But, Dad . . ." She rubbed her forehead, trying to make sense of it. "We should know *something*, don't you think?" She waved her hand. "He could be my next-door neighbor, for all I know."

Her father was quiet for a moment, and his expression was familiar. It was the way he always looked when he was sorting through his thoughts. Finally he grabbed the swing chain closest to him and took a long breath. "He's not your next-door neighbor." He sounded winded. "He's not married. He's successful and he works in Los Angeles. As far as I know, he has no children."

Ashley let the information find its place in her heart. He was in his thirties, but he wasn't married? Maybe he was unhappy, a person who had never really connected with the importance of family. Maybe that's why he was successful. She made a stronger effort to soften her voice. "What's his name?"

"That . . . I can't tell you. It's his wish that he stays anonymous."

"Anonymous?" Ashley wanted to laugh. Who would she tell? Landon? Cole? So what, right? They deserved to know and so did her siblings and their families. "Are you serious, Dad? You're not going to tell me?"

"What does it matter?" This time the pain and rejection were clear in her father's voice. "Isn't it better if we never have a name or a picture?" He gazed out at the field, to the place where Cole was still crouched near the pond. "Isn't it less painful if we just let the whole thing go?"

Ashley didn't think so, but she stopped herself from giving a quick answer. Obviously her father had spent a long time thinking about this. If he didn't want to reveal her brother's name at this point, she couldn't push him. Not now, anyway. She returned to the swing and eased herself back into it. "What about the others?"

"They should know." Her dad set the swing in motion. "I'll tell them at the reunion. The second night when we're all here. After dinner, maybe."

Ashley was surprised. Her father had thought this through. Despite the disappointment still exploding within her, she felt relieved. The secret wasn't one she would have to carry alone for much longer. "You're right." She put her hand on her father's. "That'd be a good time to tell them."

"This wasn't how I wanted the search to end." His expression was wistful, distant. He looked at her. "I tried, Ashley. I did."

She wanted to push about his name. Because maybe if she had his name she could still do her own search. She and her siblings could find him and go to him and convince him he was wrong. That no matter what his past or his life now, he was one of them. He would be blessed for a place in the Baxter family—even if only once in a while.

But again she thought the timing was wrong. Instead she touched her dad's shoulder. "Can I ask you something . . . one thing?"

Cole was skipping toward them, shouting something about tadpole eggs.

Her father looked drained. "I can't give you his name."

"Not that." Ashley rested her head on his shoulder for a moment. Then she lifted her eyes to him and pleaded, "Can you try just once more? Please?" She sat up. "I know you think you've done everything. But maybe try just once more. Okay?"

Cole ran up the steps, his face alive with excitement. "Papa, guess what?"

"Ashley . . ." He cocked his head.

"Please, Dad."

Her dad sighed. "All right." He patted her hand as he stood.

"One more time." He held his arms out to Cole, and they hugged. "Tell me, Cole, my boy."

As Ashley watched her father, she thought of her older brother, who was somewhere out there. *God, he doesn't know what he's missing. Every week that passes . . . every day. Please, God . . . change his mind. Help my dad find a way to reach him. Please.*

A strong sense of certainty filled her heart as she finished her silent prayer. She had learned long ago not to ask God for anything unless she was willing to believe it could happen. And that's how she felt right now. She had placed the situation in God's hands. Her father had found their older brother. Her brother knew about them—so the biggest obstacles were behind them. God could change the guy's mind, and He would.

Somehow, some way . . . He would bring their brother to them.

Now it was only a matter of waiting.

John thought about Ashley's request through the afternoon and into the evening. Landon and Brooke and Peter and the girls had joined them. Kari and Ryan and their kids had dinner with the Flanigan family. Ryan still coached football with Jim Flanigan at Clear Creek High School. Spring passing league was about to start, and Kari had said she was ready for an entire evening of visiting with Jim's wife, Jenny.

Even without Kari at the house tonight, the plans for the reunion were shaping up quickly and easily. The enthusiasm and anticipation for a week of being together were growing every time they talked about it.

But now, with the house empty again, John could think only of Dayne.

He'd told Ashley the truth. He'd tried everything since his conversation with Dayne's agent. Despite the man's harsh words, John had called the agent twice more, asking him to get word to Dayne. The last time the talk between them was painfully short and strained. The man had been almost rude with him.

"I gave him your last message," the man snapped. "Look, Mr. Baxter, I'm asking you to let this go. Dayne isn't interested."

That had been a week ago, and John was convinced more than ever before. He'd been to the cemetery twice and begged God for more than a dead end. But it wasn't happening, and he had to believe that God was giving him a sign. That perhaps knowing his oldest son would be worse for them—for all of them—than the shut door they were facing now.

But in light of Ashley's words, Elaine Denning's advice came back to him: *"Don't give up, John. Please try again. Maybe contact Dayne apart from his agent."*

He could still hear her voice, see the earnestness in her face. That, combined with the conversation with Ashley, convinced John that he had no choice but to write a letter to Dayne and send it to the studio that produced *Dream On*. That way John could bypass Chris Kane. Not that he doubted the agent. But maybe if Dayne read a letter straight from him—from his birth father—God would change something in his heart.

John wandered to the kitchen drawer and pulled out the box of stationery Elizabeth had kept there. Like so much in the house, it hadn't been moved since her death. As long as he lived here, her touch would remain. The way she'd arranged the furniture and the dishes and the books in the bookcase. Her curtains and tablecloths and dried-flower arrangements.

She was everywhere still, the way she always would be.

He took a piece of stationery and a pen and sat at the kitchen counter. There were so many layers of heartache where Dayne was concerned. The fact that he hadn't met Elizabeth, that he'd changed his mind hours before meeting her. The relationships he'd missed out on with Brooke and Kari and Ashley and Luke and Erin. John's heart felt heavy. Even worse, Dayne may have missed out on their faith and the faith of his adoptive parents.

If for no other reason he had to push for contact with his older son so he could do his part to help Dayne find the Lord in his life. Nothing could be more tragic than knowing they'd given Dayne up only to sacrifice his eternal destiny.

John stared at the blank page and decided he wasn't only going to send a letter. He picked up a stack of duplicate photographs sitting on the counter beside him. Elizabeth had a few small photo albums lying around, maybe in the upstairs closet. He'd use one and arrange the photos in order of Dayne's siblings, oldest to youngest.

Photos that started with one of Elizabeth and himself and moved on to Brooke and Peter and their kids and so on. They were beautiful pictures, two dozen of them in all. Whatever emotions and love John couldn't manage to squeeze into the letter would come loud and clear from these photographs he'd found. He had no doubt.

He looked at the stationery again and positioned his pen near the top. *Okay, God, give me the words.* He sucked in a slow breath and began to write.

Dear Dayne . . .

He filled an entire page before he signed his name and reread it. At the bottom of the letter John added his three phone numbers—home, work, and cell. He also included his address—though he figured Dayne probably already had it if his own PI had done a thorough job.

He found the photo album in the closet, carefully printed the information on the back of each photograph, and filled the album with the pictures. Then he stuck it and the letter into a padded envelope. He decided to address it to Dayne in care of Mitch Henry, the director of *Dream On*.

A director would know Dayne well, maybe even on a friendship basis—especially after they had just finished a movie together. Not only that, but if he sent the mail to the studio without the name of someone who worked there, it could get lost on a secretary's desk somewhere. Perhaps Henry would forward the mail on to Dayne.

The next day John took the package to the mailbox at the corner near his office, but before he dropped it in the mail slot he held it with both hands. This was it, his last chance at making contact with his firstborn son. If he didn't hear from him after this, he would have to respect Dayne's wishes and let him go.

He ran his thumb along the envelope, along the handwritten letters that spelled out his son's name. *God . . . go with this package. If You don't want a meeting between us, I'll respect that. I'll consider it Your will. I'm asking only this, Father—please let it reach Dayne. Let him open it and read it. That's it, God.*

His gaze lingered a few seconds more before he dropped the package in the box. There. He'd done it. The package would reach Dayne, because God would make sure it reached him.

After that, John's connection and future relationship with the firstborn Baxter son would be completely and utterly up to Dayne.

CHAPTER TWELVE

———— ❦ ————

THEY WERE TWO WEEKS into rehearsals for CKT's next production, *Narnia*, and Katy could feel herself finding her rhythm again. She only thought about Dayne every few hours, rather than every few minutes the way she had before. His sweatshirt was folded in a drawer now—where it would stay. Although things hadn't worked out with Terrence C. Willow, she and Rhonda had shared a good laugh.

Katy had also gone over every detail of the date with Ashley Baxter Blake when they took a walk around the track at Clear Creek High School later that week. Ashley was trying to walk a little bit every day, so she'd have an easier time with her delivery. Though they'd laughed at things Terrence had said and done, the conversation had grown serious as Ashley talked about being married to Landon.

"He's everything I ever dreamed," Ashley had told her. "I mean, sure, we have our down days. But I can't imagine anyone else for me." She looked to a line of trees in the distance, seeing images of Landon in her mind, no doubt. "Our hearts and souls are knit together. I'm not sure where I end and he begins."

Katy had thought about that line every day since.

A love so right, so real that she would blend perfectly in the arms of that man, a love so heaven-sent it would be impossible to tell where she ended and he began. That was the sort of man she was waiting for, the sort that God certainly had for her somewhere out there.

"Hey." Rhonda ran up to her. "What're you thinking about?"

They were at Bloomington Community Church, halfway through the first full-company rehearsal. Katy pinched her nose and rubbed her thumb across her brow. "Just drifting." She grinned at her friend. "You didn't tell me about Elevator Guy."

Rhonda blinked. "Elevator Guy?"

"Yeah." Katy was sitting at the table at the front of the sanctuary, the one that gave her the best view of the stage. "You know, the guy from your apartment. The one you met in the elevator."

Rhonda smiled. "You remember that?" She took the chair next to Katy and faced her.

"Of course. You and he and a bunch of people from your apartment got stuck in an elevator." Katy lowered her chin, teasing her friend. "At the time you said it was the closest you'd been to a man in months."

"Oh, that. Right." She gave a quick nod. "That's him."

"So . . . you went out last night, didn't you? How'd it go?"

Rhonda shrugged. "I didn't get out of practice here until after nine, so it wasn't a big deal. We met at the coffee shop near the university."

"And . . ."

"Well, he's six years older than me. Lived with his mother until two years ago." She tilted her head. "He says he believes in God, but I could tell by his language that it must be a kind of distant belief."

"Oh." Katy felt her face fall. "One of those."

"Yeah." Rhonda managed a discouraged smile. "He asked me back to his place for a drink afterwards. If that gives you any idea."

"Hmm. Okay, so cross him off the list."

"I already did." Rhonda pulled her choreography notes closer to her and stared at them. Her tone was heavier than before. "I joke about it, Katy, but seriously . . ." A lost look filled her eyes, and all her usual humor faded. "I was driving here this morning, and you know that little white church across from the park?"

Katy nodded. "St. Joseph's."

"Right." She put her elbow on the table and rested her chin on the palm of her hand. "There were cars everywhere, and a limo was parked out front. Just as the light turned red a bride stepped out, and half a dozen bridesmaids surrounded her." Rhonda stopped, a faraway look in her eyes. "The look on that bride's face defined love, Katy. It did." Her eyes were damp, and she made a sound that tried to be a laugh. "Look at me, all sappy."

"That's okay." Katy touched her friend's elbow. Rhonda could laugh, but Katy knew there was nothing funny about the scene. An early spring wedding . . . a glowing bride and pretty bridesmaids.

"I guess I just wanted to ask God when . . . when will it be my turn." Rhonda allowed another sad smile. "You know?"

This time she reached out and hugged Rhonda. "Only too well."

The break was winding up, and Katy had to take control of the kids. Outside, clouds were gathering, but thunderstorms weren't expected until later this afternoon. Katy was glad. This spring was supposed to have some of the most violent storms and tornadoes in recent history. The last thing she needed was that kind of drama while she had sixty-two CKT kids running about the sanctuary.

She touched Rhonda's shoulder. "Let's talk about it later." She climbed the three stairs to the stage and did the CKT clap.

Instantly the cast repeated the clap and hurried back to the base of the stage for instruction.

"Okay." Katy brought her hands together, surveying the group. The cast was talented, and Nancy and Al Helmes were back to help out with music. "I want to start blocking the battle scenes." She pointed to Al and Nancy. "Give us a little bit of the music, please."

Al was at the piano. He played several bars of intense melody, while Katy watched the reaction on the faces of the kids. A few raised eyebrows, and others nodded along. Katy had spent a few hours going over the score. For the most part, the songs were haunting and beautiful—especially when Aslan, the lion of Narnia, is killed. But during the battle scenes the music would have the people in the audience on the edge of their seats.

The music stopped, and Katy clapped. "All right, see? The reason *Narnia* is such a powerful story is because it's a battle— a battle between good and evil."

She had just said the word *evil* when the rear door opened. A man came in and took a seat in the last row. Katy stared at him; suddenly she felt her heart flip-flop. It couldn't be . . . not now. Not after so much time had gone by. A few of the kids looked over their shoulders, but the man seemed to be looking at something on the floor. Rhonda was still at the table going over her notes, so she hadn't noticed Katy trying to recover.

"Okay, so listen." Katy gulped and regained her composure. "Mr. Helmes, could you tell the kids what happens after Aslan's death? Why the battle is so important?"

"Certainly." Al didn't miss a beat. Whether or not he knew how badly she needed his help, he graciously stood and the cast turned toward him. "All the forces of evil figured they had claimed victory as the lion of Narnia lay dead."

Katy was hearing only part of Al's explanation. Her knees shook, and she couldn't exhale. She faced Al, but her eyes were on the man in the back. He wore a hooded sweatshirt, a baseball cap, and sunglasses. There was no way to tell his hair or eye color or even to make out his face. But that didn't matter. Katy would know him anywhere, know the easy walk and round shoulders, the way he slid down in his seat so he'd be less obvious. He wouldn't look at her, wouldn't look anywhere near the stage. Still, no matter how many times she shot a glance toward him, the image of the man didn't disappear. She wasn't seeing things.

The man was Dayne Matthews.

She wanted to freeze time, ask everyone in the sanctuary to leave so she could rush to him and ask him why. Why in the world was he here? But she couldn't. She had to at least get the kids positioned onstage before she could consider going to him. She pursed her lips and blew. Adrenaline was shooting darts through her bloodstream, and she could feel a fine layer of perspiration on her brow.

Al was winding up his explanation. "In fact," he was saying, "it isn't until Aslan comes back to life that the forces of evil know for certain they are defeated." He looked at his wife and then back at the kids. "That's what makes this one of the greatest battle scenes in all of theater."

Whatever he'd told them, the cast was absolutely gripped by the story. Good thing. Katy's heart was only barely finding its normal rhythm. She waited until Al was finished before she took center stage. *God . . . get me focused here. Please.* She felt lightheaded. *And hold me up; don't let me faint, God.*

Katy looked at the faces in front of her. "Okay, the battle scene involves everyone except Aslan, the White Witch, and her groupies. At least at first." She forced out a breath. She refused to look anywhere near the back of the sanctuary. "Everyone except those few characters take the stage, please."

The commotion that followed gave Katy the confidence she needed to focus on the job at hand. She arranged the children on opposite sides of the stage—good forces on the right, evil forces on the left.

"The song here is 'Deep Magic.'" Katy put her hands on her hips and paced up the narrow aisle between the two groups. "In order to give the audience a sense that the battle could go either way, everyone onstage will gradually shift stage right for several counts. Then everyone will gradually shift stage left." She looked at her friend. "Rhonda, can you come up and show them the dance steps?"

Rhonda bounded up the stairs. "All right, let me have Bailey Flanigan and Tim Reed."

Katy took the stairs slowly, her focus on the kids. The last thing she needed was to do something that would cause Rhonda to notice Dayne. Her friend was still mad that Katy hadn't introduced her the last time he was here. But this . . . this was no time for introductions. Katy's head was spinning, her stomach turning somersaults. Why would he come? Kelly would be six months pregnant by now—even though the tabloids still hadn't mentioned the fact.

Only then did anger take the front seat in the emotional ride she was on. How dare he show up now, just when she was starting to survive an hour or two without thinking about him. When she was realizing something she hadn't even had time to share with Rhonda. That being single wasn't so bad and that there was no way she could look longingly at one wedding after another until God made it clear that He even wanted her to get married.

She'd been talking to Jenny and Jim Flanigan and finding peace in the idea of being alone—maybe for now, maybe forever. And just when she felt herself letting him go, just when she'd reached the place of knowing she could live the rest of her life without ever speaking to Dayne Matthews again, he walks into her play rehearsal.

Katy reached the table below the stage and shot a look at the last row. This time Dayne was watching her. He had his sunglasses off, and his eyes told her he was sorry, that he understood the things she must be feeling. He nodded toward the lobby, stood, and made a quick exit.

Her heart raced within her.

Onstage, Rhonda was intensely involved with the actors. Bailey and Tim were running through the first eight counts of the battle dance, and the rest of the cast was standing in rows behind them, trying to figure it out. Rhonda darted from one kid to the next. "Okay, let's take it from the top and try to stay together." She positioned herself in the middle of the cast and pointed to Al at the piano.

Katy began walking slowly backward down the center aisle toward the door. If there was ever a time to make her move it was now. When she was halfway, when it was clear that everyone else in the room was too busy to notice her, she turned and walked forward the rest of the way.

She saw Dayne the moment she was through the door. He was leaning against the wall, his hands in his pockets, sunglasses on again, probably in case she wasn't the first person he saw. He lowered them now, and their eyes held.

The pain in his eyes was more than she'd ever seen before. More than merely missing her or not being sure of his direction in life. Something had happened. The hurt in his eyes was so strong she was afraid to ask. "Dayne . . . why . . . ?"

Three feet separated them, and Katy forced herself to keep her distance. Even so, she drank in the sight of him. He belonged to another woman, whether he was married to her yet or not, but she couldn't help herself. Just looking at him filled all the empty places in her heart. She anchored herself against the wall and waited.

He moved sideways and dug his shoulder into the wood paneling. "I need to talk to you."

She knew better than to be surprised that he would fly halfway across the country to talk. She glanced at the lobby door. "Deep Magic" was still playing, the scene still being choreographed. She turned back to Dayne. "I only have a few minutes."

"I know." His expression shouted his apology. "I didn't mean to interrupt. I just . . ." He took off the baseball cap and ran his fingers through his hair. "You don't answer my calls." There was no denying the hurt that flashed in his eyes. "I didn't know how else to find you."

Katy tried to will her heartbeat to slow. "How long are you here?"

"Just today. I fly out tonight."

"Dayne . . ." He would have to stop doing this, stop showing up in Bloomington and expecting her to drop everything for a single conversation. Especially when even an afternoon with him took her months to get over.

"Please, Katy." He looked like he might take a step toward her, but he changed his mind, leaving the distance between them. "Meet me at the university football stadium. I'll be there whenever you want."

She should say no. If she had a backbone at all she would tell him that she cared for him and they could talk a few minutes more here, but she wouldn't meet him. But the idea was ridiculous. If Dayne had come this far to talk to her, then maybe he needed something more than her friendship and advice. Maybe he wanted to talk about the Bible she'd given him last time he was here.

The hint of a smile tugged at her lips. "You're not easy; you know that?"

"I know." He grinned, but his eyes were still sad. "Meet me, Katy. It's important."

She sighed, and at the same time the music inside the sanctuary stopped. In a matter of minutes the kids or Rhonda or anyone else could come barreling out the door into the lobby. She had to hurry. "Okay. Give me two hours." She took a step back. "The football-field parking lot. Near the front gate."

He let his gaze linger on her a moment longer. Then he gave her the slightest nod and hurried out the double doors and into the parking lot. She watched him go, saw him climb into a silver Camry, a car no one would've expected Dayne Matthews to drive around town in.

The rest of practice dragged on. It took Rhonda and Katy most of an hour to get that many kids marching in unison first one direction, then the other—all while looking menacing.

Only after Katy had dismissed them did Bailey Flanigan pull her aside. "I saw him."

"Who?" Katy didn't see any of the cast look back more than once when Dayne first arrived. She worked to keep her expression blank.

Bailey raised her brow, as if to say that Katy wasn't fooling her. "Dayne Matthews. He came in and sat in the back for a few minutes."

Katy held her finger to her lips. "Shhh." She gave Bailey a hug and whispered in her ear, "Don't tell anyone, please. We'll talk about it tonight with your mom."

"Okay." Bailey pulled away, her eyes dancing. This was probably the best secret she'd kept in a long time.

By the time Katy met with the creative team and made her way out of the parking lot it was a quarter to two. None of the adults had the slightest idea that Dayne had been there. Rhonda was too caught up in her dance notes, and Al and Nancy had been hovering over the piano.

Katy thanked God all the way to Indiana University, ten minutes across town. Rhonda, for one, already knew about Dayne's coming baby. How was she supposed to explain his showing up without warning?

Especially when even she had no idea why he'd come.

❧

Dayne felt as if he were walking on clouds—storm clouds maybe but clouds all the same. Who was he kidding? Sure, he'd come here to talk to Katy, to tell her what had happened with the baby, and to have someone he could grieve with. But there was more to his intentions than that.

The moment he saw her he knew more than ever before. Kelly was right. He had fallen for Katy Hart at a small-town performance of *Charlie Brown*, and she'd owned a piece of his heart ever since. When he walked into the church earlier and saw her onstage, he was grateful for the closest bench. Otherwise his knees might've buckled—that's how she made him feel.

She was guarded, but he didn't blame her. She thought he was working things out with Kelly, that the two of them were busy planning for a baby. Under those circumstances there would've been no logical reason for him to come. And that's what she had to be thinking, because she kept her distance more than ever before. No hug, no touch on the arm or hand. Nothing.

Which was fine. Regardless of his feelings for her, he wasn't here to make a move on her. He merely wanted her to know what had happened, wanted her to ache with him over his loss and give him some idea what to do next. He had some ideas, but he wanted to run them by her.

Now it was only a matter of savoring the day and somehow finding the strength to leave her again—the way he always had to leave her. He had two hours to kill, so he parked near the clock tower a block from the university and walked down one of the side streets. With his baseball cap pulled low and his sweatshirt hood bunched up around the back of his neck, he could've been any college kid.

He wore the sunglasses just in case.

The clouds overhead were growing darker every few minutes, but the sunglasses worked. They told people he wanted to be left alone. He took his time, peering into the store windows, careful to look the other way if he passed someone.

He had walked by three stores when he came upon a gallery near the university. A sign hung over a group of paintings. When he read the words, he felt his breath catch in his throat. *We Sell Work by Local Artist Ashley Baxter Blake.* Dayne put one hand on the glass and steadied himself.

All the way to Indianapolis he'd thought about the Baxters, how hard it was to live with his decision not to contact them, and how tempted he would be this time—like every time—to drive by John Baxter's house or by the hospital where he'd seen his birth mother the first and only time. Somehow his feelings for the Baxters were closely woven with his feelings for Katy.

Any time he made the trip to Bloomington he had more in mind than seeing the small-town drama instructor. Always there was a chance something like this would happen. He'd take a walk or a drive and stumble upon the medical office where his sister Brooke worked or the high school where Kari's husband coached.

He often looked at the information from his private investigator, information that made him feel as if he knew the Baxters, even if he wasn't a part of them. But he never dreamed of this, of wandering down a street by the university and seeing his sister's paintings.

The PI's information stated that her work was sold in New York City. In fact, Dayne had made a mental note to look up her work next time he was in Manhattan. But Ashley's paintings were right here in the store window. He moved closer to the glass so a couple walking in his direction could pass by.

Each painting represented a slice of Americana—big expansive fields, old farmhouses, grand old maple trees, a countryside with streams meandering through, and a million colors that Los Angeles had forgotten about. Her work felt good on his eyes, and he studied them one at a time.

The first was a country scene with a white farmhouse in the background. A comfortable-looking porch wrapped around the house, and warm light streamed from the windows. In the foreground was a little blond boy, dancing through the tall grass with a butterfly net in his hand. The title was *Catching Summer*.

Next was a painting of an old lady, frail and genteel looking with a teacup in her hand. She sat at a table surrounded by two women and a man, all of whom looked to be in their late eighties. The eyes of each told an unmistakable story. The bigger woman was suspicious, the woman on the far left was timid, and the man was distant—lost in a place decades down the road. Only the woman with the teacup looked perfectly lucid. The look in her eyes could've been only one thing: pure unchanging love. The sort of love people in Dayne's generation knew very little about. The painting was titled *Love Never Fails*.

The third painting was of a firefighter in a soot-covered uniform, his face smudged with grime. He was sitting on a bench overlooking a country cemetery, bathed in late-afternoon light. His helmet sat on the bench beside him. In the man's eyes were a thousand stories, and on his uniform sleeve was a patch that said *9-11, We Will Not Forget*. The closest tombstone was anchored by a small wooden American flag and a firefighter helmet. The title of the painting was *Still Out There Fighting for You*.

Dayne was touched beyond words.

Knowing Ashley was a painter and seeing her work at close range were two entirely different things. If she could paint like this, then inside her heart stirred the same deep feelings that made up his own. He brought characters to life on the screen by reaching into a pool of empathy, a deep understanding of people and beauty and emotions.

Clearly Ashley painted by doing the same thing.

Goose bumps covered his arms, and he rubbed them. Then before he could worry about being recognized, he went into the store and straight for the counter. Inside the gallery were groupings of artwork broken up by display cases of eclectic odds and ends. The place smelled of strong spices and incense.

An older woman worked the counter. She seemed distracted, placing price tags on a stack of candleholders. "Hello," she said and smiled at him for a moment before returning to her work.

Dayne relaxed some. This was going to be easier than he thought. He tugged the bill of his baseball cap down lower on his forehead. "The paintings out front, the ones by Ashley Blake . . ."

"Yes." The woman made a dreamy-sounding sigh. "The girl is absolutely brilliant. I sell more of her work than anyone else's in the gallery."

He had thought about getting only one of her pieces, but it was impossible to decide which one. Each of them held a piece of his sister—a sister he would probably never know. If he couldn't have a relationship with her, then he could have her paintings at least. He placed a credit card on the counter. "I'd like all three, please."

"All thr—" Her tone changed. "Sir, have you looked at the price? Those paintings are eleven hundred dollars each. The frames are an extra two hundred and fifty each."

"That's fine." Dayne casually turned from the register and began looking at a display a few feet away. He kept his face from the lady. He couldn't afford to be recognized now, not when he was buying Ashley's paintings. If the woman knew who he was she'd tell Ashley for sure. *Dayne Matthews was here, and he bought three of your pieces!*

The woman was punching in numbers on the register. "Okay, get ready for this." She punched a few more times. "Four thousand, three hundred and thirty dollars. Including tax."

He barely glanced over his shoulder. "You can use the card." The Visa was perfect for helping him keep his cover. Like his driver's license, it was issued under his middle and last names. Allen Matthews. A name common enough not to stir up attention.

Dayne pretended to be studying an iron sculpture. "Oh, I need them shipped to LA. Is that okay?"

"Definitely." She began pulling packing supplies from beneath the counter. "I'll need you to fill out a shipping label."

He did as she asked—using the mailbox he had in the San Fernando Valley. The postal service company knew him and were unaffected by his star status. They allowed him to have anything shipped there—no matter the size of the package.

Just before he took his card and receipt, the woman hesitated. "You look familiar."

Dayne's answer was quick. "My brother's in here all the time. College kid at IU." He raised his hand. "Gotta run. Got a plane to catch."

"But aren't you . . . ?"

He was out the door before she could finish the sentence. She wasn't one to chase him down the street. Still, she was close to figuring it out, and that bothered him. If she told Ashley, she'd have to wonder. Or maybe she'd think it was because he'd given her a ride home one night. He could've stumbled onto her art and bought it for that reason, right?

Only why was he even in Bloomington at all? Wouldn't Ashley wonder that? Then he remembered that Ashley and Katy were friends. He allowed himself to relax. Ashley would figure he was here to see Katy—nothing more.

He tucked his Visa and the receipt into his wallet and changed his mind about more sidewalk shopping. He headed for his car, drove to the Starbucks a few blocks away, and ordered at the drive-thru window. People wouldn't expect him in Bloomington, but he couldn't take a chance. He had only a few hours with Katy. He didn't want anything to get in the way of that.

Whether he was crazy for being here or not.

CHAPTER THIRTEEN

---◆◇◆---

STORM CLOUDS DARKENED by the time Katy pulled into the parking lot and took the space next to the silver Camry, the one she'd seen Dayne drive off in earlier. Any moment lightning was bound to unleash over the campus.

"Figures," she mumbled. "You must be giving me a sign, Lord. Severe thunderstorms ahead."

She climbed out of her little red car, slammed the door behind her, and scanned the campus. Then she spotted him sitting at a picnic table beneath an overhang near the stadium's front gate. The temperature had dropped, and she wasn't sure she'd be warm enough. She wore a jacket and a white tank top beneath a black V-neck T-shirt. Her black jeans were loose, and in her flats it was easy to run the forty feet that separated them.

"It's freezing." She ducked into the covered area and stared at the sky. "That's gonna be a big one." She looked at Dayne. Her pounding heart had nothing to do with the coming storm or the run from her car.

"I know." Dayne had two steaming Starbucks cups beside him

and a bag of what looked like food. He gave her a hesitant smile. "I thought you might be hungry."

His kindness touched her. "Thanks. That was nice." The first bolt of lightning cut across the dark sky. Katy jumped and scurried to the table. "That was close."

Thunder shook the stadium and rattled the ground beneath their feet.

"Hmm." Dayne winced. "Not many thunderstorms in LA."

"No." She did a nervous laugh. "Not like this."

"What should we do?" He looked ready to run. "What's the safest place?"

Rain started suddenly, pouring down buckets on the cement promenade that separated the stadium and the parking lot.

"Well—" Katy looked around—"lightning hits the tallest object around. Still . . ." There were lots of higher places, but anywhere outdoors was a risk. "Honestly?" She took one of the hot coffee cups and moved to the edge of the covered area. "I think we should make a run for it."

As she finished her sentence, another lightning bolt shot down and hit somewhere in a neighborhood maybe a mile away. The intensity of the rain doubled.

Before the thunder hit again, Katy motioned to Dayne and shouted so she could be heard above the storm, "Let's go!"

She led the way, and Dayne stayed close behind. The thunder exploded around them just as they both slid into her car—she in the driver's seat, Dayne beside her.

Katy was breathless and drenched, soaked from the deluge. She held up her hands. "Ever notice—" she made a silly face at Dayne—"we're always running out of rainstorms?" She settled back into her seat. "Why is that?"

Dayne looked stunning. His wet hair looked darker than usual, plastered against his light tan. The effect made his blue eyes electrifying.

Katy turned the key in her ignition and tried not to notice.

"Let's go to my house. The Flanigans are running errands." She pulled out of the parking lot. "I think that'd be the safest. I'll bring you back later to get your car."

"Okay." Dayne wiped the water off his face and turned slightly so he was facing her. "Can I tell you something?"

Katy couldn't slow her racing heart. What was she doing, driving with Dayne Matthews through a pounding rainstorm, heading for Flanigans' house? She wanted to tell him yes, that he could tell her something. He could tell her about Kelly and her pregnancy and how it felt now that he was a few months from becoming a father. She kept her gaze straight ahead. "Sure."

Lightning ripped across the black sky, lighting up the air all around them.

Dayne hesitated, staring out the window. "Wow—" he chuckled—"I've never seen anything like this."

"Wait till it's mixed with tornadoes."

He rested his head against the side window. "It'd be wild, an adventure. I've watched those storm-chaser documentaries. LA has fog or sunshine, pretty much." He was quiet for a minute. "When it rains, we get about three weeks of dreary gray. But lightning and thunder are an event."

"Really?" Katy hadn't thought about that.

"Yeah." Rain dripped from his hair onto his forehead, and he wiped it again. "I think seasons would be fun."

They were almost to the Flanigans' house. Katy felt herself relax a little. Whatever had caused Dayne to get on a plane and come here, she would know the reason soon enough. In the meantime, he hadn't crossed any lines, hadn't suggested with his words or tone or body language that he was interested in more than talking with her. She let her shoulders sink back into the seat. "You were going to tell me something?"

"Oh, right." His tone was gentle, pensive. "About the kids at CKT, the battle scene of *Narnia*."

Katy was impressed, but she didn't let on. The light ahead of her turned red, though she could barely see it through the pounding rain. She brought her car to a careful stop and smiled at him. "It's a great show."

"One of my favorite series of books as a kid."

"Chronicles of Narnia?" There was no way she could hide her surprise. "I thought you didn't . . ."

"I was a missionary kid, Katy." He slung one arm up along the back of the seat. His sweatshirt was soaked through. His grin grew a little lopsided. "I knew pretty early on that it was me ver-sus God in the battle for my parents' attention. But I loved read-ing." He raised one shoulder. "Still do. C. S. Lewis was one of the masters."

"True." The light turned green, and Katy returned her atten-tion to the road ahead of them.

"Watching you and—what's her name, the choreographer?"

"Rhonda."

"Right, Rhonda. That's it." Dayne's smile filled his voice. "The two of you are amazing with those kids." His tone grew more serious. "I bet this is your best show yet. I can feel it."

"I know what you mean." Katy turned into the Flanigans' neighborhood. "The music is so powerful, and the message . . ."

Dayne remained silent, and the distance between them felt awkward for the first time that afternoon. Katy kept her eyes on the road. What had happened? The conversation was easygoing and upbeat—one more reason Dayne was so attractive to her. But as soon as she mentioned the message of *Narnia*, everything between them seemed to change.

From the moment they set out for the Flanigan house she'd been thinking about where she and Dayne could sit and talk. Not her apartment, certainly. It was little more than a chair and a small sofa. With the house all to themselves, there wasn't a sin-gle reason why they should go there.

She was still mulling over the options as she pulled into the driveway. "Well, here we are."

"Wow." Dayne peered at the house. "I never get over the size of this thing. I thought the homes in Malibu were big."

Whenever someone visited the Flanigans' house, Katy saw it with fresh eyes. The place felt like home to her, but it was a mansion, purchased with a small sum of the money Jim Flanigan had earned as a player in the NFL. Jim and Jenny had created a charitable foundation with a bigger piece of his earnings, and through it they quietly supported a dozen ministries.

More than seven thousand square feet of style and warmth painted in a welcoming taupe with white trim and a heavy black roof. The Flanigans lived on several acres, so an expanse of dense, well-manicured grass stretched out on either side of the blacktop driveway.

"Jim and Jenny think of it more as a youth center." Katy pulled up the driveway to the garage. She clicked a button on her visor, and the door began to open. "Jim says when the day comes that kids don't fill all this space, he'll sell and get a cabin on the lake."

"Jim . . . I don't think I've met him. I remember Jenny and the kids—Bailey and Connor. I don't think Jim was there that day. He played in the NFL, right?"

"Right. He wasn't here when you came by that morning." As she pulled into the garage, twin lightning bolts struck in what felt like the field across the street. "Yikes." She hit the garage button again. "Just in time."

Dayne hesitated. "They won't mind, will they? If I'm here?"

"Not at all. They'll be back in a few hours." Katy thought about the reaction they were likely to get when the Flanigans got home. Bailey would be so giddy she'd barely say hello, and Connor would be tempted to pull up a chair and ask Dayne a hundred questions about acting. She turned off the engine and looked at him. "The kids will know it's you. Bailey saw you at practice earlier."

"Really?"

"Yeah. It's okay." She unbuckled her seat belt. "I asked her not to say anything."

He grinned and grabbed both coffees and the bag of food. "She and Connor played it off pretty well when they stopped by my location shoot last October."

The memory made her smile. One afternoon last fall she had given a note to Jenny and the kids and asked them to deliver it to Dayne at his shoot downtown. The kids had pretended to be autograph seekers, and they'd patiently waited along the rope. "They were good, weren't they?"

"No one knew a thing." He winked at her and opened his door. "I think I trust the Flanigan kids."

She slipped her keys into her purse and took her *Narnia* script from the backseat. She felt a wave of fear and hesitancy. What was she doing, taking Dayne into the Flanigan house? Why had he come now? She could hardly wait to get inside and find out.

As they walked through the great room and into the kitchen, Katy made up her mind about where they would meet. The formal living room, the one with an entire wall of windows and the black grand piano. She set her things down on the counter and took her coffee from Dayne.

"Coffee cold?" He made a face and held up his drink. "Like this one?"

"A little." She opened the cupboard and grabbed two tall mugs from the third shelf. "A little microwave action and we'll be all set." The tone between them was better than before, but Katy sensed something big coming, something so serious that Dayne had to tell her in person. She poured his drink into one of the mugs and slid it into the microwave.

While she worked, he set the bag down. "Hungry?"

She looked at him. "What'd you bring?"

"Chocolate-chip muffins." He grinned. "I don't know . . . sounded like the right thing for a stormy day."

Much as she feared the conversation ahead, Katy couldn't

help but smile. "I think you're right." She slid open a drawer, took out two small paper plates, and handed them to Dayne. "Here."

He pulled the muffins from the bag and set one on each plate.

When the coffee was hot again, they sat side by side at the kitchen bar and ate their muffins. He told her about the romantic suspense movie he was wrapping up. It was edgy enough that people were suggesting it could receive a nomination for several awards.

"Best actor, even?" Dayne was popular, no doubt, but he'd never been nominated for an Oscar.

He looked down at his half-eaten muffin. "Yeah. I guess."

Katy was stunned. "Dayne, that's amazing."

"Thanks." He took a drink of his coffee. "It hasn't happened yet."

"Still . . . tell me about your role."

Lightning flashed outside, and seconds later, the thunder made a cracking sound.

He made wary eyes at the window, but he answered her question.

By the time they finished eating, Dayne was talking about the plot of the movie, but Katy was too distracted to listen. This wasn't the reason he'd come to Bloomington, to tell her about his current film project. She finished her coffee and set her mug on the black-granite counter.

He probably wanted to tell her that Kelly had agreed to marry him. Maybe he didn't want her to read the news in the tabloids, so he'd come here first. She steeled herself. That would be fine, right? Better than fine. It's what the two of them *should* do.

"Katy . . ." His expression told her he knew she was distracted. "This isn't why I'm here."

"I know." She held up her empty mug. "More coffee?"

"No, thanks." His eyes never left hers.

"Okay, then—" she nodded toward the living room—"let's talk in there."

She hadn't quite finished her sentence when lightning and thunder hit at the exact time, exploding in the air around the house and instantly knocking out the electricity.

It was still midafternoon, but the sky was too dark to allow much light through the windows. The house was suddenly bathed in shadows.

Dayne set his cup down. He went to the window and looked out. "So . . . do we need to go down to the basement, maybe?"

"No." Katy felt herself smile. "No tornadoes today. Not for a few weeks."

"How long before the lights come back on?"

"Could be a few hours." She set their mugs in the sink. "There'll be more light in the living room."

"I'll follow you."

They walked through the cherry-paneled dining area into the carpeted room where the Flanigans held most of their heart-to-heart talks. The room had a vaulted ceiling, furniture that was solid and comfortable, and a fireplace almost as big as the piano.

Katy's favorite spot to hold a conversation in the entire house was the sofa that backed up to the entire wall of windows. The couch had six overstuffed pillows, so it was comfortable no matter how you sat in it. She took one side and brought her leg up so she was facing sideways.

A foot from her, Dayne did the same.

The room was shadowy but not as dark as the kitchen. And through the window it was fascinating to see just how much lightning was piercing the dark clouds overhead.

Katy held her breath as they settled into the sofa. This was it. Whatever had brought Dayne from LA this morning, she was about to find out.

CHAPTER FOURTEEN

F OR A WHILE Dayne just looked at her.

Katy tried to deny it, but there was no question he had longing in his eyes—a longing that had been there since the first time she saw him sitting in the back of the theater today. He didn't look at her the way some guys did—as if they wanted to undress her with their eyes. No, the look on Dayne's face was nothing like that.

His was a different kind of longing—a wanting for love and laughter and family and simplicity. All the things he had never been able to find.

She exhaled and pulled one of the pillows close to her. "Please talk to me, Dayne."

The feelings evident in his eyes were so genuine and raw they almost hurt to look at. "Kelly and I . . . we're finished."

"What?" The word was a whisper, the slightest gasp. Katy had been certain he was going to finish his sentence with a dozen other choices. *Kelly and I are in love . . . Kelly and I are getting married . . . Kelly and I are working things out.* Never—not for one single moment—had she considered that this was what he'd come to tell her. She felt herself bristle, felt her back stiffen. So what if he and Kelly were through? What did that matter, given the circumstances? He was going to be a daddy after all. She found her voice. "What about the baby?"

For a few seconds, fear and regret took turns coloring his face, and as he opened his mouth, his eyes grew damp. He shook his head and dropped his gaze.

"Dayne . . ." Katy couldn't fathom what was causing this reaction. What had Kelly done? Told him he couldn't share custody of his firstborn child? She waited, her hands trembling.

His eyes lifted to hers, and there was no mistaking the pain there. "There is no baby." He blinked, and two tears fell onto his cheeks. "Not anymore."

Katy was confused. There wasn't a baby any—?

The truth hit her all at once, like a wrecking ball. She felt the blood drain from her face, felt her heart breaking. "Kelly had an abortion?"

Dayne squeezed his eyes shut and pressed his fist to his forehead. "She didn't ask me." For a long while he said nothing, couldn't say anything. When he opened his eyes, there was no denying his depth of loss. "Katy, you're the only one who would understand what I'm feeling." He glanced out the window at the storm. "Abortion's not a big deal in my world. Simple solution, a woman's right to choose." Anger hardened his tone. "But that was my baby too." He looked at her, broken. "What choice did I get?"

"Dayne—" her own heart filled with sadness for him—"I'm so sorry." This time she didn't analyze whether it was right or wrong, whether it would only prolong this . . . whatever this was between them. Instead she took hold of his hand, the one resting on his knee.

He wrapped his fingers around hers. For a long while they just sat that way. Dayne's quiet tears making paths down his cheeks, and the two of them holding hands. He was strong even now. Strong yet broken.

Katy studied him, trying to imagine what he was feeling. What she'd be feeling if she were him.

A deep, unspeakable pain filled her soul. Of course abortion would hit him this way. He'd been raised by missionary parents. The people who adopted him. Whatever direction he'd gone, whatever place in life he'd found, and whatever choices he'd made along the way, his upbringing had convinced him of this: Life was precious, unborn or not.

And in his Hollywood life, he didn't know one person who could sit with him and grieve the loss of his first child. No one except for her.

Katy tried to think of something to say, but he didn't need her words. She simply waited for him to talk.

Finally, he brushed the back of his other hand across his cheeks and sniffed. "She told me at the premiere."

"For *Dream On*?" Katy leaned forward, horrified. "Are you serious?"

He narrowed his eyes, as if he were seeing the scene play in his mind once more. "We found a private patio. She told me she was staying with Hawk Daniels."

"That's why?" The storm was still raging outside. Thunder rumbled low and long, and Katy's words were barely audible over it.

"No." He held her hand with both of his now. "She told me that the whole time she lived with me I never . . . ."

"Never what?"

He looked deep into her eyes, deeper than at any time since he'd walked into the church earlier today. "Never loved her the way I loved you."

Katy stared at him, her mind spinning. She'd spent the last few months convincing herself that Dayne couldn't have cared much for her. Not if he could leave her and months later have his leading lady move in with him. But here . . . in a single instant, he had rewritten everything she knew to be true about that part of his past.

"Look—" his voice was tender, compassionate—"I didn't come here to talk about my feelings for you, Katy. Really."

"I know." Relief came over her. Somehow it was wrong talking about whatever they felt for each other in light of Kelly's abortion. Still, in the darkening shadows and under the cover of a raging storm, they felt like the only two people in the world, as if they'd stumbled into a place where honesty reigned and no subject was taboo. She searched his eyes. "Was she right?"

Dayne brought one hand to her face and touched her cheek. "How can you ask?" He worked the muscles in his jaw and returned his hand to hers. "But it doesn't matter."

Katy could hardly exhale. She waited for him to explain himself.

"I'm not who you need." He gave her a sad smile. "I'm too much work, the two of us too different." A flash of lightning lit the room, and she could see his eyes glistening. "But believe this, Katy. All the fame and celebrity, everything people see when I'm in a role or in the tabloids, that's not who I am. Not really."

She wanted to hug him, but she kept her spot, their knees a few inches from each other. "I know." This was more transparent than she'd ever seen him.

A quiet chuckle came from somewhere deep inside him, but it sounded more ironic than humorous. "The trouble is, I'm not sure *who* I am." He released her hands, stood, and walked around the sofa to the windows. "It hit me when Kelly told me the news." He crossed his arms and stared at the sky. "I don't know if it has something to do with being adopted or that my parents died when I was a teenager. But somewhere along the way I lost everything that used to matter to me." He looked at her. "I never bothered to find out who I am."

She nodded, and their past discussions flashed through her

mind. His sudden interest in small-town America, his attempt at understanding Kabbalah, even his interest in her. "I think you've been searching."

"I have." He drew a long, slow breath and returned to his place on the sofa. This time he was a little farther away than before. "I have a friend, a guy I grew up with. He's a missionary in Mexico now." The corners of Dayne's mouth raised, but the smile stopped short of his eyes. "Same upbringing as me—boarding school, distant parents, the whole works. Ever since I heard about . . . about the baby, I've wanted just an hour or two with the guy. To ask him how he figured it out—even after his parents chose God over him." He leaned against the padded sofa arm. "You know?"

Katy pulled her knees up and hugged them. In the midst of all the sadness and uncertainty, the idea felt wonderful. "Then that's exactly what you should do."

"I am. At least I'm thinking about it. I called him. We're both free the end of March."

"Yes." Katy sat up a little straighter. "Like you said, he figured it out. Maybe he could help you do the same thing."

"That's what I thought." He gave her a partial grin. "I fly here when I need to talk to you. I could do the same to see him, I guess."

She felt her soul sing at the possibility, and the smile that tugged at her lips felt wonderful. "True. You fly here on a whim whenever you feel like it."

He angled his head, his eyes soft again. "Not hardly." Their eyes held. "If I flew to Indiana on a whim, I'd be here every week."

Dayne's words touched her, but there was nothing more important right now than his going to Mexico to talk with his missionary friend. That was bigger than everything they clearly still felt for each other. "Maybe if you go to Mexico you'll find the real Dayne." She pressed her fingers to her heart, her eyes begging him to understand. "The one no one but you and God really know."

The storm was moving away—only an occasional bolt of lightning and a low rumble of thunder in the distance. But the sky was still ominous, and the room was mostly dark.

Dayne stood and went to the window again. "From here you can see the clouds, the way they're darker in some places than others."

"Hmm." Katy rose and went around the couch, coming up alongside him. "Sort of like life."

"Yeah." He turned his shoulder against the glass and faced her. "I didn't really answer you."

They were inches apart, so close that Katy could smell what remained of his cologne. The combination of that and the nearness of him was intoxicating. She steadied herself. *Be strong, Katy . . . God, help me be strong. He doesn't need me; he needs You. That's all this is about.* She wondered if Dayne could hear her pounding heart. "About what?"

"Kelly's observation." His voice grew quiet. "That I never loved her the way I loved you."

Katy was glad for the darkness, because it hid the heat she felt in her cheeks. "Dayne, you never loved me. You liked me." She couldn't keep eye contact with him another moment. Otherwise she'd close the distance between them and wind up in his arms.

She looked down at their feet, at how they were almost touching. When she felt more composed she found his eyes. "I think you like the *idea* of me maybe even more than . . . than me." She gave him a sad smile. "Your life is so complicated, Dayne. So difficult. I think you see me—" she glanced around as if maybe the answer lay in the shadows—"like I'm some sort of image." The idea hurt more than she was willing to admit. She tilted her head, willed her tears back. "Maybe I represent the faith you're seeking, the simplicity you're craving. Maybe it's not about me at all."

At first, as she was coming up with the explanation for his devotion, his brow lowered as in confusion. But then as it became clear what she was saying, his eyes shone with hurt and then determination. "You're not an image." He gritted his teeth. When he spoke again, he had never sounded more sure about anything. "I know you, Katy. It's not what you represent that draws me to you." He touched his fist to his chest. "It's what lives inside you."

Katy didn't want to challenge him, didn't want to force him to see that his feelings for her were based more on imagination than reality. Not when his eyes were drawing her in, capturing her more completely with every passing minute.

When she didn't say anything, he moved his hands to her shoulders and drew her close—slowly, carefully, in a way that seemed perfectly natural. It wasn't the hug of two lovers or even two friends. In some ways it was deeper than that, an embrace filled with grief and most of all empathy.

Dayne put his hand on the back of her head and spoke near her ear. "I've wanted to hold you like this since I got here." He leaned back just enough to look into her eyes. "I didn't think we would."

Again Katy's face felt hot, but she wouldn't let the heat make her feel guilty. She was doing nothing wrong. Dayne was a free man, and he was her friend—even if she believed everything she'd just told him about what he saw in her. She had her hand on his chest. "I didn't either."

Neither of them said it, but the obvious filled in the inches between them. Everything was different now. Tragically, there was no baby. But that meant Dayne was as free as he'd been the last time they were together—before the phone call from Kelly that day in the LA courthouse.

They swayed a little, two friends slow dancing to the sound of falling rain. She wanted to kiss him in the worst way, but months of taking the subject of Dayne to God made her keep her distance. "Ever since that night in the parking lot at Malibu Beach—" her voice was a whisper, all she could manage as weak as she was feeling—"I've prayed about you. Prayed for you."

"You have?" His tone lightened. "Thanks." He leaned in and placed the lightest kiss on her forehead. There was no seduction intended, but they were walking a tightrope, dangling together over a canyon that—if they fell—would mean no turning back for either of them. He touched her cheek. "There's no one else in my life who prays for me."

This was it. Katy needed to make herself clear or she would lose the opportunity God was laying out before her. *Make me strong, Lord. I need Your strength.* The fact that there no longer was a baby didn't change the things that had led up to there being one in the first place. And the loss Dayne was facing didn't give her license to pretend those things had never happened.

She found her next breath. "I prayed for you and Kelly to be the right parents for your baby, and I prayed that—" she ached inside, but a strength bigger than her own pushed her to continue—"I prayed that God would help the two of us move on, to forget—" she ran her thumb along the base of his neck—"this. How it feels to be with you. Because the baby wasn't the thing that made me know I had to let you go, Dayne. The baby was what made me finally see it could never work."

The sadness returned to his face, but still he held her. "Because of my lifestyle?"

"No." She spread her fingers on the place over his heart. "Because in here you need to find what matters most."

"I feel that way." His hand came up alongside her cheek, and he worked his fingers partway into her hair. His breathing was slightly faster than before, his hand trembling. "I feel it whenever I'm with you."

Katy covered his hand with hers, and then—against every screaming bit of her flesh—she took a step backward. "Because I have what you're looking for." There were tears in her eyes, but she blinked them away. She motioned to herself. "Not what you see on the outside but my faith, Dayne. My relationship with Christ. That's what matters most."

Dayne exhaled, straightened, and shoved his hands into his pockets. "Sorry." He didn't have to specify his reasons. Clearly they could both feel how close they'd come to giving in to their feelings. He leaned his shoulder into the window. "I didn't come here for this, really."

"I know." She reached out and took his hand. "You need to go to Mexico. Let's talk after that."

Before he could say anything else, they heard voices near the front door.

Dayne looked toward the sound. "The Flanigans?"

"Yes." Relief came over her. The minutes of whispering with Dayne Matthews while a thunderstorm raged outside were over. She had known that God wanted her to avoid kissing him, and she'd succeeded. She tried not to feel disappointed. "Stay here."

He turned toward the window as she walked past the fireplace and into the foyer. Jim Flanigan was just coming through the door, Jenny and the kids behind him.

Bailey grinned and made wide eyes at Katy. "Did you hear?"

"Hear what?"

"A tornado." Jim gave her a wry smile. "Small one touched down near Clear Creek. No one got hurt, from what the news said."

Katy shivered. She had told Dayne they had nothing to worry about. What had she been thinking? This was Indiana in March. Whenever a thunderstorm like that one rolled through, tornadoes could come with it.

Shawn darted to her and tugged on her shirtsleeve. "We saw three kittens running across the road on the way home from Wal-Mart and Dad stopped." He had braces on his teeth now, and his words weren't as clear as before.

She struggled to understand. "Kittens?"

"Right." He jumped up a few times. "The storm musta' scared 'em out of their hole or wherever they live, because cats can live in fields and have babies in holes, Katy. Did you know that?" He didn't wait for her to answer. "They hunt mice and rats, and sometimes they get mean because they're living in the wild, but not these kittens because they're just babies." He grabbed a quick breath. "They're in the van in a box. Wanna see?"

Justin took her other arm. "Come see, Katy. Daddy says we can keep one."

"Maybe. If no one reports them missing." Jenny gave Jim a doubtful look and mouthed the word *thanks*.

He winked at her. "Never enough pets, right, boys?"

They hooted, and the four younger boys headed back outside with Jim. "We better find them a place on the porch for tonight. That way they'll be safe until . . ." Jim closed the door behind them, and immediately the commotion level dropped by half.

Bailey and Connor were taking off their rain jackets, and Jenny was checking the bottoms of her shoes for mud.

Katy pulled Jenny aside. She gestured to the next room. "Dayne's here. We've been talking."

Jenny knew everything about the situation with Dayne. All the details of what had happened from the beginning and right up until her meeting with him in Los Angeles, their talk at his house on the beach, and the baby he and Kelly Parker were expecting. But she showed no disdain at the news that he was in their house. "Bailey told me she saw him at practice." Jenny dropped her voice to the slightest whisper. "He's in the living room? Now?"

Katy nodded. "It's a long story. I'll tell you later. I just wanted you to know he was here."

Because the electricity was still off, Bailey and Connor hung up their jackets and walked right past the passageway to the living room without seeing Dayne. Bailey called over her shoulder, "Shawn's right. You've gotta see these kitties. They're so cute."

"In a minute, okay?" Just as Katy was going to explain to the older kids that she had a visitor, there was a clicking sound followed by a hum, and an instant later the lights were back on.

Before she could leave the entryway and return to the living room, Dayne walked through the arch that separated the two areas and waved to Jenny and the kids. "You survived the storm."

Bailey had seen him earlier that day, so she was able to hide her surprise and delight.

Connor, though, came a few steps closer. "Are you . . . are you filming here again?"

"No." He chuckled and looked at Katy. "Just needed an afternoon with your theater director."

"Oh." Connor's mouth hung open for a few seconds.

Bailey grabbed his arm, her eyes dancing. "Come on, Connor. We're supposed to go look at the kittens, remember?"

The kids left, but Connor looked back a few times. Katy felt herself smile. Of course he looked back. No matter what had happened before, regardless of the connection between her and Dayne the last time he was in town, it wasn't every day that the kids came home to find a movie star in their living room.

Her smile faded. In some strange way, Connor's reaction made her sad. This was the same reaction Dayne faced everywhere he went, in almost any setting. People staring at him, wondering if they might sneak an extra-long look or a photograph, people lined up next to him for an autograph at Starbucks or the grocery store or anywhere he went. Not just in Hollywood but here too.

It was the reason he wore hooded sweatshirts and baseball caps. And it was just one more reason why he could never share her lifestyle, not the way it was today.

"So, Dayne, how's life?" Jenny smiled at him. She had a natural way of inviting people into her home, making them feel welcome. Dayne couldn't have known by her reaction that she was privy to the details about him and Kelly.

The three of them talked for a few minutes; then Dayne checked his watch. "I have to go." When he looked at Katy, the regret in his eyes was glaring. "I wish I had longer."

Dayne said good-bye to Jenny, and they walked in a group out to the porch, where Jim and the boys had moved the box of kittens.

Katy peered inside and put her hand to her mouth. "They're adorable." They were gray with varying amounts of white, no more than five or six weeks old.

Jim looked up from the box and rose when he saw Dayne. His surprise lasted only an instant. "Dayne . . ." He reached out and shook his hand. "I hear I missed your visit last time."

"Yes. My schedule's a little strange sometimes."

Jim chuckled. "I'll bet." Around him, the boys were on their knees, reaching into the box and petting the mewing kittens. "Boys, this is Mr. Matthews."

Katy studied the way Dayne held his hand out to the younger boys. Each of them in turn said their name and told Dayne it was nice to meet him. She could see by Dayne's face that he was impressed. A few feet away, Bailey and Connor leaned against the house and tried not to laugh—probably because their silly brothers didn't have the common sense to know exactly who Mr. Matthews was.

A few minutes later when they were in Katy's car, Dayne gazed out his window at the scene on the front porch. "I love that family." He looked at Katy. "That's what I want." He hesitated, turning his attention once more toward the Flanigans. "The family, the laughter, the love. Even the kittens on the front porch."

Katy smiled, her eyes straight ahead. She didn't state the obvious. Not then and not ten minutes later when she dropped him off at his car. She was tempted to turn off the engine and linger in the dark of the parking lot, but there was no point. Not if she seriously wanted to end the visit without crossing lines. His flight was in two hours, so he couldn't wait either, which was good. It made the decision for a quick good-bye even easier.

"Thanks." Dayne leaned across the console of her car and gave her a hug that lasted a few seconds. "You were the only one

I wanted to talk to." He drew back, but his eyes stayed locked on hers. "Keep praying for me, Katy. I'm not sure I understand it, but I like it."

"Of course." She had one more question. "So you're going?"

"I have to." He checked his watch. "I have two hours, so that's an hour to Indianapolis and—"

"Dayne." She put her hand on his. "I'm talking about Mexico."

He grinned, and for the first time that afternoon, his eyes lit up. "Yes. I'm going."

"Okay, then." Her voice was low, and the electricity between them bordered on dangerous. "That's it."

"What?" He narrowed his eyes.

This time she could feel her own smile fade. "That's what I'll pray for."

"Okay." He hesitated. "Can I say how much I'll miss you?" He worked his fingers between hers.

Katy felt her breath catch in her throat. "Dayne . . ."

"I know. I have other things to take care of. But still . . ." He looked very serious. "I'll miss you like I have since the last time I saw you. More with every passing hour."

They said another minute of good-byes, and then she watched him leave, watched him walk to his car and turn around to look at her one last time. It was still strange, knowing that this guy—the one she fell a little harder for every time they were together—was America's Dayne Matthews. The Hollywood heartthrob and this man walking away from her now seemed like two different people.

He waved and held his hand in the air longer than usual. Even through the dim glow of the parking-lot lights, Katy could see his eyes glistening. She watched him climb into his car and pull away. Before his red taillights disappeared down Main Street, she set to work making good on her promise.

Then and all the way home, she prayed for Dayne as she'd

never prayed for him before. That he'd go to Mexico and spend time with his missionary friend and come away with a better understanding of mission work, that he'd find peace with the issue of his adoptive parents and their decision—the way Dayne saw it—to choose God over him. She prayed that Dayne would find out who he was, who he really wanted to be. But most of all she prayed something deeper.

That maybe—just maybe—he would allow God to find him.

CHAPTER FIFTEEN

D AYNE CHANGED HIS MIND five times in the next week.

He reserved a flight from Los Angeles International Airport to Mexico City twice and twice canceled the reservation. The principle filming for his current project was finished, but they had only four days and then the director had asked the cast to be available for reshoots. Angie Carr had invited him to spend the time at her place in the Bahamas. When he turned her down, she asked one of the other leading men—an actor living with his current girlfriend.

"Tom's going with me." She told him the last day of shooting. "Your loss, Dayne."

He winked at her. "As always, Angie." They'd survived the shoot with humor. He intrigued her, for sure. Mostly because he'd held off her advances—something very few men in Hollywood had ever done.

Even with his costars leaving town, he still figured he wouldn't go to Mexico. But every time he reached that decision, he heard Katy's voice asking him when he was going to Mexico. *"That's what I'll be praying for . . . praying for . . . praying for."*

In the end, there was no way he could let her down. He'd already done that once when he'd asked Kelly to move in with him.

When he made the airline reservation the third time, he didn't cancel. Now he was on an Airbus minutes from landing at the Mexico City Airport, wondering what he was doing.

Once he'd made up his mind, he'd called Bob again just two days ago. Like before, Bob answered the phone with the same tone Dayne remembered from their years in school together. Upbeat and eternally optimistic. "This is Bob . . ."

"Bob Asher." Dayne had felt the years begin to drift away. He'd been sitting at his kitchen table, looking out at the ocean and one of the bluest days of spring. "It's Dayne. I made up my mind."

"I knew you would." There was a youthfulness in Bob's voice, as if life continued to be one long adventure and Bob was sitting at the helm enjoying the ride. "When does your plane come in?"

Dayne had given him the details. "I wonder what old Eunice would think, the two of us together again." He chuckled. "Eunice, remember her? Bouffant hair?"

"That's right." Bob's laugh was easy and contagious. "We spent our share of afternoons with dear old Eunice."

They had talked for ten minutes before Dayne felt as though the two of them had never lost touch. Dayne could feel himself relaxing, falling into a simpler way of life, a simpler understanding of how everything worked.

"Rosa's not much of a movie watcher, I'm afraid."

"That's okay." Dayne heard the smile in his own voice. "I'm not either. Too busy working."

"I guess." Admiration filled Bob's tone. "You took that drama stuff pretty seriously, huh, friend? I watched one of your films a year ago when I was back in the States fund-raising." He paused. "You're something else."

Dayne downplayed his career and promised to tell Bob all about it when they were together.

"We have a street ministry scheduled. Otherwise the weekend's open."

"No problem." Dayne didn't want to ask what a street ministry entailed; it didn't matter. "I'll just tag along for a few days."

"I'm glad you decided to come."

"Me too."

For a beat, Bob was quiet. "Everything's okay, right?"

Dayne had his mouth open, ready to say yes. Sure, everything was fine. But if he wasn't honest now, it would be harder to be honest in person. "Not really." He sighed, and the sound traveled over the phone line. "I told you. I'm looking for something, Asher. You always . . . I don't know, you always seemed to get it better than I did. Figure I'll come and watch you, maybe talk a little and who knows? I might even figure it out."

Now, here he was—first day of the break—landing in Bob's home city. It took half an hour to get through customs, and only a handful of people gave him a second glance. He wore Dockers and a solid navy T-shirt. The hooded sweatshirt and baseball cap stayed at home, but he kept the sunglasses. Not that he'd needed them yet. This was Mexico City, not Cabo San Lucas or Cancún. Americans traveling to Mexico City weren't on vacation; they were on business—too busy to care if a movie star was in their midst.

Dayne spotted Bob as he waited for his bag. His friend was on his cell phone and looked like he was wrapping up a conversation.

Dayne was surprised at his childhood friend's appearance. He'd pictured him with long hair and a beard, wearing a gauzy shirt, maybe, and old blue jeans. The image of his parents when they were on the mission field. But Bob looked nothing like them. He was tan and clean-cut and in better shape than he'd been in when they were seniors in high school. With his khaki pants and casual, white, button-down shirt, he looked more like a geologist.

Dayne grabbed his bag and headed toward his friend, just as Bob closed the cell and scanned the crowd.

When their eyes met, Bob's face broke into a grin. He pumped his fist in the air. "Hey!"

Dayne suddenly felt choked up. Why had he let so much time pass without calling? He hadn't seen Bob for ten years, not since Bob had had a weekend layover in LA and the two had met for lunch. The people Dayne spent time with in Hollywood—at the clubs and premiere events—weren't friends. They were people with a common lifestyle. A lifestyle of glitz and fame and staying one step ahead of the paparazzi.

In a rush, everything about life as he knew it felt cheap and plastic compared to seeing Bob, compared to the genuine joy and deep recognition Dayne saw in his eyes.

Dayne set down his bag and gave his friend the sort of rough hug usually reserved for brothers. And that's what Bob had been, really. His brother. His best friend and only brother from the time he was four years old until he left the boarding school the day after graduation.

Dayne took a step back and put his hands firmly on Bob's shoulders. "You look great. Life in Mexico must be good."

"You too." Bob gave him a strong pat on the arm. "It's been too long, man. Way too long."

For a few seconds, Dayne's emotions tried to tighten his throat, but he swallowed and found his voice again. "It has. I was trying to figure it out." He reached for his bag. "That lunch in LA was what, ten years ago?"

"I think so." Bob glanced at the luggage conveyor belt. "Just the one?"

"Yep. Travel light. That's my motto."

"Well, the Jeep's this way."

Dayne kept in step with Bob. As they walked, the strain and

sorrow of the past few weeks seemed to fade away. Why hadn't he thought of this sooner? The flight had been nothing . . . and already he could sense it would be worth every minute.

They made small talk as they headed toward the parking lot. Bob explained that the weather was cooler than usual, in the seventies and only mild humidity.

"I can tell you this; for March it makes LA feel cold."

Bob opened the hatchback, and Dayne swung his bag inside.

Once they were on the road, Bob explained that he and his wife, Rosa, lived only half an hour from the airport. "Five miles, but it'll take us thirty minutes. Mexico City is unbelievable, man. Packed with people."

As they drove, Bob asked him about his latest film project.

"I worked with Angie Carr. She's one of the A-list actresses these days." Dayne stared out the windshield. Bob was right. Congestion was an enormous understatement. There were people everywhere, teeming along the highway and side streets and even in the alleyways between the buildings.

"Hmm. I've heard of her, I think. Dark hair?"

"Yeah. She's talented." Dayne left it at that. No need to get into the hazards of his job. Not yet anyway.

"I saw a magazine a few months back with pictures of you and—" Bob glanced at him—"what's her name? Kelly someone."

Dayne turned his attention to his friend. "Kelly Parker."

"Right." Bob had his right arm straight out in front of him, gripping the wheel the same way he'd done back when they first got their driver's licenses. He shrugged one shoulder. "I told you. We're pretty out of touch with the movie industry."

A smile tugged at Dayne's mouth. "You have no idea how refreshing that is." Dayne stared at Bob a moment longer. Bob really didn't know, didn't follow America's pop culture. None of the Hollywood names had a household ring to a man living Bob Asher's life here in Mexico City.

Dayne relaxed in his seat. During the next fifteen minutes he told Bob what his life was like. "My days are pretty predictable. Either filming—gone first thing in the morning and home long after dinnertime—or hiding from the paparazzi."

Bob made a face at him. "Come on. It isn't that bad."

"That magazine you saw—" Dayne gave him a wary look— "did you read it or just skim it?"

"Saw your picture, smiled big, prayed for you like I always do, and then put it back on the rack."

At the mention of prayer, Dayne hesitated. "You pray for me . . . seriously?"

"Of course." Bob laughed, the easy laugh of someone at peace with everything about himself. "All the time."

"You ever think of calling?" Dayne was teasing, resorting to what was comfortable. But in the deeper places of his heart he was reveling in the thought. Bob was praying for him. Bob and Katy. And somewhere in Bloomington John Baxter was probably praying for him too, even though he had no idea who Dayne was.

"Sure, Dayne." Bob grinned. "How many cell numbers have you had since the last time I saw you?"

It hit Dayne then that for a moment he'd forgotten he was famous. He'd asked the question like a normal person: "Ever think of calling?" As if it wasn't ludicrous for anyone to think of picking up the phone and calling Dayne Matthews. "Yeah—" he winced—"maybe a dozen."

"I knew it would happen one day." A warm breeze made its way through Bob's half-open window. It made the atmosphere even more relaxed, easier.

"What?"

Another grin. "You'd call. Every time I prayed for you I had that same sense. One day you'd call."

A chill passed over Dayne's arms and down his neck. He wasn't ready for this conversation yet, but still . . . every time Bob prayed he had the sense that one day he'd get a call from his old boarding-school buddy? "Anyway, the answer is yes. It is that bad. It's crazy bad." Dayne drew in a slow breath. "You can't believe the stuff they look for. If there's a clear shot, they'll take a picture. Anytime, anywhere. You can wind up in the tabs midsneeze or maybe picking your teeth after dinner. They'll make up their own story. 'Dayne Matthews Scowls at Waiting Fans' or 'Dayne Matthews: Does He Own Dental Floss'?"

Bob laughed, but it wasn't as lighthearted as before. "That's crazy. That why you're here?"

"Maybe." He stared through the passenger-side window at the sky overhead. Mexico City could definitely hold its own in a smoggy-sky contest with LA. "I'm not completely sure why I'm here." He looked at Bob. "It just felt right."

"Well, good." Bob grinned.

And in that grin, Dayne knew exactly what his old friend was saying.

The visit felt right to him too.

CHAPTER SIXTEEN

———◦─◆──◆─◦———

BOB'S HOUSE WAS SANDWICHED between a whole string
of houses just like his. Dayne guessed the place wasn't more than
a thousand square feet tops. There was a main room with a small
kitchen built into one corner, a table and chairs in another, and
in the front of the room, a coffee table between two thinly padded love seats. There was no TV anywhere. Bob had already told
him the place had two bedrooms, each probably smaller than
Dayne's master closet in Malibu.

But what his friend's place lacked in size and substance, it
made up for in warmth and love. Rosa met them at the door, and
Dayne was drawn to her instantly. She was a tall woman with a
beautiful dark-haired baby on her hip. Playing near her feet was
another child, equally dark-haired but with paler skin and blue
eyes.

In broken English she welcomed Dayne, kissed Bob on the
lips, put the baby on the floor, and hurried back to the kitchen,
where she had pots or frying pans on all four burners.

The little girl grabbed hold of Bob's leg. "Daddy, pick me up!"

Bob swung the child into his arms and twirled her once. "How's my little Angel?"

"I'm a happy Angel, Daddy." She had an accent, but her English sounded perfect.

He took a step toward Dayne. "This is our oldest daughter, Angel. She's three and very bilingual." He turned to her. "Say hi to Mr. Matthews."

"Hi." She hid her face behind her dad's shoulder.

"And down there on the floor—" Bob eased Angel back to the floor—"is Anna. She's just eighteen months." Bob winked at Dayne. "We don't get much company from the States. I told Rosa not to worry because it was just Dayne Matthews and—" he rubbed his knuckles on his own shoulder, his grin wide—"*I* won best actor in the boarding school's production of *Snow White* our senior year. Not you."

Dayne gave Bob a knowing look. "Because you played the mirror, and I played Prince Charming. You had the other kids in stitches from the moment you took the stage, and I got—"

"Purple tights and pointed gold shoes."

"Exactly." Dayne crossed his arms. He loved this, loved the easygoing banter he and Bob had always shared. "I still have those purple tights somewhere."

"Anyway—" Bob pointed his thumb in Rosa's direction— "she didn't care if you didn't win. Still wanted to roll out the red carpet."

"She didn't need to do that."

"I tried to tell her." Bob looked at his wife, and she—maybe sensing his gaze—did a half turn and smiled at him. It was a flirty grin, and it gave a glimpse into the private love the two clearly shared. At her feet on the floor, Angel was showing the baby how to play with measuring cups.

The picture was like something from a painting, something Ashley Baxter Blake would dream up. Rosa, working hard in the kitchen, her babies playing underfoot. Still, she shouldn't have gone to any trouble. He was no more special than anyone else just because he made movies.

Dayne leaned against the nearest wall. "Hey," he whispered, "I thought she didn't know who I was."

"Hmm?" Bob looked confused. Then a light dawned in his eyes. "Oh, you mean that you're famous? that part?"

"Yeah." Dayne gave a single laugh. "That's why all the fuss over dinner, right?"

It took a moment, but suddenly Bob chuckled under his breath. "Dayne—" he tossed out a look that said Dayne was maybe a few crayons short of a box—"what you *do* for a living isn't something that concerns her. You're my friend; you're from the United States. That's all that matters. It's like that with the Mexican culture. They're big on people."

Dayne wanted to crawl under the door, rewind the scene, and start over again. Was he that out of touch? Had Hollywood turned him into a person who expected to be recognized, someone who figured any nice thing done on his behalf was because of his fame and status?

Bob seemed to know what Dayne was feeling. He gave him a teasing slap on the shoulder. "Hey, don't worry about it." His eyes danced. "You're used to someone making a big fuss."

Before, Dayne would've chuckled and held his hands up in mock surrender. He couldn't remember how many times he'd responded that way when someone commented on what a rough job it must be, acting with Hollywood's leading ladies and being doted on everywhere he went. But he couldn't bring himself to even smile about the idea now. He felt his eyes grow distant. "For all the wrong reasons, Asher."

Bob's smile dropped off. For the first time since the airport, his eyes grew deep, more serious. "I can imagine."

They sat at the kitchen table, and Bob poured them each a glass of iced tea.

Dayne took in everything around him, drank it all in: the

smell of cooked beans, the smallness of the place, the intimacy. How wonderfully refreshing Rosa was, steeped in her culture and heritage, giving Bob private knowing glances and smiles every few minutes, happy to make a big homemade dinner simply because it was a way to honor her husband, a way to welcome her husband's friend.

"Hey, Asher," Dayne said from across the table, "you have any idea how lucky you are?"

"Not lucky." And there it was again. The depth in Bob's eyes. "Blessed. I thank God every day for my family." He spread his arms. "My home, our health. All of it."

Bob lived in a simple stone dwelling, with a hard-tile floor and three windows in the entire place. Yet he thanked God every day for what he had. The thought was enough to make Dayne's head spin. When was the last time he thanked God for everything he had? Or when had he ever done such a thing?

"Fine." Dayne laughed. He wanted to keep the atmosphere light, especially with Rosa nearby. "You have any idea how blessed you are?"

"Yes." Bob looked at Rosa, at his two young daughters, and finally at Dayne. His expression shone with a love that defied Dayne's understanding. "I definitely know."

❧

It was ten o'clock, and Rosa and the children were in bed when Dayne realized he'd made all the small talk he could make. He loved Bob, loved meeting his family and spending time in his home. The dinner had been amazing, and the conversation easy—with Bob occasionally translating for Rosa. He felt like he'd stumbled into another world, a place where he could—even for a few days—live the way other people lived.

But that wasn't why he'd come.

"So . . ." Dayne was sitting on one of the small sofas, Bob sitting on the other one opposite Dayne. "You're a missionary. Just like your parents."

"I am." Bob crossed one leg over the other. "That still eating at you, man? The whole missionary thing?"

"I didn't think so." Dayne stared at a blank spot on the wall. He couldn't get a handle on his feelings. "Last year I thought I'd worked it out once and for all. Forgave my parents for everything." He pursed his lips and focused on Bob. "I'm not mad at them anymore. I just don't understand it, you know?"

"The importance of it?" Bob's voice fell some. The kindness and compassion that had always marked him were still there. But something in his eyes showed he was ready to listen, ready for wherever the conversation might head from here.

"Right. I mean, go ahead and believe what you want. But why make a living telling other people about it?"

Bob did a slow, thoughtful nod. "It's a good question." He wasn't in a rush. He took a long breath, his expression easygoing even if his eyes held a greater intensity than before. "Can I tell you a story?"

Dayne exhaled. He still wasn't sure what he wanted to say exactly or what he was trying to find. A story from Bob would buy him time, maybe help him put his thoughts in order. "Asher telling stories?" He gave his friend a crooked grin. "Definitely."

Bob's lips curved in a smile that was as familiar as everything about their childhoods. But then his smile gradually faded. "After graduation, I spent a year with my parents in Papua New Guinea. One of the places both our parents had spent time in."

"I know the place." Dayne leaned into the sofa arm.

"There I am, a kid eighteen years old, and I'm taking my first long-term mission trip. A year in Papua New Guinea. So we get off the plane the first day, and I can't believe my eyes. The place looks like something out of a *National Geographic* spread. Tribesmen wearing bones through their earlobes and lips, men dressed in loincloths and carrying spears." He made a face that said even now he was amazed at the memory. "The only buildings were thatched-roof mud huts. Nothing else for hours in any direction."

Dayne tried to picture the area. "Pretty remote."

"Another world." Bob fell silent, as if he were trying to find his way back to the memory, to every aspect of it. "Now . . . for months before the trip while we were preparing and raising funds, I kept wondering the same thing. How do you try to explain God to other people? How do you find the words to tell them there's someone bigger than anything they can imagine yet that same someone is invisible? How do you talk about someone who is Creator and God, Savior and Friend? someone who wants to be Lord of their lives?"

A question came to Dayne's mind: *why did the tribesmen need to know?* But since Bob was on a roll, he kept it to himself. He could always ask why at the end of the story.

"I figured I'd find out how by watching my parents. After a lifetime in the mission field, they would probably have some supertrained way of introducing God to people who hadn't heard of Him before." Bob uncrossed his legs and sat up a little straighter. "But that's not what happened at all."

"With your parents?"

"Right." Bob's expression grew more intense than before. "We go out to the village people the next day and give them supplies—medical kits mostly—things they don't normally have. My parents spoke the language, of course, and by then I did too. We walked to the middle of the village square, and the tribal chief told us there were twelve groups who wanted to speak to us."

Bob took a quick breath. "I'm thinking, great. Twelve groups of three or four people each. The size would foster intimate conversation, and I could watch firsthand how my parents would explain about God." He looked straight at Dayne. "Only that's not what happened."

The story unfolded in a way that was more gripping with

every detail. "The first group consisted of more than a hundred people. I asked my parents how so many people knew we were coming." Bob's tone showed his disbelief even after all the years that had passed. "They told me it was by word of mouth. And that some of the people walked three days for the chance to be there."

"Three days?"

"Through the jungle on bare feet."

"Wow."

"Okay, so wait till you hear this." Bob explained that his parents worked with a spokesperson from the first group. "One statement was being shouted from nearly everyone in the crowd. The same thing over and over and over again. The spokesperson couldn't quiet them down. My parents seemed to understand what was being said, because they raised their hands and nodded—trying to get the crowd to quiet down."

Dayne could imagine the scene. "What were they saying?"

"They were saying, 'Tell us about God. Tell us about God. Tell us about God.'"

"So . . ." Dayne thought he was understanding. "You didn't have to worry about how to explain that there was a God because someone else had already told them?"

"No." There was a sense of wonder in Bob's tone. "No one had ever told them a thing."

Something curious stirred in Dayne's heart. "Then how . . . ?"

"See, here it is. These were people who didn't know the day of the week. They didn't know that the world's round or about television or even electricity. They received no magazines, couldn't read, and had no knowledge of Scripture." Bob patted his chest twice. "But in here, where it mattered most, they knew instinctively that there was a God, without any proof or convincing or anything at all. They knew and believed. And if we came in His name, they figured we could talk about Him, answer their dozens of questions."

Dayne twisted his face, confused. "They knew about God without being told?"

"Right!" Bob held up his hands and let them fall to his lap. "Which doesn't really work, does it?"

Dayne's voice was quiet. "No."

"Unless God put that in their hearts. God alone." He paused. "See, Dayne, the Bible says that God has set eternity in the hearts of men, and His creation stands as proof of His existence. If we doubt God, creation will speak on His behalf, so if we choose not to believe, we will be without excuse one day when we face Christ."

Gradually, Dayne understood what his friend was saying. Want proof of God? Listen to the cry of your own heart, look at the creation.

Dayne asked, "So you're saying the reason those people knew that God existed was because they had eternity deep inside them, and they paid attention to the living things around them?"

"Exactly!" Bob practically jumped out of his seat. "It was that way for each of the twelve groups that day." He seemed to realize he was getting a little too loud. He dropped his voice a notch. "Every one of them was willing to stand there a full hour until the next group needed to move into the area. There wasn't a person in that crowd who wouldn't have stayed to listen to us all day long. Just for a little more information about God." He sat back against the sofa. "I think I believed from that moment on."

"You?" Dayne was careful with his tone. "Come on, Asher. You believed from the time you were born."

"I believed because I was *taught* to believe." His words were more thoughtful. "But that first day in Papua New Guinea, I believed because, after watching the faith of those people, I knew beyond a doubt that God was real. And if He's real, then He was worth spending my life on." Bob smiled slowly, easily. "See, Dayne. None of us go to the mission field to force our beliefs on an unsuspecting people. We go because the people already know *about* God. But they're desperate for answers concerning Him. Desperate enough to walk on bare feet three days through a jungle."

Dayne felt something lift inside him. For the first time, that made sense.

"We saw over a thousand people that day, and my parents explained about Jesus twelve times —how He died on the cross to pay the price for our sins and how the people could have a relationship with Him. A friendship with God." Bob dug his elbows into his knees and leaned closer. "I saw grown men collapse, weeping on the ground because they were so grateful that my parents had taken time to tell them what they needed to know."

The scene played out in Dayne's mind. Countless people, desperate for answers about God, reliant completely on the visits of missionaries to point them in the right direction. His heart softened toward his adoptive parents. No wonder they were convinced they were spending their time the right way.

In that moment Dayne was sure about something else. He wasn't here so he could talk about his parents and their decision to be missionaries. No, he wasn't here for answers about his childhood hurts, wounds that had been healed for months. He was here—sitting with his good friend Bob Asher—for the same reason those tribesmen had walked three days through the jungle.

He wanted answers about God.

CHAPTER SEVENTEEN

T H E   S T R E E T   M I N I S T R Y was in full swing when Bob took the podium.

Dayne was sitting off to the side, out of the way of the pressing crowd. Already he'd seen Bob and Rosa act out three scenes—each showing something about the sacrifice of Christ or the joy of living a Christian life even in hard times. At the same time, Bob's church members worked various booths handing out hot dogs and carnival food. Between speakers there were games for the children and prizes for everyone who played.

A number of musicians had played for the crowd, and every half hour or so random people would come up to the podium to talk. Everything was in Spanish, of course. Dayne understood very little of the language, but over and over the message was clear. Whoever the people were, they believed they had been rescued by Jesus. With tears on their cheeks, they would look up to heaven, arms spread wide, and say, *"Gracias, Dios. Gracias!"* "Thank You, God. Thank You."

Dayne wondered why those words had never been his own,

even after all God had done for him, all the times God had tried to get his attention.

His heart felt raw, the soil of his understanding turned over and ready for planting. What had he been doing with his life? From the time he lost his adoptive parents, he'd been angry at God, alternately fighting and doubting Him.

There was a hole in Dayne's heart—one that had been there since he was old enough to remember. He'd tried to fill it with anger and fame, wild living, and Kabbalah. He'd hired a PI, believing that maybe the hole could be filled by finding his birth parents; only that hadn't worked out either. For a season he'd found some satisfaction reading the Bible, the one Katy had given him. But after a while, he'd lost track of it and forgot about how it made him feel.

Even Katy Hart couldn't make him feel complete. No matter how strong his feelings for her.

Dayne looked on as Bob brought the microphone close to his face. "Friends . . . I bring you an invitation."

The crowd grew utterly still—men, women, and children expectant for whatever Bob was about to say. They inched closer.

Dayne was surprised they knew enough English to understand, surprised too that Bob wasn't speaking in Spanish. But then, maybe his friend's part was quicker, simpler. He focused on what was being said.

"Not one of you here tonight will ever be complete until you find a relationship with Jesus Christ." Bob paused, his eyes shining with kindness and concern. "Jesus Christ, our God and Savior, the same one you've been hearing about all afternoon. The God of salvation and miracles."

In the distance, the smell of popcorn and cotton candy mixed with the pungent air from the city. The evening light was fading fast.

Dayne hadn't thought of God that way before—the God of miracles. He stared into the darkening sky. *What miracles, God?*

His question wasn't asked in anger or frustration, but more out of earnest curiosity. *What have You ever done in my life to show me that You're the God of miracles?*

There was no loud answer, but Dayne could feel a knowing growing in his heart. There was his conversation with Elizabeth Baxter the day before she died. That could've been a miracle, right? Or the fact that he'd driven aimlessly through Bloomington and walked into a theater to find a woman he could've searched a lifetime for and not found. Yes, God had been working miracles in his life all along. But until now, he'd never taken the time to look for them.

Dayne closed his eyes. *If You're a God of miracles, then please . . . please work one tonight, God. Please . . .*

Bob held his hands out to the people, his voice rising. "That same Jesus is here . . . now. He waits for you; He's knocking at the door of your heart."

Dayne felt like the words were for him alone. His heart ached within him, ached for the ways he'd tried to find peace and missed out. So many years lost, so many mistakes and wasted opportunities. If his heart had a door, then it was made of solid mahogany and steel. Not only had he refused to open it to God; he'd refused to hear even the slightest knocking.

Bob was wrapping up. "Where you live doesn't matter." He scanned the crowd, and for a moment he stared straight at Dayne. "Where you work doesn't matter." The passion in his tone built. "It doesn't matter how much money you have or whether you're the owner of a business or the one who cleans the floors. When your life here on earth is done, all that will matter is whether you heard the knock of Christ on your heart. And whether you took this chance to open the door and ask Him in."

Dayne felt the pinprick of tears behind his eyes. How many times had God knocked on his heart? Through the efforts of his adoptive parents and his birth parents—praying for him from across the country. Through people at the boarding school—

the secretary and a dozen teachers and staff members. Through the emptiness that called out to him time and time and time again.

And through the most amazing woman he'd ever known.

But every single time he'd refused to open the door.

"People, I beg you." Bob's voice rang in the still air. "If you want to let Jesus into your life, into your heart, then come forward. Come here." He motioned to a place in front of the small stage—maybe twenty feet deep, forty feet wide. A section of the street that had been roped off from the mass of people.

Dayne was breathless. Was the invitation for him too? He and Bob had shared hours of conversation. They'd talked about the women Dayne had been with and the regret he felt over the emptiness. They'd talked about Kelly's abortion and the loss Dayne felt because of it. Dayne talked about being adopted and how he had a biological family he thought about every day.

Most of all, they'd talked about Katy Hart.

For every topic, Bob listened and lent Dayne gentle feedback, wise perspective. When he told Bob he thought he was in love with Katy and that maybe she was the only reason he was feeling strangely out of sorts, Bob simply tilted his head and said, "If she's all that's eating at you, why aren't you in Bloomington?"

Touché.

Now . . . with the air cooling around him and against the background of people weeping over the years they'd spent alone without God, the truth was as obvious as the sound in his own heartbeat. The sound of someone knocking.

God, is this invitation for me too? Right here . . . now?

My precious son . . . I have drawn you with an everlasting love.

The words echoed in his soul, in the places around his heart. Dayne gulped. Okay, so maybe the invitation was for him, but if so . . . he should do something about it in private. Back at Bob's house.

Or maybe not.

Bob was explaining how people could come from either side where there was a break in the roped-off area. "Come now, friends. Jesus wants to come into your heart. He wants to stay with you; He wants to walk with you. He wants to live in your soul starting right here, right now."

A man with a guitar took the spot to the side of Bob and began to play. The sound was familiar, a hymn they'd sung a million times back in boarding school. The words were in Spanish, and they filled the air. After a few seconds Dayne recognized the song. "Amazing grace! how sweet the sound—that saved a wretch like me! . . ."

And it was on that note, with that part of the song, that Dayne felt himself crack. His eyes flooded, and tears spilled onto his cheeks.

From all over the crowd in the street, people were heading to the stage, falling to their knees, and crying out to God.

"That's right," Bob was saying. "Let God in, people. Don't wait."

Without thinking another minute, Dayne stood and joined the flow of people. Not one person gave him a second glance. Dayne Matthews wasn't the famous one now, not with all of eternity on the line. That place belonged to God and God alone. The God Dayne had spent a lifetime hiding from.

His chest hurt as he made his way closer, and he realized why. A lifetime of rust and decay had built up around the door of his heart. As long as he left the door closed, he could hide from the pain, deny the bad choices and emptiness of his life. But now—as he opened it to Jesus for the first time—it hurt.

But nothing had ever felt better or more right in his entire life.

Finally he made his way to the front of the stage. There for the first time since the beginning of his movie career, he wasn't Dayne Matthews. He was a guy who'd been alone and lost for most of his life, one of these hundreds of people desperate for a Savior. As he dropped to his knees, as he silently cried out to

Jesus and begged Him to come through the open door into his heart, into his life, he felt something he'd never felt before.

His heart was complete, and that could mean only one thing: the hole was gone.

As he knelt on that broken asphalt street in Mexico City, Dayne recalled everything rotten and wrong about his life and he gave it to God. He asked, as he'd done one time before, for forgiveness. But this time he went one step further. He asked for salvation. Redemption.

After a few minutes, Bob led them through a prayer.

When it was over, when God had filled Dayne with a peace he'd never known, and when his tears had washed away all traces of doubt or distrust, he looked around. Rosa was praying with a group of women, and after a few minutes of looking, he found Bob.

As their eyes met, Dayne could see how happy his friend looked. "You saw me down there, didn't you?"

"No." Bob's eyes widened. "So you did it? You finally let Him in?"

"I did." Dayne clenched his teeth and stared up at the sky. He could feel the tears again, but he didn't want to cry. Not now. Maybe not ever again. "I've never felt like this in all my life."

"I knew it." The intensity from earlier was gone, and in its place was a joy that spilled from Bob's eyes. "I didn't have to see you. I knew you'd come." He gave Dayne the sort of hug they'd shared at the airport. "Finally, brother. Finally." Bob pulled back and raised his fist in the air. "Thank You, God!"

The celebration felt as right as Dayne's next breath.

"Hey, Dayne . . ." Bob looked at him, his expression intense once more. "Remember when I told you I was praying for you?"

Dayne wanted to shout. He felt so good inside that he couldn't keep from grinning. "I remember."

"This, man—" he spread his hands out, indicating the street

ministry, the atmosphere, and most of all the change in Dayne—
"I prayed for it to happen just like this."

"Amazing." Dayne could hardly wait to move forward, to get
home and call Katy and get back into his Bible and find a church
where he could understand the faith that drove everyone who
mattered to him. But he had a question first. "It's a street ministry, right?"

"Right." Bob hesitated, as if he figured that much was obvious. "It's leveled right at the people on the street. People who
believe in God but who never knew they could begin a relationship with Him."

"Okay . . ." Dayne had wondered this the whole time Bob was
at the podium. "So how come you gave your talk in English?"

Bob's expression changed. Even in the dark of nightfall, the
color clearly faded from his face. "What do you mean?"

"Your talk." Dayne searched his friend's face, looking for
signs that old Bob Asher was pulling a practical joke. There were
none. Dayne's voice fell. "The whole time, Asher. It was in
English. I understood every word."

At that instant, Rosa walked up, breathless. Her cheeks were
tearstained, but her eyes glowed—much like Bob's. She said
something to her husband in Spanish, and then she grinned at
Dayne. "Good you! You give life to Christ, yes?"

"Yes, Rosa. Thank you." Dayne wanted to finish the conversation with Bob. What had caused his expression to change? And
why the shock in his eyes?

Rosa took a step closer to Dayne. "I see you come. I see . . ."
She made a frustrated sound, as if she couldn't find the right
words. She turned to Bob and rattled something off in Spanish.

Dayne was confused, trying to make sense of whatever was
being said. He looked from Rosa to Bob. "What'd she tell you?"

Bob swallowed, the shock in his face stronger than before.
"She said . . . she was surprised you came, surprised you could

make out what I was saying." He paused, unblinking. "She says she didn't know you understood Spanish."

"What? That's . . . that couldn't be." Bob Asher had given his entire talk in Spanish? Is that what Rosa meant?

Bob was nodding. "It's true, man. Not a word of English the whole time."

The ground beneath Dayne suddenly felt unstable. That was impossible. He had sat in the chair off to the side and listened to the whole thing. Every word had been as clear as—

Understanding came over him like a torrential rain.

Dayne felt overwhelmed, awed. He opened his mouth to say something, but he couldn't speak, couldn't do anything but ponder what had happened. The God who had called him all his life, the God who had met him this very night on a street in the heart of Mexico City, wasn't only his Savior and Lord. He was God Almighty, ruler of the universe. Bigger than anything Dayne could fathom. The one who had found him wasn't only the God who would bring wholeness and meaning to his existence, the God who would lead him into a new life in Christ, a changed life. God was something else too. Something Dayne hadn't thought about until just an hour earlier.

He was the God of miracles.

CHAPTER EIGHTEEN

———— ✦❖✦ ————

T ORNADO WARNINGS were in effect for counties south of Bloomington. Rain beat on the windshield as John Baxter drove to the Indianapolis airport early this afternoon. He had already called ahead to see if his kids' planes were delayed. They weren't. Apparently the weather south and east of Bloomington was more stable.

The tornado warnings didn't worry John. The forecast showed the storms heading farther north. Besides, the news he had to tell his kids tomorrow concerned him much more than any bad weather.

He and Elaine had taken a walk down to the creek yesterday. They were spending more time together—though it wasn't a fact he'd shared with any of his children.

"It's time, John." Elaine had stopped and shaded her eyes with her hand. "Isn't that what you decided?"

No matter what he'd told Ashley, he hadn't made up his mind. Not yet. He slipped his hands into his pants pockets and stared at the tallest tree on the other side of the creek. "I keep thinking

I should wait." A sigh came from the anxious places in his soul. "Maybe Dayne will write or call." He looked at Elaine. "The news would be so much easier to hear if we knew Dayne wanted to meet us. Don't you think?"

Elaine hadn't say anything. She didn't have to. As their friendship had developed, one of the things John appreciated most about her was the way she didn't rush into conversation. Instead, she let her eyes, her quietness act as a mirror. At the creek yesterday, much like other times, he could sense the right answer.

By the time they returned to the house, he'd made his decision.

John glanced in his rearview mirror now. Ashley and Cole were in their van right behind him. They would need both vehicles to bring the group and their luggage back to the Baxter house. Luke and Reagan and their two kids would go home with Ashley. Erin, Sam, and the girls would ride with him in the van Brooke had lent him. Kari and Ryan were at the house, getting dinner ready for after their arrival.

"Everything'll be all set when you get here." Kari had kissed his cheek as he left half an hour ago. "It's going to be the best week of the whole year."

John wasn't so sure.

It was the first day of the Baxter reunion, and he was struggling. The radio was off, the silence welcoming. With all the praying John had been doing, he hoped maybe God would speak to him on the ride to the airport, give him wisdom about how exactly to handle the news he needed to share tomorrow.

The day he would tell the rest of his kids about their older brother.

Two weeks had passed since he'd sent Dayne the letter and photos via the studio, and with no word, John could only assume the worst. Dayne's agent was right. The oldest Baxter son was not a Baxter but a movie star. America owned Dayne Matthews, and in the mix of people guarding his career and shaping his image, no one was willing to allow for something so crazy and unsettling as Dayne meeting his birth family.

John squinted at the road ahead. It was raining harder than before. *God, I'm struggling. I want all five of my kids to enjoy this time, to celebrate being together. I don't want anything to change between us because of . . . of Dayne.*

He heard no answer, but a Scripture flashed in his mind: Philippians 4:6-7—verses he and Elizabeth had memorized early in their marriage: *Do not be anxious about anything, but in everything, by prayer and petition, with thanksgiving, present your requests to God. And the peace of God, which transcends all understanding, will guard your hearts and your minds in Christ Jesus.*

He let it run through his head a few times, and the promised peace filled his heart—the way it did every time he thought about the Scripture. He forced a smile and drew a long breath. Worrying about tomorrow wouldn't make it any easier. And in little more than an hour he was going to meet his granddaughter Malin for the first time, the precious child Luke and Reagan had adopted from China.

Okay, God . . . I get it. Let me enjoy today. In fact, let Your presence be with us tonight, Lord, so that every one of us knows You're there in our midst.

He checked on Ashley in his rearview mirror again. Yes, this afternoon, this evening would be amazing, no doubt. And tomorrow . . . well, like the Bible said, tomorrow could take care of itself.

The rain had stopped, so Ashley barely noticed the gathering dark clouds. She and her dad had talked about the storms earlier. Everything was supposed to hit north of Bloomington. Besides, they were used to this. April was always stormy in Indiana.

It was four in the afternoon when Ashley pulled her full van into the Baxter driveway and found her regular parking spot. The excitement in the vehicle was fever pitch. Luke was sitting in the seat beside her, and in the back Reagan sat next to baby Malin strapped in her car seat. In the last row, Cole was buckled in beside nearly three-year-old Tommy. The two cousins had kept up a steady conversation the entire trip.

In the front, Ashley and Luke had done the same thing, and already Ashley felt like her brother had never left.

Luke peered through the windshield at the Baxter house. "Doesn't ever change, does it?"

"Nope." Ashley's heart sang within her. They would all be together! She only wished she could've had her baby the month before, instead of after the reunion. That way she might've gotten around a little easier.

"Hey, Ash—" Luke grinned at her—"you look great. Really. I know I told you at the airport, but you do."

"Thanks." She pursed her lips and blew out. "I feel like a house on legs."

Reagan chuckled. "I didn't miss that part with little Malin. Adopting her almost felt like cheating."

As Ashley turned off the engine, she saw her dad pull into the driveway behind her. Kari and Brooke and their kids were gathered at the door, squealing. They ran out and met the group halfway up the walk. There were hugs all around.

John glanced at the sky. "Let's move it inside. Looks like those clouds could break any second."

Cole was telling Maddie that Tommy liked him best because he was a boy, but Maddie could be second best. Ashley held hands with Erin's two oldest daughters—Chloe and Clarisse. Luke was talking to Kari about how much he'd missed Ryan, and Sam was hearing from John about the recent storms.

It wasn't any one conversation that made Ashley smile. Rather the combination, the chorus of all their voices combined that created a sound the Baxter house had been missing.

It took several minutes to get the children and luggage inside. Hayley, Brooke's younger daughter, stood just inside with her walker, grinning at everyone who walked past her.

Ashley was one of the last in, and just before she was through the door, lightning flashed nearby. She winced and hesitated, counting slowly. *One . . . two . . . three . . .* The thunder hit then. Three miles away, if the trick really worked.

Kari came to the door to find her. "You okay? Everyone else is inside."

"I know," Ashley said. "Just watching the storm. I don't want to lose electricity tonight. Landon won't be here until seven o'clock—and it'll be later than that if it gets bad."

"Well . . . I wasn't going to say anything yet. Not for a few minutes anyway." Kari studied the sky. "But Bloomington's under a tornado watch."

Ashley sighed. "Great."

"Don't worry about it." Kari took her arm and gently led her inside. "Most of the bad weather is north of here."

"Still . . ."

"Come on." Kari laughed. "You're missing all the fun."

Ashley shut the door behind her. It wasn't like her to worry about the weather. She'd spent most of her life here in Indiana, dealing every spring with the thunderstorms and tornadoes that came their way. Every year they spent a day or two in the basement, waiting out a warning, but Bloomington had never been hit by anything devastating.

Not as far back as she could remember.

Kari seemed to sense her anxiety. "Hey—" she put her arm around Ashley's shoulders—"I know how you're feeling. It's the pregnancy. Both times I was like that." She patted Ashley's middle. A smile played in her eyes. "Irrational fear is part of being a mother."

"You're right." Ashley willed herself to stop thinking about the storms. They were heading through the living room and into the kitchen. "You made Mom's Spanish casserole, right?"

"Gads of it." Kari held up her fingers. "These hands haven't done so much cooking since Thanksgiving."

"Good!" Ashley stepped away from her sister and opened the fridge. "I'll toss the salad."

Another thirty minutes passed before they were all seated around the Baxter dining-room table. Kari and Ryan had added a large folding table, so there was seating for everyone, including three high chairs—two that they rounded up from family and one that their dad borrowed from a neighbor. The setup was cozy and would allow everyone a chance to share in the same conversations once dinner got started.

The storm was stronger than before, moving closer. But the sounds of wind and thunder were drowned out by the joyful noise of the family being together, remembering days gone by and catching up on what they'd missed since the last time they had all been in the same room.

There was a knock on the door, and they heard it open. "Off early."

It was Landon!

"Daddy!" Cole raced from his chair and around the corner. They could hear the sound as Cole jumped into Landon's arms.

"Hey, sport . . . everyone here?"

"Yep, Daddy, and guess what?" Cole was holding Landon's hand when they rounded the corner. "Tommy says I'm his best cousin." Cole looked at Maddie and back at Landon. "Isn't that nice of him?"

Landon had a wary look in his eyes, and as Ashley stood and headed toward her husband she hid a smile. Landon knew Cole every bit as well as she did, knew the competition that existed between Cole and Brooke's spunky Maddie.

"Well, now—" Landon cleared his throat—"I'll bet Tommy thinks everyone's his favorite cousin."

Propped up on an old Yellow Pages book, Tommy's expression was blank—as if he wasn't sure what all the fuss was about.

The ones listening to the exchange laughed, and half the table emptied as Erin and Sam and Luke and Reagan exchanged hugs and handshakes with Landon.

Cole returned to his place next to Tommy, and Ashley waited a few feet away for her turn with Landon. Her heart soared as the scene played out, because Landon belonged here. He was part of this, the way he always should've been part of it. What if she hadn't married him? What if she'd allowed herself to remain stubborn and jaded the rest of her life? A shiver passed along her arms and at the base of her neck.

When everyone was making their way back to their seats, she stepped in and gave Landon a side hug—the best she could do with the baby taking up so much space in front of her. "I'm glad you're here," she whispered near his ear.

"Things were slow at the station, but we're all on call until the tornado watch lifts." He kissed her and then hesitated. "You okay?" He searched her eyes. "You look scared."

"The storm." She made a face.

Concern became fine lines around his eyes. "Storms don't scare you, Ash."

"I know." She let her head fall against his shoulder. "Kari thinks it's because of the baby."

"It'll be fine." This time he kissed her forehead. "It's supposed to be gone by midnight." He led her to the table. "Besides, I won't let anything happen to you."

As they took their places, Ashley noticed her father. His eyes shone, but they were distant. Probably remembering Mom. That, or thinking about how he was going to tell the others they had an older brother. She watched him, the way he surveyed each of his kids and their families. When everyone had quieted down, he smiled. "Let's pray."

Around the two tables it took a few seconds for everyone to

hold hands. Then their dad closed his eyes. "Lord, thank You for bringing us all back together safely." There was a pinch in his voice, and he hesitated.

Ashley peeked at him and saw Ryan put his hand on Dad's shoulder. She felt her own throat tighten as he continued praying.

"It's the greatest thing in the world having everyone together, Father. We thank You for allowing it. Thank You for each one here, for the lives we lead and the blessings You've given us this past year. We pray that Your hand of blessing be on this meal and on these next few days together." Again he seemed overcome by emotion. "If it be Your will, Lord, please . . . give Elizabeth a window tonight. In Jesus' name, amen."

After he finished there was a moment of somber silence, a knowing that their mom was being missed by all of them—even if they hadn't talked about her yet. The conversations would be there—the admissions from each of them about how much they missed her.

But tonight, they would celebrate being together.

The children broke the silence first. Cole looked at Tommy. "Have you learned how to jump on one foot?"

Maddie craned her head around Cole and nodded big. "I can teach you better than Cole." She stuck the very tip of her tongue out at him.

"Hey . . ." Cole looked for a witness.

But before he could say another word, Brooke shot her daughter a look. "Let's remember our talk, young lady."

"Yes, Mommy." Maddie's pout was adorable, and it brought a round of laughter that lightened the mood.

Before she reached for the casserole, Ashley allowed herself to soak in the sight of them—all of them—together in the warm Baxter dining room. The place where so many of their gatherings had happened over the years. She looked at her father at the head of the table. Next to him were Ryan and Kari, their son,

Ryan Jr. between them. On around the table sat Luke and Reagan with little Malin in a high chair beside Reagan. Next came the big kids, as Cole liked to call them. Tommy sat next to Cole, and then came Maddie, Hayley, and Jessie. Ashley and Landon rounded out the circle.

At the other table were Erin and Sam, situated on either side of their four girls—Chloe, Clarisse, Amy, and Heidi—two in high chairs. Brooke and Peter sat with them, though they were all close enough to visit with each other.

Suddenly a wave of sorrow washed over Ashley. The only one missing was their mom.

Kari turned in her seat and smiled at Erin. "Ever think we'd be surrounded by so many kids?"

"No." Erin's eyes glowed with something soft, tender. "I prayed for it." She looked at her four daughters. "But I never thought it'd be like this."

Just then, Erin's youngest took a spoon of Spanish casserole and flicked it at her sister.

Sam took a deep breath and grinned. "Can't say I did either."

They all laughed, and Ashley looked at Reagan. "Malin is absolutely precious. I couldn't be happier for you."

"Thanks." Reagan kissed her little dark-haired girl on the top of her head. Next to her Luke put his arm around his wife's shoulders. "You can pray for us come May, though."

"May?" Landon finished a bite and set his fork down. "What's happening in May?"

"The trial." Luke leaned forward so he could see Landon better. "I'll spend a week or two in LA."

"Same time my mom's headed for Iowa to visit her sisters." Reagan blew at a wisp of her bangs. "It'll just be me and the kids."

"I'm a helper, Mommy." Tommy raised his spoon in the air. "Right?"

"Right." Reagan gave the others a look. "The other day I

found him feeding Malin a bottle." She smiled at her son, then turned to the others again. "Nothing in the bottle, of course."

"So I singed to her." Tommy made a face and looked at Cole. "She had a sicky tummy."

The sisters laughed and exchanged understanding glances.

Brooke dabbed her lips with her napkin and leaned sideways so she could see Luke. "That's the trial with Dayne Matthews, isn't it?"

Luke nodded and poked his fork into his salad. "The defendant's that crazy fan, the one who tried to kill Dayne and Katy Hart."

Ashley took a drink of water. "Katy has to go out for the trial too. So far the tabloids haven't mentioned her name."

"Exactly." Thunder rocked the house, but Luke didn't miss a beat. "We're doing everything we can to keep her name out of the press for now. Eventually we won't have a choice, but at least until the trial we want to maintain her privacy."

Ashley took a bite of salad, and as she did, she caught her father's expression. The joy and sentimentality from earlier were gone, and he seemed anxious, staring at his dinner and chewing slower than usual. What was that in his eyes? Maybe conversation about the trial didn't interest him; maybe he'd fallen into thoughts about their mom instead.

But he looked more than anxious. He looked almost guilty. Ashley studied him a few more seconds before turning back to the others. She'd have to ask him about it later.

Across from her Kari ripped up pieces of a wheat roll and placed them in front of Ryan Jr. "Hey, has anyone seen that new Dayne Matthews movie, the one that just came out with the scenes from Bloomington?"

"*Dream On*," Erin said. "Sam hired a babysitter the other night, and we hit the town. Dinner and the movie." She grinned. "I thought they were going to kick me out of the theater."

Sam rolled his eyes and chuckled. "Every time there was a

scene filmed in Bloomington she would gasp and point at the screen. 'Oh . . . I know where that is!' or 'That's the park; I swear it's the park!'"

The others laughed and Reagan raised her hand. "I saw it too." She pointed at Erin. "We should go see it again, together. That way we won't embarrass each other."

"Kari and I were going to see it last week, but Jessie got sick." Ryan took their son's sippy cup, unscrewed the lid, and poured his own water into it. He handed it back and smiled at the others. "Sick kids take precedence over a movie—even one with Bloomington in it."

They all generally agreed that yes, they'd like to see the movie. Erin and Reagan both gave the film a thumbs-up.

"You know what was really weird about it, though?" Erin fed her littlest daughter a spoonful of casserole. "How much Dayne Matthews looks like Luke."

"Yeah, see." Reagan gave Luke a playful shove. "I told you so."

"Nah." Luke set his roll down and shook his head. "The guys at the office thought that too. I even thought it for a while, but it's just the hair."

"It's more than the hair."

Ashley swallowed her bite and joined in. "I saw the preview. Erin and Reagan are right. And here's something else . . ." She looked at the faces around the table, and her tone dropped a notch. "Dayne gave me a ride home last summer." She held up three fingers in the classic Girl Scout pledge sign. "Scout's honor."

There was a round of disbelieving and teasing looks.

"You were always the drama queen." Brooke grinned at her. "What, he got done filming, pointed you out of the crowd, and offered you a ride home?"

Landon chuckled. "No, it's true. I dropped Ashley off at the church to watch the rehearsal." He raised an eyebrow at her. "She comes home and tells me Dayne Matthews gave her a ride."

"No way!" Erin nearly jumped out of her seat. "Why didn't you tell us before?"

Ashley patted her round midsection. "I guess I've been pre-occupied."

"Come on, you know Ashley." Landon leaned close and hugged her neck. "She wanted an audience, that's all."

A dozen questions were fired at her at once, and Ashley explained the situation. But just as she got started she noticed her father again. He pushed back from the table and headed into the kitchen with his empty water glass. He looked pale.

She stopped her story midsentence. She felt her heart skip a beat. "Dad, you okay?"

"I'm fine. Just a little thirsty."

Ashley exchanged a look with Brooke. In a whispered voice, she told her sister, "Check on him. He doesn't look good."

Brooke stood and followed their dad into the kitchen.

Ashley continued her story. "Anyway, he was in town a few days before the filming to see Katy Hart." She didn't miss a single detail, explaining how Dayne had introduced himself using a false name and said he was Katy's friend. "At first I let him think I didn't know. But come on, Dayne Matthews? Of course I knew who he was."

A couple of the guys rolled their eyes, but the atmosphere was lighthearted, upbeat.

When Brooke and their dad returned from the kitchen, he looked better. A little more color in his face. He sat down, but he stayed unusually quiet.

"Okay, so tell us." Reagan was on the edge of her seat. "Does he look like Luke in person?"

"That's what I was getting at." Ashley paused, allowing a buildup. "The resemblance is definitely there, but it was some-thing else. His mannerisms, maybe. Half the ride home I had the feeling I wasn't with Dayne at all but that Luke was in the car with me."

"You know what they say—" Luke shrugged—"everyone has a twin out there somewhere."

The conversation shifted. They talked about Ryan's coaching and Kari's new job teaching three days a week at Jessie's preschool. Brooke and Peter explained that Hayley was making tremendous progress, and only then did Ashley notice her father being finally drawn into the conversation.

"That little girl's a walking miracle," he said. "No one at the hospital can believe how well she's doing."

"That's for sure." Peter raised his glass in the air. "Proof of God, if nothing else is."

Maddie obviously understood the conversation was about her little sister. She leaned over, pulled Hayley's face close to her own, and planted a big mushy kiss on her sister's cheek. "Hi, miracle girl."

"Hi!" Hayley grinned so big everyone around the table smiled.

Reagan shared that life was getting a little cramped living with her mom in the apartment in Upper Manhattan. She and Luke weren't sure how long they'd stay.

"The place is big enough." Reagan made a mock nervous face at her husband. "But it still feels like we're playing house."

A memory flashed into Ashley's mind. The horror of September 11 and the knowledge that Reagan's father's office had been at the top of one of the twin towers. His death had changed everything for Luke and Reagan, and in the end God had used Ashley to help Luke see that he needed to go to New York and find the girl he loved. It all seemed like a lifetime ago. "How is she, your mom?"

"She's okay." Reagan looked at Luke. "Should I tell them?"

"Sure." He took a bite of salad.

"Mom's dating." She said it with a hint of embarrassment in her tone, as if it were somehow wrong for her mother to be seeing someone.

At the head of the table, Ashley's father set down his glass.

"I think that's normal." He seemed to avoid Ashley's face as he spoke. "It's been several years."

"That's what I told her." Luke nodded. "But every time her mom's friend comes around, Reagan wants to leave."

"I'll admit it." For the first time tonight, Reagan looked more serious. "It's hard. I don't think I'll ever be able to see Mom with someone else."

Ashley's heart beat harder than before. She looked from Reagan to Luke and back to her father. What had he meant by that? By saying he thought it was normal for Reagan's mother to date? Was he saying that he felt the same way, and maybe he was thinking of dating too? Was it some way of softening them up so they wouldn't be horrified when he spent time with his friend Elaine Denning?

Another clap of thunder shook the house. Landon seemed to sense that Ashley was getting uptight. He reached for her hand and gave it a few squeezes. She felt herself relax. No, her father couldn't mean anything by it. He had already explained that Elaine was only a friend, nothing more.

Ashley sat back in her chair. Tomorrow night her dad planned to tell her siblings about their older brother—the one none of them knew about but her. A realization came over her. No wonder her father was looking strange, acting strange. He'd kept the secret about his firstborn son for decades.

But after tomorrow every one of them would know the truth.

CHAPTER NINETEEN

THE CONVERSATION WAS LIVELY and in full force the first night at the Baxter reunion. But John barely heard any of it. His heart and his breathing were both off rhythm, the way they'd been since earlier this afternoon.

Reagan was saying, "It isn't only her new friend. I think you can only live with your mother-in-law for so long, right, dear?"

Luke gave her a patient smile. "Your mom's been very gracious." He looked at John. "I got a raise, but we can't afford New York City. The firm wants to keep me until I finish law school, and then they want me full-time."

John stirred his fork through what was left of his casserole. It didn't taste the same as when Elizabeth made it. Besides, how could he eat? His emotions had been all over the map since he'd stepped out of the van at the airport. First, there was the swelling emotion of seeing his children all together again and the thrill of meeting his new granddaughter. Then the awareness that the children were growing up, changing, and the knowledge that his wife would never, ever be part of the group again.

But when Kari brought up Dayne's movie . . .

In what amounted to the acting job of his *own* life, John had focused hard on chewing his meal and pretending like nothing was wrong as his kids switched topics from the movie to the way Dayne and Luke looked alike. The whole time he wanted to stand up and shout, *Of course they look alike. They're brothers.*

And that was the part that made him feel sick to his stomach. He would tell his kids they had an older brother, yes. But he could never tell them who their brother was—not as long as Dayne didn't want to be a part of their family. The knowledge would only bring pain and heartache to his beautiful family—something he and Elizabeth had agreed they would never do.

But then Ashley revealed that Dayne had given her a ride home. His mind had been racing ever since. Dayne had hired a private investigator. He knew the Baxters were his family, and he knew they lived here in Bloomington. So chances were he knew when he gave Ashley a ride home that he was actually sharing a car with his sister.

The whole thing was stranger than John could fathom. Was it a test of some kind? Had Dayne wanted to get as close as he could to their family without actually making a connection? Or was it only a coincidence—Dayne visiting Katy Hart at rehearsal and Ashley needing a ride home? Maybe Dayne had fought the whole thing but had had no choice without making a scene.

He could picture Katy working late, knowing Dayne had a car, and asking him if he wouldn't mind taking her friend Ashley home. Even so, Dayne had to have known that the Ashley who was Katy's friend was the same Ashley in the notes his PI must've given him.

John's mind spun and raced and took him down paths he couldn't find his way back from. No wonder Ashley had asked him if he was okay. Half the night felt more like a crazy dream than the very real first night of their reunion.

When dinner was over Ashley helped her sisters make cookie-dough ice-cream sundaes for the group—something a few of their husbands had requested.

Two hours later the dishes were done and the adults were sitting at the cleaned-up dining-room table. Ryan and Landon made coffee, and the conversation turned to the events of the weekend.

"I checked online." Peter frowned. "Thunderstorms and tornado conditions all week."

"What about tomorrow?" John wrapped his fingers around his steaming mug. It felt good to have a distraction. "We're doing the picnic at Lake Monroe in the morning, aren't we?"

"Right." Ashley rested her hand on her abdomen. "I read in the paper that tomorrow's supposed to be clear until the afternoon."

"That's what weather.com said too."

"Good." Landon gave a light tap on the table. "Looks like the picnic's a go."

There was commotion in the next room, where Erin was overseeing all the children except Malin, who was asleep in her baby carrier on the floor next to Reagan. None of them at the table paid much attention to the kids, except to raise their voices so they could hear each other.

"Tomorrow night?" Brooke looked around. "Back here for Chinese food, is that okay?"

John swallowed hard and stared into his coffee cup. Tomorrow night. How soon it would be here, and he'd have to tell them the truth. *God, please . . . be with us. We're going to need You every moment when they hear the news.*

Kari was giggling. "Chinese food was my idea. Less time in the kitchen—" she grinned at her sisters—"more time talking."

Ryan chuckled and swapped a look with Landon, Luke, Peter, and Sam. "As if they need that."

Peter was saying something about a movie night during the week for the group when the big kids appeared in the doorway of the dining room. Their faces were lit with ear-to-ear smiles, and Jessie was bouncing all around, her hands clasped together. In the middle of the group was Hayley, anchored on either side by Maddie and Cole. Erin stood behind them, little Heidi on her hip. There were tears in Erin's eyes.

John turned his chair so he could see better.

Cole stuck out his chest, his eyes dancing. "Hey, we have something to show you."

Only then did John notice something. Hayley didn't have her walker.

Brooke must've noticed it at the same time, because she rushed to her feet and started toward them. "Maddie, you know she can't be up without her—"

Maddie held up her hand. "Wait, Mommy. Sit down."

"Please, Aunt Brooke!" Cole pleaded with her.

"Yeah, please, Aunt Brooke!" Jessie jumped in a small circle and then looped her arm through Cole's. "We have a 'prise for everyone."

"'Prise, Mama." Hayley grinned. Her speaking skills were still slower than they would've been if it weren't for her near drowning. But she understood what was happening around her, and every month she sounded more age appropriate.

"Maddie . . ." Brooke looked doubtful, but Peter took her hand and slowly she settled back into her seat. "Hold on to her tight. I don't want her to fall."

"She won't, Mommy." Maddie sounded calm, confident. "Me and Cole taught her a trick."

"Yeah." Cole nodded. "She's really good at it, Aunt Brooke."

The adults at the table seemed to hold their breath. Erin nodded at Brooke and smiled. There were still tears in her eyes, but her smile told them that whatever was about to happen, the kids were right. Hayley would be okay.

Cole bent around and looked right at Hayley. "Ready?"

"Ready." Hayley bit her lip and focused hard on the floor in front of her.

"Okay, here we go." Cole straightened and looked at Maddie. "One . . . two . . . three . . . go!"

At the same time, he and Maddie—moving very slowly—let go of Hayley's hands. They stayed beside her, ready to catch her. But Hayley was steady, steadier than she'd been since her accident.

Brooke gasped and put her hand to her mouth. "She's standing by herself."

"Mommy, wait." Maddie held her finger to her lips. "That's not the trick."

Jessie stopped jumping. "Go on, Hayley. Show 'em your 'prise."

With Cole and Maddie beside her, Hayley took two steps and then stopped. She grinned at Brooke and Peter. "Walk, Mama. Hayley walk."

John brought his fist to his mouth, and his eyes filled instantly.

"Dear God . . . thank You!" Brooke's words were a whisper. She leaned into Peter, her face pinched, eyes locked on their daughter. "She's walking!"

Peter couldn't speak. Tears streamed down his cheeks. He rose from his seat, ready to dart across the room and catch her. But there was no need.

"See . . ." Cole stayed an inch from his cousin's elbow. "I told you she was okay. Me and Maddie taught her how."

Maddie, on Hayley's other side, whispered at the group, "I taught her first."

This time, Cole didn't argue. They were all too busy watching Hayley. She fixed her eyes on Brooke and walked around the table with slow steady steps.

Brooke stood and crouched down, her arms open.

Hayley walked the rest of the way and practically ran the final steps into Brooke's arms. "Mama!"

Cole and Maddie did a high five.

Everyone was in shock, sitting motionless, silent. Hayley had been without a heartbeat of her own for half an hour after her drowning accident. In the weeks that followed, her doctors had explained to the family that Hayley would probably never get out of bed again. By their assessment, she would be blind and brain damaged the rest of her life.

Only here she was, walking and talking on her own.

John looked at Brooke, rocking Hayley, crying tears of gratitude while Peter and Kari and Erin and Ashley did the same.

"That's a good trick, don't you think, Mommy?" Maddie skipped over and put her hand on Brooke's shoulder.

"Yes, honey." Brooke wiped her tears. "Yes, it's a very good trick."

Suddenly John realized what had just happened. Never mind about the pain the next day would bring, about the understanding he could only hope his kids would have in regard to their older brother. Today he had asked God for a sign, proof that He was indeed with them, working in their midst. And God had delivered.

Because here and now—in a way none of them could yet begin to believe—their precious little Hayley could walk.

CHAPTER TWENTY

———————◆◇◆———————

THE FRIDAY NIGHT full-company *Narnia* rehearsal seemed like a waste from the moment it started. Al and Nancy Helmes were on a brief trip to the West Coast to see the birth of their seventh grandchild. As a result, the group had no music, and with lightning and thunder flashing outside and the building shaking from the wind, it was all Katy could do to keep the kids under control.

"Guys, come on," she heard herself say repeatedly. "We need every minute of rehearsal time."

The kids would shape into action until the next clap of thunder. Never mind that this was Indiana and they should have been used to storms. The tornado watch had everyone on edge. Halfway through the rehearsal—just as Bailey Flanigan, playing the White Witch, was hissing at young Edmond that he better find his siblings and find them fast—the lights flickered and every child onstage screamed.

A few minutes later—the electricity still fighting for survival—Krissie Schick, a board member and current CKT area coordinator, pulled Katy aside and informed her that twelve parents had called, concerned and wondering if the church had a basement and checking that Katy Hart had the sense to call off rehearsal and take the kids downstairs if the storm got bad enough.

Making it harder was the fact that Katy hadn't heard from Dayne. It had been two weeks since his surprise visit, so if he'd made time for a trip to Mexico it would've happened by now. Katy had prayed for him whenever he came to mind—which was more times each day than she could count. She'd talked about the situation at length with Jenny and even with Rhonda and Ashley.

All of them agreed. Praying for Dayne was a good thing, but dwelling on him, as if he might be a part of her life somewhere down the road—probably not.

"No matter how you think about him or how you see him," Ashley had told her the other night when they were working on sets, "he's a movie star. A gorgeous, playboy movie star."

"But if he finds God . . . if he gives his life to the Lord . . ."

"It could happen." Rhonda tried to stay positive. "But maybe you should try to forget about him for now. Until you know."

Katy had sort of expected him to go to Mexico and call her as soon as he stepped back on American soil. Every day this past week she had felt her hopes slip. Whether he'd gone or not, Dayne must still be searching for answers. Otherwise he would've contacted her.

The rehearsal dragged on, Katy spending half her time trying to get the kids to focus and the other half calming their fears. Finally, forty-five minutes before they were supposed to wrap up, she walked to the front of the stage and clapped—the special clap that signaled it was time to pay attention.

The kids fell silent and returned the clap.

Outside, the wind howled. "Okay." She held out her hands, trying to bring a extra calm to the group. "Here's what we're going to do. We're finished rehearsing for now."

Two hands shot up, and a redheaded boy shouted, "Rehearsal's supposed to go till nine, and it's only eight-fifteen."

"I know." Katy held her finger up in a sign that meant for the boy to quiet down. "Let me finish first." She pointed to the stairs at the back of the sanctuary. "We're going to go down and watch a Charlie Brown cartoon in the basement until your parents come."

"The basement?" A little girl in the front row stood up. "'Cause there's a terrible tornado like *The Wizard of Oz*, and the church is going to spin off the ground and land on a witch? Is that why, Katy?"

A few of the older kids giggled.

"No, sweetie." Katy smiled at the child. "This is more like a break time, okay?"

Several younger children looked doubtful, and one boy started to cry. But with the help of Rhonda and Krissie, they got all the children to the basement and situated on the floor in front of an oversized television. Katy started the video, and the group quieted down.

Rhonda came to her and whispered, "Good call." She looked toward the stairs with a concerned expression. "If a tornado *does* take the church building to Oz, at least we'll be in the basement."

"Exactly." Katy sat in a chair in the front of the room. She couldn't see the screen very well, but she could see the kids. Anytime one of them started whispering—especially the teens who had taken up places against the back wall—she could give them a look and get them quiet again.

She was checking her watch, praying that the minutes would speed by, when she heard hushed voices at the end of the front row of the group. A redheaded boy was motioning to another boy about his age.

The redhead gave his neighbor a mean look. Then he pointed at him and leaned forward, his eyes on Katy. "Smoking!" He said the word as loud as he could while still whispering. He jabbed his finger three more times in the direction of the boy beside him. "That kid's talking about smoking!"

Katy took a long breath and studied the boy in question. He was a heavy child named Skyler—very heavy. He had round cheeks and several chins, and sometimes he came to practice in a shirt that didn't quite fit him. Skyler was shy and took direction well. Katy often kept an eye on him to make sure the other kids didn't pick on him. So far, so good—until now.

As discreetly as possible, Katy slipped to the floor beside Skyler and looked at him with concern.

Embarrassed, the boy returned her look with wide, fearful eyes.

"Skyler—" Katy kept her voice low so the other kids could still hear the video—"were you talking about smoking?"

The boy gulped twice and gestured to the television. "See that boy there? The one with the smoke around him?"

Katy angled herself so she could see. Skyler was pointing at Pigpen, the Peanuts character who walked in a literal cloud of dirt. "Yes. I see him."

"I was saying that he looks like my mommy because she smokes, and everywhere she goes she has smoke on her. Plus, smoking's bad for her."

Katy's heart melted. She put her hand on Skyler's shoulder. "Honey, that boy on TV doesn't have smoke around him. He has dirt." She wasn't sure what to say next. Skyler's older brother always brought him to CKT, and Katy still hadn't met his mother. "Besides, your mommy probably started smoking a long time ago. Before people knew how bad it was."

"No." Skyler's eyes were big as he shook his head. "She started after she already knew it was bad. And guess what?" This was the most Skyler had said since he'd joined CKT.

"What?"

"She drinks beer too. A lot of beer."

She was about to launch into an explanation about how a person over the age of twenty-one could drink beer and still be okay, but Skyler started in again before she had a chance.

"She drinks two—" he held up two fingers—"six-packs a day. Every day. And she smokes."

Katy didn't know what to do or say. "I'm sorry, Skyler."

"It's okay." He gave her a hint of a shy smile. "She loves me and she loves Jesus." He looked at the television again. "But she looks like that boy up there."

"All right, well—"

Before she could say anything else, he held out his arms and gave her a hug.

When he let go, he looked happier than he had all day. He leaned close so his whisper could be heard only by her. "Guess what else?"

"What?" She had to work to hear him.

"You're invited to my birthday party," he said proudly.

Katy spread her fingers on her chest. "I am?" Her surprise and delight were genuine. "When is it?"

"December." Skyler frowned. "I don't have invitations yet."

"That's okay." Katy bit the inside of her lip so she wouldn't giggle. "You have eight months, honey."

He nodded. "That's what my brother said."

Katy gave the redheaded boy a look that said everything was under control before she returned to her seat.

While the video finished playing, the conversation with Skyler played over in her mind. Their talk stirred up a handful of deep emotions, all of which filled her heart.

First, she was reminded that the kids in her care didn't all come from families like the Flanigans. Christian Kids Theater was a haven, a welcoming place for anyone who loved Jesus and loved theater. Even if the practical side of living out that love wasn't quite where it needed to be.

Also, their talk made her more aware of the shy kids in their mix. Drama programs often attracted the outgoing, over-the-top children. The ones with more confidence than they knew what to do with. But it also attracted the kids who wanted that confidence but had always found themselves on the outside looking in. Kids with difficult home lives and troubled backgrounds.

Kids like Skyler.

God—Katy stared at her lap and closed her eyes for a moment—*thank You for that precious boy, for letting us talk tonight and for using him to make me see—once more—my purpose here. This is where I belong; it's where You've called me. I promise You, Lord, I'll be faithful to these kids until You tell me it's time to move on.*

Daughter . . . I know the plans I have for you.

The whisper was softer even than Skyler's, but she heard it all the same. It was Jeremiah 29:11, her special Scripture, the one that adorned her key chain and the plaque on the wall by her bed: *"I know the plans I have for you," declares the Lord, "plans to prosper you and not to harm you, plans to give you hope and a future."*

Everywhere Katy looked she saw those words these days, and it was easy to take them lightly, to think that God was saying life would be all sunshine and rainbows, good plans and easily answered prayers. What most people didn't realize about that verse was that it came in the midst of other promises—promises from God telling His people that they would also suffer great difficulties. It was what made the Christian life so dynamic. Ultimate hope and peace and joy and redemption, even in a life that would certainly have trials and temptations, tragedies and tough times.

Times like this—when she was so lonely she wondered if God had forgotten about her.

You're here, Lord. I feel You . . . I hear You. Thanks for reminding me with Skyler.

The video ended a few minutes before nine, and Katy had the kids form a circle. They held hands and Tim Reed—who was playing the oldest of the four children who stumble into Narnia in this production—led them in a tender rendition of "I Love You, Lord."

When they reached the end, and the children formed one voice singing to God, asking that He might find joy in what He heard, Katy had no doubt that He would.

Somewhere God was smiling.

It took half an hour for all the kids to leave, and only then did Katy drive home with Bailey and Connor.

"I think it's coming along." Bailey was in the front seat. "Most of the leads know their lines already."

"Yes." Katy kept her eyes on the road. The storm had tapered off, and it wasn't raining anymore. "That'll help over the next few weeks."

"Right, and there's good chemistry onstage." Connor poked his head between the two of them. "I can feel it up there."

"It helps that the White Witch's dwarf is none other than her own brother." Katy tossed him a quick grin. "You're doing great, Connor."

"Thanks."

Katy remembered what Dayne had said about the show. That it had the feeling of something special, something powerful. In fact, twice Alice Stryker had been to rehearsals. More than six months had passed since her daughter was killed in the car accident, the one that had rocked CKT and all of Bloomington. Alice seemed to be changing, growing closer to God, with every passing week. She was still attending the Flanigans' Bible study, and last time Katy saw her, her eyes shone with something that mixed sweet sorrow with unspeakable joy.

"They're coming to the show."

Katy hadn't been sure what Alice meant. "Your family?"

"No." Alice's eyes had grown damp. "The little girl who received Sarah Jo's eyes. The family wanted to stay in touch with me." There was a humility in Alice that hadn't been there before the accident. "They're praying for us."

"And they're bringing their daughter to *Narnia*?" Katy couldn't imagine what that would be like, how she'd feel looking into the eyes of a stranger and knowing they had once belonged to Sarah Jo.

"Yes. They don't want everyone knowing, but they said I could tell you and the leadership team."

Memories of that conversation lifted, and Katy drew a long breath. "Yes, Connor. I think the show's going to be just great."

When they got home, Katy and the kids met Jenny and Jim in the kitchen, and the group talked as they shared a bowl of grapes. They discussed the storm and rehearsal and how the kids wouldn't calm down.

Not until Bailey and Connor had gone to bed and Katy was almost ready to turn in for the night did Jenny give her a suspicious smile. "There's something waiting for you in your room."

"For me?" She stood and gathered her backpack and notebook. "Who's it from?"

"I told her not to look at the card." Jim's tone was light, teasing. "But you know Miss Nosy here."

Jenny gave Katy a mysterious look; then she laughed. "I can't tell. Jim made me promise."

"Okay, then." Katy was curious. Maybe Terrence C. Willow had sent a book on the dangers of cherry garnishes. He'd already e-mailed her a *Time* magazine article on the danger of pop and the likelihood of getting pepto-something-or-other from the rat droppings that collect along the top of pop cans.

Everything about Terrence had become a private joke between Katy and those closest to her—especially Jenny. By the expression on Jenny's face, she could only believe that whatever was in her room, Terrence was somehow behind it.

She waved at Jenny and Jim. "On that note, I'm off to bed."

Jenny looked like she wanted to follow her, but Jim held her back. The couple laughed, and they all said good night.

Katy trudged up the stairs to her apartment over the garage. Friday nights were always the longest—especially with Saturday morning rehearsal just nine hours away. She opened the door and caught her breath.

"What in the world . . . ?" She set her things down on the computer desk to her right and stared at her small round dining table. In the center was a bouquet of long-stemmed red roses, more beautiful and breathtaking than any she'd ever seen. Katy breathed in deeply.

The entire room smelled wonderful.

They couldn't be from Terrence, could they? He'd expressed his interest in dating her, but she'd told him three times already that she was too busy. That was easier than getting into the deeper reason—that she couldn't bear the thought of spending another hour with him.

So who would've sent flowers? Certainly not Dayne. He hadn't even called to say if he'd gone to Mexico. Were they from a parent, maybe? Someone in CKT? She took slow steps until she was close enough to see the little white envelope positioned in a plastic holder and stuck discreetly near the center of the arrangement.

She pulled a slender card from inside and began to read:

Katy . . . Mexico was amazing!

Her eyes closed, and she held the card close to her heart. They were from Dayne! He'd gone to see his friend after all. She blinked and kept reading:

Miss you more than you know. We need to talk face-to-face.
Maybe at the trial, since I'm working every day until then. You
were wrong, by the way. I do love you.

Katy's heart pounded in her chest, and tears clouded her eyes. She read the words over and over, her mind swirling. Not so much because of the roses or what he'd said about missing her and wanting to talk. Not even because of his words of love. But because of what he'd said at the bottom of the card, a single sentence that said simply this:

PS. I once was lost but now am found.

CHAPTER TWENTY-ONE

BY TEN THE NEXT MORNING the Baxters were spread out at their favorite spot on the shores of Lake Monroe.

They had a group of four picnic tables and more than a dozen folding chairs. Ashley sat in the most comfortable one and watched Landon and Cole chasing each other through the shallow water. Not far away Erin and Kari helped the little ones make sand sculptures, while Brooke and Hayley took slow steps—hand in hand—along the sand. Their dad and Luke and the rest of the group played a wild rule-free game of Ultimate Frisbee.

Ashley breathed in and savored the smell of spring.

Next to her she had country music playing softly on a small boom box, but the voices of her family were the best song of all. Storms were forecast for this afternoon, but the morning had dawned bright and warm, the skies bluer than any of them imagined. Ashley figured it was a sign. Whatever storms lay ahead, however things played out later when their father told her siblings the truth about their oldest brother, they'd get through it.

Because that's what the Baxter family did.

This sunny morning smack in the middle of multiple storm systems reminded Ashley of Lamentations 3. Those were terrible times for God's people, but in the middle of dozens of dark and stormy verses was a promise: His mercies are new every morning . . . great is His faithfulness.

Ashley studied the brilliant sky from her chair at the top of the hill. Surely, God was giving her mother a window. The way her dad had prayed.

Lord, tell her we're okay. Ashley looked at Brooke, watched the way her smile lit up the beach. *Tell her Hayley's walking now. And that we miss her so much.*

Something by Rascal Flatts was playing on the station, but there was a sudden static sound and the serious voice of an announcer. "We interrupt this program to bring you a special announcement. A tornado watch is in effect for the rest of the day for all southern Indiana counties." He rattled off a list, including Monroe County, where Bloomington was located. "We now return you to our regular programming."

The first pain hit just as the music started again. It began as an ache in her lower back but quickly shot a burning tightness across her midsection. She drew a sharp breath, closed her eyes, and pressed her hand to her middle. The pain worsened with every heartbeat, then leveled off. After ten seconds or so, it faded completely.

Ashley exhaled, opening her eyes in time to see Landon jogging up the grassy hill. "Hey." He dropped a football near her feet and stooped so he was level with her. "Everything okay?"

She smiled at him. Were they that closely connected that she could have pain and he would feel it across the beach? "I'm fine." She still had her hand on her abdomen. "It was a contraction." A frown tugged at her lips. "At least I think it was. With Cole everything happened so fast, I can't remember having labor."

"But the baby's not due for a couple of weeks."

She put her hands on his shoulders and grinned at him. "The doctor told me it could be anytime, remember?"

Landon looked anxious, his eyes wider than usual. "I know but not now . . . the baby needs this last week or two."

"Because of the reunion, you mean?"

"The reunion . . . the storms . . . the fact that I'm not ready." He sounded breathless, every bit the first-time father.

Ashley laughed. "I'll ask her to please hold off."

"Her?" Landon crawled closer on his knees and took Ashley's face in his hands. "Since when is this child a her?"

"I don't know." Ashley gave him a teasing look. It felt wonderful having him so close, breathing the smell of him. She leaned in and kissed him, remembering all the times years ago when she'd wanted to do this and couldn't. "I love you; do you know that?"

"I love you too." The expression on his face made it clear that he'd forgotten his question. He worked his fingers into her hair and cradled the back of her head as he took the initiative this time.

"Ahem." Luke gave Landon a light kick. "It's a public beach, you two."

Landon pulled back and chuckled. "She's trying to seduce me."

"Looks like it's working." Luke dropped to the sandy grass nearby and stretched out his legs. "Reagan said you looked like you were in pain."

"Wow." Ashley still had her hands on Landon's shoulders. "I must really be loved. One contraction and the whole family's ready to take me to the hospital."

Luke's eyebrows lifted. "So it was? You mean . . . you're in labor?"

"No, it's Braxton Hicks. False contractions." Ashley waved at Reagan and gave her a thumbs-up. "Go tell your pretty wife everything's fine."

Luke bounded to his feet and jogged back down the hill.

"Uh-uh, Ash . . . not so easy." Landon slid a finger along the length of her bare arm.

"What?" She found a mock innocent look for him and batted her eyelashes.

"You think I forgot, right?" Landon brought his face close to hers. "We're having a girl? Is that what you're trying to tell me?"

She couldn't make him wonder another minute. "No, silly." She closed the distance between them and brushed her nose against his. "I called the baby her so she won't get a complex. What with you and Cole calling her a boy all this time."

"And what if we're right?"

"Then this is the last time I can call him a her now, isn't it?"

They both laughed.

"Have I told you how beautiful you are? How you've never looked prettier since I've known you?"

Her feet were swollen, and freckles had broken out across her face and chest. She was carrying extra weight, and she could barely walk, let alone run along the beach. But in that moment, with Landon looking into rooms of her heart that belonged only to him, Ashley believed him. "Thank you."

"I've never been happier in my life, Ashley." He stood and grinned. "If you could get what I'm feeling onto a canvas, it'd sell for a million dollars."

"I can only try." She had stopped painting in the final months of her pregnancy, but she'd taken pictures instead. Sometimes she could capture through the eye of a camera what would take her an entire week with a paintbrush. Her favorites—photos of Cole and Landon and life at the Baxter house—were placed in a special box to use as inspiration for future paintings when her baby was a few months old and she would find her way back to her easel.

"Hey—" Landon took a few backward steps—"I'm gonna go play with Cole, but yell at me if you have more pains, okay?"

"Okay." She could feel her smile all the way to the depths of her soul. "Hey, the radio said we're under a tornado watch."

Landon looked up at the blue sky. "Looks like we still have time."

"That's what I thought."

As he ran off to join the others, a second contraction hit. But it was no stronger or lengthier than the last one. This time she didn't close her eyes. Instead she did her best to hide the pain.

And that's how she treated the irregular false contractions for the next two hours, through their picnic lunch, while she and Landon took a walk down the beach and back, and as clouds began gathering in the distance. Never did the pains get noticeably harder, and as time passed she was able to hide them better. When Landon asked if she was feeling more contractions, she kept her answer low-key.

"It's nothing much. Just false labor. My body's getting ready for the big day."

Landon was wary, but he left her side long enough to join the others for a final hour of playtime near the water. Though the kids claimed that the lake was cold, they enjoyed splashing and chasing each other along the sand.

Ashley was back in her chair, watching the others, when she noticed her dad sitting a dozen yards away, quiet and pensive.

"Dad—" she patted the chair next to her—"come sit by me."

He smiled at her, stood slowly, and crossed the distance between them. He looked better than he had the year after Mom died. Probably because he was getting out more, taking his daily walks, and making time to work on the property. She dismissed the possibility that his friendship with Elaine Denning had anything to do with his improved appearance.

"How're you feeling?" He stopped in front of her, his hands on his hips. "Luke said something about a contraction?"

"I'm fine." She made a face. "They're way too irregular to be anything serious. False labor, I'm sure."

Concern shone on her father's face. "Are you sure?"

Ashley smiled. "Definitely."

"Well, keep track. You're early, right?"

"Two weeks."

"So, not really." He gave her a look that showed his excitement. "How wonderful if you had the baby this week while everyone's here."

"Except I don't want to spend the time in the hospital."

"You'd be out in twelve hours." He settled into the chair beside her. "Landon must be so happy."

"He practically glows in the dark." Ashley grinned and looked down the hill to where Landon was standing with Cole on one side, Maddie and Jessie and Hayley and Clarisse and Chloe on the other. He was picking up rocks and showing the kids how to skip them across the water.

"Just one at a time." They could hear his voice, kind and gentle, teaching them the age-old skill. "Careful so you don't throw them anywhere but at the water."

"Hmm." Her dad watched Landon, his eyes wistful. "You know what I sort of hoped?"

She turned to him. "What?"

He gazed at the men mixed in with the others playing along the sand. "I hoped your older brother would be something like Landon or Ryan, something like Luke."

They hadn't talked about the oldest Baxter sibling for the two weeks leading up to the reunion. Every time Ashley wanted to ask, she'd changed her mind. Her dad had told her she'd be the first to know, and when he didn't mention anything, she figured his last efforts with her brother had amounted to nothing. "You never heard from him?"

"No." Regret colored his tone. "I wrote to him. Sent him photos of everyone in the family. Nothing."

Ashley let that thought sink in. She watched her family running and laughing on the shore, watched how the lake rippled and sparkled with the last bit of sunshine as the clouds moved in. Maddie and Jessie now sat on either side of Hayley, with Chloe and Clarisse finishing off the circle. The five girls were building a sand castle, clearly in competition with Landon, Ryan, Cole, and Tommy, making one a few feet away. Erin and Brooke and Kari sat with three of the babies on a blanket twenty yards off, lost in conversation. At a table nearby, Sam and Peter played chess. Luke and Reagan sat closer to the shore.

Wasn't there some place in the mix where their older brother could fit in? Even for a onetime visit? Whoever he was, he didn't know what he was missing. She frowned at her dad, still not sure she should ask. "You're telling everyone tonight, right?"

He didn't hesitate. "Yes. After dinner."

She had more questions, like whether he'd be able to mention the guy's name now or whether it was still important to keep his identity a secret. But before she could ask, heavy raindrops began falling.

John looked up. "Storm's coming." He stood and cupped his hands around his mouth. "Okay, everyone. Let's pack up."

At the same time, another song on the radio was cut short. "We interrupt this program to bring you a special announcement. Weather officials have announced a tornado warning for several counties in southern Indiana." He rattled off a list of names, and again Monroe was among them.

An arrow of fear pierced Ashley. The tornado watch hadn't seemed too ominous under blue skies. But now . . . a tornado warning? She tried to listen over the suddenly loud pounding of her heart.

"We repeat, conditions have formed a tornado that has been sighted in this area. Stay tuned for more information as it comes in. This tornado warning will be in effect until five o'clock this evening. Please stay tuned to your local forecast for updates as they are available."

In the far distance, a siren began to wail. Slow and mournful, the sound was unmistakable and known by everyone who lived in the part of the country known as Tornado Alley. It was a tornado siren, the alarm that confirmed what the radio had just announced. A tornado warning was in effect. Everyone should take cover.

How crazy was this? Tornado watches were common this time of year, but a warning? When they'd had beautiful weather all morning? Ashley watched her siblings and their spouses stand a little straighter, pausing briefly to listen to the distant siren. Then—the way people in Indiana were used to doing—they moved quickly, packing things and hurrying children to the vans in a manner that was calm and efficient.

Landon was at her side. The rain was coming harder now, and already his hair and shirt were wet. "Don't panic." His eyes were bright with humor and a hint of fear.

A single laugh slipped from her throat. "You, either."

"No, really." He glanced at the sky, folding chairs and blankets as he talked. "Warnings happen every week around here."

She stood and collapsed the chair she'd been sitting in. "I know, Landon." The teasing felt good. It was better than being scared to death. "I live here too, remember?"

"Right." He was breathing faster than usual. "And you're not in labor, are you, Ash? Tell me you're not in labor."

"I'm not in labor." She handed him her chair and picked up a bag of leftover chips. She felt a sheepish grin lift the corners of her mouth. "At least I don't think so."

"Great." He set the chairs on the closest ice chest and heaved the entire load into his arms. "My wife goes into labor just as tornadoes are spotted coming our way."

"Just don't get called in to work."

Landon groaned and headed down the hill. "God . . . get us through this." He looked over his shoulder. "Cole, come on. Let's get going."

Despite the chaos and commotion around her, Ashley was

touched by Landon's concern. Here he was, a big strapping firefighter, a guy who had spent nearly three months cleaning up the debris at Ground Zero while looking for the body of his firefighting friend, and now he was coming undone over the idea of contractions and tornado warnings.

She grabbed two blankets and the food bag and followed Landon. Halfway down the hill she realized it had been nearly thirty minutes since she'd had any contractions. Definitely false labor. One less thing to worry about. It was pouring now, the drops so big they stung her shoulders.

Luke ran up from behind her. "Ashley, I'll get that."

She stopped and handed the large bag to her brother.

Kari ushered Cole down the hill toward the vehicles.

Landon dropped off one load in the back of his Durango and jogged back toward Ashley. He took the blankets from her and looped his arm through hers. "You okay?"

"Definitely. No more pains."

"Good."

They made it down the hill—Landon on one side, Luke on the other. There were no pains, but she felt nauseous, and suddenly she remembered that she'd felt that way before Cole came too. Landon helped her into the Durango and followed both vans out of the parking lot.

Ashley wasn't sure, but far against the horizon one of the clouds looked as if it were trying to form a funnel. "Exactly how bad is this storm?"

"Bad." Small beads of sweat dotted Landon's brow. He looked in the rearview mirror at Cole and Tommy. Luke and Reagan and Malin were in the back. He could see the concern on the faces of Luke and Reagan, but they were busy in conversation with the kids.

Ashley put her hand protectively on her protruding stomach. *Please, God . . . not now, not tonight. We need to take shelter, Father. Be with us.*

Landon was quiet, intent as they drove to the Baxter house. Lightning and thunder moved in, and rain fell in sheets that made it almost impossible to see the road.

When they finally pulled into the Baxter driveway, Ashley heard Reagan sigh. "Thank God we're home."

"I agree. This is one wicked storm." Luke sat up straighter, his hand on Ashley's shoulder. "You okay, Sis?"

"I'm good." She covered his hand with her own. "At least we're back."

They gathered the children and whatever food needed to be refrigerated and dashed into the house, while everyone from the vans did the same thing. Once they were inside, the storm seemed to hit even harder.

Erin and Reagan and Kari put the younger children down for naps, and the adults gathered around the dining-room table, with the kids playing in the next room, the way they had the night before.

An hour later the storm abated. And Ashley's nausea seemed to fade also.

She and Landon held hands, and silently she thanked God. Not just because the storm had passed, but because the labor pains she felt at the lake had been false. This was definitely not the day to have a baby. Especially after the radio made another announcement.

The most serious tornadic conditions in years were only a few hours away and headed straight for Bloomington.

CHAPTER TWENTY-TWO

DAYNE WAS LISTENING to a talk station, jogging along Malibu Beach when he heard the news. Some of the worst tornadoes of the decade were brewing in the Midwest, most of them centered in southern Indiana.

He slowed his pace and looked at the sky. It was already six o'clock in Bloomington, so whatever storms were forming, the people he cared about must already know the news.

Three girls in bikinis were walking toward him. One of them pointed at him and said something to her friends, and the three of them picked up their pace.

Not today. He increased the volume on his radio and doubled his pace, refusing eye contact as he passed them. For half a minute, they turned around and tried to keep up, and from the corner of his eye he saw them waving, heard them screaming. Other people sitting along the beach also took notice.

But eventually the girls wore out, disappointed and out of breath. They never could've caught him and neither could any of the other beachgoers. He was used to running the beach, miles at a time and faster than the average fan.

Finally, he slowed to a walk. When his heart rate was back to normal, he sat on a dry patch of sand, pulled off his T-shirt, and looked out at the ocean.

Life had been good since he'd come home from Mexico.

Dayne could feel the difference, sense the presence of God's Spirit inside him. He and Bob talked every day—sometimes for an hour. He had questions about his future and what he was supposed to do with the feelings he had for Katy Hart. With every ounce of his desire, he wanted to pack his things and move to Bloomington. But that wasn't possible—not now. Maybe not ever.

Bob's advice was consistent. "Talk to God about it, yes. But more than that, wait for His answer. If she's the one . . . when the time's right, God will show you. He won't leave you in the dark—not if you're asking Him for wisdom."

Dayne had been praying about the situation as if his life depended on it. So far, he sensed no real answer or direction, and if Bob was right, that meant he was supposed to wait. Which he needed to do anyway, because he was too busy with work to think about going to Bloomington. Even for a weekend.

He spotted a sailboat on the horizon and watched it for a while. His mind drifted, going over the details of the past couple of weeks and especially a conversation he'd had with his agent, Chris Kane. They'd met in Chris's Hollywood office, a glittering place on the twenty-third floor of the Bank of America Building. A wall of windows behind his desk offered a view of Hollywood Hills.

"Things good for you, Dayne?"

The room smelled of leather and expensive cologne. Dayne gripped the arms of his chair and gave his agent an easy smile. "Looks like I'm making you rich enough."

Chris raised an eyebrow and lobbed back at him. "Looks like I'm making *you* rich enough, you mean."

"Whatever." Dayne didn't care about the money or fame. Not anymore. He still loved acting, loved bringing a story to life on camera. But he was ready to walk away from everything that went with it. "I need to know my obligations, how many films I'm committed to."

Chris was a deliberate man, best in the business, the top agent in Hollywood. Everything he did was well thought out, intended to elevate Dayne in the way he was viewed and admired, the way he was sought after. The price he drew for a single film. Chris Kane controlled all of it.

He had leaned his elbows on his desk and given Dayne a strange look. "Ready to go to contract again—is that what you're saying?"

Dayne could tell by his agent's tone that the man knew full well that wasn't what he was saying. He'd chuckled, keeping the atmosphere as light as possible. "You know what I did last week, Chris?"

"Watched your old films, looking for ways to improve?" His words were slow, calculated.

It occurred to Dayne why some of the people in the business found Chris a little cold. "Wrong." He felt his grin drop off. "I went to Mexico."

"Oh." Chris took a paper clip from a container on his desk. He began to work it into a straight line. "I sort of hoped you'd go to the Bahamas with Angie. She invited you, didn't she?"

"She did." Dayne nodded slowly. "Yes, she did."

"You've been absent in the tabs lately." Chris leaned back. He was still working the paper clip. "A trip to the Bahamas with Angie would've made the cover of every rag in town."

"Yes. Exactly."

"If you didn't take Angie's invitation, what'd you do in Mexico?" A hint of frustration had crept into his agent's voice.

"I accepted a different invitation." He smiled bigger this time, complimenting himself for his play on words. "I have a friend in Mexico City, a guy I went to school with."

"Mexico City?" Chris frowned. "Not many senoritas and sunny beaches there."

"No." Dayne had gradually grown more serious. He wanted to keep the air between them light, but what he had to say was important. "My buddy's a missionary. He and his wife. They're amazing people."

"Missionary . . . meaning, *Christian* missionaries?"

"Yes." Dayne listened to his agent with fresh ears. "Christian missionaries."

This was something Bob Asher had warned him about. He'd get back to Hollywood, and no one would understand. Christianity represented something foreign and dangerous to people in Dayne's business. Hollywood saw Christians as the religious right, supporters of President Bush, close-minded bigots without any sense of political awareness.

Dayne didn't know about any of that. He'd simply handed over the reins of his existence to God, and in the process his entire life felt whole. But that wasn't how his agent was bound to hear his news.

"So . . ." Chris waved his broken paper clip in the air. "What did you do . . . get born again—or whatever it's called?"

Okay, God, give me the words. Dayne cleared his throat. "Yeah, I did." He nodded, giving his agent the easy grin that people around the world had come to love. "No brainwashing or anything. Just a surrender. Time for God to take over."

His agent froze, unblinking. "You're serious?"

"I'm still me." Dayne lifted his hands and gave a nervous chuckle. "Don't flip out."

Chris leaned across his desk. The paper clip fell to the floor. "You haven't told anyone, have you? the press or anything?"

"Of course not." Dayne gave him a strange look. "It's not like that."

But his agent had acted differently the rest of the meeting, trying to talk Dayne into going clubbing with Angie and some of the cast from his current film and telling him he needed to keep his image sharp. "People want their Hollywood stars edgy, Matthews. Not churchy."

The comment had stayed with Dayne every day since.

He squinted at the way the sun shone against the ocean water now. The place where he was sitting was far enough down the beach that there were no other people nearby. Even his house was half a mile away. The privacy felt wonderful—even though the paparazzi couldn't be far behind.

Edgy? Meaning the only way he could maintain his star status was by staying out until three in the morning and having his picture in the magazines with any one of a dozen starlets? That's what should define him?

Well . . . it was too late for that. He had God in his life now. The only relationship that was going to take him into the life he wanted was the one he was starting with his Creator. Forget the tabloids. If they truly weren't interested in him, then so be it.

He was finishing his thought when he heard the rapid click of a camera nearby. *Yeah, Chris Kane,* he wanted to say, *they've completely lost interest in me.* He looked up, feigning boredom, his grin in place automatically. "Come on, guys . . . my backside's never my best."

The photographers didn't know what to do with him. Half the time he was brilliant at evading them, and other times he practically invited them up for snacks.

He turned toward the sound of the clicking. "You can come out."

"You're no fun." It was the big guy, the one who had been there the day Katy fled the parking lot. "And you're wrong. The girls love your backside." He shuffled out from the bushes and held his hands out in surrender. "Okay, who was she, Dayne? The girl who ran that night."

"I told you. She was an actress." The paparazzi still didn't know about Katy. If they did, her picture would've already made the magazines.

"We talked about it." The photog came a few steps closer. "Everyone thinks she's from out of town."

Dayne shrugged. "It's a mystery, I guess."

The man snapped another dozen photos. "How am I supposed to make a living off a picture like that? Dayne Matthews sitting on the beach—alone?"

"That's your job." Dayne had talked with the guy long enough. No matter what he pretended, the paparazzi were bloodsuckers. They'd chased Princess Diana to her death, and they'd do the same to him and his colleagues, given the chance. He stood, grabbed his shirt, brushed the sand from his shorts, tipped the bill of his baseball cap at the guy, and gave him one last smile.

The photographer snapped pictures until Dayne was too far down the beach to hear the sound. Chris Kane was wrong. As long as Dayne was making hit movies and maintaining his six-pack abs, as long as he looked tanned and toned without a T-shirt, the paparazzi would put his mug in the magazines.

Even if he was a Christian.

Dayne jogged another five minutes and then—with the photographer out of sight—he slowed to a walk. With all his heart he wished his agent was right. Because if there really was a danger that the paparazzi were losing interest, then his freedom might actually be achievable.

It happened to the older guys eventually. The media lost interest in following their every move. But he was just hitting his prime. That might not happen to him for another decade, and by then . . . well, by then the Baxter family would be ten more years removed from ever knowing him. And Katy Hart? She'd probably be married with three kids.

The question he'd asked his agent was the only one that really mattered to him. How many movies were left on his contract? The answer was something Chris finally gave him before Dayne left his office that afternoon. Five. He was obligated to star in five more films with his current studio—each for more money than anyone had a right to earn. Altogether, the commitment would take nearly three years.

More than two more years of living and working in LA, being chased by photographers, who watch his every move, every expression, looking for even the slightest bit of dirt. He'd asked Chris about the timing, if there was a way to space the movies out so he could spend half a year somewhere else.

The answer was no, of course. The studio wanted two hit films a year starring Dayne Matthews. A hot star was a busy star, and if Dayne wasn't hot, the films he starred in wouldn't be either. The formula was pretty simple.

He would go home, spend an hour on his balcony reading his Bible. The one Katy Hart had given him. He hadn't heard from her since he'd sent her the flowers. But she knew about the change in his life, the understanding he'd reached about God. There was no reason to badger her. Besides, he would see her in a few weeks when the trial started.

Dayne dropped to the sand and leaned back on his elbows. The setting sun burned away what was left of the fog, and the warmth felt good on his stomach. The trial was something he prayed about often, every time the thought hit him. No matter what his legal team did, they wouldn't be able to keep Katy Hart's name from the media. Her part in the trial would become public record.

Depending on how deep the paparazzi wanted to dig, there was no limit to the type of stories they could write. He shuddered at the thought. *God . . . protect her. Protect the friendship between us.*

Sometimes when Dayne prayed, he could almost sense an answer, hear the small whisper of God's response echoing somewhere in his soul. But now he only had the overwhelming knowledge that God was here . . . with him, inside him. And if that was all the answer he ever received again in his life, it would be enough. He remembered the tornadoes then, the storms that were supposed to hit Indiana tonight.

It was Saturday, so Katy would've had *Narnia* practice this morning—the story with the message that had frightened Dayne before his trip to Mexico City. He smiled and sat up. He needed to get home, but he couldn't shake the sudden strange feeling in his heart, an uneasiness he couldn't explain.

Storms came through the Midwest all the time. This night wouldn't be any different . . . or would it? Not long ago he'd watched a special on TV about tornadoes, about how an F-5 or an F-4 could level a town. Drop it to the ground, so that all that was left of the town's existence were piles and piles of rubble.

What if a tornado like that went through Bloomington?

He had the urgent feeling that he needed to talk to Katy, maybe call her when he got home. Or maybe not. Maybe this was God's way of reminding him to pray, not just for her but for everyone in Bloomington who mattered to him. But not here, not on the beach with paparazzi probably closing in on him again.

He slipped his shirt on and began jogging toward his house. If he could will it, he'd be there now, in Bloomington, taking cover with the rest of them. In fact, he'd be at the Flanigans' house, talking with Katy and Jenny and Jim and the kids and perhaps even making plans to visit the Baxters.

Thinking of his biological family always raised the same questions. Would they ever connect? Could there ever be a time when his presence in their lives wouldn't ruin things for them? He jogged faster, pushing himself until his sides heaved.

Not until he was home, not until he was out on his deck with his Bible in his hands did he do the thing he was dying to do.

He bowed his head and prayed with all his heart for the people he loved in Bloomington—people he might never have in his life, but people who mattered to him more than anyone or anything else. He prayed that they would be safe and that they'd find shelter tonight.

No matter how terrible the storm about to descend on them.

CHAPTER TWENTY-THREE

⟨⟩

TORNADOES WERE DROPPING all over southern Indiana.

John Baxter had kept the battery-operated radio nearby, and when the tornado warnings came again he made the decision. Everyone would move to the basement. They could stay there and play board games, and if the lights went out, they could use flashlights and keep the kids calm.

As soon as the decision was made, his kids snapped into action. Kari and Erin and Brooke gathered food for the downstairs refrigerator, and the guys moved the cribs and high chairs to the basement. The big kids made a number of trips down with sleeping bags and blankets and pillows—in case they all had to spend the night. When that was set up, the guys moved a number of cots down. Landon was concerned that Ashley have a place to stretch out, a way to get comfortable.

Overall the atmosphere was calm and controlled. But the news coming through the radio was not encouraging. Tornadoes had left a path of devastation in a town just twenty miles south of them, and more were expected to touch down in the next few hours. It was a phenomenon weather experts called an outbreak. Dozens of tornadoes spawned from a single series of storms. People were being told that conditions were ripe for a major twister, an F-3 or an F-4. The warnings were repeated every few minutes.

John hadn't stopped praying.

It wasn't until they were all safely in the basement that the wind began howling in earnest. Minutes later the electricity went out. His kids were smart; they engaged their children in games and conversation, but even by the glow of half a dozen large flashlights, he could see the fear in their eyes. They'd spent time in the basement during tornado season before—but tonight's warnings seemed more ominous than anything they'd ever faced before.

They all had places to sit, either on the old sofas already in the basement or on the cots. The younger children were asleep except for Malin. Reagan was trying to get her to quiet down by pacing along one wall of the room, giving her a bottle.

At one point, Luke came up to John, his voice low so the others wouldn't hear it. "Any updates?"

"There're tornadoes everywhere. They've spotted four in Bloomington alone."

Luke looked around the basement. "Are we . . . are we safe here?"

"Yes." John had no doubts. "A tornado could tear the house from the foundation, and still we'd be okay." He thought back to when he and Elizabeth built the house. The door leading to the downstairs was stronger than usual, a storm door. But it was the one at the bottom of the stairs that would save them in an F-5 tornado. It was made of steel, and it bolted in six places to steel posts on either side. John felt himself relax just thinking about it. "Your mother and I built this basement to withstand any tornado."

"Good." Luke breathed a sigh, and relief filled his voice. "What about Ashley? Any more labor pains?"

"She hasn't mentioned any."

"Let's pray that baby holds off. At least until the storms pass."

"I am." John gave his son a troubled smile. "Believe me, I am."

Time passed slowly. The big kids settled in finally, hunkering into their sleeping bags and falling asleep while their parents whispered reassuring words to them, patted their backs, and stroked their foreheads.

By ten o'clock, the radio announcer confirmed that at least two more tornadoes had touched down in Bloomington.

A moment later the news got worse. Landon made his way around the sleeping children and took hold of John's arm. "She's in labor, Dad. She didn't want me to say anything until she was sure."

The doctor in John came to life, pushing his fears aside. "Let's keep her calm." He walked a few feet to the nearest wall and the small window well. Through it he could see the trees bent nearly in half and lightning zigzagging across the dark sky. He could hear the wind screaming through the branches. John looked at Landon, his voice quiet. "We aren't going anywhere. Not in this storm."

Landon's face was tight, his expression worried. "What are we supposed to do? I don't want her to have the baby here."

"Listen—" John took hold of Landon's shoulder—"you're a trained medic. I'm a doctor. Brooke and Peter too. Combined we've delivered hundreds of babies."

For the first time in half a minute, Landon drew a breath. "True." Alarm flashed in his eyes. "But that's at a hospital. Here in the basement? We can't have her deliver here."

John cast another look at the storm outside. "We can't have her deliver out there either."

"So what do we do?"

"Landon, you already know the answer." John heard the calm in his own voice, felt himself relying on a power far greater than anything he might've possessed.

For a moment Landon looked unsure. But then slowly peace returned to his expression. They would do the only thing they could do. They would pray. It was then that John heard a crackling on his radio. He moved the few steps to the box and held it to his ear.

The news was still worse, bigger even than Landon's announcement that Ashley was in labor. An F-4 tornado had been spotted on the outskirts of Bloomington. If the announcer was right, they were about to find out if the storm door would hold the way it was supposed to.

The twister was headed straight for them.

❧

Ashley knew she was in trouble, both her and the baby.

While the winds outside built and the house above them shook, her contractions came at her full force. Landon was timing them, and so far they were twelve minutes apart. That part wasn't bad, but they were lasting nearly a minute each, and even between pains Ashley couldn't catch her breath. The experience with Cole had been nothing like this—at least she didn't remember it this way.

She lay on one of the cots and clutched Landon's hand, blowing out, trying hard to empty her lungs so she could take a full drink of air. "Why . . . why am I . . . so out of breath?"

"Honey, it's the pain. Sometimes it can do that." Landon was doing all he could. Every minute or so he took her pulse, and even now he seemed to be watching her for signs. "I'll be right back."

He went to her father, and the two spoke in whispers. But at least once Ashley heard the words *high blood pressure* and *racing heart*. She willed herself to be calm. She didn't need either of them to tell her what the next step should be. If they were worried about high blood pressure and a racing heart, then it was time to take her to the hospital.

But the sounds outside were like something from a horror film, creaking and groaning and pounding. Sounds she'd never heard in all her life in Bloomington. Whatever was going on with her body, she knew they couldn't go to the hospital now.

Landon and her father returned to her side. Her father checked her vital signs.

"Hang in there, Ash," Landon said. "Please . . ."

"I am." Another contraction hit. She tightened, her back lifting off the cot as she tried to survive the knifelike pain slicing through her body. When it was over, she felt a rush of panic. She couldn't catch her breath, not a single one. "Help me . . . Landon, help."

He squeezed her hand and leaned over her. "Breathe out, little breaths."

"I . . . I can't."

"Father God . . . we need You now . . . please!" The intensity of his words told her just how worried he was.

Again she considered that maybe this was more than a difficult delivery. Maybe she and the baby were facing a life-or-death situation. She couldn't bear the thought. She wanted to grow old with Landon, live a full life of raising their family and watching their kids become adults. She wanted what her parents had, what dear sweet Irvel from Sunset Hills had with Hank, her lifelong love—decades and decades of memories, enough to last into life's very darkest midnight.

God . . . help me. Hold me! I don't want to die!

Landon was still praying, his voice urgent. "Calm Ashley, Lord. Help her breathe. Right now, I beg You."

Kari and Brooke and Erin must've heard him, because she noticed that they'd gathered with their dad, holding hands and praying. She made a circle with her lips and pushed out the smallest bit of air.

"That's it, Ash . . . blow out. You have to blow out." Landon hovered over her, his eyes more serious than she'd ever seen them. "God, help her . . . please."

She could feel her heart racing inside her. In the background the wailing wind reached another level of intensity. It no longer sounded like a storm but more like a freight train bearing down on them. Ashley wasn't sure if it was her contractions or her fear that was making it so hard to breathe, but she closed her eyes.

Focus. God, give me Your peace.

And then, despite her terror, she heard His voice—still and silent yet louder than the wind and storm combined. *Daughter, I am with you. Do not be anxious about anything. Peace I leave. My peace I give you.*

For the first time in four minutes, Ashley felt herself fully exhale, felt the supernatural peace flood her body, and felt the air slowly filling her lungs. "There." She wanted to shout for joy. "I got a breath."

"Thank You, God." Landon breathed the words against her skin. He gently kissed her forehead, his concern not one bit less than before. "Keep breathing out, Ash. Please."

"It's the Lord, Landon." She could sense Him. "He's here. Everything's going to be okay."

They held on that way as the sound of destruction filled the air outside. Her contractions were getting closer together, and she heard Landon and her father talking. If they couldn't get her to the hospital soon, they might have to stage the delivery here. In the basement. With twenty people gathered around.

The sound of breaking glass mixed with the screaming wind and pounding thunder. The kids were awake now, sitting up and whimpering. Then—in a way that seemed impossible—the intensity grew.

Kari and Ryan had their two children and Cole between them. In between the blinding white-hot contractions, amidst efforts at exhaling, Ashley caught glimpses of him.

Cole looked scared to death, and each time she looked his eyes were glued to hers. He mouthed the word *Mommy.* Once he even held his little hand out to her. *"Mommy."*

Kari rubbed his back, and now and then she would lean close and whisper something in his ear.

Outside the wind sounded like a terrible monster, an evil presence. There was a loud crash, and Maddie cried out, "Jesus . . . help us!"

Next to her Hayley's eyes were big. Brooke and Peter had the girls tucked close between them. "It's okay. Jesus is with us." Brooke breathed the promise again and again.

Ashley let the words wash over her weary body. *Jesus is with us . . . Jesus is with us.*

All four of Erin and Sam's girls were crying openly now, and Sam worked next to Erin to keep them calm.

Just as the next contraction hit, the house above them seemed to shudder. More breaking glass, more thuds and crashes.

"Mommy . . . it's the end of the world!" Cole jumped up and ran to her and Landon. "Daddy, I'm scared!"

"Cole . . ." Ashley ran her tongue along her lips. They were so dry, same as her mouth and her throat.

"Son, it's okay." Landon was still hovered over her. He kept one hand on her wrist, and he placed the other over Cole's shoulder.

Cole buried his head against Landon's chest. "Why won't God make it stop?"

Across the room, Ashley heard her dad's voice rise above the others. "Jesus . . . we beg You to keep us safe. We thank You—" another crash shook the house—"for being with us. We need You, Father."

The entire family seemed to brace itself, as if the worst was just ahead. Another pain gripped Ashley's middle, making her dizzy from the way it seized her.

Then, as quickly as the storm had descended on them, it stopped. The wind and rain, the lightning and thunder—all of it settled into utter, eerie silence. The only sound was that of the children crying softly, the adults making quiet reassuring sounds.

Across the room, her father let out a sigh. "Thank You, Jesus."

Ashley glanced at him. He lifted the radio close to his ear.

Between contractions, Ashley sensed that her siblings were finally able to calm the kids. But she could just barely hear her father whispering to Luke. The news was horrific. The F-4 had turned and headed east, just missing downtown. Another tornado—an F-3, weather officials were guessing—had gone through the Clear Creek area of town.

"What was that?" Ashley wasn't able to say much. Her breathing was fast and irregular.

"Everything's okay," her father answered quickly. He was trying to keep the news from her, trying not to upset her further.

Landon still had Cole pressed up close to him. Finally Cole felt safe enough to return to his sleeping bag and his place near Kari and Ryan.

Landon stayed beside Ashley, talking her through each contraction, praying over her, and helping her stay calm enough to keep breathing. But the contractions were too close to wait another minute.

Finally her father joined them. "How far apart?"

"Seven minutes. Six and a half, maybe." Landon's voice was strained, his words clipped. "I'd like to take her if you think it's safe."

"We're still in a watch situation, but the worst of it's passed." John looked weary, beaten. "It's after midnight, and the phones are out. I tried calling the hospital. There's no telling what things are like there, but I think we should go. It's bound to be better than waiting here."

Ashley listened to their conversation, listened and prayed while another contraction took hold of her body. No matter how calm she felt or how strongly she sensed God's presence, she agreed with both of them. "Please—" she was breathless again— "let's go."

They got her to her feet, and each of her sisters whispered

from the shadows that they'd be praying for her. Ashley felt weak and dizzy. Her father unbolted the storm door, and they made their way up the stairs by flashlight. She was sure they were all terrified about what they would find.

Her father creaked the top door open. He stepped inside and shone his flashlight around the living room and kitchen. "Amazing."

"It's still here." Landon had his arm around her, supporting her almost completely. "Come on, Ash. Let's get you to the car."

The Baxter house was still standing! On the way through the kitchen toward the door, Ashley was shocked at how little damage there was. Despite hours of furious tornado-force winds, the rooms were intact, the walls still holding firm. Only several windows were broken. When they reached the garage, they saw that a ten-foot section of the roof had been stripped away.

"We'll find more damage in the morning." John hurried ahead of Landon and opened the door for Ashley. Landon helped her into the backseat before climbing in beside her, and minutes later John was heading the car toward the hospital.

Ashley spent most of the ride staring down at her abdomen, praying for her baby, staring at the place where Landon had tight hold of her hand. She felt awful, like she might be sick if she looked up. But when she did, she saw devastation was everywhere. Hundred-year-old oak trees were uprooted and tossed into gullies or lying at strange angles across the road. Street signs and vehicles and roofs were twisted and littered the pavement. Several times her dad had to stop and maneuver around debris so they could continue on.

Finally, when Ashley didn't think she could take another contraction, they wheeled into the hospital parking lot and pulled up outside the emergency-room entrance. The place was packed, but her dad would know what to do. He ran inside, and in what felt like seconds, he rushed out with a stretcher. He and Landon helped her onto it.

Landon kept close to her face. "Keep praying, baby. . . . Everything's going to be okay."

But she could tell from his face that something was wrong. Very wrong. Black spots danced in front of her eyes, filling in the light and making it impossible to see him. "Landon . . . where are you?"

"I'm here, Ash. I won't go anywhere."

She wanted to tell him that she loved him with all her life, that nothing could happen to her because she wanted to spend forever loving him, and she hadn't had nearly enough time. But she could feel herself slipping away, falling . . . falling . . . falling, and for the first time that night, the pain began to dim.

It grew more and more faint until she wasn't sure anymore. Was she in the hospital, really? Or was she at home? Maybe the entire night was only a bad dream, and she'd wake up ready to go to the lake, ready for the next day of the Baxter reunion. Or maybe she was already dead . . . being taken to heaven.

Please let me live, God. And where was Landon—where was her husband? *Landon, can you hear me?*

Her mouth wouldn't work, not at all. She wanted to scream that it couldn't be so; she couldn't be dying. The baby wasn't even born yet, and she didn't know if it was a boy or a girl. How could she die when she hadn't met her second child?

But then a peace came over her, a calm even greater than the one she'd felt earlier.

For the second time that night, she felt God's presence and the certainty of something she hadn't thought of before. She felt herself relax deeply, completely. Everything was going to be all right, because she loved the Lord, and He loved her. She was safe in His hands now, and forevermore she would be healthy and happy, safe and loved and completely cared for.

Whether she ever woke up again or not.

CHAPTER TWENTY-FOUR

FINALLY THE STORM HAD PASSED.

Katy Hart and the entire Flanigan family used their flashlights and crept carefully out of the basement and up the stairs. The storm had raged for hours, but upstairs they found little damage. At least from what they could tell in the limited light.

The electricity was off, and probably would be for a while. Days, maybe. But she'd gotten a cell-phone call from Rhonda. Some mobile phones were working. The CKT families were starting a phone chain, and anyone with service was being asked to call three people until they were certain everyone was okay.

Times like this, if someone was in trouble, it was better to find out immediately. That way they could bond together and do what they could to help. Families might be missing people or in need of shelter—or worse.

Jim and the boys made their way from room to room, checking the ceilings and windows. Jenny stayed next to Katy in the kitchen, making phone calls. All of them were shocked by the violence of the storm. Jenny kept saying the same thing: "I could feel the hand of God over us. Every minute while we were down there."

Katy had felt it too. But what about the others? As many families as there were involved in CKT, someone was bound to be suffering that very minute. She couldn't relax until she knew every one of them was okay.

The basement at the Flanigan house was nicer than the homes most people had, so they'd been able to eat dinner and drink water. They even had a battery-operated television downstairs, so the kids had been able to watch videos after the electricity went out. Only during the last few hours, when the winds screamed and the thunder crashed, did they turn everything off and form a prayer circle.

It was the first time Katy had ever seen Jim look scared. Now, between phone calls, Katy couldn't thank God enough for keeping them safe.

One after another, she and Jenny went down the list of names and numbers. And one after another the news was good. People had lost cars and roofs and in one case half a house. But they were okay and accounted for. All except the Reed family.

Next to the Flanigans, Katy was closer to the Reeds than anyone in CKT. She'd called them three times, but no one answered. She was about to dial them for the fourth time when her phone rang in her hand. She jumped and checked caller ID. It was Rhonda. "Hello?"

On the other end, Rhonda was crying, so upset her words were barely understandable.

When Katy could finally make out what her friend was saying, the news knocked the wind from her. "Rhonda, say it again. Say it slow." Katy was on her feet, pacing the kitchen floor. "The Reeds . . . are you sure?"

"Yes . . . their house . . . it's gone. There's no . . . no sign of them."

Katy pressed the phone tight against her ear, not wanting to miss any part of the conversation. "Let's try to meet over there. It should be safe to go out. You and I and maybe Jenny. We can pray and look around and—" she raked her fingers through her hair and tugged at her roots—"we have to do something."

"Okay. I'll leave in five minutes."

There was no talk about what they might find or how the news could go from bad to worse. Their friends were missing; they were in danger—their house destroyed. Of course Katy would go. She closed her phone and looked at Jenny.

Her friend came to her and hugged her. "I'm sorry, Katy."

"Come with me, please?"

Jenny hesitated. Then she nodded and went to tell Jim.

Ten minutes later Katy and Jenny were driving around debris and twisted house parts, swerving around cars that had been tossed around like toys. Even at one in the morning, the darkness couldn't hide the obvious. Bloomington had been devastated by the tornadoes.

When they reached the Reeds' neighborhood called Autumn Trace, Jenny slowed her Suburban. The place looked like something from one of those storm-chaser videos on the Discovery Channel. On either side of the street, where rows of houses had stood just hours ago, the entire block was leveled. Only an occasional chimney or partial brick wall was left standing. Emergency vehicles filled the streets, and a police officer blocked the way ahead of them.

Jenny rolled down her window. "Our friends' house is gone." She motioned ahead. "They're missing. We want to help find them."

The officer looked like he was going to turn them away. But clearly there weren't enough emergency personnel. "We have units coming from as far away as Illinois, but for now . . . I guess we can use all the help we can get."

Jenny thanked the man and inched ahead, careful not to hit

fallen trees or cars mangled along the road. "It's hard to tell where to go."

But just then they spotted Rhonda's car forty yards in front of them. Two fire trucks were parked across the street.

"There." Katy pointed to the spot where crews were working. "That was their house!" Katy's heart pounded so loudly it seemed to echo through the Suburban.

This couldn't be happening, not again. They'd already lost Sarah Jo Stryker and little Ben Hanover. And now the entire Reed family? CKT couldn't take a blow like this. She peered into the darkness, afraid to climb out of the SUV. Her teeth chattered, and she clenched her fists. "Why . . . are we here again?"

Jenny reached over and squeezed her knee. "Come on. We can start looking around the area, checking for victims."

"Maybe I c-c-can't do it." She felt sick and faint, unable to move, let alone begin a search for the dead bodies of her friends. "Jenny, I can't."

"You can." Jenny's voice was calm, stronger than before as she prayed, "God . . . be with us. This is a night of terror and loss, but You are still God. Give us Your strength; we ask in Christ's name."

Katy still didn't feel strong, but her teeth stopped chattering. Jenny was right. God would meet them here, no matter what lay ahead. "All right." She swallowed back her nausea and opened the door. "Let's go."

They walked slowly toward the place where the Reeds' house had stood. The piles of rubble were smaller than Katy would've figured. Entire houses were gone, but the debris amounted to little more than a few dump-truck loads.

For over an hour, she and Jenny and Rhonda walked by flashlight, scouring the area around the Reeds' property. Rhonda agreed to go one direction, Katy and Jenny, another. Meanwhile, firefighters worked with equipment to unbury the collapsed pieces of wall and roofing that lay over the place where the Reeds' basement was.

They were maybe a hundred yards away when Katy heard a faint crying sound or maybe a cooing. She looked at Jenny, and her heart began to race. "Did you hear that?"

Jenny stopped, silent. The sound came again, and she nodded. "Sounds like a baby or maybe an animal."

They closed in on the noise, and there in the middle of an area wiped clean of all other debris was a wooden baby crib. And inside . . .

"How can it be?" Jenny rushed forward. Carefully she put her hand on the baby's forehead and arm, checking for injuries. "Katy, get help."

For a single instant, Katy stood planted in place, trembling. Her teeth were chattering again. "It's impossible . . ." She shone her flashlight at the square of ground where the crib was standing. There was nothing. No house, no car, no people. Only a few scattered bricks and tree branches.

She turned and ran as fast as she could back to the emergency crews. "Help!" she shouted.

Two of the medics searching through debris stopped and looked up. They jogged in her direction. "Did you find something?"

"A baby . . . alive." Katy couldn't talk, couldn't catch her breath. Her heart was racing so hard that all she could do was point and start moving back toward Jenny and the infant.

The medics used their own flashlights to look ahead. Once they spotted Jenny near the crib, they took off running toward her.

Katy felt her lungs relax, and she drew a full breath. As she walked up, one of the medics had the baby cradled in his arm.

He was an older guy, maybe in his fifties. He stared at Katy and shook his head, disbelief etched in every line on his face. "She's fine. Completely unhurt."

All of them seemed to realize at the same time that the situation was impossible. The other medic, a young guy maybe eighteen or nineteen, pointed toward the sky. "God saved this baby. There's no other answer."

The men thanked Jenny and Katy and took the infant to a waiting ambulance.

Jenny bent over and put her hands on her knees. When she straightened, she seemed faint, her voice weak. "I think it's just hitting me. Where's that baby's family?"

Katy pointed her flashlight in a slow circle, taking in the devastation around her. "Where are all these families?"

"And where are the Reeds?"

Without any discussion on the matter, Jenny reached out and took Katy's hand. There in the middle of the block—with sirens and the sounds of firefighters and paramedics searching for victims—they begged God for a miracle for the Reeds, for the tiny baby in the crib, and for every family touched by disaster tonight.

When they were done praying, Jenny released her hands and aimed her flashlight at what used to be a line of houses.

For a long time neither of them said anything. Katy still didn't want to be here, in a place where they might find any imaginable horror. But at least they'd found the baby—the single sign that somehow, someday, the terrible tornadoes of this April night would be a distant memory. Life would go on—God would see to that.

"Let's walk the rest of the block." Jenny sounded stronger.

The Reeds' neighborhood had one entrance and maybe forty houses in a small square, all of them gone. Other developments connected to theirs were still standing, though block walls and fences that had separated them were missing. Katy and Jenny walked in the middle of the road, using their flashlights, passing other people doing the same thing.

There were no more discoveries, and after ten minutes they

met Rhonda back where the Reeds' house had stood. Katy told Rhonda about the baby, and the three of them fell silent, too amazed and terrified to speak. Firefighters and paramedics had brought in a crane to lift heavy sections of their house off the entrance to the basement.

Katy approached a police officer standing nearby. "Why this house? How come they're not working this fast to move debris off the other basements?"

The man tightened his lips into a straight line and crossed his arms. "You know these people; is that right?"

"Yes." The officer must've heard from his partner that she and Jenny had been given the okay to enter the area. Katy held her breath, waiting for his answer.

"When the tornado hit this area, we received a 911 call." He gestured to the Reeds' crumbled home. "It came from here. The woman was frantic, said that her house had collapsed into the basement. The whole family was trapped down there. Five of them."

A surge of hope rose in Katy's heart. "So . . . so they're okay? You're just trying to reach them?"

"That's the problem . . . we've lost contact with them. Either their cell phone is dead or . . ."

He didn't finish his sentence; he didn't have to. The truth was clear. Either their cell phone was dead or they were. The way countless other people in this neighborhood were probably also dead.

"We're working as fast as we can."

Katy nodded her thanks and returned to Jenny and Rhonda. They exchanged a look that said the other two had heard everything. There was nothing more to say. Even if there was, Katy couldn't talk, couldn't watch the rescue efforts. The sound of machinery and scraping metal, of debris crashing to the earth as the pile was moved one piece at a time . . . all of it made her sick.

How could it have happened? *God, please be with them. Don't let them suffer down there, please.*

She closed her eyes and leaned her forehead on Jenny's shoulder. On her other side, Rhonda put an arm around her shoulders. The three of them clung to each other, too afraid to move or cry or do anything but stare at the awful scene taking place near them.

Jenny leaned close. "Pray, Katy."

"I am."

They stayed that way for what felt like half an hour, praying, whispering, begging God that someone might find the Reeds alive.

Katy was barely clinging to hope when she heard one of the firefighters shout, waving at the other guys to join him near the base of the pile.

The area was lit by emergency floodlights set up by the rescue crew, so it was easy to see the man's face. He was smiling.

"Jenny . . ." Katy took a step forward, clutching her friend's jacket sleeve. "Did you hear that?"

"I did! I think it's good news!" Rhonda advanced forward also.

Jenny studied the man's face. "I can't make out what he's saying."

"I know but . . ." Katy could still barely talk. "But it sounds happy, right?"

Someone cut the engine on one of the machines, and suddenly the voices became clear. The same man was yelling for ambulance crews to move in. "They're alive, all of them!"

Katy collapsed to her knees and covered her face with her hands. "Dear God, thank You . . . thank You." She was still shaking, but now her despair was being replaced by a burst of adrenaline and hope. She could feel Jenny and Rhonda at her side, hear them whispering words of thanks also.

The commotion twenty yards away intensified, and slowly Katy and Jenny and Rhonda stood, arms linked. Bits and pieces were still being shouted back and forth, and they picked up enough to get the important details. Everyone was conscious; a beam had protected them from the collapse of the house. No obvious major injuries.

They were placing each member of the family into an ambulance and hurrying them off to the hospital for tests, but the sense around the rescue scene was one of shear elation. Mission accomplished!

The three friends couldn't get close enough to speak to the Reeds. If they wanted to share in the moment, they'd need to meet them at the hospital. But that could wait until morning. For now, all either of them wanted to do was go home, fall into bed, and spend the rest of the night relishing in the victory at hand.

The Reed family was found!

CHAPTER TWENTY-FIVE

LANDON HAD NEVER BEEN more scared in his life.

He stayed at Ashley's side constantly, even while John Baxter and one of his coworkers hovered over her, trying to stabilize her blood pressure. He still wasn't sure exactly what had caused the problem, but he'd seen the signs back in the basement. Even before the big tornado hit.

First she was suffering from a dramatic rise in pressure. John had verified the symptoms back in his basement—her rapid pulse and breathing and the redness in her face. But as her pains had increased, her pressure dropped, and that could mean only one thing—her life was in danger. Hers and the baby's.

The hospital was a zoo, with victims from the tornadoes streaming in. But Ashley didn't need the emergency room. John hurried her to labor and delivery, where things still felt chaotic but not nearly as crowded. Another doctor worked with John, and the two had her hooked up to machines and an IV in minutes.

Ashley was unconscious by then, but Landon still held her hand, still whispered to her. "Hold on, baby . . . fight for us, okay? Fight for everything we have ahead of us."

He hadn't realized he was crying until one of the nurses handed him a box of tissues. Even then his eyes never left Ashley. A million moments flashed through his mind, the mosaic that made up his memories of Ashley Baxter. When they had graduated from high school and he'd tried everything to tell her his feelings, even making it clear that he'd wait for her to come home from Paris. Later the realization that she was home again, but she'd come back pregnant—and the heartbreak he'd felt when she wouldn't return his calls.

He'd finally run into her at the coffeehouse near the university, the place where they would see each other every few months after that. He was so struck by seeing her that he stumbled over his words. But that wasn't what stayed with him.

It was the wall, the fortress she'd built around her heart. The thing was so massive, so impenetrable. A smart guy would've seen a girl like Ashley Baxter, seen the walls, and run the opposite direction. What point was there pursuing someone who didn't want to be chased?

Still, with each chance coffeehouse meeting, Landon felt his attraction to her grow. He spent more time talking to God about her than talking to her, and eventually they struck up a friendship. But not until he was nearly killed in a house fire in Bloomington did he hear her words of love for the first time.

He had been in a coma, his lungs severely damaged, but her words rang out clear: *"I love you, Landon. I've always loved you."* After that, there was no denying that something had grown between them. Of course, with Ashley not one step of it was easy. There was his stint in New York City and her health scare. But throughout the journey, Landon had always known one thing.

There would never be any other woman for him.

He was alone in the room with her now. Her contractions were still steady, but they'd eased off with the medication she'd been given.

John had explained the situation to Landon as honestly as

possible. "We want her to regain consciousness before she delivers. Otherwise . . . there'll be concern about a lack of oxygen—both to Ashley and the baby."

Landon couldn't understand how things had gotten so terrible. He'd been with her every step of the way. So how had she suffered a lack of oxygen? The only time it could've happened was in those minutes after they'd reached the hospital. She had been groggy, but by the time they put her on the stretcher, she'd fallen unconscious.

They'd rushed her to labor and delivery as fast as possible, right? How could she have had a lapse of breathing during that time?

Landon ran his fingers lightly along her arm, the way he often did. "Don't give up, Ash. . . . God has so much more for us, for our kids." He rested his head on her hand. "You can't leave me."

And that's when he heard it.

The slightest moan came from her throat.

He was on his feet immediately, searching her face and watching the machines. He wanted to find her father or one of the other doctors, but he couldn't leave her. "Ashley . . ." He brought his face low, close to hers. "I'm here. Wake up."

She moaned again and moved her head a few inches to either side. "I . . ."

This time Landon felt his tears. "Ash, it's okay. You need to wake up so you can have this baby."

Her response wasn't in words or open eyes. Instead she squeezed his hand, squeezed it with all the strength she could've possibly possessed in that moment. Then she worked her mouth, clearly trying to speak.

"You don't have to say anything, Ash."

John Baxter walked in then. "How is—?" He stopped short, studying the monitor. "She's coming out of it!" He hurried to the other side of the bed and leaned close. "Ashley, it's Dad. Wake up, honey. We need you to wake up."

Slowly, as if the movement took more effort than running a marathon, Ashley began to move her eyes, and finally she opened them just enough to see them. The beginning of a smile played on her lips, and she worked her mouth again. "Is . . . everything okay?"

Landon kissed her forehead, his tears falling onto her face. "It is now, baby. It is now."

Her father took over, and with his eyes he told Landon that Ashley wasn't out of danger yet. Her blood pressure was still dangerously low, and they were giving her all the medication they could without harming the baby. John mouthed the words *keep praying* to Landon.

Landon nodded and turned his attention back to Ashley. He kissed her forehead. "Stay awake, honey. We need you to be awake."

She nodded, but her eyes were heavy. "I'm . . . trying."

John gave orders to the crew of staff who had entered. They began working around the room and preparing Ashley for the delivery. For a moment John studied his daughter.

Landon had never seen him look so desperate. "Stay with us, Ash. Come on," he pleaded.

As Landon remained by Ashley's bedside, the medical staff moved quickly, talking in a language Landon understood but couldn't focus on. All he could see or think about was Ashley. *Please, God . . . let her get through the delivery. Please . . .*

"Come on, people." John was back at the center of the action. "We need to get that baby delivered."

Landon released her hand. He turned away, walked to the wall, and let his forehead rest against the cool plaster. *God, You gave her to me. The way You've always given her to me. I can't believe this is how it's all going to end, Father. Please . . . I'm begging You. Give her back to me one more time. Please.*

At that exact moment, a technician said the words that sliced through Landon like a knife. "Hurry. We're losing pressure fast."

Ashley had no idea how long she'd been asleep, but now that she was awake things were happening fast. Her father was nearby and Landon too. She heard her father say something about a C-section and getting the baby out as quickly as possible, but then his voice mixed with Landon's.

"Let's not take any chances. If a C-section's smarter, let's do it."

Before she could make sense of what was going on, she was being wheeled into a small room with bright lights. Someone placed a mask over her face and told her to breathe normally. Only then did it dawn on her what was taking place.

She had survived! Someone was saying something about dropping pressures, about a danger of something Ashley couldn't quite make out. But none of that mattered. She was here, and she was having her baby.

But something wasn't right. Once more she could feel herself slipping away, feel the life being sucked from her. *God, I know You can hear me! Please, God . . .* The words no longer formed, but she knew what she was praying for. Another chance, more time with Landon and Cole and this new baby. A miracle.

Then, slowly, her vision cleared. The voices around her grew gradually clear again, and she could hear Landon standing over her.

"It's okay, Ashley . . . your blood pressure's coming back. God's working everything out."

Tears burned her eyes and slid down the sides of her face. She couldn't talk, not with the mask on, and she couldn't put her arms around Landon the way she wanted to. But that was okay. If Landon said she was making a recovery, then she was. *Thank You, God . . . thank You so much.*

She blinked slowly, and over the next minute the staff in the room became clear. But this time Landon was gone. She shifted her gaze, and there was her father, looking down at her.

"Dad . . . where's Landon?" Her words got trapped in her mask and sounded like a garbled moaning.

Her dad leaned closer, wanting to understand.

An idea hit her. She lifted her left hand and pointed to her wedding ring.

Her father grinned. "Landon? He's talking to Cole. Erin's cell phone works, so he has a way to tell everyone back home that you're okay." Her father gave her hand a quick squeeze. "I'll get him." He held up a finger, then hurried off. Less than a minute later he returned.

Landon was with him. He took her hand. "Sorry, baby . . . I'm here. I won't go anywhere."

Someone rolled her onto her side and gave her a shot near her spine, and then they returned her to her back. She was having a C-section; that's what was happening. One of her dad's colleagues set up a screen over her chest area so she couldn't see the operation. Off to the other side, her father took his position, ready in case she needed him for anything at all.

It was happening—it actually was. She and Landon were about to have a baby together, and God was being gracious enough to let her live to see it happen. She willed herself to relax. There was no pain now, and her breathing was much easier than before.

In minutes, she felt a strong pulling sensation, a tugging almost. Landon still had hold of her hand, but he had moved far enough down the length of her to see the delivery. Watching his reaction was like watching the birth herself. His eyes glowed and sparkled, and then he looked at her, awe and amazement shining on his face.

Their baby's first cry filled the room—a healthy, lusty wail that told her everything she already knew. That the problems were behind them.

"Ashley . . ." Landon's eyes were wet. "It's a boy. He's . . . he's beautiful."

The doctor held him up, and for the first time Ashley saw for herself. She brought her fingers to her mouth. "He's perfect." Her words were barely a whisper, mixed with tears and joy and a lifetime of hoping that somehow, someday she might share a moment like this with the man she loved more than life itself.

A nurse took the baby a few feet away, where she cleaned him and wrapped him in a blanket. The whole time, Ashley allowed herself to be lost in Landon's eyes, in the miracle they'd just witnessed. Not just that she had survived and lived to see her baby's birth. But that God had used the love between her and Landon to bring this precious child into being.

When their baby was ready, the nurse handed him to Landon.

"Congratulations!" Her father came up beside them and peered over Landon's shoulder. "He's perfect."

Ashley's tears came in earnest then, because her mother should be here too. Standing nearby, sharing this moment with them. "I wish . . . Mom were here."

Her father came a step closer and took her hand. "She is, honey."

Sorrow and great happiness more than she'd ever known mingled and fell like rain from Ashley's eyes. Her dad was right. Somewhere in heaven, her mother was rejoicing with her over this new little boy, this child who was God's blessing to her and Landon, His way of saying that every bit of struggle along the way had been worth it because here they were.

Landon brought their tiny son closer, and the three of them huddled together. She kissed his minutes-old cheek and nuzzled against his face. Then she kissed Landon. "I can't believe it."

"I'll remember this . . ." Landon kissed her again; then tenderly he stared at their son. "I'll remember it as long as I live."

The nurse was waiting; Landon gave their son one last kiss before handing him over. The infant needed to be weighed and checked, cleaned more thoroughly, and run through a host of tests. But before the nurse left she grinned at them. "He's fine. There's nothing to worry about."

Her father went with the woman, leaving the two of them alone with the other doctor.

Ashley lifted her eyes to Landon's. "You're a daddy!"

His eyes held more depth and meaning than she had believed possible. "Yes." His smile held an understanding. "For the second time."

Right then, Ashley knew she was part of not just one miracle but a series of miracles. She had survived, and the baby was healthy. But even more, she was married to a man who loved her precious Cole and had been a father to him as far back as she could remember.

For this was the greatest miracle: that somehow, out of billions of people in the world, Landon Blake had found her and loved her totally.

❧

Cole was the first to see the new baby.

The entire Baxter family—even the children—were in the waiting area down the hall with Landon's parents. But Ashley had asked her dad to bring Cole in before the others so they could have a few minutes as a family. Ashley was propped up in bed, their baby bundled in her arms and Landon at her side, when Cole came bounding into the room.

He was breathless and red-cheeked, and the moment he saw the infant cradled against her chest, he stopped. Ashley watched the transition happen in his heart. For years, he hadn't needed to share his mommy with anyone. Now, though, the picture of life as he knew it had changed forever. He didn't look jealous or angry, just aware, understanding that things were different now. Then just as quickly, he flashed his parents his biggest grin and hurried to her side. "Papa said it's a boy!"

"He is." Landon let him squeeze in front. He put his hands on Cole's shoulders and kissed the top of his head. "He looks just like you."

Cole angled his face, studying the baby. "He's redder than me."

"Yes." Ashley bit her lip to keep from giggling. "I think Daddy means his eyes. He has your eyes, Cole."

"Yeah." Cole leaned in. "Hi, little brother!" He brushed his finger across the baby's cheek. "I knew you were going to be a boy."

Neither of them could argue with that. "God must've known you needed a brother, Coley." Ashley reached for him and pulled him close. "Brothers are very special."

"I know." Cole hugged her, then straightened. His eyes danced. "'Cause we already have Maddie and Hayley and Jessie." He wrinkled his nose at Landon. "That's probably enough girls, don't you think?"

"And Chloe, Clarisse, Amy, Heidi, and Malin."

Cole smacked himself on his forehead. "I forgot about all those ones."

They all laughed, and Cole leaned toward the baby again. "He sure has little fingers." His expression was earnest. "I don't think he can throw a ball for a long time, Mommy." He lifted his little brother's arm. "They don't make balls small enough for hands like that."

Ashley savored every moment of this first meeting, the first time the four of them were together as a family. "Your daddy and I picked a name for him. Wanna know what it is?"

"Not Brent, right? 'Cause Brent at school made that a bad name, I think."

Landon coughed to cover his laugh.

Ashley swapped a grin with him, and then she looked at her older son. "No, Coley, not Brent."

"We named him Devin Anthony Blake."

"Hmm. Devin is nice. The best soccer player in all of fifth

grade is named Devin." Cole nodded and brought his face close to the baby's once more. "Hi, little Devin . . . grow up fast, okay? I wanna teach you how to throw a ball with me and Daddy."

Ashley felt a tug on her heart. Because Cole didn't need to worry. Devin Anthony would grow up fast, just the way Cole had. Too fast. But there would always be a considerable age difference between the boys. When Devin was five, Cole would be starting middle school. She ran her fingers along Cole's brow. "I pray you'll always be the best of friends, Cole."

"We will." He smiled at his tiny brother, and it was the smile of an angel.

Her father poked his head into the room. "Ready for the others? They want to come in groups of four or five."

Ashley laughed. "Even that'll take an hour."

"It's your fault." Landon swept her hair off her forehead, his voice full of teasing. "You're the one who moved the reunion to the hospital."

After Landon's parents had a chance to meet their new grandson, Luke and Reagan were the first of the Baxters to come in. Malin was in Reagan's arms, and Tommy held Luke's hand.

Luke blinked and gave his sister a wide grin. "He's a little miracle; that's for sure."

Reagan took a turn. "He looks like Cole."

"But redder," Cole interjected. "I'm not that red."

Laughter filled the room, and Luke caught them up on the news outside the hospital. Seven people were confirmed dead in Bloomington, mostly residents of a trailer park that had been straight in the path of the F-4. Six people were still missing, but police expected to find them alive.

The Autumn Trace area, just outside of downtown, had taken the hardest hit. But, fortunately, everyone there had had time to take cover.

"We ran into Katy Hart in the lobby."

"Katy?" Concern sounded in Ashley's tone. Katy had dealt with enough lately. "Why is she here?"

"One of the CKT families—the Reeds, I think she said—lived in Autumn Trace. Their house was leveled, everything destroyed. For a while the whole family was missing. She was at the scene when they were found."

The enormity of the storm was something Ashley hadn't thought about since waking up. All that mattered in her own little world were her baby and sharing him with the people she loved. But outside these hospital walls, the people of Bloomington were reeling. She knew the Reeds, of course. They were a wonderful family, and now—though they were all alive—they had lost everything.

Ashley's heart hurt for them. "Please, Luke, tell Katy to stop in later. Tell her I'm glad everyone's okay."

The visits from her siblings continued in a stream of congratulations and admiration. Little Devin did indeed look like Cole, but he looked like his daddy too. It was something they had both noticed, and she found herself praying that he would be like his daddy in other ways also.

Finally, after everyone had met the newest member of the family, the Baxters headed home. The reunion agenda was a little altered now. They had already missed church and instead of a game day, they were going to check out the Baxter house and begin making whatever repairs were needed.

When they were gone, Landon pulled up a chair and settled in beside Ashley, and a nurse brought in a portable bassinette for the baby. Only then did Ashley realize something. In the craziness of the night, her father hadn't had time to tell her siblings about their older brother.

The only Baxter who didn't know there was a new little addition to the family.

She thought about asking Landon to call her father. Maybe they could set up a meeting tonight in her hospital room, and her dad could carry on with the news the way he'd planned. But she gradually let the idea go. They couldn't squeeze more than twenty people into the room, and even if they could, this wasn't the time for a conversation like that.

Next to her, Landon dozed. Poor guy. He was exhausted from the emotional roller coaster of last night. Same with her father. No, this wasn't the time for her siblings to find out about their parents' secret.

And maybe that was part of God's plan too. Her father had wanted more time, hadn't he? Well . . . now he had it. Another year could pass before they were all together again, but so what? Maybe by then their older brother would change his mind and want to meet them, want to take his place at their family reunion. God had worked one miracle after another in their lives, hadn't He?

Maybe a year from now He would work another.

CHAPTER TWENTY-SIX

DAYNE WAS SOUND ASLEEP when the phone next to his bed started to ring. "Ughh." He rolled over and squinted at the clock. Seven thirty. Who would be calling so early?

He'd been doing reshoots with Angie until ten the night before, and after working with the director in the editing room, he didn't get home until after one in the morning. It had to be work related, because his friends always called his cell.

He reached for the phone and brought it to his ear. "Hello?"

"Dayne . . . Mitch Henry here." There was an urgency in the man's voice, which was often the case.

Still, the director's tone made Dayne sit up on his elbows. "You woke me. What's going on?"

"You're lazy, you know that, Matthews? We working slobs are in the office by seven but not you A-listers." He chuckled. "Want me to call you back?"

"No. I'm awake now." Dayne sat up a little more. "Let me guess; you're casting a movie and you want me to go to Bloomington to find a woman with pale blonde hair and transparent blue eyes, right?" He yawned. "A woman whose innocence is as genuine as summer."

"That's not why I'm calling, but if you can get her here for a film, I'll give you a bonus. Her too."

Dayne smiled. That was the beauty of Katy Hart. Money couldn't attract her to Hollywood, not as long as God was calling her to stay in Bloomington. "Okay, so other than to get my lazy self out of bed, why'd you call, Mitch?"

"Because—" Mitch hesitated—"I received a package this morning from the mail room at the studio. Apparently someone sent it here, hoping I would get it to you."

"Fan mail?" Dayne rubbed his eyes. Mitch needed another movie. If he was getting people out of bed over fan mail, the guy clearly had too much time on his hands. "Why don't you forward it to my agent? Isn't that how it usually works?"

"Well, this one's different, Dayne. It's from Bloomington, and it's got *Private* and *Confidential* written all over it."

Mitch had his attention. Had Katy put something in the mail to him? And if so, why would she send it to the studio with Mitch's name on it? "Who's it from? Any name on it?"

"Yeah. The sender's a guy named John Baxter."

Dayne's head began to spin. Was he dreaming? Was that how he could explain what he'd just heard? He looked at his clock and at the sunshine streaming through his blinds. No, he wasn't dreaming. It was a new day, and his former director was on the phone telling him that he was holding a piece of mail for him. Mail from John Baxter. But how had he found out? How could anyone have known?

"Dayne . . . did you hang up?" Mitch was a smart man. His voice made it clear that he had questions about the piece of mail. "Do you know the guy, or what?"

"Uh, yeah." Dayne was already getting out of bed. "I met him on location last fall."

"Okay, so do you want me to forward it to your agent? I'm just trying to clear my desk."

"No!" Dayne's answer was fast. His heart thudded hard against his chest, and he had to work to sound calm. "Actually, I have to run a few errands. I'll be by to get it in twenty minutes."

❧

Dayne was dressed and on the road in record time.

His agent and his PI were the only people who knew about his connection with the Baxters, so how could John have figured it out? Katy couldn't have said anything. She knew he was adopted but nothing else. Not even that his birth family lived in Bloomington.

He drove as fast as he could without being unsafe. Clearly Katy knew nothing about John Baxter's discovery. Dayne had talked to her briefly after the tornado outbreak. He knew about the Reed family's house and that everyone else was okay. That was days ago, so by now the town was probably knee-deep in the cleanup efforts.

Why would John send a letter now?

Dayne reached the studio, parked his car in a tow-away zone, and dashed inside. How long had he wondered about this moment, dreamed about it? And was it possible the package was some sort of strange coincidence, maybe something from Luke Baxter pertaining to the upcoming trial? Could it be that Luke had asked his father to send the package, and John had written his own name on it by mistake?

Or had his biological father truly found him?

Mitch was sitting at his desk. He looked surprised when Dayne rounded the corner, breathless. "Very nice." He gave Dayne a once-over, his voice laced with sarcasm. "Sweats and a ragged T-shirt. Bed hair. The paparazzi will have a field day with this look." He handed Dayne the envelope. "Did you even *check* the mirror?"

"Very funny." Dayne took the package. He didn't care what he looked like. This was a moment he'd wondered about for years.

He stared at the large envelope. It felt lumpy, as if there was more inside than legal documents. His hands shook so badly he could barely make out the words. One thing was certain: he wasn't about to open the package here. He had one more question for Mitch. "When did it get here? Yesterday?"

"No." Mitch leaned back in his chair and studied Dayne. "Three weeks ago, I guess. I've been working at another studio, so the mail room held it for me."

Three weeks! Whatever was inside, John Baxter had sent it the same week Dayne found out about Kelly's abortion, the week he had never felt more lonely and lost in all his life. He held up the envelope and grinned at the director. "Thanks, Mitch. I owe you one."

"Okay, so who's John Baxt—?"

Dayne was already out the door and down the hall. There was only one place he wanted to go, one place where he could feel alone with whatever was in the envelope. Even if it was only legal papers and maybe cassette tapes from Luke, the package had been sent by his biological father.

In his Escalade out in the parking lot, he scanned the area for paparazzi. There were none—too early for them. He set the envelope on the seat beside him, and fifteen minutes later he pulled into Pepperdine University. He parked in the same lot where he and Katy had been when she was considering the role in *Dream On*.

The lot overlooked the Pacific, and on a clear blue day like this one, there was no better view anywhere. He thought about getting out, walking to the small stone bench thirty yards down the narrow footpath, the one by the duck pond. But that would leave him no way out if paparazzi found him here.

Instead he rolled down his windows and stayed in his Escalade.

He picked up the package and turned it over in his hands slowly, tentatively, as if its contents might explode in his face. And they could, couldn't they? Whatever the envelope held, if it truly was from John Baxter, his life would be changed from this moment on.

God . . . You brought this to me. He could feel adrenaline rushing through his veins, feel his brow getting damp. *Whatever's in here, let me react with Your understanding, Your wisdom.*

There was an assurance that came with a prayer like that. No matter what lay ahead, God was with him. Because of that, he could handle whatever he was about to find. He slid his thumb under the flap and ripped open the top of the envelope. Now that he was ready to read it, he couldn't get the contents out fast enough.

Immediately a small album fell onto his lap. What was this? He opened the cover, and the first photo was one of John and Elizabeth Baxter. Just like the one that had been on Luke's desk in his New York office when Dayne realized they were related.

He turned the page as it hit him what he was holding. John— or someone else—had put together a collection of photographs of the Baxter family, a way of showing him who they were—the people he was related to. He looked at the photos quickly, because he wanted to get back to the envelope. There had to be a card or a letter, some sort of explanation.

He set the album on the seat beside him, then slipped his fingers into the package. The letter was at the bottom, and Dayne pulled it out. No doubt at all, this package wasn't sent by Luke. It was sent by John Baxter, his biological father. Dayne couldn't imagine how the man had found him, but it didn't matter. He needed to read the letter before he could ask another question.

He unfolded the paper and let his eyes find the beginning. It was dated the same day as the premiere.

Dear Dayne,
This is my final attempt.

He stopped there and reread the sentence. The letter was John Baxter's final attempt? What could he possibly mean by that? When had he ever tried to make contact? Dayne's fingers shook as he found his place again.

> The last thing I want to do is cause you grief and frustration—especially now, when so many years have passed since we gave you up for adoption. I guess you've talked to your agent, and you know that I hired a private investigator. I found out who you were, and I was taken aback. Not that you were a celebrity but that you'd been right here in Bloomington twice.

The details were coming at him like a battery of flying arrows. What was John Baxter talking about? Dayne's agent? Chris Kane? Had Chris known something about John hiring a private investigator, and if so, how come Chris hadn't said anything? Dayne blinked and remembered to breathe. Once more he returned to the letter.

> My PI told me you know who we are, that you'd come to our town and perhaps even made contact with my wife—your birth mother—before she died. But your agent told me no, that didn't happen. He said you changed your mind after you arrived in town and that you wanted nothing to do with us.

Anger had begun to build in Dayne, but it became a hot, raging fury in as many seconds as it took him to read that last part again. Chris Kane had talked to John Baxter? told his biological father that he had no interest in meeting the Baxter family? He felt dizzy with rage, and he took hold of the door to steady himself.

John must think he was awful, a pompous celebrity who considered himself too good for regular people like the Baxters. He felt nauseous, but he kept reading.

> Dayne, I want you to know I respect that. But I can't let you go that easily. Thirty-six years ago I had no choice but to let you go.

> Now, though, I feel a loss for every year you weren't a part
> of our life.

The words tore at Dayne's heart. He stopped and held the letter to his chest, his emotions coming at him like a series of battering waves. Anger gave way to an aching loss. His birth father cared about him, just like Elizabeth Baxter had told him. Dayne had avoided them only to protect them, but in the process they'd all lost. His eyes stung, but he refused his tears. Slowly he lowered the letter and found his place once more.

> Only one of your siblings knows about you—your sister Ashley.
> And she doesn't know your name or what you do for a living. I've
> kept you anonymous. The way your agent asked me
> to do.
> I guess I'm writing so you'll know we have no ulterior motive.
> Your agent said a lot of people want things from you—money or
> connections or fame. I can tell you sincerely that the only thing
> we want with you, Dayne, is to give you a hug and tell you we
> love you.

The sobs welled up within him, floods of them, but still he held them back. His agent had no right to make this decision for him, no right to tell John Baxter that Dayne couldn't be bothered with their family because they might want something—money or fame. The idea was appalling. Only by God's divine intervention had this final attempt from John Baxter even made it to him. Dayne was reaching the end of the letter, and despite the hurt inside him, he finished it.

> Every day since I found out about you, I've wondered and
> thought of you. No matter if you want to keep your distance from
> us, I'll still think of you, my oldest son, and long for a relationship
> with you. I know that your adoptive parents were killed on the
> mission field. I'm sorry, Dayne. So sorry. You smile well for the
> cameras, but there's a lot more they don't catch. I can see it in

your eyes—because they are the eyes of our younger son, Luke. The eyes I see when I look in the mirror.

I'm sending a small collection of photographs. The names and ages of your siblings and nieces and nephews are on the back of each picture. As you read this and as you look at the pictures, please consider meeting us. Or at least meeting me—even just once.

If I don't hear from you, I'll know this is a closed door and that you don't want contact with us. That's what your agent has already told me, and I will respect that. But I'm hoping to change your mind, Dayne. I'm praying about it.

Having never met you, I love you. Please consider my letter.

In His light,
John Baxter

At the bottom of the page were several phone numbers.

Dayne stared at them, stared at the words his birth father had written.

And the tears came then.

Alone in the empty parking lot, Dayne hung his head against the wheel of his SUV and wept for all that he'd lost, for all his fame had cost him. They weren't hopeless tears; rather they were tears drenched in rage. John Baxter had hired his own private investigator, and the only real contact information he'd been given besides Dayne's identity was the name of his agent.

Chris Kane.

Dayne thought about John Baxter, grieving the loss of his wife, hearing from his PI that maybe Dayne had met her, only to have Chris tell him he hadn't. That Dayne had changed his mind. That he wanted nothing to do with them. Was that what his life had amounted to? Some sort of puppet show controlled by his agent?

He gritted his teeth, and in a rough single motion he dragged his hands over his wet cheeks. Enough crying. Before he could look carefully at the photos or read the letter again or try to contact John Baxter, he needed to make a phone call. He whipped out his cell phone and pushed a few buttons.

Chris Kane answered on the first ring. "Hey, Dayne . . . what's up?"

Dayne clenched his jaw. "John Baxter . . . ring a bell?"

His agent missed a beat but then forced a laugh. "I was going to tell you about that."

"Sure you were." Dayne kept his tone even, kept the anger to himself. "When did you talk to him, Chris? How long ago?"

"Well, let's see." His agent exhaled hard, as if he were working his brain for the detail. "A month, maybe two." Another laugh. "I meant to tell you back then, Dayne. I mean, I figured you didn't want anything to do with the guy. You were in Bloomington after all, so you could've met him if you wanted to, right?"

"That wasn't your decision." Dayne closed his eyes. He pinched the bridge of his nose and massaged his brow. How could this be happening? How could his agent have told John Baxter those things? He never should've involved his agent in the search for his birth family; then none of this would've happened. He took a slow breath. "I'll contact John Baxter if I want to."

"Contact him?" Worry crept into Chris's tone. "You're not serious, are you? Who knows what the guy wants from you. You're a celebrity. You don't just call up people like John Baxter and make contact."

Dayne was glad the conversation was happening over the phone. Otherwise he would've punched the guy, and overall that wouldn't be the best proof of his newfound faith. "Look, I'm busy, Chris. I have a call to make."

The agent sighed again, heavier this time. "Really think about this, Dayne. You're not like everyone else . . . you don't just look up your birth parents and go knocking on their door." He sounded nervous. "You're not mad, are you?" Chris tried to chuckle, but it sounded more like a cough. "I'm just looking out for you. If I don't look out for your image, who will? I mean, if I don't—"

"Chris." Dayne's voice stopped the agent midsentence.

"Yeah?"

"You're fired." He waited, but Chris remained silent. "My attorney will send you a letter later today. My agent has to be someone I can trust."

Chris hung up without saying another word, and instantly Dayne felt relief. There were other agents, people who wouldn't try to control his actions, shape his image. He was who he was. One of Hollywood's top leading men, whose personal life had done an about-face.

Whoever his next agent might be, that was all the personal information he needed to know.

Dayne wanted to sort through the pictures, take them from the album, and read the names and ages the way John Baxter had suggested in his letter. But he had more to do first.

He contacted the airlines. It was Friday, and the next available flight into Indianapolis didn't leave until early in the morning. He would go, and he would make sure the paparazzi didn't follow him. Even if he only met John Baxter and not the others, he had to go—if nothing else, so he could look him in the eyes and apologize for the things Chris Kane had told him.

Once his reservation was booked, he decided his next call would be to John's cell. No telling who would answer at his office. He dialed the numbers, and after four rings a voice came on the line—the voice of his father.

Though it was just a recording, a few simple sentences asking him to leave a message, Dayne was mesmerized by the sound. The tone of his voice, the timbre of it were the same as his own. He swallowed hard and hesitated at the beep. "Uh . . . this is Dayne. I received your letter today from Mitch Henry."

His words weren't coming easily. They were bottled up in his heart and throat. "Chris Kane, my agent, gave you some bad information, John. I'd like very much to meet you. I'll be on a plane first thing in the morning." He looked at his notes. "Arriving in Indianapolis around one o'clock. I'll rent a car and drive to Bloomington."

His mind raced. "I'll be at the . . . at the park. The one by the downtown theater. You can call me on my cell, but I'll be there. I'll try you again tomorrow afternoon." What else? How should he end it? He stared out at the ocean. "Thanks for the letter. It meant . . . more than you know."

He snapped his phone shut and looked at the other numbers. John lived alone now, right? All Dayne's siblings were married and raising families, and with Elizabeth gone, John would probably be the only one home. Late on a Friday morning, he might still be home getting ready for work. It was worth a try. He opened his cell and tapped in the numbers.

On the third ring, a girl answered. Or maybe a woman. "Hello, Baxter residence."

He opened his mouth to speak, but then he changed his mind. It was probably Ashley, stopping by with her little boy. His cell-phone number had a feature that blocked the caller ID, so he wasn't worried about that. "Hi. John Baxter, please?"

The girl sounded puzzled. "He's not here. Can I take a message?"

"No." His answer was quick. "That's okay. I'll try him again later." He hung up before she had time to ask another question. His heart pounded so hard he could feel it in his throat. He needed to be careful. Just because John knew about him didn't mean it was time to put the rest of the family at risk, to make it public knowledge that he was their older brother.

Dayne picked up the photo album and returned to the first page. It was still impossible to believe what Chris Kane had done, that he'd been so callous to John Baxter. If John hadn't taken time to write this letter, to try and find a way around his agent, they might never have connected at all.

God . . . this was Your doing, wasn't it?

I know the plans I have for you, My son.

The quiet whisper no longer caught him off guard. If he listened, if he focused on the very real presence of God Almighty, he could almost always sense His response being breathed into his soul. Yes, God had plans for him. Some days that was all that kept him from hopping on a plane and showing up at Katy's front door. He missed her so much, missed everything about her.

But with her and with the Baxters, he had promised to wait on God's leading. He stared at the photo again. Now that's exactly what God was doing. Leading him to make a connection he'd wanted as long as he could remember.

It was hard to believe. Tomorrow—if God allowed it—Dayne would meet his birth father, a man he had thought about and imagined for half his life. If his letter was any indication, John Baxter was a kind man, warm and loving. By the sounds of it, the act of giving him up had been as hard on him as it had been on Elizabeth.

A car pulled into the parking lot, and Dayne watched it, watched the driver move slowly toward him. Paparazzi, no question. A few of them knew he liked this spot, and since his Escalade was easy to identify, they probably had Pepperdine on a list of places where they regularly looked for him.

He turned the key in the ignition, backed out, and sped away. The car followed him, staying close behind until he pulled into his garage. Dayne waved out the window at whoever was chasing him, then closed his garage door behind him.

That's fine. They could sit out there all day.

Just as long as they didn't follow him to Bloomington come morning.

CHAPTER TWENTY-SEVEN

————————◆◆◆————————

IT WAS TIME TO SAY GOOD-BYE.

Ashley had been released from the hospital a couple days ago, and now she rested on her parents' living-room sofa. Bags were packed, and the vans loaded with suitcases and strollers and car seats. Brooke would drive her van and her dad would drive Ashley's. Kari was staying with Ashley to help care for the baby and to watch the other kids.

Everyone was gathered in the living room, more somber than they'd been all week.

John had Malin cradled in one arm and Tommy on his knee. "Well, I don't think any of us imagined a reunion like this one."

"Definitely not." Luke was standing nearby. He put his hand on their father's shoulder. "I think we'll be talking about it forever."

Reagan looked at Ashley. "I'm so glad everything worked out."

"We were worried about you, Ash." Erin had a baby on her hip and another one playing near her feet. Her two older girls were at the kitchen table playing cards with the big kids. "I don't think I've ever prayed that hard."

"I'm amazed at how the town looks after only a few days." Brooke shook her head. "You can already see the cleanup efforts of all those working around town. Only that one trailer park and Autumn Trace were really leveled."

Landon was at work—his first shift since the baby had been born. He had said the same thing. His buddies at the fire department were amazed at how fast road crews had come through and cleared away trees and building parts. Across town, churches and work groups and families were pitching in and beginning to repair and rebuild the homes that were lost.

Ashley cuddled Devin closer to her and looked at him. "It could've been so much worse."

"Okay . . ." Luke glanced at his sisters. "So when are we doing this again? I think we waited too long for this one."

"Christmas, maybe?" It was Sam's suggestion. He stooped down, grabbed a pacifier from the floor, dusted it off, and put it back in the mouth of the baby in Erin's arm. "Most of us have time then, right?"

"My mom's having her college girlfriends out to New York." Reagan frowned. "Sort of a reunion she's been planning."

"Us too. Peter's family in California wants us to fly there for Christmas." Brooke shrugged. "I know it sounds like a long time, but next spring might work best for everyone."

"Maybe so." Erin's eyes grew watery. "It just seems like such a long time away."

"We'll keep in touch." John kissed Malin on the cheek. His voice told them he was struggling with good-bye, but he was trying to stay upbeat, happier than he felt. "We can have the conference calls over dinner, like we've done this past year."

"Right." Luke messed his fingers through Tommy's light brown hair. "And I'll keep everyone posted about the big Los Angeles trial coming up in May."

"Yeah, do that, Luke," Erin said. "I wanna know every detail before I see it in the magazines."

They shared smiles and a few easy laughs.

John looked at his watch and drew a long breath. "Well . . . it's about that time."

Ashley felt herself grow sad. She didn't like having Erin and Luke so far away, not being a part of their daily lives, not having the chance to know their kids better. The mood changed, the sorrow there for everyone.

Erin came to her first. She leaned down, and they hugged for a long time. "Take good care of Devin." Erin pulled back, her eyes shining. Then she kissed the baby on the cheek and did the same to Ashley. "I'll call you."

Ashley's throat was tight. She hated saying good-bye, not knowing when they might all be together again.

Sam brought the other kids into the room, and Ashley gave kisses to all four of their girls. Erin did the same with Kari and Brooke, and then she and Sam led the girls outside toward the vans.

Reagan came to her next, and the two hugged. "One of these days, we'll have to find a way back to Bloomington." She tickled Devin under the chin. "Tommy can't stop talking about Cole and his little brother."

Ashley laughed, but it was tinged with tears. "That would be amazing."

"Yeah." Reagan took a step back. "Maybe after Luke finishes law school." She ushered Tommy close and instructed him to say good-bye.

Cole was waiting off to the side, his eyes red and swollen.

After a few more kisses and hugs, Reagan took both her kids outside.

Only Luke remained. Ashley had known from the beginning that his good-bye would be the hardest of all. They shared a special bond, one that had been there since they were little kids. No matter how much distance or time separated her from Luke, when he came around she would always feel like a little girl again.

"I can't stand this part." Luke shoved his hands in his pockets and stood beside the sofa.

"Yeah." She ran her thumb over Devin's blond brow. "You and I were going to have houses next door to each other, remember?"

He gave her a sad smile, his eyes shining more than before. "Maybe someday." He leaned down and wrapped his arms around her. "I love you, Ashley."

"Love you too, Luke." She held on to him. "Maybe we'll come see you in New York."

"Okay." He pulled back and sniffed, brushing quickly at his eyes so she wouldn't see his tears. "Tell Landon bye for us."

"I will."

Her brother waved one last time, turned, and walked out of the room.

And just like that, the house was quiet. Kari had the kids in the kitchen for a snack, and only she and Devin remained in the living room. It would be easy to give in to her tears, to cry and grieve the fact that life had taken them away from the days when being together was something they took for granted. But instead, Ashley smiled at her newborn, at all that lay ahead of them. Life was full of seasons. In this one—where she and her siblings lived in different states—she wouldn't be sad for what she was missing but grateful for the time they had together.

Even if a week was never quite long enough.

John's eyes were dry as he drove home from the airport. Brooke had left a few minutes before him—in a hurry to get back to her office. But John wanted to take his time. The weather was clear and warm. It was hard to imagine how terrible the storm had been until he saw the evidence of destruction that still remained.

In all, it had been the worst tornado outbreak the area had ever seen. Not since 1925 had a series of tornadoes caused so much damage to Indiana, and tornado season had just begun. Experts were on the news every day talking about the tragedy, the efforts that had already begun to rebuild the areas of devastation, and how amazing it was that so few people had been killed or injured.

A newspaper story in this morning's paper explained how the CKT families were donating all door receipts from their upcoming show to help the Reed family rebuild their house. Bloomington had pulled together, and as always with a town like theirs, what hadn't killed them would make them stronger.

Luke was right. They would never forget their time together, huddling in the basement while Ashley was in labor, praying for a break in the storm, praying for Ashley to breathe, praying for the baby. God had answered all their prayers and given them days of laughter as they had repaired the broken windows and a couple areas on the roof.

Good-byes were always hard, but this time John felt somewhat relieved. The storm had given him a reason to dodge the thing he'd dreaded most—the meeting with his kids, the one where he would've told them about their older brother. Now that moment would have to wait—maybe a year. And in the process, he could only pray that Dayne would change his mind.

He was halfway home, anxious to spend an afternoon with Ashley and Devin. The newborn was so precious. John agreed with his kids—the baby looked just like Cole had as an infant.

John was about to turn on the radio when the phone on the console between the two front seats began to vibrate. He picked it up and read the message in the window. Three new messages.

"Crazy phone." He shook his head. He'd had the thing with him the whole morning and all of yesterday. How could he have missed a call? Maybe it was time for a new phone, because this had happened before. He'd get no messages for several days and then—as if some switching station just realized he had messages waiting—several would be thrown his way at once.

He sighed and punched in the numbers for his voice mail. He entered his code and pressed the phone to his ear. The first message was from Elaine, congratulating him on the birth of his latest grandchild. He smiled. He'd call her as soon as he was finished with the messages.

The second was from one of the doctors at the office, calling to check on Ashley and the baby.

There was a beep, and the third message kicked in. "Uh . . . this is Dayne. I received your letter today from Mitch Henry."

John's heart dropped to the floor of the van. Dayne Matthews? His son? He kept his hand steady on the wheel and listened.

There was a coughing sound and then Dayne's voice again. "Chris Kane, my agent, gave you some bad information, John. I'd like very much to meet you. I'll be on a plane first thing in the morning." He paused. "Arriving in Indianapolis around one o'clock. I'll rent a car and drive to Bloomington."

John couldn't believe what he was hearing. Dayne was coming to Bloomington? When had he left the message? He used all his concentration to hear the rest.

"I'll be at the . . . at the park. The one by the downtown theater. You can call me on my cell, but I'll be there. I'll try you again tomorrow afternoon." Dayne hesitated, and his voice seemed to grow softer. "Thanks for the letter. It meant . . . more than you know."

John couldn't concentrate on the road. He took the next exit and pulled into a gas station. He checked the date and time of the message. Dayne had left it yesterday, even though he hadn't gotten notification of it until now. He worked his jaw, frustrated. So Dayne was maybe on this very freeway headed for Bloomington? Could that be possible? He was flying in today, possibly passing his sister and brother at the gate or on the concourse without ever knowing it?

John ran back through the message again and exhaled. Dayne hadn't left a number. He checked the list of missed calls, but the one that must've come when Dayne would've called said Restricted.

If the private investigator had been able to get Dayne's private cell number, John would've called it a long time ago. That meant he had just one choice. He looked at his watch. It was after two o'clock. If Dayne had followed through with his plans, then he might be waiting at the park now.

John turned the ringer on loud, closed his phone, and stuck it back on the console. He spent the next thirty minutes driving and praying that the meeting might actually happen.

When he pulled into the parking lot at the old downtown park, the place looked empty. It was too early for the farmers' market, and other than a few kids playing baseball on one of the diamonds and a few couples strolling the tree-lined walkways, he didn't see anyone.

But then, just as he was getting out of the van, he saw him.

There at the other side of the park, sitting alone on a park bench, was a guy who had to be Dayne. His size and build were familiar, not because John was a moviegoer so much as because it was the build of Luke. The build he himself had. As he stared, as he wondered if it really could be him, the young man stood and shaded his eyes. In that moment, John had no doubt. The thing he had prayed about since Elizabeth gave birth was finally happening.

He was about to meet his firstborn son.

CHAPTER TWENTY-EIGHT

———— ❖ ————

DAYNE SAW A VAN pull into the parking lot.

He'd been sitting on the same bench for nearly an hour, dressed in jeans and a sweatshirt, his baseball cap pulled low over his forehead. A few people had passed by, but no one looked twice at him. The paparazzi hadn't followed him, and there was no reason for anyone to suspect that a movie star might be sitting alone on a park bench in downtown Bloomington.

He had his photo album with him.

By now he'd looked through it a dozen times, studied the faces of Brooke and Peter and Maddie and Hayley, smiled at the way Kari and Ryan and Jessie and Ryan Jr. looked like they belonged together. He had gotten familiar with Erin's and Sam's pictures and the photos of their four daughters, Chloe, Clarisse, Amy, and Heidi. Of course he recognized Luke's picture—the one with Reagan and Tommy and their daughter, Malin.

But it was Ashley's photo that tugged at his heart the most.

Ashley and Landon and Cole.

In the photo, Ashley was pregnant, and every time Dayne

looked at it he remembered taking Ashley home and wishing with every fiber of his being that he could go inside and meet her family. He had come so close. . . .

Every time he looked at the pictures he was struck by one overwhelming thought: the Baxters were huge supporters of adoption. Erin and Sam had adopted their four daughters—John had written as much on the back of their photo—and Luke and Reagan had adopted Malin from China. Little Cole was adopted too—by Landon, the guy in the photograph. And Ryan had adopted Jessie. Dayne's PI had told him those details.

Even though adoption had been a painful thing for John and Elizabeth, their children had turned it into something beautiful. That hour in the park, as he'd looked at their faces, Dayne had come to understand that his birth parents really hadn't had a choice. And that his adoptive parents had only been acting in love when they chose him. By their standards, they saw nothing wrong with taking a four-year-old to Indonesia and placing him in a boarding school.

Every so often, he would look up and search the parking lot, and finally—this time—he saw a man step out of a van and scan the grounds. Dayne narrowed his eyes, but he knew almost immediately. The man was John Baxter, his biological father. The man who would've been his dad if Elizabeth's parents had given them a chance.

Dayne stood, slipped the photo album into his pocket, and tossed his baseball cap on the bench behind him. He shaded his eyes.

John seemed to notice him. He began walking toward him. All the while Dayne couldn't look away, couldn't even blink. John Baxter walked just like he did, the way Dayne would walk when he was in his sixties. John was tall and strong with broad shoulders, but the closer he came the more Dayne could see something else.

John Baxter was broken.

Dayne took a few steps in his direction. As the distance between them closed, he could see that John was crying. Not weeping, not anything that could be mistaken for weakness. But quiet tears that simply streamed down his cheeks and told Dayne more than the man's words ever could.

As John came closer, his steps slowed. Dayne felt almost as if he were seeing a ghost, someone who had only existed in his imagination. His birth father. He wondered if he had avoided this meeting so much because of the paparazzi or because he was afraid of being rejected, afraid John wouldn't love him the way he clearly loved his other children.

John stopped a few feet away. His lips quivered, and he put his hands in his pockets and shrugged, apologizing without words for his inability to speak. For a while he struggled, trying to find control. When he did, he said simply, "Dayne."

"Yes." Their eyes held, and a lifetime of regret and sorrow passed between them. For every time Dayne had wondered about this man, he could see in that instant that John had wondered about him too. He could think of a hundred things to say, and at the same time no words seemed big enough.

Then, at the same time, they did what they must've both wanted to do—the only thing that made any sense. They held out their arms and came together in an embrace that erased the decades. John held him so hard, so tight that Dayne could barely breathe.

Dayne imagined what it would've been like having someone love him this much all his life. What would it have been like to play catch with John Baxter? to have him in the front row at his drama performances? or to have late-night talks with him when he was making decisions about his life? John appeared to be a solid man, a man of character and conviction.

Dayne knew something in that instant. The years he'd lost with John Baxter—with the entire Baxter family—would forever be the greatest loss he would face. Right up there with the trag-edy of losing his own unborn child.

When John finally pulled back, he kept his hands on Dayne's shoulders. He was still struggling to speak, still fighting a life-time of emotion. But he managed to speak anyway. He searched Dayne's eyes. "I can't believe . . . I found you."

Dayne's heart raced the way it did when he sprinted on Mali-bu Beach. His throat was tight, and he fought to find the words. "It's . . . been a long time."

"Yes. Too long." John sniffed and shook his head, desperate for control. He stared at Dayne, looked deep into his heart, to the place where the little boy inside him still lived. A place only a father's eyes could find. "I'm sorry, Son." John's voice broke, and he hung his head. When he looked up, there were fresh tears on his cheeks. "I've asked God all my life for the chance to say that."

"I'm sorry too." Dayne blinked back his own tears. His heart was racing ahead of his words. He pressed his fist to his mouth, waiting for control. "My agent lied to you. I never . . . never once knew you called."

John studied him. A sound of disbelief came from him, and it broke the ice. "I had a feeling." He narrowed his eyes. "You look exactly like Luke."

"Yeah." Dayne grinned. "I've been told that a time or two."

"So . . . you've been here before." John's eyes held what must've been painful questions. "Can you tell me about that?"

"Yes." This was bound to be the hard part. Okay, so they'd met. That didn't mean anything had changed in Dayne's life. So where exactly did that leave them? Where did it leave his rela-tionship with any of the Baxters? He nodded to the bench, the one where he'd been waiting. "Can we sit?"

"Please." John led the way to the bench.

Dayne was dizzy with the feel of John beside him. Never mind that they'd never met before. This meeting—the closeness he was feeling from John—was exactly what he'd always hoped for. Now if they could only find a way to hold on to it.

John sat a foot from Dayne, facing him. "Talk to me, Dayne."

Suddenly his argument sounded crazy. So what if he was famous? Who cared if the paparazzi figured out he was adopted or that he'd made contact with his birth family? He looked at the damp ground, at the new grass poking its way to daylight. If he was ever going to make sense of the situation, he needed to share it with John. "It all started with Luke."

"Luke?" John put his arm over the back of the bench. "You mean at the law firm?"

"Yes." Dayne looked at the sky, at the sun filtering through the branches of an oak tree. "I was sitting in his office, and he had this picture on his desk." He took the photo album from his pocket and turned to the first page. "This picture."

Dayne could feel the wonder of it, see it playing in John's reaction. Only God could've led to such a meeting; he had no doubt. "People at the office kept saying we looked like brothers, so I took the picture."

"You took it?" John's eyes were gentle, without an ounce of judgment.

"I thought it looked like a picture I had in my storage unit. A picture of my birth mother. When I compared the two, I knew Luke was my brother." He stopped and let the breeze brush against his face. A mother and four children were playing at the swings a ways away. Their laughter carried on the wind.

Dayne breathed in slowly. "That's when I hired the private investigator."

"So you found out about us, right about the time Elizabeth was getting sicker."

"Exactly." Dayne explained about the call from the investigator and the message that his birth mother was terminally ill. "I knew I didn't have much time."

Pain burned in John's eyes, a pain so strong it seemed to force him to look away. "It was her dying prayer that she might meet you. I only wish . . . you would've gone in to see her."

Dayne leaned closer, his eyes locked on his father's. "My agent lied about that too."

John blinked. He slid to the edge of the bench. "Meaning what?"

"I went in. I did. I spent an hour talking to her." Dayne's voice was softer than before, touched by the memory of sweet Elizabeth. "I thought she'd tell you."

This time, John let his body fall against the back of the park bench. He looked straight up and whispered, "Thank You, God . . ." After a while, he shook his head. "She did tell me. But she was so sick, and with all the drugs they were giving her . . . I didn't think it was true. I figured she was . . . hallucinating. Especially when she mentioned your name. See . . . Luke had just told us about having met you, working with you. He told us people thought you looked alike." Peace came over John. It seemed to soothe the lines on his forehead and lighten his eyes. "God answered her prayer, Dayne. She begged Him for the chance to meet you before she died."

A shiver ran down Dayne's spine. It was one more sign, one more bit of proof that God had been there all along, working in their lives. "That's what she told me."

Gradually, John's expression changed, as if the memory of that time was replaying in his mind. "But you didn't stay. And then . . . then you came back here to film your movie but still nothing. No connection with us."

It was time to get to the point of the matter. "I needed all my strength to stay away from you—from all of you. But believe me, I did it for one reason." He hesitated, praying that John Baxter would understand. "I did it to protect you."

"Protect us?" John didn't doubt him; that much was clear in his tone. But he didn't understand either.

"Okay." Dayne anchored his elbows on his knees, ran his fingers through his hair, and tried to find a way that would help John know what he was talking about. He decided to do what Bob Asher had done with him. He turned enough so he could see his father's eyes. "Let me tell you a story."

John waited, never once looking away.

Dayne began without waiting another minute. He told John about flying to Indianapolis and renting a car, about coming to the hospital and parking in the back row. Just as he was getting out of his car, he saw a family leaving the front entrance, heading to the parking lot.

"Luke was one of the people, so I knew it was you. The Baxters. My birth family." He smiled, remembering the joy he had felt, the elation at the chance of finally meeting them. "I was going to walk up and pull you aside, tell you who I was. I figured maybe it would be a time when we could all meet—assuming the others knew about me."

Instead, as he went to climb out of his rented car, he heard the rapid click of cameras. Paparazzi had followed him to the hospital, and now they were going to shoot him relentlessly, speculating at why he might be there and who he could possibly be visiting at a small regional hospital in southern Indiana.

"In that moment I had to make a decision. I could go to you, talk to Luke, and pull you aside, tell you who I was. But the photographers would have captured every moment of it. Within a week, the entire story would have been splashed across the front pages of every tabloid in the country."

Slowly, like the sunshine after a thunderstorm, understanding dawned on John's face. His expression grew serious, troubled.

"I saw that one of your grandchildren was in a special wheelchair, that she was handicapped, and I wondered about the rest of them. I know a lot about you. And if I can find out the dirt, so can they."

John was intrigued now. "What, Dayne? What do you know?"

He didn't have to think about it. The information was deep in his heart, woven into the fabric of all he knew to be true about the people he considered family. "I know about Kari's husband having an affair with a student and how he was shot and killed by a college kid on steroids. I know about Peter's brush with pain-pill addiction and his stint in recovery. And I know about Hayley's near-drowning accident. Two of your kids had babies out of wedlock—Ashley and Luke—and Erin struggled with infertility until she and Sam adopted."

John looked as if he might topple off the park bench. "How in the world could you . . . ?" He wasn't angry, just amazed. The information wasn't something even he had probably ever put together in one sentence.

Dayne raised his brow. "Even you and Elizabeth had your secrets." He gave his father a sad smile. "Right?"

Two birds landed not far from them and took turns tugging at a worm.

John put his arm on the back of the bench again. "So you're saying all that information could become public knowledge."

"No." Dayne gave a sad laugh. "It *would* become public knowledge. The tabloids are ruthless. I promise you, they'd want everything they could find on the birth family of someone like me."

"So—" a greater understanding seemed to be filling John now—"you didn't contact us because you wanted to spare us that scrutiny."

"You're private people. People who love God and family and who have stuck together when times weren't easy." Dayne's voice was thick with emotion. He begged God that his birth father might understand. "I wanted to meet you so badly. But I didn't think it was fair. I couldn't put you in that kind of limelight."

John exhaled long and tired, in a way that sounded as if it came from deep inside him. "I guess I never thought about it." He scanned the grounds, the parking lot. "Did they follow you this time?"

"No. I'm smarter now." He gave John a crooked grin. "More careful."

"Then . . . couldn't you meet our family, be a part of us, and keep it a secret?"

It was the obvious question, the one even Dayne had wrestled with. "We might be able to pull it off at first, but it would get out. The tabs don't miss much." Dayne's voice fell a little. "Can I ask a question?"

"Yes."

"How come only Ashley knows about me? Why . . . why haven't you told the others?"

"Ashley found a letter your mother wrote to you before she died. She . . . she had written *Firstborn* on the envelope, and Ashley thought it was for Brooke. She took it, forgot about it, and a week later she read it."

Dayne couldn't help but smile. "Ashley's a spunky sort, isn't she?"

John grinned. "You could say that." He stared at the sky and gave a sad shake of his head, his grin fading. "We had a family reunion this past week. Did you know that?"

"No." Dayne felt his heart sink. Why was it always this way? He showed up just in time to know there would not be a meeting with his family. There couldn't be a meeting. He hid his disappointment. "I prayed for you . . . the day of the tornadoes."

John blinked and stared at Dayne. "You . . . you prayed for us?"

"Yes." He smiled, warmed by the memory of his recent decision. "I have a friend here. Katy Hart. She gave me a Bible and that led me to Mexico City—where my old boarding-school buddy is a missionary. It happened recently. Right after you mailed me the letter." Dayne could feel his eyes glowing. "I gave my life to the Lord, the way I should've done years ago."

John took hold of Dayne's shoulder and gave him a gentle squeeze. "Elizabeth always knew you'd make that decision one day." He looked deeply at him. "I'm happy for you, Dayne. Choosing Christ will change your life."

"I know. I can already tell." He still wanted an answer to his earlier question. "So the others, if they were all together last week, why didn't you tell them?"

"I was going to, but Ashley went into early labor and had a baby. The night of the tornadoes, of all things."

"Wow." Dayne hung on every word, every bit of update about his siblings. "I didn't know that."

"But really, I didn't want to tell them because of what your agent said. He told me you wanted nothing to do with us." John shrugged, his smile lost in a surge of defeat. "How could I tell them that they have a brother they never knew about, but he wants nothing to do with them?"

"You'll be happy to know something." Dayne cocked his head.

"What's that?"

"I fired my agent yesterday."

John laughed. "Sounds like a good call."

Dayne looked at his watch. "I have to leave in fifteen minutes. I only had today to make this happen." He hated the thought of leaving now. Especially when he hadn't seen Katy and wouldn't have time to see her. "I couldn't go another day letting you think I didn't want contact with you. This town, all of you . . . Katy. I'd leave everything in Hollywood tomorrow for this life if I didn't think it would hurt all of you in the process." He thought some more. "That, and the five movies I'm still under contract to make in the next few years."

"I . . . I had no idea." He covered Dayne's hand with his own. "Wouldn't that be something?"

They were quiet for a minute, each of them processing all that had gone on this afternoon.

Finally John stood. "You have to go. Let me walk you back to your car, Dayne. And let's both pray about what lies ahead."

Dayne rose and walked beside his father. They talked about

John's career as a doctor and how Dayne's life was spent running from photographers. Dayne felt the connection, the bond between them. There was an easy rhythm to the way they were together—something that made it feel as if they'd known each other their entire lives.

When they reached the car, John stopped and faced him. "You have no idea the peace, the hope you've given me today, Dayne. I've longed for this from the first minute Elizabeth told me about you."

"I wish . . ." Dayne looked down at the ground. With the toe of his shoe he kicked at a loose bit of gravel. "I wish her parents would've understood."

John's eyes welled up. "Me too."

They thanked each other for coming, and they each promised to pray.

Dayne felt the pain in his heart and knew it would only get worse when he drove off. In some ways, this good-bye reminded him of his adoptive parents, catching stolen moments between flights and never really having enough time with each other. Dayne stepped back and studied John's eyes. "I want more than this."

Then, without any pretense, John put his hand on Dayne's shoulder and began talking to the God they both believed in. "Lord, I bring You my firstborn, my oldest son." His voice cracked, and when he found the words, there were tears in his voice. "Fame and celebrity aren't real, God. So please . . . show us a way around the snares that seem set for us. Give us a way to be a family. We beg You, in Jesus' name, amen."

With that, they hugged one last time, and Dayne climbed into his rented car and drove away. The tears came then, and he didn't stop them. But for the first time when it came to the Baxters, they weren't tears for all he'd missed, all he'd lost along the journey of life. They were tears of longing, because he had found his father and just as fast, he had no choice but to say good-bye.

He had to find a way out of Hollywood. He didn't belong there, not anymore. Life wouldn't be right again until he could come back to Bloomington without hiding, without watching the clock and always rushing back to the airport.

As his tears dried on his cheeks, as he watched Bloomington disappear in his rearview mirror, Dayne realized something remarkable. Here and now, he had found something else, something besides his father. Something he hadn't even known was missing.

He had found his way home.

A WORD FROM KAREN KINGSBURY

D E A R   R E A D E R   F R I E N D S ,

Okay, so yes, this book has been a long time coming. There were weeks and months in the past year when I kept wondering how in the world my schedule had gotten so jam-packed and how I could've let this book fall so far down the list of things demanding my attention.

The obvious answer, of course, is that my publisher—Tyndale—asked me to take a break from the Firstborn series to write *Divine*. If you haven't had a chance to read it, I hope you will. It's a story about a modern-day Mary Magdalene, a woman who was so thoroughly saved from such great evil that her Rescuer could only have been one truly divine. It's a story that defends the divinity of Christ at a time when so many other sources are calling His true nature into question.

Anyway, even in the midst of asking God to help me handle that amazing challenge, I was aching to get back to my friends in Bloomington. I could hardly believe I'd left Dayne with a Bible and a hundred questions about God or John Baxter with the phone number of a PI and little else in the quest to find his son.

I feel much better now.

Isn't there something wonderful about the word *found*? It implies that something was lost—something or someone. But now, everything's okay. That's the beauty of being found. While I took Dayne down the journey of finding Christ, of allowing God to find him, I thought about my own life—the lives of the people I love. What would my life be like if someone hadn't prayed for me, if my husband hadn't taken the time to show me God's Word? I might be writing books; I might even be selling a lot of copies. But I would be completely and utterly lost without Jesus.

We are all lost until we meet Christ, aren't we?

In a discussion with our kids the other day, one of them said something sort of blunt. "All roads lead to hell except Jesus." The sound of that sentence set us back for a minute. It had a harsh sound to it. The room fell silent as we pondered that thought. But just as quickly we came to realize the truth in it.

There are many good people in this world. Many roads that seem fruitful and successful. People on those roads may have found their motivation in great works or charity, in helping people or succeeding at something wonderful. There are athletes and lawyers and businessmen and mothers, artists and singers and teachers and students—all going about their business in a way that seems pleasant enough.

It's not often that we take another look and realize that for every one of them—for every one of us—the life that has us getting up each morning, smiling and succeeding and returning to our beds at night—is a road that leads nowhere without Jesus.

That was something Dayne had to figure out.

He thought maybe his emptiness came from his loneliness, from wild relationships, and from the loss of his first child. He wondered if maybe Katy Hart or the Baxters would somehow make him feel whole. And while those were wonderful possibilities, the truth for Dayne is the same truth for us. Wholeness is always and only found in finding that relationship with Jesus.

I guess the thing that stayed with me as I wrote *Found* was this—we need to pray for the people in our lives who haven't yet found their hope in Christ. Dayne had people praying for him. Katy Hart, John Baxter, Bob Asher, and even Ashley—who still doesn't know his name but prays for him anyway.

There is power in prayer, power enough to move mountains or give someone a miraculous translation when the message that would change their life is being spoken in Spanish. By the way, I used that miracle in this story because when I was a reporter, I did a story on a girl who was drowning in a wind-tossed lake.

Her rescuer spoke only Spanish, but she heard everything he said and understood it.

Because she heard it in English.

Our God wants a relationship with us, and He's willing to make miracles happen to turn our heads, to make us finally see that He's been there all the while—waiting for us to find Him.

So be encouraged. If you or someone you love hasn't found the One who will make life whole and complete, don't give up. Keep praying. God wants us all to come to a saving knowledge of Him—and until we do, He wants us to pray. Please know that I'm praying for you also. If you're not sure how to find Jesus, get ahold of a Bible and read the book of John in the New Testament. Using the yellow pages, find a Christian church—one that teaches only what the Bible teaches. Nothing more, nothing less. As it was with Dayne, so it is with every one of us. God is waiting . . . there's no time like now to make this decision.

Deep breath. You won't believe what I'm off to do.

Between hugs and kisses and time spent with my kids and my husband, I'm starting work on *Family* tomorrow morning! I promised I'd bring you this series in quick installments—and this one was hardly quick. But the next one will be released this fall if all goes well. I can't wait. Only God will be able to get the Baxters and Dayne and Katy Hart through the challenges of the coming two books.

By the way, I'd love to hear from you. Stop by my new Web site at www.KarenKingsbury.com and see what's coming up or use it as a place to meet other readers and book clubs. You can also leave prayer requests or take on the responsibility of praying for people. So often people ask me what ministry they might be good at—especially if they're home a lot or not able to get out. Prayer is a very important ministry. Remember, it was prayer that turned things around for Dayne. Your prayers could be crucial in the lives of someone else, someone God is calling you to lift to Him in prayer.

Thanks so much for sharing in this journey, the journey of the Baxter family. I pray that God is using the power of story to touch and change your life, the way He uses it in mine.

Until next time, blessings in His amazing light and grace,

Karen Kingsbury

Discussion Questions

Use these questions for individual reflection or for discussion with a book club or other small group. They will help you not only understand some of the issues in *Found* but also integrate some of the book's messages into your own life.

1. What were the signs that Dayne was feeling empty about his life, even before his phone call from Kelly Parker?

2. The call from Kelly triggered much in Dayne's heart and soul. Explain at least three things that Dayne felt as a result of learning his former girlfriend was pregnant.

3. How do you feel about the way Dayne handled the news about Kelly's pregnancy? Do you think he believed he could make things work with her? Why or why not?

4. When Katy heard the news that Dayne was going to be a father, she believed it was God's way of giving her a message. What was that message, and what changes did Katy make as a result?

5. What was wrong with Terrence C. Willow? Explain what would make a person act that way. What is the best way to handle such a person?

6. Do you know anyone struggling with being single? Halfway through the book, what realization was Katy reaching about singleness? Do you think God calls some people to be single? Why or why not?

7. Explain how Dayne felt when he heard the news about Kelly's abortion. Do you think his feelings were genuine? Why or why not?

8. What role did the loss of his first child play in driving Dayne to look deeper at his adoptive parents' faith? What was he hoping to get by going to Bloomington and finding Katy Hart?

9. What surprised Dayne about his boyhood friend Bob

Asher? How have you viewed missionaries in the past? Did reading about Bob's understanding of missionary work change your mind? Why or why not?

10. Dayne's time in Mexico City was very powerful. Give three reasons why you think his time with Bob and Rosa was life-changing.

11. How did Dayne feel about being important to Rosa because he was Bob's friend and not because he was a celebrity? How did he feel in the midst of the street-ministry crowd, knowing that he was merely one of the people in attendance?

12. Bob's message was in Spanish, but by some miracle, Dayne heard it in English. Do you feel a miracle such as that is possible or believable? Why or why not?

13. What was the turning point for Dayne as Bob was giving the final invitation of the evening? How had God prepared Dayne's heart—not just in those few days but all his life—for hearing that specific invitation that night?

14. Seeing Hayley walk without assistance for the first time since her accident was another miracle in *Found*. Do you think miracles still happen today? Tell about a time when you or someone you know experienced a miracle.

15. Katy Hart felt that God used Skyler to teach her something about her place with the CKT kids. Describe what God was telling her and how she reacted.

16. John Baxter thought it was very important to take time for reunions with his kids and their families. When was the last time you took part in a family reunion? Why do you think they are important, or why not?

17. Dayne's agent, Chris Kane, made decisions about Dayne's life without asking him. What was this agent trying to accomplish? Did you agree with his decision to try and protect Dayne's reputation?

18. Tornadoes played a big part in the Baxter reunion this

time. How has a storm ever affected something important in your life? How are storms symbolic of our lives
and God working in our lives?

19. What was Dayne's reaction when he received the letter
from John Baxter? Discuss how his emotions changed
that day and what made them change. Was Dayne
wrong to fire his agent once he knew what the man had
done? Why or why not?

20. In the final scene, John Baxter and Dayne finally find
each other. Describe the ways the word *found* was used
in this book. How have you or someone you know been
lost and then found—literally or spiritually? How does
the word *found* make you feel? Why?

Turn the page for an exciting preview of

F A M I L Y

the fourth book in the

FIRSTBORN SERIES

by Karen Kingsbury

Available fall 2006
ISBN 0-8423-8746-3
www.tyndalefiction.com

From

F A M I L Y

by Karen Kingsbury

CHAPTER ONE

KATY WAS FIVE MINUTES from landing at Burbank Airport outside Los Angeles. The trial was set to begin in the morning.

For weeks, Katy had been talking to Dayne on the telephone nearly every night. Something was changing between them, strengthening their friendship and making them both dizzy with possibilities. On the good days, anyway.

On the bad ones, Katy would go to the local market and pick up a tabloid. Always there was something about Dayne—at least on the inside. Rumors about who he was seeing and who was falling for him, talk about a mystery girl meeting him at the beach or driving with him along the Pacific Coast Highway.

Katy never mentioned what she read. But it gave her reason to wonder, reason to think that whatever was happening between them, she'd be crazy to think it could turn into a relationship. A normal relationship, the kind that Ashley Baxter Blake and Jenny Flanigan had with their husbands.

Still, their recent conversations had been wonderful.

Dayne had told her the news—that he'd made contact with his birth father. He still hadn't told her his name or any of the details, but the difference in Dayne was undeniable. He seemed stronger, more confident. Between the news about his birth father and Dayne's growing faith, Katy considered the changes nothing short of divine, the sort of work only God could've brought about.

She had shared the details with Rhonda and Jenny, and she wanted to share them with Ashley. All three of her friends had prayed for her all along, for the most part gently suggesting that Dayne couldn't possibly be the right person for her. But now . . . now even Jenny was beginning to wonder.

There were issues to be resolved, of course. The greatest was the paparazzi and the fact that Dayne needed to stay in LA until he finished his current contract—five more movies with the studio who was backing him. Katy had no idea how either of them could survive being apart that long, not if their recent conversations were any indication.

The simple fact was this: Dayne was in love with her, and the longer he talked to her, the more he shared about how God was working in his life and how he was taking walks along the beach every morning praying for her, the more there was no denying her own feelings.

She was falling for him harder than ever before.

Now, as the plane landed, as she gathered her bags and rented her car, she could hardly wait for their plans to pan out. She checked into her hotel and waited until the right time. According to Dayne, the paparazzi had been quiet around him lately. But he still made the interior spreads of every magazine, even though he wasn't hitting the nightclubs or showing up at the usual restaurants and haunts.

"My old agent told me this would happen," Dayne had told

her on the phone the night before. "He said photographers stay away from Christians."

"But do they know?"

Dayne had to think about that. "I haven't found a church yet, so I guess not." He paused. "Maybe it's something they sense. I'm being too well behaved, and they're losing interest."

Katy had been tempted to say something about the tabloid rumors, but she kept her thoughts to herself. He owed her nothing. If he spent time with other women, with his leading ladies and supporting actresses, so be it. She wouldn't complain, wouldn't bring it up.

But because the photographers hadn't been lurking in the bushes beneath his Malibu house, he figured it was safe to try what they'd tried before, to meet at the beach and see each other for the first time since his visit back in March. Her first night in town would be safer than any of the others, since the trial hadn't started and the paparazzi had no idea who she was. Not yet, anyway.

"Besides, we need to talk about that, about how you're going to handle them." Dayne sounded worried about her. "You need a plan, Katy."

She believed him.

The weather was warm as she headed out to her rental car. She wore capris and a tank top under a pale blue, long-sleeved blouse, the kind that tapered in at the waist. Bloomington had been warm for a couple weeks, and she'd helped Jenny in the garden, so her cheeks were more tanned than usual.

She parked in the Malibu Beach parking lot, not far from where she had parked before. It was dark, and she looked around the way Dayne had told her to—in case there were transients or photographers, anyone who looked suspicious. If so, she was supposed to pull into his driveway. He would open his garage, and she could park inside. But they wouldn't be able to go outside, because the paparazzi would be desperate to know the identity of whoever was visiting Dayne at his house.

Okay, she told herself, this is just a couple of friends getting together and having a talk, catching up on all they'd missed in the past couple months. But no matter what Katy told herself as she stepped out of her car, the truth was as clear as the hint of perfume she left behind her.

She moved quickly, looking around and making sure no one was watching her. There were people scattered across the parking lot, washing off surfboards near the outdoor showers along the bathroom building. As soon as she hit the sand, she saw several couples here and there along the beach. The beach was definitely more crowded than it had been a few months ago.

The sand felt good, and she liked the way it pushed up between her bare toes in her sandals. She wished she could stop and take her shoes off, but Dayne had told her to keep walking. She reached the shore and turned left, heading north along the beach. She was maybe ten yards into her walk when a guy came down the sandy hill toward her.

Just as she was about to pick up her pace, the man whispered, "Katy . . . it's me." Dayne appeared from the shadows and fell into step beside her. "Keep walking."

The feel of him next to her heightened her awareness, made her notice everything about him, how tall and big he was beside her and how good it felt when their arms brushed against each other every few steps. "Are they out . . . the photographers?" She kept her eyes straight ahead. Strange how being with Dayne in public was like playing a role, and she remembered the part in *Dream On* that she'd read for almost a year ago.

"No. But I couldn't let you walk the beach by yourself. This time of year there're more people out." He slipped his hands into the pockets of his shorts. "I watched you park, made sure you were okay." He shot her a quick grin. "I'm just not willing to take chances with the paparazzi."

They kept a steady pace and after a few minutes, Dayne slowed down. He scanned the dark beach in both directions and then turned toward the surf. There were no people. "I think we're alone."

She kicked off her sandals. "Mmm. The sand feels so good."

"Not as good as seeing you." He met her eyes before looking back at the moonlit surf.

He was keeping his distance on purpose; Katy could feel that much. It was hard to believe how the threat of photographers ruled everything about his public moments. She breathed in the ocean air and worked her toes deeper into the sand. "You look good." She angled her face, finding his eyes again. "Something about you is different."

"Different?" He smiled and kicked a bit of sand at her foot.

"Don't worry—it's a good thing." She straightened and let the breeze wash over her. It felt wonderful after a day in airports. "I think it's your eyes." She felt shy telling him this. "It's like I can see Jesus in them."

"Mmm." He fell quiet for nearly a minute. Then he groaned. "I can't stand this."

He didn't have to explain what he meant. Katy felt it too. Being together this way and not at least hugging. It wasn't natural. She looked at the sand around her toes and then at him.

Once more he glanced around. Then he turned to her and did what they were both dying to do. He slipped his arms around her waist and eased her into his embrace. "Katy—" he brushed his cheek against hers—"I've missed you so much."

Her hands came up around his neck, and she looked into his eyes. They shone with a love that could have only come from God, and that—mixed with the moonlight reflecting off the water—was more than she could take. She let herself be pulled in closer, and she rested her head against his chest. "Why is it—" she looked up and let herself get lost in his eyes—"I never feel complete until I'm in your arms?"

At first he looked as if he might answer her, but the air between them changed in the time it took him to blink. He brought his hands to her face, and with the most tender care, he touched his lips to hers.

But before he could kiss her, before they could express the feelings they were both clearly feeling, there was a movement in the bushes, a rush of feet, and the clicking of a camera. In a blur of motion, two men appeared—one of them the same as last time she was here.

Katy held up her hand, but it was too late.

The men blocked their way to Dayne's staircase and began taking rapid-fire pictures of them.

"Put your hand down, Katy." Dayne tried to shelter her. He took her hand and pulled her close, wrapped his arm around her, and hurried her around the photographers to the door that led to his stairs.

The cameras didn't stop clicking until they were inside the private staircase. Even then the men banged on the door shouting at them. "Tell us her name! Come on, Matthews. She's not an actress. Just tell us who she is."

The other one chimed in. "She's the mystery girl, right? The one who'll be at the trial tomorrow?"

Only then did Katy realize what had happened. The paparazzi had figured it out. They might not know her name—not yet. But the pictures they'd taken would show her entire body—her face and her surprise—and the fact that she had been locked in an embrace with Dayne Matthews. And that could mean only one thing.

Life as she had known it was about to come to an end.

The **Best-Selling**

REDEMPTION SERIES

by Karen Kingsbury and Gary Smalley

Novelist Karen Kingsbury and relationship expert Gary Smalley team up to bring you the **Redemption series,** which explores the relationship principles Gary has been teaching for more than thirty years and applies them to one family in particular, the Baxters. In the crucible of their tragedies and triumphs, the Baxter family learns about commitment, forgiveness, faith, and the redeeming hand of God.

REDEMPTION
a story of love at all costs

REMEMBER
a journey from tragedy to healing

RETURN
a story of tenacious love
and longing for a lost son

REJOICE
a story of unspeakable loss and
the overwhelming miracle of new life

REUNION
a story of God's grace and redemption,
His victory even in the most difficult times.

Other Life-Changing Fiction by

KAREN KINGSBURY

have you visited
tyndalefiction.com
lately?

Only there can you find:

» books hot off the press
» first chapter excerpts
» inside scoops on your favorite authors
» author interviews
» contests
» fun facts
» and much more!

Visit us today at: tyndalefiction.com

Tyndale fiction does more than entertain.

» It touches the heart.
» It stirs the soul.
» It changes lives.

That's why Tyndale is so committed to being first in fiction!

TYNDALE FICTION